What the Moon Did

a novel

Jessica Barksdale Inclán

Flexible Press
Minneapolis, Minnesota, 2023

Print ISBN: 979-8-9862459-2-8
eBook ISBN: 979-8-9862459-3-5

Flexible Press LLC
Editors William E Burleson
Vicki Adang, Mark My Words Editorial Services, LLC
Cover via Canva

For my mother

I don't know why it is given to us to be so mortal and to feel so much. It is a cruel trick, and glorious—Louise Erdrich

Jenny Bradford Pine
February 2018

DID IT START with her mother's pie crust?

For most of her life, Mary Jo Bradford had been a pie maven. But now, her famous flaky crust—golden brown, crisp, a snap in the mouth—was suddenly crumbly and sour with a mouth-puckering tang, as if she'd dumped cream of tartar into the dough, each bite metallic. The crimps were lumpy, uneven; the bottom both soggy and burned. At least the pumpkin custard came out all right, and those gathered at Jenny's house for Thanksgiving that year ate the pie anyway, scraping out the sweet goodness with dessert spoons.

"This is disturbing, Mom," her older son, Dom, had whispered as he dumped the ragged pie remains into the sink.

Jenny patted his shoulder and shrugged. Something was up. How many rounds of dough had her mother rolled out on tile, Formica, granite? How many crusts had she witnessed baked golden? Jenny's grandmother Ginny and her great-grandmother Gert—pastry queens in their own rights—perfected the rich, crispy crust made with butter and shortening. This crust was a touted family treasure, a family favorite, a pastry prize-winner back in Saint Helen, Iowa, where Jenny's mother had grown up.

When Jenny was in fifth grade, her mother taught her classmates' mothers how to roll pie dough thin and light, and then transfer it as if by magic and without sticking to the pie plate. Crimping? A cinch. Baking? A breeze.

Turns out, making a piecrust was as scary as math.

Pumpkin, cherry, apple—apple was what Jenny's father wanted instead of chocolate cake on his birthdays—her mother made them all. Mary Jo baked cakes and tarts and sheet cookies when needed, but she loved pie. Fluffy strawberry spy pie, chocolate mousse pie, pecan pie. Mary Jo spent years making pies.

Then Mary Jo gave it up. After the metallic Thanksgiving pumpkin pie, Mary Jo began to fear the holidays, her worries mounting immediately after the new year.

"I can buy a pie," she told Jenny. "Anyway, no one likes pumpkin pie anymore."

"The boys love your pie, Mom," Jenny said. "There would be a revolt without it."

"I've lost all my pie plates," Mary Jo said.

"We can go buy one at Safeway right now."

"I've forgotten the recipe," Jenny's mother said, waving a hand to mimic her memory whisking into the air.

"Mom, the recipe is on the back of the can. Right under the *Libby's, Libby's, Libby's.*"

"The crust recipe. I can't find it."

"It's in your red recipe box."

"That's lost too."

"Mom, it's around here somewhere." Jenny scanned the counter, which was mounded with stacks of magazines, cable and water bills, and an odd assortment of rubber bands, paper clips, and thumbtacks.

"Tricia would go buy me a pie," Mary Jo said.

"Tricia lives in Australia," Jenny said flatly. "She won't fly home to buy you a pie."

"If Joy were here, she'd make the pie for me."

Jenny closed her eyes. This again. Always this, that old pain. She swallowed and found her breath. "She's not here, Mom. You know that."

"She loves me best."

Verb tense, Jenny thought, saying nothing.

Her mother stared at Jenny, waiting for something. Jenny shrugged a little.

"Well, fine," Mary Jo said. "When the time comes, I'll buy one at the bakery."

"Mom—" Jenny started.

"If only your father were here." Mary Jo crossed her arms, taking on that distant look as if she could see into the future, into a place where her husband was level-headed, one to help in a crisis. "I hate pie. I'm never going to make a pie again."

With each new disaster in the kitchen, and soon in other rooms, Jenny headed over to her mother's condo, as she had more and more often as things broke beyond repair or simply disappeared. The hourly helper Jenny had hired, Mo, dealt with veterinary appointments for the cats, furnace repairmen, library visits, but on the weekends, Jenny was on call.

As she fixed and found things, Jenny uncovered mysteries. In her mother's closet behind a wall of shoeboxes filled with brand-new shoes, Jenny found stacks of Post-it Notes, dozens of pens, varying sizes of Ziploc bags, including one that could accommodate a small child or a dead cat, chilling thoughts. Unwrapped picture frames, eyeglasses dating back to the '70s, unworn blouses still in plastic. Most surprisingly, a case of SweeTarts, a container of Mentos, a commercial-sized supply of Good & Plenty.

"Shut down her damn Amazon account," Tricia said when Jenny complained on the phone.

It worked.

Nothing was where it was supposed to be. Jenny's heart thrummed with worry when she dug around for Mary Jo's missing passport, birth certificate, car title, insurance forms, all eventually located in one envelope that had slipped behind the desk.

She put new batteries in her mother's remote controls, but the gadgets still didn't work right, at least according to Mary Jo, who bashed one to bits in anger when she couldn't turn on the news. When her computer was finally so slow, broken, bad, horrible that Jenny ordered a new one, it was, according to Mary Jo, worse than its predecessor.

The mechanical world was against her, Mary Jo claimed. She had been betrayed by technology. Her car doors stuck, the sunroof locked permanently in the open position, the rear view camera fuzzy. That's the damn reason, Mary Jo insisted to anyone who would listen, she crashed into the bushes.

"It really wasn't my fault."

Back at home, Jenny's husband, Steve, made compassionate noises, but one night he said, "Listen, you need to take her to the doctor. This isn't normal aging."

"She's eighty years old," Jenny said. "What should she be like?"

Steve raised his eyebrows and cocked his head toward the left. "Look at our neighbors." John and Barbara were seventy-six and seventy-eight, and spent their weekends fishing, riding bikes, and gardening. The summer before, they had traveled to Italy for a pasta-making tour in Parma, Modena, and Lucca. Sure, John had that tricky knee and Barbara was a bit forgetful, but Steve was right. Mary Jo lived on a different elderly planet.

But still. Mary Jo Bradford had never been a hiker, biker, runner, walker, or swimmer. Outdoors was made for sitting and drinking a cocktail, preferably when the weather was fine. Travel outside the country was too dangerous, enough that Mary Jo hadn't seen her daughter Tricia for years. Jenny shot her husband a look. There wasn't a schedule for aging. And there certainly was no manual. Wasn't this how they would all fall apart, one skill set at a time?

Before Jenny could reply, Steve held up his hands. "You don't have to do it right away. But this is getting out of control."

One day in February, Jenny found herself on her stomach on her mother's kitchen floor, one arm deep into the back of a cupboard as she searched for the missing pie plates. Meanwhile, Mary Jo paced the kitchen in a wobbly gait, opening drawers and not closing them. Cutlery and serving spoons rattled. She talked incessantly, but Jenny tuned her out as she searched the backs of the lower shelves. On the television, Fox News blared, the station on every waking moment except when Rush Limbaugh squawked through the radio. MeToo was the topic on the news, more allegations against more men. Jenny tried to tune that out, but she was trapped by the constant noise, dust, and the ridiculously high temperature her mother kept her condo at. Sweat slicked under her sweater.

Aside from Mary Jo's holiday command performances, it was clear she had stopped using her kitchen except for the sink, microwave, and fridge. Most of the glass bowls and cake tins dated back to a time well before Jenny.

"Mom, can you turn that thing off?" Jenny called up from the floor. "Too much bad news."

Her mother was silent, but her scurrying had stopped.

"Mom? Do we have to listen to this all day long?"

Mary Jo was still, the newscaster hurling accusations at the women who had come forward, actors and models and businesswomen.

"It's all a sad grasp for publicity," the newscaster was saying. "They are trying to wreck reputations."

Finally Jenny's fingers touched it—glass, slightly curved. A pie plate, shoved into the back, as if her mother had hidden it there on purpose. Then her fingers grazed the recipe box. Mary Jo didn't want to make pies, so she lied and hid things. When had she become so secretive?

"It happened to me," her mother said, her voice thin and light.

"*What* happened to you?" Jenny pulled the plate and box out of the cupboard and sat up on the floor, wiping her forehead with the back of one hand.

"That," she said, pointing to the television. The image had changed to a sea of pink hats, women holding up signs. The screen flicked to different images of the marches after the last presidential election. Then there he was, that man, smiling out at the world, chin jutted. Yes, *that* had happened to her mother, though, of course, Mary Jo had voted for him.

"I know," Jenny said. "We have a horrible president. But the good news is I found your pie plate."

"No." Mary Jo looked down at Jenny, her eyes wide. "Me. Me, too. MeToo."

Mary Jo Johnson
June–December 1949

MARY JO WASN'T making it up. She was twelve years old and knew the difference between fairy tales and real life. This wasn't a story, something in a book. It was true. Mr. Bradfield had been watching her. All summer.

His gaze was attention. Attention was gold. Mary Jo wanted to reach out and touch its shine.

But it hurt too, made her cower, ashamed. She wanted to run away from its sharp spines.

On dusky late June evenings, the day's heat dissolving into a lush sultriness, her parents, he, and his wife, Betty—a newlywed couple years younger than her parents—leaned back on patio furniture, lightning bugs popping bright into the twilight, dotting the space over the lawn. Mary Jo played with her younger brother, Bobby, both of them hiding in the grass, counting stars. He was three years younger than she was, but he knew things about the night sky Mary Jo had never paid attention to. Later, her neighborhood friends Margie or Diane would come over, all of them hiding behind the black maples that grew at the back of the house, screeching when tagged. The moon rose, full and white, flickering between the branches. As Mary Jo ran, her arms outstretched, his gaze became her shadow, her second skin, cupping her.

She might fly up and over the trees, his attention pulling her along.

When she turned to face the house, he sat on his lawn chair, taking a sip of bourbon or laughing at something her father had said about farm wives and their big bottoms. But even turned away, he was watching her, his gaze confusing and awful. And wonderful. He was old, of course. But tall, with a full head of dark hair. Bigger than her small, slight father, he had strong shoulders and long legs. He walked like he owned the very stones or floorboards or grass he strode on. His voice was deep, serious, but also filled with laughter. She could hear him now, telling a story, pulling everyone into his good mood.

Even in the growing darkness, even in the dull yellow porch light, Mary Jo felt his stare, his large eyes trained only on her, eyes so dark she couldn't see his pupils. Eyes like caves, wells, tunnels.

Last summer, the first time it happened, he lifted a hand to lightly skim her waist as she passed by, pulling on the leg of her shorts during a family-style picnic at the creek. The *crick*, as her father said.

One time he came into the kitchen while she stirred the soup pot for her mother, one hand on the spoon, another holding a book.

"What are you reading?" he asked, his eyes not on her book or her face but on her breasts that had begun to grow. He glazed over, his fuzzy expression taking in all of her, arms, legs, body. Mary Jo imagined she could feel things in her opening. Her breasts bloomed, her skin fleshed out against her blouse. The pain of it, this emergence, enough that she wanted to scream.

When she held up her novel, her hand shaking, he whistled. "Charlotte Brontë. Aren't you the smart one?"

The words. *Smart one.* The way his eyes moved over her as if she were a longed-for landscape. She could feel her own hills, smooth undulations of golden grass moving in whispers. Mary Jo almost stopped breathing, wanting something else.

But Roger Bradfield winked, dark eyes bright again, watching, and then he left the room.

"Oh, my, Virginia. Mary Jo surely is growing," Betty said to her mother as the three of them rolled out pie crusts for the Fourth of July party at the town square. "And that new hairdo. My word! She looks like she's in her twenties."

"Hardly that!" Her mother shook her head, wiping flour from her right cheek. "All it takes is one look at that bedroom of hers to know she's a child. Books higgledy-piggledy all over the floor. And that closet! Does the girl know what a hanger is?"

Betty laughed. "Maybe a fact, but it's about time to head down to Hedda's for a fitting."

"My thoughts exactly," her mother said, giving Betty an approving look, a glance Mary Jo craved. "Made an appointment for next week. She sure doesn't get bustiness from my side of the family."

Her mother and Betty laughed, though Mary Jo didn't get it, as usual.

"Her time is coming." Betty raised her eyebrows.

"She's owlie as all get out," Mary Jo's mother said. "I would suspect it's just around the corner."

What was *it*? Mary Jo wondered, her face flushed. Whatever *it* was, it wasn't good. And whatever it is, she was going to keep it secret from everyone.

He kept watching, staring at her from collarbone to hipbone to thigh bone, lingering on her breasts, which were now carefully held in her new bra from Hedda's. Her legs were summer lean, her hips wider, her hair growing blond at the tips from the relentless sun. She, Margie, and Diane didn't go to the public pool because of the polio scare, but they turned on the garden hose and ran through arcs of cool spray. They lay on towels in golden afternoon heat and closed their eyes, listening to the grasshoppers sing and the wind whisper through the corn patch, a rustle, a scratch, scratching. The skin on Mary Jo's neck burned. The sun arced up and over them, the day turning still and lazy and so hot they hid under the salvation of the cherry tree's shade. They lay on their backs, eyes closed, listening to nothing but the electric hum of growing grass. The birds stilled in the bows. Even the katydids slept.

Later, Diane and Margie whispered stories about junior high and how forward the eighth-grade boys would be at the dances.

"They'll put their hands all over you," Diane said, giggling and clutching at Margie's shoulders. "My sister told me. If you let them do it, they'll call you fast."

As Mary Jo listened, she felt those hands over parts of her that pounded under her shorts and blouse. Her thighs and belly felt fleshy, hot to the touch, round and sticky with sweat. Mary Jo knew hands, but she didn't tell her friends about Mr. Bradfield, everything about him barreling toward her as fast as a runaway boxcar.

"Boys are idiots," Margie said, as if she knew anything about boys. She didn't even have a brother. Margie had no idea about anything and didn't know the secret things Mary Jo understood under her skin.

Mary Jo had lived in California. And Mr. Bradfield had picked her.

He watched her on the weekends. During family outings. He was always with them.

"Such a great couple," both of her parents said. "That Roger is the life of the party."

"Do call the Bradfields," her father said when her mother suggested a dinner, party, movie.

"Why do you always invite them?" Mary Jo asked.

Her mother turned to her, a hand on her hip. "Don't be rude, young lady. The Bradfields are our best friends in town. They met right here at our dinner table. That's not something to take lightly."

Mary Jo didn't understand that at all. And she wondered if her mother would take what Mr. Bradfield was doing lightly. What was he doing though? Mary Jo had no words to explain it.

There he always was, smiling, a wink as she walked past. When she accompanied her mother to his downtown grocery store on busy summer mornings, he would come out of his office, black eyes wide, gleaming, and ask, "What can we do for you today, Virginia?" but as he said the words, he was watching Mary Jo, his gaze burning past her skirt, blouse, bra, panties. He was like the X-ray machine in her father's office, exposing her down to the bone.

What he was doing was wrong, but something inside her held his wrongness close. She wore it like a necklace, the locket smooth between her breasts. It was hers.

"Don't be silly," her mother would have said if Mary Jo had told her. "You? Why would Roger Bradfield watch you of all people?"

But he did. He did watch her.

He watched her in the buffet line, in the library, and at parades. He watched her from the corner of his eye and straight on, his eyes wide and focused only on her. When no one else was in the room, he came closer, enough so that she smelled him, a darker, deeper odor than her brother or her father, a man smell of paper, the meat counter, aftershave. He smelled like summer heat and the pomade he used to keep his thick hair straight and flat.

Roger Bradfield stepped too close, his body inches, seconds, from hers, his heat shimmering between them, a skimmer of fabric, flesh. All she could see were his shirt buttons, shiny, white, and small. She wondered if she saw his heart beating under the breast pocket. Parts of her body that had recently opened up and bled seemed to flame in a way that made her want to run. Made her want to stay.

"You're growing up," he said one afternoon in late August. They stood in her parents' kitchen as she filled up the water pitcher to take out to the patio. Mary Jo's hands clenched the glass handle, her breath shallow, air hitching in her throat. She wanted to cry, great wrenching sobs caught under her ribs.

He went on. "You're really filling out that blouse."

Then after looking out to the group in the back yard, he stepped forward so quickly she flinched. He took her hand in one of his and brought an index finger to her chest, between her second button and her throat, his fingertip burning her skin. "I bet you look amazing with it off." He looked at her, his gaze locked tight. He held her, freezing her in place, forcing her eyes on him. He moved his hand toward his pants zipper, and she couldn't look down. She didn't want to see, but she heard the sound of flesh rubbing on fabric. Her mouth opened, air ripped from the back of her throat.

Slowly, he took her hand and brought it close, holding her gaze as he rested her palm on him. A part of him. Hot and smooth.

One second. Two. His pupils were great dark circles. Time held itself still, invisible, breathless. Outside, though, people. Danger. At any moment, her mother or Betty would swoop into the kitchen and shriek, hands to mouth. Mary Jo wanted to wrest free, but she couldn't move, both of them underwater, Mr. Bradfield swimming toward her, unwavering.

And then he stepped back, zipped up, and snatched a snicker-doodle from a platter and left. As he walked outside, Mary Jo heard Betty tease him about eating dessert before lunch.

In a near collapse, Mary Jo let the pitcher clunk to the bottom of the porcelain sink. Her badness was eating her up. She was as ugly as the latest photo her father had taken, her face brown and sweaty, her hips disgusting and big, her ugly short hair like a curled helmet. Mary Jo was ugly in and out, red and black and boiling, like the devil in his cauldron. She was Satan tempting Jesus. But what was she offering Roger Bradfield?

"Mary Jo?" her mother called. "We're parched!"

She wiped her face and brought the pitcher out to the patio, ignoring Mr. Bradfield and then running to play with the other children in the woods. the night air wrapped around her, warm and wicked.

He kept watching her, up until those first days of September when the leaves began to turn, sycamores and maples flaming yellow and red-tipped. But then school started, and the weather shifted—no Indian summer that year—and Mary Jo was caught up in the newness of junior high, and then bored with it, all her classes and classmates too slow. But there were books to read and Latin to learn. She was the *smart one*, after all.

Diane had been right about the boys, who were suddenly inter-ested in carrying Mary Jo's books between classes and walked her home in the afternoons, even if they were a good three inches shorter, had buck teeth and cowlicks. Even so, Mary Jo felt a little smug when Peter Hughes held her hand for a minute behind the library.

In October, Principal Skort announced the first dance to be held in the gymnasium. Now that Mary Jo understood these boys were fumbling, confused boys, she didn't worry about their hands. None of them had Mr. Bradfield's hands, sure and confident. None of the boys had his glittering eyes.

Her new pleated skirt and slip swished as she walked down the stairs, her brand-new saddle shoes—fresh from their stiff cardboard box—shone. Everything she wore was clean and fresh, all hers. Finally, she'd figured out her new hairdo, the way to force it to curl under, just like her mother's.

Sometimes when she stood in front of her bedroom mirror with her brush, she heard Mr. Bradfield say, "I bet you look amazing with it off."

"Don't you look nice," her father said as she headed to the front door to catch her ride with Diane's mother.

Mary Jo shivered.

What did *nice* mean? And wasn't her father a man in the way Mr. Bradfield was a man? She'd never noticed her father looking at her mother the way Mr. Bradfield looked at her. She'd heard her mother say to her friends, "A girl and a boy. We're all done."

Did that mean with children or with the act that created them?

But did that *thing*—the heat that burned inside Mary Jo when Mr. Bradfield looked at her—die away after children were born? Was that feeling even related to anything? Mr. Bradfield's stare made something happen. Was Mrs. Bradfield used to those stares? Mary Jo had never noticed that look passing between the Bradfields, not ever. What did it mean that he would talk to Mary Jo that way? Was there something so terribly wrong with her that he would pick her out? Was she the only one? Maybe she wasn't. Maybe he did it to everyone. That's why no one but her seemed to notice.

Mary Jo coveted the bad thing inside her that had made Mr. Bradfield notice her in the first place.

She burned for her badness. She wanted his gaze again. All the time.

***

The fall was flat and boring, filled with dopey boys who could barely move on the gymnasium dance floor and the incessant giggles of her friends, Diane and Margie finding everything so exciting. No, finding the boys exciting.

"He smiled at me! Didn't he?"

Margie nodded at Diane. "It's your new dress. Tight you-know-where!"

Who cares? Mary Jo wanted to say, but instead, she nodded along, wanting only for the school break to start. At home, her mother was already preparing the house for their annual Christmas party. Right after Thanksgiving, the ten-foot tree was delivered, and her mother had spent days decorating it, shooing both Mary Jo and Bobby away.

"You'll just ruin everything," she snipped.

The night of the party, the guests started to arrive at five, the drinking hour, though Mary Jo was sure her mother had started earlier. In her organized and exacting fashion, Virginia had laid out a full spread on the gleaming and perfectly set walnut dining room table. The buffet table was stacked with thirty plates, bowls, cups, saucers, and dessert plates, Virginia's wedding china sparkling. Wanting everything to be perfect, Virginia brought out platter after platter of marinated pork tenderloin, Jezebel dip, cheese balls and pimento logs and crackers. In the fridge, frothy eggnog loaded with brandy, a whole cold ham studded with pineapple rings and cloves, three lemon meringue pies. The entire house was decked out in full Christmas splendor. Bobby's model train had been set up to run around and behind the tree. Lights shone, the fireplace burned bright, ornaments and bobbles flickered in the glow. Frank Sinatra's Christmas hits crooned on the Hi-Fi.

"Why are the Bradfields arriving so late?" her father asked as he brought in a case of beer and set it with a *thunk* on the kitchen table. Mary Jo's mother gave him a look and then shrugged.

"Catholic celebration," Virginia said. "The Feast of Saint Somebody. They'll be here after Mass."

Mary Jo backed out of the kitchen and fled upstairs. Should she stay in her bedroom the entire night, locking her door and finishing *Cat of Many Tails* by Ellery Queen? Or should she flounce down, smile, act as if nothing were on her mind but Santa Claus and his many reindeer? What should she wear? Maybe her new blouse, dark green with buttons down the front, tight you-know-where. For the holidays, her mother had insisted on two new skirts, one black, one red, both of which looked good with the green blouse. Just thinking about getting dressed reminded her of Mr. Bradfield in the kitchen, the way he'd reached out for her, his finger strumming her skin. Sometimes, when she was in the bathroom, she brought a hand to her chest, her breasts, her belly, imagining what it would feel like for someone else—him, of course—to touch her. He'd touch himself too, the way he had while staring at her, something happening not only to her, but to him.

Something she made happen.

Slowly Mary Jo got dressed, feeling the fabric graze her prickly skin. She thrummed like Bobby's guitar, which he hadn't put down since his birthday. She wished she could drink alcohol along with the adults, all of them laughing after their first glass. As people began to arrive, Mary Jo heard them from her room, the gaiety of conversation, the laughter echoing from the kitchen. As the house filled up, cigarette smoke clung to the ceilings, slipped under her door.

Sitting down at her vanity, she opened the top drawer and pulled out her brush, stroking her thick hair, still light at the tips from the summer sun. Soon she wouldn't be able to call herself a blond, the bright white hair she was born with slowly turning as dark as her father's. But her hair was growing in thicker and gleamed in the dull bedroom light. She wished her mother let her use perfume or lipstick, but she tskked and said, "There will be time for that yet."

At 8:45, the Bradfields finally arrived. While Mary Jo was in the kitchen helping her mother spread pimento cheese on toast points, she watched them bundle in and hand their coats to Opal, the Johnsons' housekeeper, who had brought along her sister Hazel to help for the night.

"Oh, Virginia," Betty said, swooshing in to give Mary Jo's mother a kiss on the cheek. "The house looks simply wonderful. A winter wonderland!"

Hazel and Opal came in and picked up trays of tiny Swedish meatballs and bowls of clam dip. Both of them rolled their eyes, but Mary Jo's mother didn't notice.

"Put the dip by the soda crackers," Virginia called after them. Then she raised her eyebrows at Betty and whispered, "I have to remind them about everything."

Betty gave her mother a quick smile and then turned to Mary Jo, patting her arm. "Look at you. All grown up."

Mary Jo blushed, flooded with guilt. Or jealousy. One of the deadly sins, for sure. Betty was so beautiful, glamorous next to Virginia, who was attractive, but older and pinched around the lips from all her smoking. Tall and blond with dark brown eyes and smooth, apricot-colored cheeks, Betty, a former nurse at the hospital her father did rounds at, had met Mr. Bradfield when he returned from the war, a set-up right here at her parents' table. Mary Jo remembered that first meeting, her mother starching her up and pulling her braids tight, wearing a new dress, her shoes shined, her dress pressed and crisp.

"Aren't you a sweetie," Betty had said and gently pressed two fingertips on Mary Jo's cheek, chin.

The rest of the night, she'd sat as close to Betty as she'd been able, Mary Jo right in the center of a romantic courtship the whole town watched play out. When the Bradfields were married last year, Betty wore a beautiful silk gown with a train. Mary Jo was able to see her upturned face when Mr. Bradfield removed the veil, the way her eyes closed when he bent down to gently kiss her.

"What a gentleman," her mother had whispered near Mary Jo's ear as they sat pressed together in the pew. "Storybook ending."

"Betty Bradfield is a princess," Diane had informed their friends at school.

Mary Jo was the only one who rolled her eyes, but Diane was right. Betty Bradfield was Cinderella and Betty Grable smushed together.

While eavesdropping on her mother and Betty two weeks ago, Mary Jo discovered Betty was expecting her first baby in late spring. So far, Mary Jo couldn't see any evidence, Betty lean and stylish, her lips a shiny red bow.

Virginia took a break and sucked on her perpetual cigarette. "Mary Jo, put Jupey in the garage for the night and then go out and see what needs replenishing."

Betty laughed. "Roger's so hungry, he probably ate all the ham and half the pecan pie Opal laid out. When he gets hungry, nothing is safe."

Popping a toast point into her mouth, Mary Jo whistled to Jupey, who wagged her tail and followed Mary Jo out into the garage and to her banishment dog bed. At least that's what Mary Jo liked to call it. Whenever there was company or too darn much going on, Jupey was relegated to the garage with her tattered blankets and metal water dish.

"It'll be over soon," Mary Jo said, stroking Jupey's nose. "I'll come back when they all leave. Then you can come sleep in my room."

Mary Jo went back in the house and headed first to the dining room and then to the living room, which seemed about as big as a shoebox. There were so many people in the house, she couldn't see the tables or couches or chairs. Groups had spilled out into the covered patio, the entryway, and the first-floor hallway. A group chatted in front of the downstairs bathroom, and outside the large living room picture window, she saw a group of bundled-up men standing in a circle, holding cigars and drinks. Smoke swirled around them.

Nothing needed replenishing. Her mother, Opal, and Hazel had piled so much food in the dining room, the party could go on all weekend. And because it wasn't snowing—the night barely at freezing, the sidewalks dry and shoveled—people could drink all they liked and walk home, leaving their cars parked here 'til morning. That was always the sign that her parents' party had been a success—the line of cars out front.

Mary Jo smiled at her parents' friends, neighbors, Mr. Deming, the local pharmacist. She waved at Diane's parents and a few people she recognized from the country club. As she moved through the stifling living room, she realized she was looking for Mr. Bradfield, waiting for him to turn and see her, but he was nowhere in the house, at least down here.

Circling the rooms twice, she peeked into the kitchen for her mother, but she and Betty were in the middle of a group of women in the dining room. Laughter burst from them like bouquets. Her father was on the patio, telling a story, using a cigar like the pointer Mary Jo's history teacher used to indicate landmarks on the maps that rolled down in front of the blackboard.

Bobby had gone to Ralph Jamison's house to spend the night, the housekeeper in charge. Mr. and Mrs. Jamison sat smashed deep in the living room couch, both with drinks in their hands and plates on their laps. Opal and Hazel were moving a mile a minute, handing out drinks, taking plates back into the kitchen, bringing out platters now filled with sand tarts, sugar cookies, gingerbread, and snickerdoodles. Pies orbited the table like planets. Cakes towered on the buffet. The music seemed too loud, and the whole house smelled like mulled wine, pine boughs, and cigarette smoke.

While partygoers drank, ate, chatted, and smoked, Mary Jo snuck down the hall and up the stairs, the noise peeling off her with each step. When she reached the landing, she paused, listening carefully. In the quiet, she was alone, maybe a bit lonely. It would be nice to sit on the top step with Bobby right now, comparing notes about the guests and eating gobs of cookies. Mostly, she'd do all the talking, but he'd be at her side, crunching away and begging her to play checkers.

The way this party was going, it was better he was gone. A couple times, Mary Jo had discovered adults up here during a party, men and women, not necessarily in the couples she expected. They had pushed past her, and Mary Jo lowered her eyes, trying not to think: Mr. Jarrett and Mrs. Gustafson; Mr. Vidal and Mrs. Hughes. In the wreckage of after-party mornings—ashtrays heaped with butts, the kitchen clinking with glasses and plates that not even Hazel could handle—there wasn't a way to tell her parents. Later, when she saw the adults on Main Street, at the country club, or in the next pew at church, she pretended nothing had happened.

Mary Jo let out a long sigh, and then something shifted, moved, a noise from down the dark hallway. Slumping, she wished she wouldn't have to watch another sad parade of parents slink past. But then she heard, "It's me. Come here."

"I—" she began, but then she felt his hand on her wrist, and he pulled her into her mother's large walk-in linen closet, a room no parent had ever emerged from before.

He held her tight by her wrist, her arm, her shoulder, and then Mr. Bradfield pulled her against his body, picking her up, her back against the shelves, the wood hard on her spine. She exhaled, her whole body tingling. This was the time he would finally touch her gently, hold her close, and say nice things. She started to smile in the darkness, anticipating his words, something about her filling out her blouse or her hair being so soft.

But as he closed the door, he shoved her against the wood, too hard, and she yelped. His strong hands gripped her body, his hands hard on her ribs, hip bones, shoulders. That was okay. Finally, they were close together. He would tell her more about how she looked. He would stare at her, even in the closet, maybe seeing her with his hands, moving over her brand-new skirt and blouse. He'd brush a finger along her cheek or her throat, like he had in the summer. They should go to her room, she thought, shrugging him away a little so she could see him in the gloom and tell him that.

Before she could get out a word, he slammed his mouth on hers, and for an instant, she wondered how she would breathe, her whole life sucked up into his mouth. In what felt like survival mode, she inhaled ragged breaths through her nostrils, taking in the stuffy air of the closet, towels, soap, old blankets. Then she stilled, her heart stopping, stunned by what was happening. This wasn't what she imagined, but how could it be? She didn't know what to expect in the first place. Mary Jo stiffened, relaxed, and then pushed against his chest until she realized that she had no ability to stop this thing that hadn't been anything before right now. This thing she must have willed into existence.

Mary Jo struggled to stop him, but it was no use. He held her up, gripping her hard, pinning her tight. Yanking down her skirt zipper, he thrust one hand down the front of her body and then slid up into her. He opened her, every part. Her mouth, her blouse, her panties, his fingers yanking them down, his hardness—that part she'd seen through his pants that day in the kitchen—near her, hot, hard, horrible, and then, oh! he shoved and thrust inside her, ripping and pushing, pushing, pushing against her, nothing feeling good or right, all of it impossible.

He rammed on, his hot, horrible breath in her ear, one hand iron around her waist, the other bracing himself against the shelves. Mary Jo squeezed her eyes shut, gripping his shoulders with her fingernails. She wanted to go back to minutes before, back when she was on the stairs, thinking about Bobby and cookies. She wanted to return to the kitchen with her mother and Mrs. Bradfield, talking about the party. Further back, further back to when she was little and would sit next to her mother on the couch and listen to stories. Mary Jo wanted to be anywhere but here, in this prison, cave, grave. She struggled against him, desperate to cry out, but he kept his mouth on hers, his tongue too heavy for any of her words to emerge.

Help, she thought.

Mommy, she thought, a name she'd never used for her mother, or if she had, she'd been so little, she'd forgotten. Mommy!

Dad!

Mr. Bradfield grabbed her with hands like claws. Daggers ripped up her private parts in tearing yanks. Finally, with three intense shoves, he seemed to freeze, a yell in his throat unuttered because he stayed clamped to her face. His movements stuttered, and then she was filled with wetness that didn't belong to her, unless he'd hurt her so badly, she was bleeding. Or her tears—she realized she was crying—had covered her from top to bottom.

Another thrust, slower, and another. Finally, he took his mouth away from hers, panting into her face, each breath a waft of alcohol. Her mouth free now, she searched for sound, but the scream she had craved seconds before had curled up and disappeared like smoke, sneaking under the closet door and disappearing in the crowd of partygoers.

As he panted, he lowered her to her feet, tucked in his shirt, smoothed his hair, moving against her in the closet. Then he took his two hands and put one on either side of her face.

"Don't tell anyone about this, Mary Jo," he whispered. "This is between us. This is our secret. Just us. You and me."

He put his mouth on hers one more time, a small kiss, now soft, almost kind, a kiss cousin to the lovely kiss he'd given his bride at the wedding.

He whispered, "You're the one I love the most. My favorite. You will always be my favorite."

Mary Jo didn't look up, but she started to whimper, a wounded sound that seemed to come from somewhere else. A puppy in a corner. A lost gosling. A baby bird fallen from the nest.

"Don't worry," he whispered. "Don't be sad. We'll do this again. As many times as you'd like."

Then he opened the closet door and closed it behind him, leaving her to sink to the floor, a mess of open clothing and ripped, wet underwear, blood and something else. She grabbed a pillowcase from the closest shelf and put it between her legs, staunching the liquid flowing from her. She closed her eyes, breathed. In a minute, when it was safer, she would sneak back into her room and get into her pajamas. She'd lock the door and stay hidden for the rest of the night. Only Jupey would miss her. Her parents and all the partygoers would have had too much to drink by then. They'd had too much already.

Virginia Johnson
January 1950

THE FIRST SATURDAY after the new year, Virginia told the whole family to leave the living room and then the house. Larry sputtered, protested, and then relented, agreeing to take the kids on a drive to see the countryside in winter, and soon doors slammed, the car roared, and they were gone. Relief settled over Virginia wide and calm. Finally, she could put everything back in order.

After last weekend's New Year's party at the country club and her slow Monday slog around the house as she waited for the aspirin to kick in, Virginia hadn't been sure she'd ever get the tree taken down. But by Tuesday, she had a to-do list as long as her right arm. Thank goodness the kids were old enough to make their own lunches and do chores. Now that Bobby could slap together a bologna-and-cheese sandwich, Virginia could really get her house organized.

If only Bobby would stop playing that silly "Rudolph the Red-Nosed Reindeer" song on his record player, strumming along with the damn guitar Larry had been silly enough to buy him. Maybe next time Bobby went on a sleepover, she'd sneak in his room to find the album and the guitar and tuck them away where he would never find either one again.

Carefully, Virginia picked each ornament off the tree, dusting the glass, crystal, wood, or fabric and wrapping them with tissue, the exact way she had done for years. Even the tissue from five years ago looked ready for a drippy nose, barely wrinkled. Her mother had given her three Bavarian crystal ornaments, bright and glittering, that Virginia wrapped in soft pieces of flannel cut from a pair of Larry's old pajamas.

Last year, she tried to show Mary Jo how to help her, but the girl didn't dust properly. The child couldn't decorate or undecorate a Christmas tree! Sometimes she even left the hooks on. And the tinsel! My goodness, the child couldn't be bothered to pick it off the branches. What was the point of teaching her? It was best for Virginia to do it herself.

After a coffee and cigarette break, Virginia turned on the radio, letting the music keep the beat as she worked. She had finished with the ornaments and was slowly unwinding the strings of lights when an alert caught her attention, the mention of Davenport, Iowa, pulling her out of her task.

Tragedy struck today in Davenport at the women's psychiatric ward at Mercy Hospital. A quick burning fire killed forty patients trapped inside the locked building...

Virginia sat down hard on the ottoman, a fist clutched at her breastbone. She listened to the last of the story, barely able to breathe. Twenty-five women had escaped, but those forty! Virginia couldn't even imagine. Or she could, feeling the fire, tasting the smoke on her tongue, seeing her hand reaching out to grab the woman closest to her. A decade earlier, her sister Katherine could have been trapped at Mercy Hospital. Katherine bound on her bed, locked in her room, locked in a ward, no visitors, not yet, not now. When the family was finally allowed to visit during specified hours, Katherine was lank, oily-haired, blank, wrapped in an ill-fitting gown.

Later things improved. She seemed to wake up, a light coming back into her eyes, her sorrow—which had started before she was twenty for no reason Virginia ever understood—lifting, mostly. Katherine now worked at a doctor's office in Charles City and lived in her own apartment. She had a couple of friends from work, her own television, and spent time with their mother on the weekends.

"She'll never be independent," the doctors told their mother, Gert.

Katherine had proved the doctors wrong, but there was no chance for these poor creatures now burned to a crisp. Virginia lit another cigarette, her hands shaking. Goodness, she hadn't thought about Katherine's hospitalization for years. It was all so long ago, but she could still see her sister on her small twin bed, looking up at the ceiling, her eyes fixed on mysteries she never shared with anyone, though once she came home, no one ever talked about it again.

For Katherine's entire hospitalization, Gert's mouth was clamped as tight as a fist. Not even their closest neighbors had an inkling.

"A schizoid break," the doctors said.

Katherine had proved her diagnosis wrong too.

Virginia took another puff of her cigarette and then stood, brushing away nothing on her skirt. She wanted to get in the car and drive home to Charles City and visit Katherine. She wanted to ask the questions that had always troubled her.

What was wrong?
What happened?
How did it feel?
What made it start?
What made it end?

Of course, it was likely the drugs had chipped away Katherine's wicked sense of humor and her raucous laugh as well as the illness, but did her sister finally decide enough was enough? Did she want to disappear into nothing because of something that had happened?

Virginia needed to know these answers because what if the same thing happened to Mary Jo or Bobby? What if she was missing what was wrong with her own children, not seeing the terrible spark that ruined Katherine's life? What if Virginia had skipped over the start of what would be the end?

It was too late to ask Katherine. And mostly, what happened in the past wasn't worth worrying about now. Onward, as her mother always said to them as they were growing up. The moment Gert had wiped tears or wrapped a finger with a plaster, it was time to make do. They'd fail a test, lose a friend, skin a knee, break a heart, and the cry was *Onward!*

Virginia walked over to the radio and turned it off. With a stab, she ground her cigarette into the ashtray, smoke curling in the air. She didn't need to hear any more. What was done was done. Maybe she'd put on Bing Crosby instead, letting his voice smooth away the tragedy. Truth was, those poor women were gone. There was nothing anyone could do about it now. She would finish with the tree and the decorations and then pack Christmas away in basement shelves where it belonged, ordered, neat, and in its place.

Mary Jo Johnson
Spring 1950

MR. BRADFIELD HAD hunted her down at the Wallingfords'
New Year's Day party and yanked her into a bathroom, the incident lasting only minutes. Alone, she slumped on the toilet afterward, Mrs. Wallingford finally knocking on the door, calling in with
concern, "Is everything okay in there?"

When Mary Jo slipped out, she shrugged and said something
about "her time."

"Let me know if you need anything, dear." Mrs. Wallingford
patted her shoulder. "You're almost a woman."

If she were almost a woman, what would being a full woman
bring? Who else would drag her into small rooms?

In February, he showed up when he knew her parents were at
the McCurdys' for cards, this time taking advantage of Bobby's
Boy Scout snow camping trip to pull her to the family room sofa.
This time it went on for longer, Mr. Bradfield taking off all her
clothes and doing things to her that made her clench her eyes shut
against his face, lips, body. Not that it worked. She felt it all, his
warm hands pushing open her thighs, his fat, horrible fingers digging into places she didn't want touched, his fingernail pressing
hard into her nipple, her mouth full of salt, blood. Her breath
stabbed her throat, her lungs.

Mary Jo's body was stretched and pulled in ways she never
imagined possible. But at least it had stopped hurting as much, the
pain after the time in the family room only lasting a day or two,
and she didn't bleed much, not like the first time.

But from that point on, Mary Jo contrived to never be home alone ever again. If Bobby was going to be out for the day or evening, she asked to accompany her parents to the country club or to whatever house they were headed, ignoring her parents' confused looks and silent communication. *Is this the girl who wanted nothing more than to read a book at home alone?* If tagging along with her parents wasn't possible (meaning, they were headed to the Bradfields'), she managed to spend weekend nights at either Diane's or Margie's house, enough that Diane's mother christened her an honorary member of the family.

She stopped going to the grocery store with her mother, citing homework or a stomachache or a migraine. She opted out of the fabric store and the five-and-dime excursions. For one weekend, she finagled two nights at her grandmother's house in Charles City, catching a ride with her Aunt Fiona and staying until her Uncle Dave headed through and could drop her back at Saint Helen. All she needed to do was keep up this ridiculous, hopping schedule until Mr. Bradfield grew distracted or bored. Until he forgot about her. Until what started in the summer and ended in the winter was nothing but a memory. Forgotten, a horrible part of her life that she no longer had to live. All Mary Jo had to do was live through it, and then it would be over. All she had to do was wait until he stopped looking. Then she would never have to think about it again, tucking these past months into a box she could hide for the rest of her life.

"Mary Jo is getting a little broad in the beam," Mary Jo heard her father say as she walked toward the kitchen. "Ginny, you might want to cut back on the mashed potatoes. Put a few more vegetables on the table instead."

Mary Jo leaned against the wall in the hallway, her breathing shallow, body still. She heard her mother tsk. The oven door closed. It was Sunday. Pot roast, mashed potatoes, and roasted carrots. Gravy and horseradish sauce. Mary Jo's stomach growled.

"It's puberty." Her mother's voice carried an undercurrent of irritation. But about what? The idea of having to cook more vegetables or her husband telling her what to do?

"That's more than hormones," her father said. "She's put on ten pounds since Christmas. Her face is as round as a MoonPie."

"It was a long winter." Something clattered onto the counter. There was a pause, the sound of ice clinking in a glass. Then there was the crackling, salty smell of pot roast in the air, a meaty waft filling the hall. "She didn't get out as much."

"She was downright odd," her father said, but he didn't offer up any proof. What had she been doing?

"You try to be a girl these days," her mother said. "So many things going on at school. It's all so social."

"She only went to one dance."

"Would you go to a dance with those farm boys?"

Her father laughed, the sound warm and happy, though Mary Jo felt nothing but sadness at his disapproval of her and her body.

"I don't think I would," he said. "Point is, we want to nip this weight gain in the bud. I can't tell you what I see day in and day out—"

"Don't start with me about the farm wives eating the big meals along with their husbands, morning, noon, and night. I know, I know. I can throw together a green salad if you really think it would help. But go roust the kids. Dinner in fifteen minutes."

Mary Jo turned and rushed up the stairs and into the bathroom, closing the door behind her. Light off, she leaned against the door. When her father called up the stairs about dinner, she yelled back, "Okay!"

Broad in the beam, one of the worst criticisms her father gave out. He never said fat. Or pudgy. Or stout, like the pants that were sold at Merten's Department Store. Farmer's wives were broad in the beam, and that was bad, leading to heart failure and stroke. The angina, she heard her Grandmother Gert call it. Her father was slight, short, and strong, muscled, his arms as tight as the climbing ropes in the gymnasium at school. When he came back from the war—he was a doctor on a war ship—he'd given up smoking and went light on the butter.

"I want to live to the twenty-first century," he told them one night at the dinner table. "Watch me."

Maybe she wouldn't make it to the twenty-first century. Mary Jo hadn't thought once about giving up butter. Worse, sometimes she and Margie smoked stolen Camel cigarettes behind the Duttons' barn on the way home from school, though they hadn't done that since early fall. Lately she'd been hungry, her stomach telling her it was time to eat on the hour. Also, when it wasn't. Her stomach let her know when what she ate was wrong. Last week she'd raced out of her world history class to throw up.

"No wonder," Margie had said after Mary Jo told her. "Your mother made you a liverwurst sandwich! With mayonnaise. Yuck!"

"Disgusting," Diane agreed, though Mary Jo was pretty sure Diane had never eaten liverwurst in her life.

Mary Jo wished she had a liverwurst sandwich now, though, and she slid to the floor, tears on her face. The winter had hung on forever—snow drifts still humped on the lawn and piled on the sides of the streets, the rain a mixture of hail and sleet. Every day was cold and an obstacle course—a complicated plan of how to avoid being alone or close to Mr. Bradfield, who still caught her eye when they were anywhere near each other. He would hold her gaze, wink, smile, his dark eyes on her. Her stomach burned.

"Mary Jo?" Her father knocked on the door. "Time for dinner."

I'm too fat for dinner, she wanted to say, but she was hungry, already tasting the stringy, salty, fatty pot roast, the melted butter dripping down the creamy potatoes before she poured gravy over everything. "I'll be right down."

A month later, the weather shifted, and Mary Jo was finally outside in a slash of sudden warmth and sun, sitting in a metal chair she dragged out onto the lawn. When they all walked home from school the day before, Margie and Diane had begged Mary Jo to go to the park to meet up with some boys. One boy, Jimmy Hayes, was a freshman and really swell.

"All those curls!" Diane said. "Dreamy."

"Luscious curls! And he wants to talk to you," Margie said.

Mary Jo pretended to be excited about Jimmy, but then shook her head, citing chores, watching Bobby, and homework.

"I'll let you know what he says about you," Diane said.

Mary Jo waved, but she didn't care what Jimmy or anyone said. She wanted to stay home, protected by doors and locks, safe from everyone. She wanted this year to be over. She wanted to move back to California, where they had lived during the war, where it was always hot and the sun always shone. At their house at the base, they'd had an actual orange tree growing in the front yard. The beach had been a quick walk down the street and then a short trek over a sand dune, the air tasting of seaweed and salt. And what a view, water out to the end of the world. Seagulls overhead. Her mother seemed lighter there, as if all that weighed a hundred million pounds in Saint Helen weighed a half-ounce in San Clemente. When she was five, nothing mattered, not even when her father shipped out. He'd been so handsome in his brand-new uniform and white cap. They'd cried, of course, but he would be all right. He was on the right side of things. The whole country was. And hadn't the big bombs dropped on Japan saved his fleet, not to mention the entire world?

"If we hadn't bombed the Japanese," her mother told her and Bobby, "your father wouldn't be alive today."

Her father had come home in one piece, his medical practice now stronger than ever. It was all because of California and its constant dream of heat and sun and blue skies.

It was all because of the bombs.

Iowa was heavy, cold, and deep with snow. Iowa was her extended family and all the people who had tied her parents to this place: schoolmates, college pals, in-laws, friends. Like a spider web, Mary Jo thought as she sat down and leaned back against the chair, closing her eyes. She heard her mother moving around in the kitchen. The phone rang, and her mother's voice was a pattern as constant as the first of the crickets. Who was on the other line? Betty Bradfield? One of Mary Jo's three aunts? A committee emergency? It wasn't long distance because she kept talking for a while, not rushing the conversation and hanging up on the expense with a clang. Then there was silence, save for the whine of insects and the flicker of leaves. A door opened and closed.

"Hey there, sleepyhead," Mr. Bradfield said.

Mary Jo jolted straight up, her heart beating in panic. He loomed, blocking the sun, his face darkened, but even so, she could see his intense stare. She strained to hear her mother's voice.

"She's next door at the Vidals'," Mr. Bradfield said, stepping closer. "I told her I'd run around back to borrow your father's pickaxe from the shed. No worries, I told her."

Pickaxe, she thought. What would he do with it?

Swallowing, Mary Jo stood and moved behind the chair, clutching the top. Her knees trembled. Mr. Bradfield held her father's pickaxe at his side, the metal glinting and sharp in the afternoon light.

"Hey," he said.

She stepped back, the chair now on its back legs. Without looking toward the Vidals' two-story house, she wondered how long it would take her to zip past him and out of danger. She could run across the wide lawn, through the verge, and over the fence, like Bobby always did. But she wasn't a runner or anything physical. Mr. Bradfield would pin her down in a second.

"Hey." He moved even closer, and she swallowed down her scream. Mary Jo needed her mother to appear, but also, her mother couldn't know about this. Either way, Mary Jo was going to get caught and punished. Either way, she would be in terrible trouble.

Then as he always did, he started to take her in and swallow her down, his eyes on her lips, throat, body. His gaze lingered on her belly, staring, staring, something in his face changing, growing slack and then sharp, like a hawk spying a baby chick. But in his face there was something awful, his eyes wide and hollow, filled with a bad ending.

"Mary Jo," he began, his voice urgent, cracking. "Why are you hiding from me?"

"Yoo-hoo," her mother called out, walking around the house and into the back yard. "I see you found it."

Mr. Bradfield slapped the axe against his leg, a whack, whack. Mary Jo dropped the chair, and it toppled to the lawn.

"Goodness," her mother said. "Roger, let's go inside and have a cocktail. It's five o'clock somewhere. And Mary Jo, either sit on that chair or put it away."

Her mother and Mr. Bradfield walked off, the grass smashed by their steps. Heat beat down on Mary Jo's head, gnats spun around her face. She dragged the chair to the side of the house and then walked around to the front and headed down the street, hoping she still had time to meet up with Diane and Margie. Hoping there was a place for her anywhere but home.

"She up and left without telling me," her mother was saying, holding a serving spoon in her hand. "I heard from Vera—Diane's mom—that they were with a bunch of boys. From the high school."

Mary Jo poked at her meatloaf with her fork. Her stomach churned as her parents talked over her, as if she didn't exist. Jimmy Hayes had been there, and he was friendly and cute, his *luscious* curls bobbing. But all Mary Jo had been able to do was tamp down her terror.

"She came home, didn't she?" Her father had been golfing at the club all day, his face glowing with sun and time off from patients.

"That's not the point." Virginia, still holding the spoon, turned to Mary Jo.

Her father wiped his mouth with his napkin and sat back. Bobby snickered into his scalloped potatoes. Their mother had been so upset with Mary Jo that she hadn't noticed Bobby had come to the table with his hair sticking up straight and his finger-nails rimmed with dirt.

"You should have told your mother where you were going," her father said. "Facts are facts."

Her mother turned her wedding ring round and round on her finger and then sighed. "You don't know what might happen out there. And—my heavens, Bobby, what in good graciousness is the matter with you? Your hands! Look at your nails! Go wash up right now."

Bobby snorted, pushed away from the table, and headed toward the bathroom.

"Young man," her father called out, but Bobby disappeared down the hallway and slammed the bathroom door.

"I'm sorry," Mary Jo said as she carefully placed her fork on her plate. She breathed in and out slowly, trying to keep her tears inside. All she needed to do was get up to her room and close the door. "May I be excused?"

"No dessert?" her mother asked.

Mary Jo wondered if this was a dig about Mary Jo's weight gain. But her mother seemed serious, maybe even concerned.

She shook her head and pushed back from the table, and something in the way she moved pulled her skirt tight against her belly. Or she turned oddly, giving her father a look at her. That's all she needed, she thought when she heard him suck in air. She was that horrible. That huge. A dirigible floating over the table, seconds away from crashing and burning. A big, giant farm wife balloon in the Macy's Thanksgiving Day Parade.

"My god," her father said, his voice hollow and full of air. "My good god."

"What is it, dear?" her mother asked, and then, in a short second, she exhaled as she followed her husband's gaze. "Oh. Oh, my."

Bobby never made it back to the table, packed up with a sleeping bag and a ham sandwich and sent to Timmy Rawlins house.

"I don't want to go!" Mary Jo heard him whine, but then the door closed, and Mr. Rawlins's car glugged down the road.

Mary Jo's mother had taken the phone off the hook, tucking the receiver into a drawer to keep things quiet. Now they all sat silent in the living room, one light on. They stared at her, and her father cleared his throat. She heard him turn into his doctor self, the voice he used on the telephone when patients called.

"Do you know how girls get pregnant?" he asked Mary Jo.

"Larry." Her mother reached out a hand to his knee, but she didn't say anything else.

"Mary Jo," he said, starting again. "Do you know how babies are made?"

All these months, Mary Jo had pretended she didn't know where babies came from. But of course she did. Her parents owned a large farm outside of town, renting it to a farmer who raised corn and sorghum and all sorts of animals: chickens, geese, pigs, cows, and horses. Once when they all visited, she and Bobby had watched in amazement as a gander hauled after a goose inside the barn, honking as he did whatever it was. Something that the goose didn't want at all.

Mary Jo nodded and looked down at her hands. Her body felt as if she were filled with bees.

"You had your first period, right?" Her father looked at her earnestly, eyes wide behind his glasses.

She nodded.

"And since?"

Mary Jo took in a breath, unwilling to admit to what she had suspected. Something had gone wrong. She'd had that first menstruation, and then she'd waited, prepared for it, sanitary napkins in the drawer by the toilet and in her school bag for emergencies.

But she'd never bled again. She shook her head.

Her mother put a hand to her mouth and began to sniff.

"Ginny," her father said, voice firm.

"What happened…?" Her father's doctor voice faltered, and Mary Jo looked up to see his eyes heavy with a look she'd never seen before, not when he left San Clemente to fight the Japs in the Pacific Ocean. Not over any really sick patient. Not over anyone.

Then there before her was Mr. Bradfield, staring, looking, pulling her close. All those months, she'd never told one soul. She could have stopped it, but she hadn't.

"Mr. Bradfield," she said. "He did it."

Her mother sat back, confused. "Roger?"

Her father stared at her. "Surely not."

"Roger Bradfield?" Her mother asked. "Not a boy at school? Maybe from the high school?"

"A high school boy," her father repeated.

"Those boys from last night. Was that the first time?" Her mother's voice was high and thin like a tightrope. "Is this why you've been keeping secrets?"

Mary Jo shook her head. "Mr. Bradfield," she began, not knowing how to start or even end this story. "He was looking at me."

"What do you mean 'looking at you'?" her mother asked, sitting back, irritation and maybe disgust spreading across her face. "When was he looking at you? Why was he looking at *you*?"

"At the Christmas party," Mary Jo said, not including all the other days when Mr. Bradfield had watched and touched.

Her parents sat back together as if her words had been a giant hand slapping them into silence. Mary Jo looked down at her hands again, wishing she could melt away like snow. What could she tell them that would keep her out of trouble? But she was already in trouble.

"I'm not having a baby," she said suddenly. "I heard you tell Mother I was broad in the beam."

Her father stared at her, something in his throat sticking. He swallowed and swallowed again and then rubbed his forehead.

"Did Mr. Bradfield...did he touch you?" Her father faltered. "Did he put his body next to...into yours?"

"What time did this happen?" Her mother suddenly stood up, her arms crossed over her chest as if she were freezing. "Where was I?"

"You were in the kitchen," Mary Jo blurted. "He..."

"He what?" her father asked, calm again, smooth, the doctor's voice Mary Jo had heard her entire life.

"He trapped me in the linen closet upstairs and did it. To me. He grabbed me. He did. He did it." Mary Jo started weeping, wiping her eyes with the back of her hands. Her entire body began to shake, sobs strumming her sternum. For a second, she could barely breathe, as if she were in the linen closet once again, smashed against him, trapped. Trapped. She sobbed, wishing someone would reach out, but her tears pushed her parents away. They turned toward each other, locking eyes.

"My god," her father said again and again. "My god."

"They came late that night because of the service," Mary Jo's mother said.

"Roger drank a lot," her father said. "Didn't eat."

"Hunger and alcohol," her mother began.

"I've seen this happen before," her father finished. "People lose control. They black out. They don't remember a thing."

"Of course. He didn't know what he was doing. How could he? Could he?" Her mother turned back to Mary Jo. "Has he done anything else to you since? Has this happened again?"

Mary Jo stopped breathing. In fact, everything inside her seemed to stop, hanging on this question. He had done so much more. He'd keep doing more too, if she let him. Except—except maybe he'd seen something too. His face, the way he'd stepped away, turned off his beam, eyes dropping from hers.

But if she said once, once only, it would all be a terrible mistake. Everyone would know, but he would leave her alone. If there really was a baby. A baby. Her baby.

"He wants—" she started before she crumpled.

They stared at her. "Has he done it since?" her father asked.

Heart thudding in her ears, breath frozen, Mary Jo shook her head.

"Did he say anything? After…" her mother began. "Did he apologize?"

Mary Jo's mouth went slack, and she stared at her mother, who looked away.

Her father ran a hand over his hair, sighing. Then he stood and walked to the wall calendar in the kitchen, the one on which her mother wrote all their lessons and appointments, the parties and social engagements and birthdays. He flicked through the months.

He let go of the calendar and took off his glasses, rubbing his eyes the way he did after a long day, thumb on the side of one eye, middle finger on the other. Then pressed tight, as if pressure could keep him from seeing anything else.

After a long moment, he came back and sat down, smaller, it seemed, than when he'd gotten up.

"We have to call them. We have to tell them both," her mother said. "Oh, poor, poor Betty."

Poor Betty.

"Let me take her into the exam room. Probably too early to hear a heartbeat…"

If her father bothered to listen to her body, he'd hear something. Mary Jo's heart was beating, beating, her body, her head, remembering how she hit the linen closet shelves, hard, the pain in time with his ugly, horrible rhythm. Mary Jo reached a hand to her throat, knowing that she might die here, right now.

Neither of them was watching her. Her father kept talking. Mary Jo could perish on the spot or stand up and walk out of the room. They wouldn't notice.

"What will we do?" Her mother grabbed her father's arm.

"One step at a time, dear." And in that instant, there was affection, her father leaning close to her mother. Their foreheads touched, then their lips. A kiss.

Her parents whispered to each other, nodding and holding hands. She looked down, the only place her gaze belonged. She needed to pee, her thighs trembling as she pressed her knees together. She wanted to cry. Things would never get better.

Her father kissed her mother one more time and then stood up. "Come on, Mary Jo. Let's go to my office."

And she followed.

All Mary Jo's life, her father had kept a home office, perfect for seeing patients who lived nearby or who were having late-night emergencies. Sometimes her father treated people who came straight from the fields. People who couldn't pay except in bushels of tomatoes, bags of string beans, or buckets of strawberries. Once he was paid in a side of beef, which Mr. Bradfield stored for them downtown in the grocery store freezer.

The office was cozy and warm, but the thing Mary Jo liked the best was that on his desk in the small consulting room next to the exam room was a bowl of butterscotch candies. When she was taken in there for a first-rate wound cleaning or splinter removal, her father would urge her still with a promise of one, maybe two, of the crunchy amber sweets.

She was sure she wouldn't get one tonight.

"I'm going to have you lie down on the table. That's right." He helped her up and then to recline on the table. She'd only ever sat on it before, and it was funny to be looking up at the ceiling.

"Could you lift up your skirt? Over your belly button," he said as he turned and put on his white coat.

Mary Jo's skin burst with heat. She hadn't been in her underwear near her father in years. Maybe ever. But he took out a sheet and pulled it up over the band of her underwear and then pushed both down a little, the skin of her belly prickling in the cold exam room air.

Mary Jo turned toward the wall. Her mother had decorated the office with hunting scenes, three paintings she and Grandma Gert had discovered in an antique store in Latimer. "A steal!" her mother had said.

"A find," her grandmother had said.

Mary Jo sniffed. Her father turned the faucet on and off, wiping his hands. What else? An eye chart that Mary Jo couldn't read because she wasn't wearing her glasses. A weight chart she knew too well.

"Five pounds over average," her father had told her last month.

On the counter, a head mirror, a stethoscope, and a small wooden thing that looked like a cup. Mary Jo looked at her father, who showed her his hands and then touched her stomach. Mary Jo flinched, closed her eyes, forcing herself to not cry. How long had it been since her father had touched her?

Turning to face the wall, she focused on his gentle pushes on her abdomen.

"Does this hurt? Does this? Here?"

At each question, she shook her head.

He slumped a little into his doctor's stool, staring at her for a moment, a question somewhere inside him. Ask, she thought. Let me tell you the whole story. But instead, he turned to grab the little wooden cup, placing the base of it on her skin, his ear on the open part, his face looking at her, but not. He was listening, thinking as he did, waiting for something, waiting, waiting, and then his face closed down, crumpled, and he stood up.

"Go upstairs and go to bed, MJ," he said as he put the cup back on the counter, the sound a tiny click. He shrugged off his white coat and hung it up. "We will all talk tomorrow morning."

MJ. He hadn't called her that since before she started first grade, when her mother had insisted they all use her full name, Mary Jo, proper and lovely and so grown up, now that she was a big girl going to school. MJ was for toddlers.

Can you call me that forever? she wanted to ask. MJ would never find herself in this mess. MJ would have run away from Mr. Bradfield fast as a wink. MJ would have battled him with a sycamore branch or Bobby's pirate sword. MJ would have run like the dickens to her father and told him everything. MJ was strong and lean and had long beautiful hair.

MJ was everything Mary Jo was not.

Quietly, Mary Jo closed the office door behind her. She stared into the empty house, dark now, only a tiny light in the stairway casting a pale glow. Heaviness filled her like lead as she stepped into the stairwell. She had to concentrate on each step, carrying her horrid, weighted self up each stair, one by one, even though all she wanted to do was sit down and wail.

She pushed open her bedroom door and stood in the darkness at the center of the room, moonlight flooding through the window and lapping at her shoes. Wind blew through the tree branches, the moonlight flickering. Cool air whisked over the tops of her hands, her neck, her ankles, and then she heard the great heater at the core of the house ignite, whirring and pushing out hot air. On her bedside table, her alarm clock beat out time, every second taking her further from the time when none of this was true.

She flopped on her mattress and lay in the pale darkness, listening to the tap of leaves on her window. Maybe in the morning something good would happen. She'd wake up bleeding, as she had that first time. Blood would take the baby and all her problems away.

Mary Jo Johnson
Summer 1950

MARY JO USED to love her family home, the large three-story house outside the center of town on a tree-lined street, the sycamores so tall their top branches touched, creating a barrow. On hot summer days, the coolest spot was the middle of the road, wind pushing down the packed gravel, rising up through the branches and emerald leaves, whirling from tree to tree to tree.

Across from her house, through a gate, and down a grassy path were a park, a creek, and then the pond it fed into, home to wood ducks and white herons and beavers. Sometimes in the summer, her father carried his canoe down to the creek and sat Mary Jo and Bobby down, one in front of him, one behind, and they would paddle as far as they could before the creek petered out. Her mother always packed them a basket of sandwiches, sliced apples, and a thermos of coffee, their father carefully pouring out cups they sipped as they were buoyed by the slight movement of the water. Cattails swayed, water bugs scuttled, and they ate to the sound of air and water.

Her mother had the decorator's touch—or so she told anyone who offered her a compliment about the curtains, rugs, or wallpaper—and each room on the main floor was full of gleaming wood furniture, some with richly upholstered cushions and covers. Most of the time, Mary Jo and Bobby weren't allowed in the living room, which seemed ridiculous to Mary Jo because it was her parents' friends who spilled glasses of Scotch on the sideboard or ground cigarettes into the thick wool pile of the big carpets. "That's not the point," her mother snapped once when Mary Jo managed to say just that.

She and Bobby had learned to treat parts of their own house like a museum, something to visit quickly before heading to the kitchen for a snack.

Snacks? Well, her mother had those in spades: great glass jars of cookies, pans of brownies, pie plates full of fruit pies and lemon tarts. In the fridge, pickled peaches and pears, cucumber dills, fresh tomatoes sprinkled with sugar. When Grandma Gert came to stay, the oven never stopped producing sweet treats and savory roasts, the whole house full of the sizzling aroma of fat and salt and heat.

Summer was Mary Jo's favorite time: school was out, the air heated up, the world turned all the greens and bright blues and whites. In the morning, she would complete whatever tasks her mother had for her and then go outside with a book, climb the cherry tree, and read for hours and hours. Jupey would curl up at the base of the tree and wait for Mary Jo to finish the last line of the last chapter. Then Jupey would stand up and wag her tail, ready for dinner.

After an evening meal of fresh corn and summer squash, fried pork chops, and homemade vanilla ice cream with chocolate sauce, Mary Jo played with her brother and friends, every summer except during the war years, all the summers until the last when things went wrong.

After the night of her father's examination, things changed fast, starting with the meeting her parents had with Mr. Bradfield at the grocery store the next day. Mary Jo was not invited, but she felt each minute her parents were gone, half expecting to hear the wail of a police siren headed toward the grocery store. Didn't things like that happen on *Call the Police*, that crime drama her father liked to listen to? Someone was always trying to clean up crime in the city.

Maybe her parents would do it the quiet way: Mr. Bradfield led off in handcuffs, pushed into a sedan, rushed to jail. That would do it. He'd be gone, and her father would take care of everything.

As she waited for her parents to return, she sat with Bobby while he listened to the radio and played with his train set. But she couldn't hear anything but static, her thoughts on fire. If he weren't arrested, would he and Mrs. Bradfield have to move away? Sell the grocery store? Leave the state? No one would ever talk to them again, would they? They'd have no friends. Their church would kick them out. They'd have no other choice than to leave.

Or would she be the one who had to leave? She the one with no friends?

"I'm bored," Bobby wailed.

"Shut up!" Mary Jo snapped. "Go play your stupid guitar."

"I don't want to play my guitar. I'm hungry."

"You're always hungry."

"Am not. But I'm hungry now."

After lunch passed and the afternoon stretched to breaking, Mary Jo relented and slapped together cheese-and-pickle sandwiches. She and Bobby sat together at the kitchen table, Bobby babbling on about large pileated woodpeckers and guitar picks. She pressed a hand against her mouth and pushed her sandwich to the middle of the table, blinking hard.

Finally, after hours and hours, her parents returned home, sent Bobby to bed, and sat Mary Jo down again in her father's office.

"Thing is," her father said, "Mr. Bradfield is very sorry for what happened."

"Sorry," Mary Jo repeated.

Her mother held up a finger, her constant signal to be quiet. "He'd worked hard from dawn to dusk at the store and then went to church. He came to the party without eating a bite since morning. Then he drank too much, very quickly."

Mary Jo stared at her mother, but Virginia would not meet her eye. Instead, she sniffed and continued. "He barely remembered the party. When we asked him, he was astounded. Then ashamed. Horrified. He thought that he'd pulled his wife into their bedroom at their home. He didn't really know where he was or who he was with. He was so confused, and…well, he…"

"He violated you," her father said, his words a slap, but he avoided Mary Jo's gaze as well, his face pale, lips white. "He is truly sorry and wishes to make amends."

Amends. The word sounded like something from church, something you would do to be forgiven for the worst of sins like murder. And he was a liar, another sin. He hadn't thought she was Betty, his wife. He'd called Mary Jo by her name! *Don't tell anyone about this, Mary Jo*, he'd said. He'd been planning it all. He'd been watching her all summer. He'd touched her. Then he'd done all those things, and he'd done them again and again, and now he was lying again and ruining her life.

And she'd never told anyone. She was as big a liar as he was. They'd blame her for not telling. Mary Jo clenched and unclenched her teeth, the truth in the tiny space between her molars. But if she told, she would be caught in her own lies like a bug, crushed and sucked dry.

"Are they going to have to move away?" Mary Jo finally asked.

At that, her mother gave her a strong look. "Why would you ask that?"

Mary Jo's throat felt thick, as if she were about to cry. Was she? She rubbed her nose. "Because of what he did."

"He did something very wrong," her father said, looking at a spot above her right shoulder. She wished she could lunge forward and pull his face to hers like she used to. Hadn't they played together on the rug in the family room before dinner? He was a pony or a car. She could still feel his face under her palms, his face prickly with beard.

"But it's wrong."

Her father nodded.

"Aren't you going to call the police?"

Her father looked down at his hands. He clenched them once, twice. "He didn't mean for this to happen."

"It's wrong."

"It was." Her father nodded.

Mary Jo stared at her father, neither his words nor his actions making one bit of sense. All her life, her doctor father, Larry Johnson, had told the God's honest truth, hand on the Bible. But what he was saying now was nothing but a lie.

"But—"

He held up a hand. "The Bradfields have a child of their own, Mary Jo. Their little boy, Harry. If we take care of this ourselves, it can turn out all right."

Mary Jo blinked, swallowed hard, the lump moving into her chest, all of her clenched now, sore, from holding on so tight. But to what?

"How can anything be all right?" she asked, gripping her hands together.

"We have a plan," her mother said.

"What do you mean, 'plan'?" She wanted her father to save her. She wanted her father to be like men in books, the kind who break down doors and save people in burning buildings. A firefighter, policeman, fighter pilot. The men who swing on ropes across snake-filled rivers. The kind who save their daughters from the neighbors. He was supposed to save her, even when there wasn't a fire. When the fire was inside her.

"This baby will be your mother's baby," her father said.

"What?" Mary Jo stared at her parents. What were they saying?

"You'll go stay with your grandmother in Charles City."

"Grandma knows?" Mary Jo asked, horror-struck at the thought. Her bespectacled, gray-haired grandmother was strict and followed every rule. If the Bible or President Truman said something, Grandma Gert was first in line to behave and then enforce. All during the war, she had planted victory gardens and canned every vegetable and fruit she grew. Her lips were never loose, so she never sank ships. She sold war bonds and dragged Mary Jo into the effort one summer afternoon, both of them walking the neighborhood and knocking on doors.

"Don't be shy!" Grandma said. "Ask them to donate to the greatest fighting men in the world."

In the nights toward the end of the war, Grandma Gert wrote letters to soldiers abroad, urging them to hold a steady strain. *It will all be over soon.*

Mary Jo having a baby was out of order, followed no Grandma Gert rule. Had this even happened before? This was nothing that anyone had done in this family.

Her parents nodded. "She knows." Her mother pressed her lips tight after she spoke, her face pale.

"How will the baby be…" Mary Jo looked at her mother.

"We will pretend," her father said. "It's our only solution. And when your time comes, I'll take care of the delivery. When you come home, well, you'll be the big sister. And then you can start school right on schedule."

The air seemed alive with silver insects, wings clacking. Her father looked at her, blinking to the beat of their noise. Mary Jo blinked back, waiting. Pretend? Was her mother going to go around with a pillow under her dress the way Mary Jo and her friends sometimes did to pretend they were fat? How was it going to work? "What if something goes wrong? What if…"

What if? What if she couldn't have the baby the right way and something bad happened? To her or the baby? What if someone discovered the lie, the stacks of them? What if her father didn't make it to Grandma Gert's house on time? What if, what if, what if?

"Nothing will go wrong."

But Mary Jo had heard enough stories to know something always did. The boy who was run over by a tractor. The woman whose appendix exploded. The man who took too many pills.

"Let's think one step at a time." Her mother stood up, as if that were quite enough talk. "You are going to leave school. A medical reason. But you won't fall behind. We'll ask for your assignments."

Mary Jo was going to skip school, live with her grandmother, and be pregnant. Pregnant, an ugly sounding word, so hard at the end, uncomfortable on her tongue. She'd never really thought about the word. She was pregnant.

"Do Aunt Fiona and Uncle Dave know?"

They nodded again.

"Aunt Katherine?"

"Oh, no," her mother said, a strange look on her face. "Not Aunt Katherine."

Why not Aunt Katherine? She was always at Grandma Gert's. How would they be able to keep such a secret from her? From anyone?

"What about my friends?" Mary Jo asked.

Her mother took in breath. "Don't say a word to them, especially Diane. That girl talks too much. Mouth as big as a bullfrog's."

"Time for your friends later." Her father stood up too, busying himself with papers on his desk, his hands rustling through them as if they were dried leaves. "But you won't want to tell anyone about this...situation."

"Bobby?"

"Bobby is going to have a little brother. He won't know otherwise."

"What will the baby think?"

Her father reached out a hand, pressing her arm. "He won't feel any different from you or Bobby. He will be a Johnson through and through."

She shook her head, her breath held deep inside, a dark stone. How would her mother make anyone believe the baby was hers? And wouldn't that baby deserve to know who he was? Isn't that what everyone wanted? She had always known she was Mary Jo Johnson, daughter of Larry and Virginia Johnson, sister to Bobby. She would always know she was mother to this baby, but he would be disconnected from her and never know this story.

Mary Jo swallowed, a terrible lump in her throat. But how could she tell the baby what had happed in the linen closet. The baby deserved better. All her life, Mary Jo would hold this secret for the baby alone. Not for the Bradfields or her parents. Or even herself.

"Go upstairs now," her father said. "Pack your bag but don't worry too much about it. Your mother and I will bring what you forget."

Maybe she could forget the baby, right now. Leave it here. But nothing was safe in this house with these people. Look what had happened to her upstairs? She hadn't been safe for a year.

In her room, Mary Jo stood in the middle of the floor, eyes on the carpet, forgetting what she was supposed to do. Nothing made sense. Her mother would pretend to be pregnant. Her father would be a terrible doctor, doing what he shouldn't. Her grandmother would hide Mary Jo for months in her house like a German spy or a Communist.

She put a hand on her belly, right in the spot where her father had pressed that cup to hear the baby's heartbeat. The baby was inside her, beating into life, growing and turning into itself. That heartbeat was changing everything. School, her friends, her every single day. She was left with nothing except the baby, the only thing she had left.

Betty Bradfield
Summer 1950

HARRY STIRRED IN her arms, his mouth clamped on her right nipple, sucking hard. It was 2 a.m., the feeding she loved most. She and the baby were alone in the nursery, in their bubble, one light casting a yellow glow that warmed the room. Though it was hard to wake up after only a few hours, once she sat in the rocking chair Roger had bought before Harry was born, she was at peace.

A baby was all she'd ever wanted. Of course, she'd wanted a husband too. But babies. Five of them. Maybe six. A big family, noisy, rambunctious, full of energy. Probably mostly boys. The house would be electric.

But now Betty wasn't sure her marriage would make it past this baby's infancy. She always had her work. She understood life inside a hospital. Though she hadn't been a practicing nurse since the day before her wedding to Roger Bradfield, Betty still understood patients, heard her patients, those she'd tended at Saint Helen's Hospital. Those she'd tended during the war at the naval hospital in Norfolk, Virginia. She knew the difference between a cry of pain and that of sorrow. Betty knew the difference in the sounds of men shipping out and those who had shipped in.

Betty sensed the difference between the sounds of hunger, despair, and physical pain. She could read the language of each.

Outside, a light wind blew by the window, leaves scratching the glass. Harry's suction loosened, his open mouth white with milk. Betty understood this baby, sensed when Harry was angry or gassy. The moment she first held him, she felt him, deeply, internally, his personality radiating to his skin. Now she could tell when he was hungry before he could.

After only two years of marriage, Betty could tell when her husband's workday had been successful or a bust, the list in his left step, a scuffing, a lurch.

What Betty hadn't known was the sound of her husband raping a child.

That she'd not expected or trained for that. No one had ever told her this was an area she should focus on, wait for, anticipate.

After Pearl Harbor, Betty had been recruited to nursing school right out of high school, sent to Norfolk, and trained in surgery. She had helped doctors put bodies back together as well as take them apart, but she was unsure how to mend the jagged wound in her own life.

Harry stirred, his eye on her as she moved him to the other breast. He latched on, and she sat back. No other Saint Helen mothers Betty knew breastfed their babies, but she'd had a strong, straightforward obstetrics teacher, a doctor who believed childbirth and breastfeeding were natural processes. Nurse Davis had walked to the front of the classroom wearing her starched whites and prim hat.

"Eschew the formula! Help the mother," she'd said, holding her hand up as if clutching a breast. "Guide the nipple to the baby. Once, twice. That's all it will take."

Nurse Davis had been right. At the naval base, she'd never worked with mothers, but when it was time, Betty guided her own nipple to Harry, and he'd latched on hard and fast in his first moments of life. And Betty had been awake for it, waving away the gas the nervous nurse had offered before, during, and after labor.

"I want to pay attention," Betty had panted. "I want to see."

She hadn't seen everything, apparently. She hadn't noticed that her tall, dark, and handsome husband had pushed tiny twelve-year-old Mary Jo Johnson into a linen closet and raped her, enough that she was pregnant with Harry's half-sibling.

It was as if her ears had turned off the moment Roger had sat her down on their living room couch.

"Something's happened," he began, taking her hand in his.

"The business?" she'd asked, the crash of 1929 still in her bones. A banker who had invested his life savings into the market, her father had been hollow for the rest of his life, empty of cash and emotion. Betty's mother had started taking in washing and mending, enough to get Betty through high school. They'd made due as her father faded into the wood-paneled walls of the house, dying just before the war started.

Betty Bradfield knew how to survive a cataclysmic financial crisis. After all, hadn't her own mother kept them in evaporated milk and potatoes for years? Trouble now? They'd consolidate, condense, convert. They'd survive together. They could sell this big house, pack up, and move to Des Moines and rent an apartment. She'd go back to nursing. She'd pull her weight.

Roger shook his head, that gorgeous head, his hair thick and dark and shiny with a slight wave. He was perfect, well, except for his nose, which was a bit too large to be silver screen ready. But she liked that imperfection, he not too good for her by a flare of a nostril.

"Not the business." His voice was low and hoarse, as if he'd been crying. Betty had never seen her husband cry. "Something much worse."

"Your parents!" she cried out.

He looked up at her, this time not dropping his gaze. His eyes were bloodshot, filled with despair. The creases on his forehead were deep and cavernous; his face was wet from sweat or tears or both.

As she thought of her husband's face, Betty shuddered out a large sob, the movement wrenching her entire body. In a million years, she would have never guessed what her handsome husband had done. She let out a moan and then another. Harry startled, stilled, and then his mouth began to form his own sob.

"No, no, no," Betty whispered in his ear, holding him tight. "Oh, no. It's all right. It's all right."

She was lying. It would never be all right. This horror would follow Harry for the rest of his life, whether he knew about it or not.

After Harry finished the second breast, she stood and burped him and then placed him back in the crib, patting his back as he settled. Then she walked over to the lamp, flicked it off, and settled onto the camp cot she'd brought up from the basement. Remembering, she stood and bolted the door with the lock she'd bought at the hardware store and installed herself. The bolt slipped in smoothly with a metal click. Of course, her husband could beat down the door if he wanted to. But that wasn't how he worked. No. He hid in the darkness and snatched under-aged girls from hallways.

She sat back down on the cot, letting the darkness surround her. The house was silent, Roger sleeping the sleep of the damned or insane. Why was she still here? Betty's first instinct had been to run back to her mother, Harry in her arms. She needed to wait. To plan. But she knew one thing: Roger Bradfield would never touch her again.

The week that Mary Jo was whisked away to her grandmother's in Charles City, Virginia Johnson showed up unexpectedly on Betty's porch, rapping on the front door.

"Betty," Virginia called, "I need to talk with you."

Betty stood stock still in her foyer, barely breathing. If only Virginia would go away. How could Betty face her? Virginia was full of nothing but politeness, but she didn't take the hint, knocking, knocking, knocking until Betty was sure her neighbor to the left, Mrs. Vander Meer, would come over to see what the racket was all about. Besides, Harry had finally gone down for his nap.

Betty pulled open the door and tried to glare, but tears filled her eyes and soaked her face. Her husband had raped this woman's daughter. She wanted to throw herself at Virginia's feet and beg for forgiveness.

"Oh, dear," Virginia said, stepping inside and taking hold of Betty's elbow. "Come on, now. Let's go into the kitchen and sit down."

Instead of Betty tending to Virginia and making tea and pulling out lemon icebox cookies, Virginia made do in the kitchen, setting the kettle on the stove and arranging cookies on a plate. Then they sat silently for a few minutes, steam rising from the teacups. Virginia had pulled Betty's wedding china from the middle shelf, using teacups Betty hadn't thought to use herself since first putting them away.

"This is a horrible situation," Virginia began, wiping the corner of her mouth after taking a delicate bite of a cookie. Somehow she'd managed to eat a cookie and not disturb her red lipstick, expertly applied. Somehow she'd managed to eat a cookie, even while talking about this. So polite. So proper and put-together. For parties, Virginia arranged her hair in short, shiny auburn curls and did up her face, all big brown eyes, perfect eyebrows, and pouty mouth. She was of medium height and slim and could wear the hell out of a pair of trousers with wide legs, like Katharine Hepburn, really. And she could talk, sipping her bourbon and waving her cigarette. Virginia could slice a comment. Throw it like a knife.

Would she blame Betty for this?

"I'm not—"

"I'm so sorry," Betty interrupted. "I don't know how this is going to work out."

Virginia nodded, looking absently at the tabletop for a moment before reaching out to press the pad of one index finger to a cookie crumb. For an irrational second, Betty wanted to take Virginia's finger and lick it. What was wrong with her?

"Men," Virginia began and then stopped.

Men. Betty knew men. She'd been in close quarters with no one but men at the naval hospital for three long years. She'd listened to them, held their hands, staved off their advances, even when they were mortally wounded or desperately ill. She'd listened to them wheedle and cajole. She heard them crying at night when they thought the rest of the men in the ward were asleep. During ministrations, she'd avoided their erections, paying close attention to their bandages instead.

Men were men. But Roger was not only a man but her husband. A man she thought she knew.

"Well," Virginia said.

"Mary Jo?" Betty reached out a shaky hand to her teacup.

"At my mother's."

Betty had met Virginia's mother once before, a stern woman with a knot of gray hair pinned tight at the back of her head and small spectacles. Gert hadn't left the kitchen the entire visit, and when Betty conjured the woman, she thought about a white apron, barely smudged. Poor Mary Jo.

"And Larry will tend to her…when her time comes." Virginia paused, wiping her cheek. "She will come home after the baby does. And in a couple of years…"

Betty brought a hand to her chest. The baby would be here? She'd have to watch the baby grow up? "Not adoption?"

Virginia looked down at her teacup, swirling the liquid. "We surely thought about it. Larry's father was adopted, and he never knew, well, who he was. Larry doesn't want to do that to this child."

"But he won't know who he is really—"

"It will be close enough. Family, no matter what. That's why Larry said we should raise it as our own."

Betty looked down at her hands. "Not something else? Another alternative?"

There was a long pause. When Betty looked up, Virginia was staring at her, her lips pressed tight. Then her shoulders slumped, and she smoothed out her cuff. "No."

"All of us here in one place. This tiny town." Betty shook her head. Nothing changing. Everything changing. They were crazy.

Virginia shrugged. "It seemed the best way."

Betty almost laughed. "For whom? Certainly not me. Harry." *Mostly me. It's not best for me.*

"Let me put it this way," Virginia said. "It was the best we could think of."

From her tone, Betty wasn't sure if Virginia really thought that. And really, the best they could do would be to invent a time machine and stop this from happening in the first place. Conjure up some science-fiction madness and fling them all back in time. But when, exactly, was the right time to land? On that holiday party night? Or was there something deeper, darker, and worse in Roger?

Maybe Mary Jo wasn't the first time Roger had made a *terrible mistake.*

The mistake might be hers too. She'd missed something, hadn't she? All those times at the Johnsons' house. Roger must have glanced at Mary Jo. Things like that don't just happen. The poor child. Betty should have stood up and beat him to the ground.

But she hadn't done anything.

Betty shuddered and tried to take in a breath. Time beat its wooden spoon in the kitchen, a dull *thwap thwap* as Betty stared at Virginia. Outside, the breeze, the voices of the mailman, Sidney, and Mrs. Vander Meer, a car blustering past, backfiring as it turned onto Franklin.

"Roger knows about this?"

Virginia nodded. "I thought he might have told you."

Betty pushed back a bit from the table to slump against her chair. "We aren't speaking. I'm not even sure I will stay."

Nodding, Virginia met her eye again. "Your mother's?"

Betty shrugged. "I don't think I could bear to tell her the story. I can't even bear to think about it myself."

"I'm not letting Roger off the hook—"

"You are," Betty said. "After what he did…to your own daughter."

Again, Virginia nodded, but her face flushed. "He was drunk. He didn't know."

Didn't he? How could someone not know that?

Virginia kept talking over all of Betty's thoughts. "We can make this right. Mary Jo won't have to wonder all her life what happened to her baby. She will be with her baby. She'll be able to watch her baby grow up and go into his or her life. And she will also be able to have a life. She can graduate from high school and go to college and have a real family of her very own. But only if we do this now."

Horror gripped Betty's chest, her breathing ragged. Watch the baby grow up. Harry's half-sibling. They'd be in the same grade at school. And Roger. Had he really not known? He was always so insistent, so sexual. It was a miracle she hadn't gotten pregnant two months before her wedding, when she finally relented, gave in to his persistent pursuit. And since the wedding, all he could talk about was children. She'd kept telling him she wanted to finish up her job, get the house ready, feel like she truly lived in Saint Helen before starting a family. But every night, sometimes more than once, so much that she was sore and at least twice had suffered from bladder infections. If she wasn't a nurse, she wouldn't have known how to take control of her own body, making sure she kept clean and drank a lot of water. The writing, though, was on the wall. Her life would be a long string of children, which was okay. But his constant need for sex? It was an obsession. A sickness. A disease.

Had he turned to Mary Jo Johnson on purpose? Did he seek her out? How was any of this possible?

She shuddered, wanting to run fast and far. If she were smart, she'd stand up from the table, pack up Harry, and drive away for good. But where?

Virginia sipped her tea as if this were a regular social call on a regular day, but Betty noted her hands were shaking.

"How will you do it?" Betty asked finally. "How will you make people think this is your baby? How will you keep this from the neighbors?"

Virginia put down her teacup, the china *click* so delicate, so contrary to the conversation. "That's one of the reasons I'm here. I need your help."

For a second, Betty wanted to hand over her entire life. Here, have it, she would say. Whatever you need.

Betty picked up a cookie and popped the entire thing in her mouth, the sugar making her back teeth ache. Then she drank half of her lukewarm tea.

"What do you need?" she asked.

"A couple of your maternity blouses."

"Why?" As the word left her mouth, she knew. She could actually see it: Virginia walking down the street a bit slowly, a hand to her lower back, an A student in a drama class. Virginia was going to fake a pregnancy, one that was starting to show. A surprise pregnancy, long after another baby had been expected. A surprise. A happy accident. Oh, those Johnsons are so in love. Then Virginia would go into "labor" during a random visit to her mother's house, and Larry would deliver the baby. So lucky! Can you believe how it all worked out?

Betty would have believed it. She almost believed it now.

"What about Bobby?"

"Bobby doesn't see anything but his Boy Scout manual and his comic books," Virginia said. "And that damned guitar."

"And Roger?"

At that, Virginia's lips pressed together. "He's agreed to this idea."

There was more to this agreement, Betty knew. Maybe it was a threat. Or the whiff of a threat. Larry might be a short man, but he was an important man. A doctor with a thriving post-war private practice, hospital privileges, and powerful friends on the board and in town. He knew everyone at the country club. One call, and Roger would be behind bars.

Betty had met Larry before she'd met Roger. During her first day of work, a swift, slight man came rushing down the hospital corridor, spectacles on, reading his clipboard while making his rounds. Once introduced, she and Larry struck up casual conversations, chatting now and again, enough so that she was invited to the Johnson home for weekly dinners. One night a young grocer, a bachelor, a veteran, was in the chair opposite her, he with the big nose and bigger smile.

This was all the Johnsons' fault.

"So much could go wrong."

With sad, dark eyes, Virginia looked up from her teacup, the china sparkling brilliant blue in the morning light. "It already has," she whispered and then cleared her throat. "But we can make this right."

Betty's mother used to say, *Time heals all wounds.* Did Virginia really mean that after months and years, Betty would forget about Roger's drunken crime? Now, though, there would be no forgetting. Roger's baby born of rape would be eating peanut butter-and-jam sandwiches at the lunch table with Harry. Playing baseball on the same team. Dating the same girls. No matter where Betty turned, there would be the crime she was now agreeing to hide. The lie she was going to promote. Until Mary Jo went off to college or got married, Betty would have to look at her and smile, pretending that she was like all the other teenage girls in town.

Outside, a garbage truck clacked by, metal cans clanging. Virginia pulled a handkerchief from her bag and wiped her eyes, sniffing into the silence. On the wall, the clock ticked. Was time working yet? It was still moving. And in about five minutes, Betty was going to get up and bring down her three favorite maternity dresses and two blouses. She and Virginia would confer on how best to create a pregnant look: pillow or batting? When she shopped at the stores on Main Street, she would nod when Gloria Blunt handed her a pack of baby blue rickrack trim and said, "Did you hear about Mrs. Johnson's surprise package coming due in September?"

"I know!" Betty would put a hand to her cheek, feigning amazement over and over and over again. For months, she'd be putting on a fake smile, a happy demeanor. After all, she and Roger were the Johnsons' best friends. They were over the moon about the new baby.

Betty would smile and nod. "Oh, my, yes. What a blessing."

Larry Johnson, MD
September 1950

LARRY SAT AT his desk in his home office, the door shut. Without meaning to, he kept glancing at the black phone on his desk. He wasn't waiting for it to ring. It always rang. He was waiting for *the* ring, the call from Gert.

"Larry," she would say, haste and worry making her voice light and warbly, an old sparrow. "It's Mary Jo. It's time."

Three times since Mary Jo left, Larry had made the quick run to Charles City in his Chrysler—not the old Mercury sedan he drove down to the office and hospital. He wanted to see how fast his brand-new car would roll when he was nervous and when he needed nothing but speed.

Each time, he made it in under an hour, even the second time when there was a fender-bender in Aredale and a cow in the road in Greene.

"You have to call me right away," he told Gert. "At the very first pain."

One hour was nothing during a first labor. There wasn't enough time for things to go sideways.

Gert had literally wrung her hands, something Larry had only read about in books. Looking old and grim and despairing, Gert sat on her couch and shook her head.

"Oh, Larry. How can we do this?"

Now Larry stood up and began to pace the rug between desk and door. Gert didn't know the half of it. As a GP in a farming town and with a practice that serviced the county, Larry had seen his share of things. A few girls pregnant at too young an age and by men who had no business interfering with any of them. He'd ground his teeth over those cases, but the babies had been born and two fostered out. The third? The girl and her family moved away after harvest.

Larry wished he still smoked. He wished he could see the ocean again, the huge ship under him pushing through the Pacific. If he closed his eyes, he could be leaning against the taffrail with Sergeant Howard at his side. At least in that instant. No dangers on his imaginary horizon. They'd both be smoking, and Howard would tell a joke or two before they went back to work. Howard hailed from Decorah, enlisted even though he was thirty-two, seven years younger than Larry. But they were the old guys, both from Iowa, and they made much of their collective wisdom and know-how.

Know-how, Larry thought. What did he know?

In one quick procedure, right here in this office, he could fix everything. Yes, he'd call in Betty to assist, putting her back in her role as nurse. Not as wife to the man who did this to Mary Jo, their patient. Together in all things, she and Larry could anesthetize Mary Jo and scrape this horrible situation out of her body. There was still time; at least, Larry thought so.

Larry clasped his hands, staring at the wall in front of him. In the house, the sound of the radio, Virginia in the kitchen. He'd never performed an abortion, not even when women had begged, one holding onto his shoes as she wept on the floor. Not even when a father dragged his teenager through the waiting room, dumping her on the exam room table. Larry knew how, of course. But on Mary Jo? A child? His child? For a horrifying, frozen second, he saw his daughter bleeding out on the table, Betty shrieking, Virginia at the door, her face graying past pale.

At the door, a light knock. Virginia knew how jumpy he'd been these past three days.

"Dinner in ten." Her eyes were wide, waiting. They were all waiting. All but Bobby, who had managed to live in his own world without even realizing it. All he'd needed were his comic books and trains. Lucky boy.

Across town, was Roger Bradfield waiting? After the scene he made, weeping face down on his desk at the grocery store, imploring, red-eyed and snotty.

"I blacked out," he'd wailed. "I had no idea."

Now Larry bit down hard on his molars. He should have killed the man right then.

"Is everything all right?" Virginia asked in her quiet voice, the one she used when he was working, reading, sleeping, being. She tamped it all down until things exploded. She glanced at the phone, as if she could conjure or repel an incoming call.

He nodded, wishing he weren't lying.

She closed the door and left him alone, the space closing around him.

There was no need for an abortion. He could call one of his contacts at the county orphanage. An adoption agency in Des Moines. Whisk the baby away once delivered, once safe, once Mary Jo fell asleep. Drop off the child, no questions asked or answered. Tell Mary Jo later that the baby hadn't suffered. Bring his child home and go on with life. Maybe shoot Roger Bradfield in the dead center of his forehead somewhere in between.

But other than that, the Johnsons would live their lives.

Larry wiped a hand over his face. He couldn't let the baby go. His father had been adopted, always joking, "We could have been Smiths instead of Johnsons," a polished story about a fight between two families vying for his cherubic face.

A furniture salesman who died on the showroom floor months before retirement, Larry's father was never bothered by his lack of lineage. He'd become a Johnson, and that was that. But Larry had always wondered, especially when it was clear there was a story in his father's pretty baby face. While Larry was short, wiry, and dark, his brother, Frank, was over six feet tall, broad shouldered, golden haired. Frank had been the athlete—football, track, baseball—and the more successful doctor. A surgeon in Iowa City, he vacationed in Palm Beach and owned a fishing boat. When the war started, he'd been too old to enlist, so he hunkered down and built up his practice.

That wasn't how things had gone for Larry. He'd struggled, developing TB during med school, missing a whole year and then making it up. He'd lurched into a practice in Saint Helen, getting it going despite the Depression. When the war came, he turned out to be the youngest practicing doctor in the county. So off he went to war, leaving his aspirations behind.

Point was, he was the dark horse, a collection of unknown genes, the runt of the litter. He was the grandson in whom the unknown grandparents made their presence known, their random heredity making him an also-ran, the boy not like his brother. All his life, Larry had wondered who he was and why. When he looked in the mirror, he saw a place that wasn't Iowa. Wasn't, sometimes, the United States. He was from a darker place with a brighter sun and ripe lemons and figs.

Larry couldn't do that to another baby. Maybe the relationship wouldn't be honest, but the child would see himself reflected in the people around him.

Outside, shadows reached across the broad expanse of lawn. The office filled with dusk, the air darkening past gold. But he didn't flick on a light or turn on the radio, not wanting to hear more about the war in Korea. He needed to focus. But could he? His plan was insane. Girls should not have babies because they were physiologically able. Mary Jo was no string bean, and her hips weren't shaped like her mother's, slim, like a boy's. No, she was of farm stock, like Gert, wide in the hips and broad in the beam. She'd filled out. She was healthy.

Didn't matter. Both she and the baby could die. Mary Jo was still growing herself, bones and organs. All these months that the baby was growing, it was sucking away calcium and nutrients from its mother, a relentless vampire. Worse, on its way out, it could tear Mary Jo from stem to stern, ripping in a way Larry had never seen. Anchored in Tokyo Bay, Larry had been in Japan during the surrender, privy to stories about Hiroshima and Nagasaki from other doctors, but watching his child have a child was beyond any horror he could imagine.

One more time, he opened the bag he'd packed and repacked and set by the office door. Pinard, bulb syringe, cord clamps, stethoscope, flashlight, lubricant, scalpel, apron, gloves, soap, sterile OB packs, morphine, thermometer, suture kit, umbilical and surgical scissors. And, oh, God, forceps.

If he reached for those during her labor, Larry would stop and gather up Mary Jo and head to Franklin General, no longer caring which one of Gert's biddies or Virginia's childhood friends found out. He would do the same if labor failed to progress. He should revise the plans right now before the worst happened, which it was, barreling right for Charles City like a Kamikaze pilot.

They were all crazy. It was Roger's fault. Mostly, it was Larry's. He hadn't been watching. He hadn't protected his child. By God, he would this time. And he'd protect her child—his child, his child—too.

"Larry?" Virginia called again.

"Coming." He closed the bag and put it back by the door, tapping it once, twice, forcing himself to not look again. He left his office and left the door open, ready for when the phone rang.

Gertrude Church
September 1950

THE PAST TWO weeks, the only time Gert felt close to normal was when Mary Jo went to bed, trudging—a twelve-year-old trudging!—up the stairs to the guest room. After she put on her nightgown and brushed her teeth, Mary Jo closed the door, yellow light slipping out from under the door. But she was in her bed, and all Gert could do was fall into her chair next to the big radio and pretend to listen to *The American Album of Familiar Music*, which used to relax her to no end. But not anymore. Oh, all she wanted was a sweet song to pull her out of her worry.

Then she'd remember. When Mary Jo first arrived, it was business as usual. A summer visit but with some chores. Shopping in the morning, work in the garden, housework after lunch. Then the two of them would take a walk around the neighborhood and end the day sitting together in the parlor reading and listening to a radio show. On the weekends, they would go over to Katherine's house for sandwiches on white bread and iced tea in tall iceless glasses. Mary Jo had always been good company: smart and a good listener. She asked her aunt questions and got a laugh out of her now and again. Katherine had no idea why Mary Jo was staying for a while, though last month, Gert suggested to Mary Jo they not visit.

"Katherine has had such a taxing work week."

Mary Jo nodded, and they stayed busy. She was quick with card games and crossword puzzles. She wrote letters home. Sometimes Gert's sister Edie came by, and the three of them sat on the porch watching the summer night fade into gray.

After a month of that, Mary Jo's condition was more difficult to conceal, so she was stuck with Gert, inside or in the back yard, a gloomy girl in a horrible situation. Poor child. Poor, poor child.

There was nothing to do about it though. Doing something would have involved the law and the ruination of two—maybe more—families. All of this was true and made sense, but even so, Gert had bitten every nail down to the quick, enough to bleed.

Why had she said yes?

The phone suddenly rang, and in an irrational moment, she thought maybe Mary Jo had gone into labor. Of course, she would be the one calling Larry. What a loon. Gert chuckled and headed over to the table in the front hall where the phone sat jangling.

"Is the coast clear?" Edie asked.

"I can see for miles," Gert said. "Cruise ship in the distance."

"I'll be right over," Edie said. "I'm bringing a bottle of elder-berry wine."

"Oh, my," Gert said. "I'll get out the party hats."

She hung up the phone and headed for the kitchen, using tiny mouse steps, willing Mary Jo to stay asleep despite the phone, but the darn thing hadn't stopped ringing. Larry had called her twice today and Virginia once.

"Anything?" they'd both asked.

Don't wish for it, Gert thought as she hung up from each call. As soon as that baby is born, there will be no putting it back. A mother of three, Gert understood what babies brought with them: sleeplessness, waves of feeling less than incompetent, anger about the way a woman's body was slave to a baby's needs.

Eventually, all that dark upset dissipated, turned by mother magic into the uncommon common love that came with having a child.

"It's the hormones," Edie—childless—had told her.

It was more than that, Gert thought as she pulled two crystal wine glasses from the hutch in the dining room. But this baby? This poor, wretched baby, whose conception was inconceivable, whose mother was a child, whose grandparents were concocting a charade that would have to last for what? Eighty, eighty-five years until the baby was an old person drawing last breath. What kind of life was that? Larry might not want the child to feel different, but those were simply words. The child would know, deep in his bones, that something wasn't right.

"What would you have us do?" Virginia asked almost savagely during her last visit. "What is your great plan? How would you do anything differently?"

Gert held her daughter's gaze, refusing to be intimidated by Virginia's fear of the truth, of the neighbors, of Larry's patients and colleagues, of Saint Helen's hoity-toity folk. But then Gert sighed. Of course. She'd taught Virginia the way to hide things right here in this house. What had she repeated all those years? *Don't look back.* No mulling, worrying, or upset.

Now it was easy to see her own mistakes, especially with her children. With Katherine certainly, but even with Virginia. What had Gert done to let all this happen?

Gert took in a deep breath. "Adoption," she said, putting one hand on Virginia's knee. "We take Mary Jo to Des Moines. She and I stay in a hotel. I take her to the hospital there. Then you and Larry sign the papers to let the baby go to a family who won't be harboring an ugly secret."

For a second, Virginia's eyes filled as she looked at Gert. Then she sighed and took a deep breath as she settled against her chair. "It makes more sense."

"Of course it does!" Gert said, encouraged by the admission. "And it's not so different than what we are doing here in Charles City. A drive and a big hotel bill, but—"

"We've already decided. And what am I supposed to do about—?" She waved a hand around her fake pregnancy, Virginia carrying low and slow for this third child. Such a surprise! *I didn't even know I was pregnant! Our happy accident baby! A miracle!*

"You lose the baby," Gert said, such a fierceness in her words, she pressed a hand to her mouth. Then she took a breath and kept going. "Lose the baby now. Here. With me. Lose it and go home in tears. I'll take care of everything. For land's sake, Ginny, I've had three babies. You and Fiona have six children between you. I know my way around a pregnancy."

Virginia had argued, citing Larry's commitment to the baby and even concern for that despicable Bradfield man. Gert had sat next to Roger Bradfield on several occasions, impressed by his hearty laugh and shining dark eyes. So personable. She liked him! But after what he did to a poor, defenseless girl, why was he part of the equation?

"His family," Virginia said quietly. "His wife. Because—"

If they made Roger Bradfield a villain, something bad did truly happen right there, in their home, to their firstborn. Larry and Virginia had allowed it to happen. They should be punished.

They were protecting themselves. And who would suffer? Mary Jo and her baby, from now until the end. Gert would be gone for most of it, but somehow, her spirit, her ghost, would feel the pain of the living.

Gert lost the argument. As she watched her daughter drive away with a pillow stuffed under her attractive blue maternity blouse, Gert saw the acrid black lie follow behind the car like exhaust.

Now as she set out the wine glasses on the coffee table in the living room, Gert stilled, listening to the house, waiting for a moan, a cry. Or something softer, the toss of a blanket. But Mary Jo did not waddle down the stairs, a sight that always took Gert's breath away. Nothing moved but the soft push of fall wind and leaves outside, crackling over the eaves and tapping the windows. Then Edie knocked once and let herself in.

"Anything?" She peered into the room as she took off her coat and hung it up. "All's well?"

"For now."

Gert put a plate with a few oatmeal cookies on the table and sat down next to her sister. After so many years, here the two of them were, two biddies on their tree limb. Both recently widowed, they were back to their old pattern, the pair of them in the thick of things. Gert hadn't told Larry or Virginia this fact, but Edie was in on the plan, ready to help. Edie had never had children, but she'd been at Gert's side during three pregnancies, labors, and deliveries.

Before Edie had arrived, Gert had been ready with hundreds of comments for her sister, most of them complaints and barbs about

Virginia, but now she found she had nothing but silence. Together they sipped wine and nibbled on cookies. Finally, Gert brushed a couple of crumbs into her palm and stood up.

"Let's see what's on the radio." She tipped the crumbs onto the empty plate and started to cross the room when she stopped dead.

"What?" Edie asked.

Gert held up a hand, her heartbeat a roiling ocean in her head. But even over the crash of fear, she heard her granddaughter's call.

"Grandma," Mary Jo cried out from the second floor. "Come here."

Edie rose from the couch and gripped Gert's hand. "I'll call Larry," she said. "Go, Gert. I'll be up in a second."

Gert took the stairs faster than she had in years. She burst into the room to find Mary Jo curled around her belly, tear-stained.

"It hurts," she whimpered.

"Oh, it does," said Gert, sitting on the edge of the bed and taking Mary Jo's hand. "That it does. But tell me how often the pains are coming."

Mary Jo wiped her eyes and sat up a bit against her pillows. "Maybe ten minutes? I thought I was having a backache."

Back labor, Gert thought grimly. Oh, that wasn't good.

Carefully, Gert put a hand on Mary Jo's big, unnatural belly, wanting to feel what? A contraction? The baby moving? She had no skills but the practical.

"Let's get you to the bathroom. Have a tinkle. Then I'll set you up in this bed to wait for your father. He's on his way now."

Mary Jo's relieved look could have cracked January river ice. Poor child thought her father would save her. If only he had started out earlier. If only Gert had checked upstairs a half-hour ago instead of drinking wine.

"Come on. Walking is good for you anyway when the pains come." Gert held Mary Jo's elbow as they walked across the room. Downstairs, Edie talked on the phone, the conversation twirling up to the second floor. Gert couldn't grab any of the words, and the trip down the hallway to the bathroom seemed to take forever, Mary Jo wiping away tears, grabbing her belly, crying some more.

"All the mothers in all the world have done this," Gert murmured as she pushed open the bathroom door. "Your mother. Me. My mother, all the women in this family back to the days in England. All the women all the way back to the beginning of time."

"But it hurts," Mary Jo said, as if she were talking about a skinned knee or raft of splinters from an accidental slip down the backyard fence.

"Here, sit," Gert said as she adjusted her on the toilet. Privacy time was over for now. "Relieve yourself. We'll get you back into bed."

Gert started to move back, but Mary Jo latched onto her wrist, gripping tight. Her hands were baby hands, soft and small, her fingernails trimmed, short, and clean. Hands that should be writing papers, turning book pages, picking out the best chocolate from the sampler.

Edie sidled up behind Gert as Mary Jo went to the bathroom and said low, "Larry is on his way. He said to not leave her side until he gets here."

Gert rolled her eyes. Did he think she'd go to bed and lock the door? Besides, Mary Jo had her gripped close and tight. Anyway, where had Gert gone these long months? Her trip to Quincy to visit her cousin Shirlee had been cancelled. Fiona thought it wisest to stop coming by once Mary Jo started to show. Even the weekends had shut down tight. Gert hadn't bothered going antiquing in the countryside since Mary Jo moved in. Too much worry. What if Mary Jo started bleeding? What if she fainted? What if, what if, what if?

Mary Jo was done on the toilet, panting a little, her brown hair in front of her face. Gert smoothed it back. So soft. This girl was as new born as a newborn.

"Okay, there you go."

Mary Jo stood up from the toilet and leaned into Gert, wincing as another pain ripped over her. Then, as the three of them stood under the yellow light of the bathroom, Mary Jo's water broke, a whoosh on the tile floor. The girl gasped.

"Oh, my," whispered Edie.

"All part of the process." Gert heard herself almost clucking into her granddaughter's ear. "Natural as can be. That baby is ready to come on out into the world."

Over her shoulder, she nodded toward a towel. Edie got the message and put it on the floor, stamping on it as Gert and Mary Jo left the bathroom.

"Take a breath," Gert said as she guided Mary Jo back into the bedroom, grabbing a clean towel from the linen closet as they passed by. "That's it. Breathe. It will all be over soon."

Of course, it wasn't over soon, not even close. After her water broke, Mary Jo's labor slowed, barely registering when Larry showed up, his short hair on end, his face pale. Gert wondered if it was the child's relief that brought on the strong contractions that seemed to do nothing but cause pain.

Gert and Edie were up and down the stairs with water, blankets, towels. They took turns wiping Mary Jo's forehead and wishing they could evaporate like steam right out of the house.

"The neighbors will think you're running a speakeasy," Edie said at one point, dead serious.

Gert went around the house and pulled down every shade.

Finally, around six the next morning, Larry called Gert's family physician, Dr. Clark, and the two of them brought the squalling, small, very much alive baby boy into the world.

Then it was over. The baby in Dr. Clark's arms. Larry delivering the placenta, checking for excess bleeding or tearing, finding neither. Mary Jo pale and asleep on the bed, but breathing and healthy too. Both children were alive.

How could this be happening, Gert thought over and over again, even as she held the tiny, so real baby boy in her arms, his eyes shut tight, fingers curled around the blanket.

Now she and Larry sat at the table with coffee and the coffee cake Gert had made the day before, back in the world before this had happened. But neither of them had taken a bite, the flick of cinnamon in the air making Gert nauseous. Edie was asleep in the big stuffed chair next to Mary Jo's bed. Gert imagined Dr. Clark went home reciting parts of his Hippocratic oath (*I will respect the privacy of my patients*) and clutching a healthy check for the clinic. Within the next half-hour, Virginia was to arrive, still pillow pregnant and ready to deliver her third child, who, lucky for Virginia, had already been born in blood, sweat, and tears.

Within two weeks, Mary Jo would return home from her recovery from whatever illness Larry concocted for her and go back to school. Virginia would jump back into her mother role. Bobby would run his train set, construct model planes, and raise general mischief, his childhood unaffected. Yet how could it be? This huge shift was subterranean. Anyone living in that house would feel the shaking.

"The baby needs feeding," Gert said. "What are you going to do about that?"

Larry wiped his face with one hand. "Brought the formula."

"What about Mary Jo?" Gert stared at her son-in-law. "That's not a pleasant experience on top of what she's been through."

"Lactation suppression—"

Gert slapped the Formica table, the sound echoing. "I mean her not being able to nurse her own baby. Not able to treat him like her own. Having to go home to a house where she can't do what her body will want her to. How do you expect a twelve-year-old girl to separate her heart from her actions?"

"Most women don't nurse these days," Larry started vaguely. Gert wanted to thrash him up one side and down the other. All these years, she'd thought he was an intelligent man, but here he was rationalizing the tender hearts of his family.

"You find a way to make this right for that girl," Gert said. "You're so worried about that baby boy and his identity. But what about your own daughter's life? How will she go on to mother anyone after this? How will she bear the split?"

Without her permission, tears trickled down Gert's face. She batted at them with the back of a hand and sniffed. "How can you pull this off?"

Larry shook his head. "I have no idea. I don't want that little boy out there all alone."

"He wouldn't be alone, Larry. He'd have a family."

"But he'd be without us."

As if they were a prize, Gert thought. Any of them.

"If you are dead set on this plan, here's how you do it," Gert said. "You let Mary Jo be the mother inside the house. Make it so that the baby is a big fancy doll. She's at that age to love babies. She can nurse the baby at home, starting right here and now."

"But the baby won't know who his mother is."

"Let her nurse for a couple of months. By that time, Virginia can take over feedings."

"I don't know," Larry said.

"Guess this never came up before in your practice."

Larry was quiet for a moment, fiddling with his coffee cup. "Not exactly."

Gert stood and picked up her coffee cup and carried it to the sink. Her family stretched back to before this country was one, and Gert had never heard of what was happening in her own home. But then, who would have told her?

She turned around. "This will work. And eventually, Mary Jo will get married or go to college, and that baby boy will live his life too. If this is the way you're going to do it, it makes the most sense for everyone, especially Mary Jo. There's no way she'll ever forget, so you might as well let her remember something good."

Larry sat back and looked up at Gert. He was a small man but handsome, with bright eyes and a whole lot of smarts. Maybe this plan was not Larry at his best, but if anyone could pull off this charade, he could.

"Let's go give her the baby," he said, looking up at Gert with sad eyes.

Gert almost cried out. Instead, she swallowed back the sound. She walked back to the table and sat down, poking at her coffee cake with her fork, allowing time to flow around Larry's words for a few quick seconds. She took a bite, hoped she could eventually swallow. She put down her fork, wiped her mouth.

"Good idea," she said, scooting back her chair.

Mary Jo Johnson
October 1950

THE BABY WAS hers. Her father said. He was her baby in the house. Her grandmother said so too. Mary Jo could care for him. She could feed him. She could change his diapers—once her mother showed her how. She could sing him songs, read him books, and tuck him in at night.

"I'm sick of the baby," Bobby said the second day Mary Jo and the baby were back, his voice muffled by the closed bedroom door. "I hate that little kidney bean."

Neither Mary Jo nor her mother said a word, both of them staring at the baby.

"His face looks red enough to explode," Bobby added. "A volcano!"

There was a pause, and then he knocked. "I want to see!"

"Bobby, go play," her mother called out.

"I'm bored!" he said from the other side of the door. "What are you doing?"

Mary Jo heard him thump a soft fist on the wood.

Her mother pulled up the cloth diaper and held up the pin. "Put your finger under the pin like this."

The baby squirmed, but the pin slid through the fabric and out the other side. Her mother snapped it into place. "Now you try the other one."

Mary Jo took the pin and opened it, exactly as her mother had. The metal tip looked sharp and dangerous. Why would anyone put something like this next to a baby's skin?

"Go on," her mother urged, kinder than she'd been to Mary Jo for months. "Put your finger in—that's right. Now in and—yes! Now snap it shut. That wasn't so hard, was it?"

It wasn't. Having the baby had been hard, and her body was still recovering, every trip to the bathroom bloody. She wedged the giant pads between her thighs and then worried about her breasts leaking, which they did. Her mother cut some of the pads into squares that she could wear in her bra. At school, girls giggled about other girls who "stuffed" their bras. What would they say when Mary Jo showed up at school, breasts pushing out of her blouse? Her whole body was bigger, as if the virus her father told everyone she had was an eating disease. Now she really was broad in the beam.

"Your grandmother," Virginia had sniffed when Mary Jo came home from Gert's. "Can't stop making the pasties."

Mary Jo held back her tears then, and now, even as she hid the tiny prick the pin had given her index finger.

Her mother continued dressing the baby, slipping on a thick pair of plastic pants and then a soft knitted sleeper. The baby pulled his fists to his eyes and whimpered.

"He's hungry again," her mother said, nodding toward the rocker in the corner.

Mary Jo swallowed, her breasts reacting to her mother's words and the baby's soft, mewling cries. She was like a cow, the ones that she and Bobby had petted at the farm, all of them with dangling pink udders.

She sat down, unbuttoned her blouse, and loosed her bra, the new one her mother had bought her that made nursing easier. Her nipples surprised her, suddenly dark and huge, as if placed on her body overnight by somebody stupid. How horrible every single part of her body was, swollen and ugly.

But then the baby was in her arms, warm and squirming. Bobby wasn't lying. The baby was still reddish, but not as much. His cheeks were soft but dotted with tiny little spots. "Baby acne," her mother had told her. It didn't matter. He was so cute and warm, and when they were together like this in a closed room, nothing seemed wrong for at least an hour.

"Do what we practiced," her mother said, this time not bending close to help Mary Jo angle the nipple into the baby's mouth as she had for all the other feedings.

Mary Jo swallowed back some fear, then squeezed her breast in the exact way to…yes! She yelped as the baby latched on. Mary Jo took quick breaths and grimaced at his insistent tugs as she waited for the tingly, all-over feeling her mother called "letdown."

"That's perfect!" These days her mother was almost friendly. Mary Jo wanted to laugh, but she didn't dare. Tears were waiting behind every thought and emotion. But she wondered for a second if she should have had a baby earlier. Maybe her mother would have liked her sooner.

Her mother gave her a big smile as she turned back to the changing table to tidy up. Mary Jo watched the baby, felt as the milk came, noted how he had a rhythm to sucking, as if he knew exactly what to do with every part of his day: sleep, cry, poop and pee, eat, sleep. Had she ever been this content and sure of herself? She wanted to ask her mother, but it would ruin the moment.

Holding up the diaper pail and nodding, her mother walked out of the room and closed the door behind her. Mary Jo heard Bobby ask, "Where's the baby?" though the rest of the conversation faded away as they walked down the stairs together. Then she heard the radio—her mother was trying to keep Bobby busy.

Mary Jo relaxed even further, adjusting her arms so slightly the baby didn't even notice. He needed a name. Her parents were going to let her name him, but she didn't have any clues. Bobby's real first name was Lawrence, like her father's. Lawrence Robert Johnson. So Larry wasn't an option. Last year she'd read a histori-cal novel set in Scotland, and there had been a Robert the Bruce, a Scottish king. She liked Bruce, though it was oddly spelled. There was Benjamin, but she always thought of Ben Franklin, who was old and long haired and portly. Maybe she needed to get off of B and head to a letter way down the alphabet but not as far as her mother went.

What about Thomas? Tom was a good name for a man, strong sounding. Her mother sometimes said, "Don't be a doubting Thomas." Mary Jo wasn't even sure what that meant. Maybe her mother would stop saying that if Mary Jo named the baby Thomas. Tommy until he became Tom. Thomas for when he was a doctor, like her father. But not *his* father. He could never be like his real father.

Thomas Bruce.

The baby pulled away from her nipple, eyelids fluttering. Mary Jo looked up for her mother, who had not returned. She waited one beat, two, but then all by herself, she followed the steps, putting the baby up on her shoulder and patting gently, waiting for the burp before moving him to the other side.

The baby fussed as Mary Jo arranged the cloth under his cheek, so she stood, starting to sway a little as she patted his back, waiting for the burp and hoping to avoid the spit-up, which seemed to be splatted all over her these days.

The air stilled, and so did the baby. Had her mother done this with her? Had she sat in quiet rooms with Mary Jo on her shoulder, giving away all that precious time? Vaguely, Mary Jo remembered Bobby as a baby, but he was only two years younger, the images indistinct.

Her father hadn't come into the nursery since they'd come home from Grandma Gert's late the third evening after he was born. He'd examined him in his office (checking the shriveled umbilical cord stump), but mostly he'd stayed away, leaving any room Mary Jo walked into with the baby.

The baby. Thomas. She had to start thinking of him by his name.

Thomas burped as if in response.

"My goodness," Mary Jo said, carefully sitting back down and arranging him next to her left breast. All of this was so strange, and she didn't understand how her body knew how to do any of it. Grow a baby. Push it out. Feed it. All of it seemed so natural and so wrong, but in a good way. She really couldn't explain it.

Thomas latched on fast, ready for another round. Her mother was still nowhere close. In fact, Mary Jo breathed in the aroma of browning meat. Maybe Mary Jo had had enough training.

"He's your baby in the house," they had said. "Yours to take care of."

What about me, she wondered. Were her days of being cared for over and done with?

Thomas settled in, lips and jaw moving. What had they said to her about Mr. Bradfield? It wasn't his fault. It was the alcohol. He thought he was with his wife. He was so very upset.

He was a liar. But now it was too late to do anything about it. Thomas was here. In a month when her "virus" was finally gone, she'd go back to school, as if all were well. By then she would have stopped bleeding, and the cut her father had made in her, well, parts would have healed. Her mother had her on a reducing plan so no one would wonder why a virus made her fat. Or they would think she was broad in the beam as usual. Until she was back in shape, she wasn't to see anyone, not that Margie or Diane had tried even once to come by. They'd all forgotten about her. No one really cared, not even Roger Bradfield, who'd wrecked her life and lied about it.

Thomas lifted his hand, and she took it in hers. He was so little, fingers like a doll's, face like an angel's. Her baby. He was her baby in the house, until he wasn't. He'd have to not be her baby before he started to remember, but how would she be able to forget?

No one had an answer to that.

Thomas started to slow, his mouth open and slack. Careful not to wake him, Mary Jo put him back up on her shoulder, patting until he burped again. Then slowly, she laid him down in the crib, on his back, but then she thought he was supposed to be on his front. But he was so fast asleep, she left him, covering him up with the blanket Grandma Gert had knitted all summer, a lovely pale yellow, warm and soft.

"Good for a boy or a girl," she'd said, barely looking at Mary Jo in that way she'd not looked at her the entire time Mary Jo lived there, as if she had no idea what to do with the situation.

Mary Jo sat in the rocking chair and began to cry. All the adults had decided things for her, and nothing felt right. It wasn't fair, and she hated her whole family, even Bobby. She wished they'd all go away, except for Thomas. In his crib, Thomas made a cry, tiny as a chick's. Mary Jo looked up, terrified he was still awake, but he'd only brought one tiny hand to his mouth. She relaxed and then walked to the bed, the one her mother had set up for her.

"You can take the night feedings this way," she'd said earlier in the day. "I've done them the past two nights. But you can take over."

She hated this bed and her mother, but the pillowcase was freshly laundered and smelled crackling and clean from the huge dryer in the basement. Mary Jo closed her eyes, wishing for anything but this. One day she would leave and never come back.

Maybe she would take Thomas. Maybe she wouldn't. Maybe by then he would be a boy in his Saint Helen life, unaware that his sister was his mother. He'd be more like Bobby was now, a boy who liked to play outside and cause trouble, who hated homework and would rather listen to the radio day and night. A little boy in his own life.

The house's furnace rumbled on, a sharp wind bringing the first arctic chill of the season. Soon it would be winter. Then spring. A year would go by, and maybe she could forget about everything.

Roger Bradfield
October 1950

ROGER SAT BEHIND his big walnut desk in the grocery, going over invoices, flicking through one, another, another, but he couldn't read a word or concentrate on totals. Beef sides, canned goods, wax paper bundles.

He slammed his hand down and tossed the pages to the side.

"May," he called to his girl, the new one he'd hired after Zora Soames quit the week before, totally out of the blue. "Will you get in here."

It wasn't a question. He shouldn't have these on his desk. Zora would have known what to do, but she wasn't even-keeled. Roger was better off with May, but she needed a lot of training.

Where was the damn girl? He needed to focus on the deal he and Dick Jensen were putting together to buy the local bank. That flighty bitch Zora had put him in a real bind.

"May!" he roared, feeling something other than irritation welling inside. Rage. A hot, ugly feeling in his chest, under his throat, something he had not been able to swallow for months.

"Yes, Mr. Bradfield," May said, running in with notepad in hand. "I'm sorry. I was…indisposed."

Roger stood and glowered. "Zora took care of the invoices. I need you—" He waved at the desk. "To figure out her system. It's all out there somewhere."

"In the filing cabinets?" May asked, voice wavering.

"Figure it out. If you can't, I'll find someone who can."

He waved his hand again toward the front office where Zora had sat for two years, wearing those tight, formfitting skirts and post-war pantyhose. God, those legs.

Roger ran a hand over his face. What he needed was his wife. Betty had helped out when Roger and she were first married. That kept things steady. Easy. Also kept Betty in front of him all day, which kept him out of trouble, at least for a while.

"Close the door," Roger said.

May wiped her face, trying, it seemed, to arrange her expression into something secretarial as she shut the door. She was no Zora, but she was pretty in a round, apple-pie type of way. A true daughter of Iowa. Something in Roger relaxed, loosened.

He gazed out the window to Main Street, bustling by as usual. But other than May, who would know if he ran out of the building and followed behind the shoppers and businessmen, walking briskly down the street until he made it to a neighborhood. Maybe he'd go by the Johnsons' house and peek through the window to look at the baby. Betty had told him the baby was a boy. She'd spit it out during one of their nightly battles. All Roger wanted was one glimpse.

Screw them all if they cut him out and took everything. Screw them all. He'd keep going. He'd survive. He'd head to the highway, where he could hitchhike his way somewhere. Anywhere. Anyplace but Saint Helen, where his wife wouldn't talk to him and he had not one but two babies, one with a twelve-year-old girl.

In front of him, May sniveled.

"Look," he said, exhausted by it all. "I know this is hard. Here."

Roger picked up the pile of papers, stood, and walked toward May, putting an arm around her waist. He heard her take in a breath, but he didn't stop. He pulled her close and handed her the papers. As he did, he squeezed a little, feeling a luscious little layer of fat under her blouse. God, he could paddle around in that. She was a true sweetmeat, this one.

He walked her into the front office and then slowly let her go, feeling her warmth slide away as she sat down behind her desk. "Go over these invoices, and then start looking around. Today that's all I want you to do. I'll get the phones. You take stock. Get the lay of the land. Really take your time. Don't worry, I'll get my own coffee too. You settle in."

May glanced at him in astonishment. "Are you sure, Mr. Bradfield?"

"I should have done it sooner. I'm sure sorry I didn't." He gave her his brightest smile, the one that always worked. "Don't mind me. I've got matters on my mind, but that's not your fault."

May sat, a bit wide-eyed and stunned.

"I'll bring you a cup of coffee, and you get started. All right?"

May pushed her bangs back from her forehead, flustered, nervous.

Roger sat on the edge of her desk and patted her arm. So soft. How old was she? Twenty? A corn-fed farm girl wanting life in town. He opened his eyes wide and gave her the look again, taking her in, letting her know he really saw her, all the parts she wanted hidden. He wanted those parts, the ones she didn't want to share. Someday he'd have all of them.

She blinked, her red lips slowly parting into a smile.

"That's right. That a girl. Trust me, everything is going to work out fine. You and I are going to make this work. It's going to be great."

May smiled at him, the worry whisked clean off her face. "Thank you so much, Mr. Bradfield. This job means the world to me," she gushed, her face as open as a child's. Her bright blond hair glowed under the office light.

My word. She was a true Golden Delicious, a crisp Pippin, sweet and juicy all the way through. Roger could tell. He could already taste her, luscious juices on his tongue, his lips, his chin. But he'd watch himself this time. He'd wait. He'd go so very slow.

At home that night, Roger pulled on the face Betty required from him now: not happy but not woeful or full of regrets or sorrow or anger. He thought of it as his *happy dog in the doghouse face*. That way she could be right about Roger's inherent evils but not be reminded about them all night long.

She hadn't left him yet. All he needed was a few more weeks. Two months tops. He'd do everything she wanted.

Every morning, whether snow, blizzard, or bright sunshine, Roger walked the ten minutes to work. When they were first married, Betty had scolded him about taking the Cadillac such a short distance and parking it behind the grocery all day for everyone to see.

"What does that say to your employees?" she asked. "You walk to work like an average person, as they do."

His mother would have said, *Don't take on airs.*

So he came into the house not through the side door, but through the large front door like a man should. He wiped his feet, hung his coat and hat, and slicked back his hair in front of the entryway mirror. Looking good, Bradfield, despite everything.

Without calling out as he used to—"Back home!" or "Your sweetheart is here"—Roger headed to the kitchen. Betty was at the stove, frying a deep pan of chicken, the oil crackling, heat and smoke wafting into the vent. Over by the kitchen table, far away from any potential accidents, Harry sat in his playpen batting together two stuffed toys.

On purpose, Roger ignored Betty and went right to Harry, picking him up and holding the solid little boy in his arms. The baby gurgled and smiled, burrowing into Roger's chest. He smelled like soap and something Roger couldn't explain: a new sheet or a soft blanket or a summer day. He breathed in deeply, and without warning, a rip of feeling he'd never known flooded through him. For a second, he held onto Harry tight, not wanting to be parted from him. This child was so innocent. So pure. And Betty was the perfect mother for him. For all the kids they were going to have. Five. Maybe six.

Harry struggled a little in his father's unfamiliar tight grip. Afraid he'd drop the baby from an overabundance of feeling, Roger put him back down, almost panting. He wiped his face with his handkerchief and hoped Betty hadn't noticed anything.

"The heating oil was delivered today," Betty said factually, her words flung at him in an ordered staccato since the day he'd told her about the Johnsons' party. "Bill's on your desk."

"Good." Roger walked over to the fridge and took out a Coke. He'd stopped drinking since he'd found out about Mary Jo. At least, he'd stopped around Betty.

"Harry's going to see Dr. Wilson tomorrow." Betty began to pull the chicken from the pan, salting the hot drumsticks and thighs. At least she kept serving him the food he liked. On the stove top, mashed potatoes, gravy, and sautéed greens.

"Regular checkup?" Roger downed half of the soda.

Betty nodded as she put platters, bowls, and cutlery on the table. She filled the crystal pitcher with water and poured two glasses. This was some dry house, Betty the total teetotaler. Then she picked up Harry and strapped him into his highchair, cinching him up as if he were about to take off for outer space.

Without looking at Roger, Betty sat down and served up his plate, heaps of food covered in hot gravy. Roger was famished and tucked right in. Between bites, he noted that Betty dolloped small portions onto her plate and mysteriously produced a blanched-looking piece of chicken, placing it bald and bare on her plate.

Roger chewed a bit longer—the chicken was delicious—wiped his mouth and sat back. He took a sip of the blasted water and put on a smile. Betty kept her eyes on Harry and her demurely portioned food. Her hair was neat and swung under her jawline.

Roger cocked his head and stared at his wife. Was that lipstick? Was she giving up on her hatred campaign? At least Betty was taking care of herself. About time.

Roger put down his water glass. "Great meal." He picked up a drumstick, salty and barely greasy, and took a big bite. The meat melted like butter in his mouth. From the corner of his eye, he saw Betty giving him furtive glances, but he knew what to do now. His patience had paid off. She'd made him sleep alone for months now, but here they were, sitting around the table with their baby, Betty dressed up and ready for show. Those lips. That hair. Just like when he'd met her at the Johnsons'. Crisp and clean on the outside, soft, silky, and wild on the inside.

He put dropped the chicken bone on his plate and shifted in his seat. "Do you want me to go to the doctor with you?"

Dr. Wilson was their new doctor. They'd needed one, obviously, once Larry Johnson was out of the running. At least for now.

Betty looked up surprised, but then she rearranged her face. "I don't think so."

"I'd sure love to see how he's growing. This kid looks like he's busting up the charts." Harry banged his cup on the chair tray, mouth wide with a toothless smile. "See? Even Harry agrees."

Roger kept his eyes on his son, reaching out a hand and making small talk. He handed Harry a mauled and mushy Zwieback stuck to the tray. "A football star in the making!"

He beamed at Harry and then turned back to his plate, finishing his potatoes and greens with a high school senior's gusto. He waggled his fork at Harry who gummed his cookie.

"You're going to be something," Roger said to his son, his peripheral vision on Betty. "Can't wait for the doctor to see you."

Across the table, Betty relaxed. She'd held her body so tight for so long, he could almost hear her spine unhinge as she sank against the chair back. Thatta girl. That's the way.

Betty reached over to pat Harry's arm, and for a second, she smiled at Roger despite what he had done. Despite the other baby across town. Thomas. His name was Thomas.

Roger felt a calm sweep through him. Right now, in his kitchen, he saw the future. He would make peace with Betty. He'd get back in with the Johnsons too. They had no idea what a slutty vixen that Mary Jo was, all big eyes and swishy ass. Roger Bradfield wasn't going to be the one to tell them. They'd have enough on their hands once she got into high school. They'd find out what she was really like. So until then, Roger simply needed to go through his paces, never making that kind of mistake with a girl like Mary Jo again, at least that way. He'd be much more careful.

He'd tried to push her out of his mind, but he could still see her honey-colored eyes widen, lips part, cheeks flush. Oh, what a gumdrop.

Roger breathed, shifted in his chair, pushed his hair back once, twice.

"Harry has such a good appetite," Betty said, her voice faraway.

He gulped his water. "Like his father." Again, Roger laid on his big, wide, happy smile that took in the whole kitchen and family scene. "He's going to be at least six-two. Mark my words."

His wife pushed her hair behind one ear, a pearl earring glimmering. She'd had her nails done, the first time since the baby, at least as far as Roger could tell. The pale pink shone under the kitchen light. God, she was a beautiful woman.

No time for that now. Roger nodded and scraped up every last bit of his dinner. He'd be nice and nice and nice some more. "That hit the spot."

Betty would cave. Betty would fall. Not tonight. But in the next week or two, she'd unscrew the lock from the nursery door and come back into their bedroom at night. Roger would charm her silly until then.

"Let me do the dishes," Roger said, putting his napkin on the table. "You've done so much already. You go give Harry his bath. I've got everything under control."

Jenny Bradford Pine
February 2018

JENNY STOOD UP and put the pie plate on the counter with a soft click. Her mother stared at the TV, eyes vacant, mouth open slightly.

"What do you mean, Mom?" Jenny asked. "What MeToo?"

Her mother turned to her, dark eyes glittering. Was she crying? "You remember Mr. Bradfield."

This was how her mother started most conversations about the past, as if Jenny's remembering parts of it made it worth telling. *You remember Saint Helen, your Grandmother Gert, Payday candy bars, the summer you ran away.*

"Of course."

The Bradfields had been a constant in Jenny's grandparents' lives. There were shoeboxes full of photos in her mother's storage closet with Larry and Virginia Johnson posed with their best friends, Roger and Betty Bradfield. Whenever Mary Jo took her daughters to Florida to visit their grandparents, they had one or two nights out with the Bradfields. Once, the Bradfields had visited California, staying at the Mark Hopkins Hotel in a fancy suite. Jenny had been seventeen at the time, all Farrah Fawcett hair and bright colors. Jenny, Tricia, and Joy had sat on a couch together, Mr. Bradfield across from them, watching, his eyes dark, his laugh loud.

"I always liked Betty," Jenny said. "He was nice too. A little intense maybe."

"When I was twelve," her mother said, "he took me into a closet and kissed me."

Jenny stilled. "What?"

"My parents were having a party. He and Betty had shown up late. He was hungry and drank too much. It wasn't his fault."

"He kissed you?" Something stopped inside Jenny: breath or blood or thought.

"It wasn't his fault. He hadn't eaten—"

"It wasn't his fault? What do you mean by that?" Jenny walked toward her mother, wanting to hold her still, hold her. "How could kissing you not be his fault? You were twelve years old!"

"He didn't mean to," her mother said, backing away. "Never mind about this. Forget about it."

"You can't say something like that. You have to tell me what happened. I mean, I grew up knowing that man," Jenny said. "He was there when we visited Grandma and Grandpa. We visited him. How could they be his friend after that?"

"He never did it again," her mother repeated, rushing the story. Mary Jo started to pace, frenetic, jangly, walking toward the coffee table and picking up the remote, pressing buttons that did nothing as usual.

"Mom, if he did that to you…there isn't an excuse for that. I can't—"

"I should never have told you. I wanted you to know it happened to me." She kept pressing the volume and channel controls, the sound suddenly going up and down, the screen flicking fast.

Jenny's whole body filled with something: anger or confusion or fear. Maybe rage. What was coming out of her mother's mouth was a nice and tidy explanation, handed to her by an adult, probably Grandma Ginny. All these years later, Jenny could imagine her grandmother's explanation, hear her needling, slightly whiny voice: "He never meant to do that, dear. He'd had too much to drink. It was an accident. It really wasn't his fault."

Jenny's hands shook, and she struggled to calm herself as she watched her mother lift and point the remote over and over again like a broken robot. Press, press, press. She stamped her foot when the screen stayed the same. Stamped her foot when one channel after another flashed by. But Jenny couldn't move. This was horrible. And worse, so much worse, was that Roger Bradfield never went away. He hadn't been banished from Saint Helen or even her grandparents' house. There the bastard was, year after year, smiling into the camera, lifting a glass, holding a Christmas present, his arm around her Uncle Tommy. There he had been for football games and harvest festivals.

Her mother banged the remote on the bookcase. "I wish I could tell Joy."

"She's not here," Jenny said, taking in a breath, holding it lightly in her lungs.

"It should have been you." Her mother shot Jenny a hot, dark glance, eyes narrowed.

What should have been me? Jenny wondered. What happened to Joy? Or me in the closet with that bastard Roger Bradfield?

How easy it was for her mother to pass off the worst things.

"Mom," Jenny began.

"I can't turn off the TV." Mary Jo threw down the remote. The thing skittered across the kitchen linoleum and wedged under the stove. "I'm hungry. I want to go get a hamburger."

"Mom," Jenny said. "I—"

"I don't want to talk about it anymore," she said. "Where's my purse? Have you seen my purse? I can't find my purse."

Mary Jo Johnson
December 1950

WEARING HER NEW red wool dress under her winter coat, Mary Jo walked toward the school bus that huffed at the bottom of the driveway like an ice dragon. She carried her book bag, which was full of all the assigned reading material from the summer and first part of the school year. Her mother had delivered her completed homework and tests to the office, and right now, while not having been in school for months and after having a secret baby no one knew about, Mary Jo still had straight A's as she always had.

A light dusting of snow fluttered and swirled, as if the house, the bus, and Mary Jo were inside a snow globe. She reached out a mittened hand to catch a few flakes. Then she heard a tap tap, and turning, she saw her mother on the other side of the picture window. She stood holding Tommy, who wobbled a little as he looked out at Mary Jo. Was he really looking at her? Or was she imagining things? Would he miss her? Her body panged in a way it never had before, a heavy sadness in her chest like a bad cold. Like the pneumonia she'd had when she was six. How could she leave him home alone?

But she waved, and her mother lifted Tommy's hand to wave back. From somewhere inside the house, Jupey barked.

Tears filled her eyes, but it was too cold to cry.

Behind her, Bobby kicked at the snow drift at the bottom of the driveway. "Stupid school," he said, the same way he muttered "stupid baby."

Mrs. Soames tooted the deep, bellowing bus horn. Mary Jo turned away from Tommy, trying to find an expression that would make sense. A back-after-a-long-illness face that Diane and Margie would believe.

"Welcome back, Miss Johnson." Mrs. Soames sat large but tidy in her blue uniform behind the great steering wheel. She wore a knitted cap under her bus driver's cap and a huge black coat that hung around her like a witch's cape. "Good to see you among the living."

Mary Jo blinked. Had people thought she died?

Bobby scuttled by, pushing at her coat and sitting by Timmy Rawlins.

Mrs. Soames shrugged. "Oh, come on. It's an expression. Go sit by your friends."

Mary Jo took each jolt of her old life like a hard crack in the face. She'd forgotten how anything could be funny. Her grandmother hadn't broken into a smile the whole summer except with Aunt Edie, and her parents had walked around the house stiff and solemn like one of Bobby's toy robots. Mary Jo had been afraid to say anything unless it related to how she could take care of the baby. Because she'd been nursing and was still too fat for more weeks than she should have been, she'd stayed in the house or in the back yard, but winter had come early, so she was forced to hide in her room and the nursery to keep her secret away from Bobby.

Right now she didn't even know how to walk down the dark black aisle of the bus.

"Hi," she said when she got to the seat where Margie and Diane sat, both of them looking up at her with wide eyes.

"Are you still contagious?" Margie asked. "My mother said to watch out."

Mary Jo sat down in the empty seat across from them, her legs shaking. She glanced at them from the corner of her eye. Her friends looked so clean and new and fresh, their hair shiny, blue and brown eyes clear, as if they hadn't been up at night with babies. They smelled different too, like a present kept under wraps at the back of a sacheted wardrobe or a special, precious object brought out only during celebrations. Not like Mary Jo, who was beaten and mashed, old and ugly and worth nothing. She was like her ancient doll Flat Susan who was forgotten in the back of her closet under a stack of blankets, her smile barely visible after all these years.

Mrs. Soames closed the bus door and headed toward Main Street. Mary Jo breathed in and blinked back the tears that were defrosting in her eyes.

"Not anymore," she said, remembering what her father had told her about her *disease*, symptoms that lingered for months, mighty convenient for their present lie. Fatigue, sore throat, and fever, all combining to create the perfect excuse for going to Grandma Gert's and hiding out. *Infectious mononucleosis* her father wrote on the note to Principal Warren in the late spring.

Case resolved, he had written on the note in her bag right now. *Thank you so much for accommodating Mary Jo's needs.*

"You look okay," Diane said.

"I stayed with my grandma," Mary Jo said.

"Meet any nice boys?" Diane asked. Margie looked on, interested.

Mary Jo shrugged. She never wanted to meet a nice boy. "I slept mostly. That's all I wanted to do."

She could hear her father's approval of her storytelling. "And my throat was sore all the time. My grandma had to stay in the room with me. That's why I went to her house."

"That sounds horrible—" Diane began.

"That's not nice! Her grandmother isn't horrible!" Margie said.

They all laughed, the movement an awkward, stretchy feeling on Mary Jo's face.

"That's not what I meant," Diane said. "I meant you didn't have to go to school!"

The bus rumbled to another stop, the brakes squealing, plumes of exhaust billowing in front of the windows. "Jimmy Hayes asked about you the whole time," Margie said. "Didn't seem to matter that you had a terrible illness. He kept asking when you were coming home."

Mary Jo pretended that was good news. Margie kept talking, telling Mary Jo about the start of football season and how Jimmy Hayes was on the varsity team.

"Let's all go to the next game. We can sit together and cheer for him."

Mary Jo nodded, agreeing that they all could go and see Jimmy after the game was over, but how was she going to go anywhere in the late afternoon? How could she leave the house except for school? Her baby was at home, and if she wasn't there, her mother wouldn't pay him enough attention. She might forget to give him his bottle. He would cry in his crib because Virginia was too busy mixing her father a cocktail. He was the one who would end up like Flat Susan.

"Friday will so fun!" Margie squealed.

Mary Jo flinched at her stupid voice, the high-pitched whine so immature. Margie had nothing to squeal about. Neither of them did. Neither had one clue about feelings, not like Mary Jo. Neither of them knew what real pain was like, the kind she felt when giving birth. They were so idiotic. Tears rimmed her lids, and she sniffed.

"Don't be scared," Diane said. "School is the same as always."

She reached across the aisle and patted Mary Jo's arm. With a jolt, Mary Jo realized that aside from Thomas, this was the first touch anyone had given her in weeks.

"Thanks," she said, wiping her nose with her hankie. "I'm kind of nervous."

Diane gave her a quick smile but then began to follow Margie's jabbering about the Christmas dance and who would dance with whom. Mary Jo clutched her book bag to her chest and, eyes forward, focused on the long road ahead, the sound of the bus under her, and the jittering of her entire body.

After school, Mary Jo jumped on the first bus rather than staying late for her academic decathlon club and raced into the house, tossing her bag on the floor by the front door. She heard her mother on the phone and peeked into kitchen, only to see her mother at the table with a cigarette, phone pressed against her ear. Bobby was already home, sitting at the table, eating a slice of chocolate cake and reading the latest Joe Palooka. He glanced up darkly and then went back to his comic.

Mary Jo raced up the stairs to the nursery, heart pounding, certain that the worst had happened: Tommy was wrapped in his blanket, suffocated. Tommy was on the floor. Tommy was dead. She flew into the room and then stopped dead. The air around her was quiet, still, and Tommy was asleep, wrapped perfectly in his crib, her mother's sure swaddling holding him tight.

She stared at him, moved closer, listened to his soft breathing. He was alive. Everything in her relaxed, and she sat in the rocking chair.

"He's fine," her mother whispered from the doorway, motioning Mary Jo out of the room. "Come on."

Mary Jo stood and gave Tommy one last look, heading out the door. Her mother closed it behind her and pulled Mary Jo by the shoulder toward her parents' bedroom.

"Sit down," her mother said, patting a space beside her on the bed.

Mary Jo wished she could change out of her school dress, her skin itchy and awful. She wished she could go into her room and close her door to everything and read for hours. For a terrible second, she wished it were last summer when Mr. Bradfield first looked at her. In that moment, she was special. He was the only one in the whole world who thought she was worth something. But that went wrong too. Now she was worth nothing.

"I took care of two babies before Tommy," her mother said.

Mary Jo nodded. Her mother sighed and smoothed her skirt over her thighs, even though there wasn't a wrinkle in sight. There never was.

"I let some bad things happen," her mother said, avoiding Mary Jo's eyes. "That's a fact. But we're moving on. And what you need to do now is go to school. Go to your club meetings. Spend time with your friends. You don't have to rush home as if I've lit the crib on fire. He's going to be fine."

Mary Jo looked at her hands, dry and cracked from the heat, the cold, the heat, the cold. The constant washing she had to do because of diaper changes.

"But I'm supposed to be his mom in the house," she said.

"You don't always have to be in the house. I'm here already."

"He'll forget," Mary Jo said. "He won't remember."

For a second, her mother put a hand on Mary Jo's hand, her mother's touch warm. Mary Jo leaned closer, just a little, pressing into her mother's shoulder.

"He has to forget. At least partway. He has to know there are two of us. And then he needs to know there is only one."

Her mother. That one. Not Mary Jo.

Mary Jo stared out her parents' bedroom window. The sky had broken free of the grip of clouds, a hazy, barely golden light coming through the sycamore trees. It was football weather. Even Mary Jo knew that.

"Stay late at school like you used to," her mother said. "We'll be fine. Now go do your homework. I'm making chili soup and corn fritters for dinner."

Her mother left the room, turned a quick ear to the nursery, and then headed down the stairs. Mary Jo got up and did the same, praying that Tommy would cry out, but he didn't. The house was silent except for the furnace. Downstairs the front door opened and closed, Bobby off to his trombone lesson. He'd taken up the instrument over the summer, the sound more annoying than his guitar. Why had her mother agreed with a baby—their baby—on the way?

In her room, Mary Jo changed out of her school clothes into a plain skirt and old sweater that smelled like dried breast milk and Tommy—soap and powder and baby lotion. She pushed back her hair with a headband and put on her slippers. Her mother was right, though not one part of Mary Jo wanted her to be. At the end of all this, Tommy had to have one mother, not two.

Downstairs Mary Jo settled at the kitchen table with her books, a slice of cake, and a glass of milk. Her mother was on the phone again, this time to Grandma Gert. The room filled with the smell of browning beef and onions. Outside, the wind blew, scattering leaves across the lawn, still green.

Friday afternoon, Mary Jo sat with Diane and Margie on the bleachers, a heavy tartan blanket spread across their laps. They shivered together, pressing their wool-clad shoulders close, sipping from the thermoses their mothers had filled with hot chocolate. The stadium filled with Saint Helen High fans waving red-and-white flags. The bleachers on the other side of the field were filling up with Thurston High fans, who began waving their flags, theirs blue and gold. The afternoon beat back the snow, mostly, though now and again, flecks pinged Mary Jo on her cheeks and nose. She rubbed her mittened hands together and watched the players run onto the field, past the junior varsity team headed back into the locker room.

And there was Jimmy Hayes, lean in his red-and-white uniform, hoofing it behind the starting lineup. The crowd began to clap, following the cheerleaders' rhythm.

"Oh, my goodness, there he is!" Margie clapped her hands together. "Aren't you excited?"

Before Mary Jo could answer, Diane grabbed her arm. "He's so tall! He's like a man."

Was he? When he sidled up to her at the drugstore counter two days ago, his face looked like a boy's, almost like Bobby's. Smooth, rosy, and fresh, Jimmy could have no idea what men were really like. Could he?

"Don't you think?" Diane insisted.

"Right," Mary Jo lied. "He could probably grow a beard!"

As she spoke, Mary Jo felt the harsh roughness of Mr. Bradfield's afternoon face, the scratch and burn he left from his kisses.

"He's so handsome," Margie wailed into the crowd. Thank heavens no one could hear her over the thrum.

At the drugstore, when Jimmy had put an elbow on the counter and looked at her, saying, "Hi, there," she'd thought the same thing. Jimmy Hayes was handsome. Then she thought, Why is he talking to me?

As Mary Jo lay in bed that night, she wondered if what was deep and dark inside her showed on the outside. She pressed a palm into her ribcage, half expecting a hot spot or bump or wound. Could people tell what Mr. Bradfield had done to her? Did they see something she couldn't in the mirror? After all she had been through, why would Jimmy Hayes pick her out of a crowd and ask her to come to the game to watch him?

"You'll be my good luck charm," he said.

"Oh, my goodness!" Diane and Margie had whispered into her neck, pushing aside their soda glasses. "You are going to be so popular."

Was she?

The crowd roared as the marching band honked onto the field, lurching with brass and drums. Mary Jo couldn't help but pick out the trombone player, obnoxious and loud. Somewhere in the crowd, Bobby was probably watching, mouth open in amazement.

The team began to run drills, throwing balls back and forth. On the other end of the field, the opposing team did the same. The sky turned orange with dusk, and Mary Jo shivered into all that suddenly felt normal.

Just then Jimmy Hayes ran past, a hand outstretched as he headed to the coach.

"He's so dreamy," Margie said.

"He's not yours," Diane said. "You've got Stan Dugan."

Margie pushed her arm. "Do not!"

"Do so!"

Diane's excitement was tinged with sadness. So far she didn't have anyone.

They dissolved into bickering and giggles. Mary Jo watched Jimmy, the way his body sailed over the turf, each movement deliberate but spontaneous, smooth and easy and clean. He took off his helmet and glanced up, smiling at her from the field. His dark hair buzz-cut but with a hint of curl. Mary Jo smiled back, the air around her stilling.

Jimmy Hayes. Older boy, football genius. Boy who moved in his body as if he knew what he was going to do before he did it. Mary Jo could tag along behind him until he left for college. He could protect her. He could be her excuse for everything. Jimmy would be at every party and event. Jimmy would drop her at home and walk her to her door. There wouldn't be anyone Jimmy Hayes couldn't fend off.

Mary Jo would do everything in her power to keep him for herself. Now, after everything, she understood what boys wanted.

He was so much older, but maybe she could skip a grade, start high school early. In four years instead of five, she could be done with Saint Helen for good. Tommy would be her mother's boy by then, one hundred percent. These last couple of months would be erased; Mary Jo an older sister off to school, nothing more. That's what she'd do. She'd apply to every college in California and never come back.

A whistle blew.

"It's starting!" Diane squealed, and the girls clapped their hands. How ridiculous, Mary Jo thought. But how necessary.

Two large boys met in the middle of the field as a referee flipped a coin. Heads or tails. Didn't matter who won the toss or the game. Mary Jo had a plan.

Bobby Johnson
August 1953

BOBBY GLANCED OUT the window, a hot breeze blowing in. He was supposed to be mowing the front lawn, but his mother had made him blow a gasket, so now he was in his room, sitting quietly on the bed as commanded.

As Bobby brought out the lawn mower and then the rake, his mother said to Tommy, "Look at your brother," like he was a boring television program: *Big Brother Mows Lawn.*

Meanwhile, Mary Jo was off in her show: *Sister Pretends to Not Be a Mother.*

Three years ago his family returned from his grandmother's house with the new baby who squalled and puked and peed everywhere. Bobby was supposed to have been at the front door, wearing a big smile, ready to say stupid stuff about how cute the baby was and how happy he was to have a baby brother, who wouldn't even be old enough to play with before Bobby left home.

He wasn't happy, not one bit. And brother? Sure. Brother.

They all thought they'd gotten away with it, but Bobby wasn't an idiot. Didn't they remember he was a Boy Scout? He had his stalking badge, for one. He could creep up on things. Interpreting too. Morse code! And he understood enough German that he could listen in when Grandma Gert said mean things to his mother.

"Du must eine bessere Mutter sein!"

"How can you say that? I'm doing my best. You don't know what it's been like."

There was a long silence before his grandmother said, "Du hast nicht genug aufgepasst."

"I was paying attention. But it's not all my fault. That girl. She's sneaky. She would never have told us anything unless Larry spotted it."

His mother hadn't been careful enough on the telephone either. Pulling it into the hallway to talk wasn't enough when Bobby was around. He knew stuff.

"It's not going well," his mother had said. "She's having trouble letting go of the baby."

Bobby wanted to say, "Duh!" What did his mother expect, anyway?

At least that's what he had thought, but Mary Jo hadn't been careful enough at night, closing and opening doors, turning on lights in the nursery. Then not closing doors that should have been, Mary Jo sitting in a chair and—Bobby still couldn't believe it, something deep in him shuddering.

He stood up, pacing his bedroom floor, wishing walking could take away the truth. But there was no way to erase what he'd seen. That night, it had been late; no lights shone in from outside, not even the moon. The air had been still, his parents not stirring, Jupey asleep somewhere, maybe in her bed in the garage.

Sneaking up quietly from down the hall, he had hovered outside the triangle of light coming from the partially open door, breath hovering outside his body. Putting one eye to the warm fan of golden light slipping out from the nursery, Bobby blinked and then sucked in sharply, his lungs flat, airless, empty. There in the chair, the baby in her arms, Mary Jo sat nursing Tommy.

He closed his eyes and then opened them again, a spangle of stars in his field of vision. Mary Jo's nightgown was open at the neck, and her right breast—Bobby looked down and then back at his sister—in Tommy's mouth. The baby was drinking. There was milk. Mary Jo had milk?

Stumbling away from the door, he'd looked around for his mother, assuming this was some kind of mistake only she could explain. Maybe this is what women—and big sisters—did to stop babies from crying sometimes. It wouldn't have been anything he'd have known from Boy Scouts. No badge for that. No one would have told him. But his mother never appeared, and deep inside himself, he understood that this was secret, forbidden, and all wrong. Things inside him twisted.

Bobby had crept back to the door and crouched down, taking in everything, as if there would be a test later. Sucking, murmuring, burping, diaper changing. Before Mary Jo turned off the light, he slunk away, slipping down the hall into his own room, watching her from a tiny crack. It was Mary Jo, moving as if there was nothing wrong. As if she were doing what was natural and normal.

As if she were Tommy's mother. And if she were Tommy's mother, who was the father? It could only be Jimmy Hayes—if she liked him now, maybe she had liked him three years ago. The thought stuck in Bobby's throat, tears pricking his eyes.

Now Bobby balled his fists, pressing them to his thighs. He wanted to slam out of the house and never come back. And when he was home, he wished he could put on an astronaut helmet and snuff out the sounds around the dining room table. All that stupid, fake chatter, nothing that was real. Better yet? What about going to the moon himself. Mars. Getting out of this house, which was like an alien planet. Green men, but they lived here in his house and said the stupidest things ever.

Noise came in through the window with the breeze. Bobby should go back and mow the lawn. Maybe his mother would stop pestering him about making friends and combing his hair the *right way.* Maybe Tommy would stop pulling on his arm and asking him questions. But first, Bobby needed to think. Things hadn't been right for months, and not just with his family. For one, even Jupey seemed confused, wandering the rooms of the house as if searching for something. Something inside Bobby seemed off too, though he couldn't put his finger on what. It was as if there was an older boy in his head telling him what to do and how to act. Then there was himself who wanted to get in his father's canoe and fish. Or walk to the pool and swim for hours and not worry about polio. Or he could take his pellet gun and go into the woods and hunt rabbits. The normal part of himself wanted to pack up a few things, count out his savings, and run away, and not to Grandma Gert's house. Somewhere far away, where he could wait out these terrible years and then join the Navy and be like his father.

But this older boy had rules and ideas about what was correct, most of which Bobby didn't agree with. That's the real reason he was camped out on his bed. His mother wasn't paying attention to anything. Besides, she was irritating. So his bossy older boy self had to be taught a lesson. No, he would not mow the lawn this minute. Certainly not on command.

In the maple outside the window, an Eastern phoebe chattered and peeped. Bobby knew all the birds in Saint Helen. He had that badge too. The bird wanted to go to the creek with Bobby, to swoop and fly and catch gnats.

Sighing, Bobby stood up. In the front yard, his mother pulled weeds from the flowerbed while Tommy tumble-ran across the lawn, pulling a kite on the ground, Jupey behind him. Things almost looked normal.

Finally Bobby left his bedroom and walked down the stairs, his hand gripping the handrail. If only he could talk to someone. He wished he could talk to Jimmy Hayes, that boy Mary Jo liked. But what would he say? If only he knew exactly what question to ask, the one that would give him the perfect answer. He wanted to help, he really did. Bobby was prepared and ready to do a good turn daily. But no one wanted him for the hard things, the big things, like understanding his own family. Mary Jo needed help, but Bobby didn't know for what exactly. If he did—if there were a badge for that—Bobby would do it, even if a part of him was a severe, rule-bound boy telling him, "No, no, no."

Bobby had knives, ropes, notepads, and binoculars. He had patience and could decode confusing directions and foreign languages. He could chart a course, read the stars, probably even drive a car if he had to. All anyone needed to do was ask.

Virginia Johnson
September 1953

VIRGINIA JOHNSON SAT on a small wooden chair in the cafeteria at Saint Helen Grammar School. All the mothers were in a semicircle, while the toddlers played on the cushions usually reserved for gymnasts. Mothers took turns engaging the children, two at a time, throwing balls and offering up big stuffed animals. In a couple of corners, older children sat listening to stories. In a half-hour, they'd all be brought together for cookies and milk, and then three-year-old Tommy's prekindergarten socializing would end for the week. Next year he'd be in the corner listening to books, though he could already sound out some letters.

"I-C-E," he'd sounded out while staring into the freezer at Bradfield's grocery. At night when Mary Jo read to him, Virginia heard him following along, sounding out words. *Bear, hat, hello.*

Mary Jo was a good mother. *Sister,* Virginia reminded herself, cringing. Even though she came home so late most days—all those clubs and practices and events—Mary Jo took time each night to be with Tommy, though Virginia was sure that whatever feelings he had for Mary Jo were completely filial.

"Sister," Virginia told him. "Big sister."

He looked at her with Mary Jo's short-sighted honey-colored eyes. "Sister."

"Tommy," Virginia said suddenly, reaching out a hand as he galloped by holding a large stuffed cat.

Sister or not, Virginia knew Mary Jo felt all the motherly feelings Virginia could not. This was not what Virginia had ordered up for her life menu. She wasn't meant to be sitting on a little chair in a preschool class at her age, for goodness sake. She should be at the garden club meeting or the social for the Daughters of the American Revolution society—Gert had asked her to come with her, the annual meeting in Charles City. Virginia should be sitting at her kitchen table with a cigarette and a magazine and her third cup of strong coffee. She should be just about anywhere else but here because this was not supposed to be her life.

But it was.

Tommy was running around like a crazy person. Most of the other children walked, barely balanced on the cushion, wobbling side to side. He was always running, starting about a month after his first steps at barely a year old. Today, though, another boy had started chasing him. Bigger and taller, the other boy gave Tommy a good chase, both of them squealing. Virginia turned to find the other mother in order to give her an acknowledging smile. But the other mother was Betty Bradfield, sitting uncomfortably on a similar wooden chair, pregnant with what must be her third child, her maternity blouse billowing around her.

Betty's baby would Tommy's sibling, Virginia thought. Another one. She squinted. Was that one of the blouses Betty had lent her? The memory of those months and her lie slid over her skin like cooking oil.

That damn Roger Bradfield couldn't keep his hands off anyone, not even his wife. Chances were nothing had stopped that man. Rage flooded Virginia's skin, a heat welling from her heart. But she had to push it away because there was nothing to be enraged about. She was here with her son, Tommy, at play group. He would learn how to toss rubber balls and play with all the other children.

All of it was very confusing.

She gave Betty a quick nod and turned back to the boys. Her throat was tight and dry, and she struggled to focus. She wanted to run over to Betty and tell her everything. To let her know the plan had worked, but it had failed too. She was living in a secret, and the secret hurt. She had to keep it alive, every day, making the world imagine that Tommy was her son, hers and Larry's, the spitting image of both of them. Forcing the world to see that she had not neglected her daughter and allowed such a tragedy to play out in her own home.

But it hadn't been Betty who had forced Virginia to live a lie. Virginia could be friendly with Betty, but she had to stay apart, away. And that hurt too. Regrets Virginia felt only at night crowded her thoughts. If only, if only, if only.

Thankfully, the Bradfields had pulled away from the Johnsons, finding another doctor, putting their country club membership on hold, and spending holidays with Betty's family in Illinois. Whenever there was a chance the women would encounter each other, both Betty and Virginia found ways to mitigate. Betty prepared the care packages for the soldiers in Korea at home. Virginia baked for the holiday celebration fundraiser but didn't sit at the table to sell. Betty did. Virginia stopped playing bridge on Thursday evenings, citing Bobby's various projects and groups (such a busy boy. Oh, yes. The trombone!). Betty dropped out of the garden club. It was a terrible dance, one of them always out of sight of the other, though both knew exactly where the other was.

Except for today.

Virginia smoothed her skirt, feeling old and out of place, as she usually did when taking Tommy to see Dr. Treasure, the new pediatrician in Larry's practice. Old and out of fashion, as she did when pushing Tommy through the aisles at the grocery store, the only place Virginia was certain to run into a Bradfield. But until the Fareway market was completed at the end of Main Street, she was forced to shop for everything at Bradfields, looking away from Roger's office each time she needed rice and oatmeal. She didn't dare ask Mr. Huff behind the meat counter for a special order four-bone roast at Christmas or Mr. Saalborn in produce for a pineapple, flown in special order from California via Hawaii.

She didn't know what she would do if Roger Bradfield ever looked at her again. She might use her car keys or a fountain pen to gouge out his eyes.

But of course, Virginia wouldn't do that, though she might do something, with words maybe. Of course, then she and Larry would have to move out of town, the whole secret blown to smithereens.

Not once, never, God forbid, did she let Mary Jo go grocery shopping, even though the girl would be driving soon, and it would be so handy if she could run out and grab a few last-minute items: butter, baking powder, Worcestershire sauce. Worse, it wasn't just the store but the bank too. That darn Roger Bradfield was at two corners of Main Street, lurking like a monster. They all had to hang on. In another couple of years, Mary Jo would be gone. Only then would Virginia be able to breathe again.

Tommy waved as he ran past for the eighth time, and Virginia waved back. Such a happy boy. Less like Mary Jo and more like Bobby, though puberty had made her older son a bit sullen and dark, and it was only a matter of time before he bloomed into acne and greasy hair. All the activities helped. It was likely near on to impossible to be an introvert and play the trombone.

"All right, mothers," Mrs. Reed said. "Let's have another two of you in the mix."

Virginia nodded and put her bag on her chair and stepped into the play ring. Tommy ignored her, continuing to chase Harry. Balls rolled past, and Virginia avoided stepping on a tower two boys were building with wooden blocks. A little girl sat in the middle of the cushion by herself playing with a very worn doll. This was the Huff girl. Doris, Virginia thought. Her mother, Janice, was closer in age to Mary Jo than Virginia and sat on a chair in a cotton dress that made her look about twelve. Damn men. Janice's husband had picked her right off the family farm like an apple and brought her to town, getting her pregnant the second the wedding vows were uttered.

"Can I meet your doll?" Virginia asked Doris, not wanting to meet either, but knowing that she had to act the part and keep busy, lest she find herself gazing at Betty.

Doris stared up at her with green eyes, her eyebrows an impossible red, as was her hair. She held out her doll. Virginia took it, her arm suddenly weary. How sad it was, all of this. Janice and Doris, her and Tommy, Betty and Harry. These children's lives were fraught, as her mother would say.

"Sure is pretty," Virginia said. "A real nice little doll."

Doris nodded, taking back her doll and recommencing her play, which was so quiet that Virginia had no idea the motive or outcome. With Bobby, there had always been so much noise—revving of train engines, blowing of brass instruments, strumming of the GD guitar, yelling in the back yard over bows and arrows—she always knew where he was. She'd thought she'd been on top of Mary Jo. The child had always had her nose in a book, no matter where she was. Up in a tree, at a party, on a picnic—Mary Jo was halfway through a novel.

Take your eye of a child for one second, and she ends up pregnant. For a moment, the world tilted, and Virginia sat down next to Doris.

"Are you all right?" a voice said above her.

Virginia nodded and took in one of the deep breaths Larry always told her to when she was "het up."

One breath, two, and then she opened her eyes. Betty Bradfield leaned over her, Harry in her arms. Her maternity blouse billowed around them both.

"I had a sinking spell is all," Virginia said.

Doris stared, her doll clutched tight in one hand. Virginia patted Doris on the head and stood, coming eye to eye with Betty, who unleashed Harry back into action.

"He's enjoying this," Virginia said, wishing she didn't have to be so damn sociable. Wouldn't it have been acceptable for her to turn on her heel, grab Tommy by the hand, and walk out the door? She'd send her regrets to the center and never come back. But no. What would Gert say? That was not how Virginia was raised.

"My cousin in Chicago sends her boy to a nursery school. Tells me it socializes them," Betty said. "But Harry needs more than that. Maybe I should sign him up for track-and-field now."

There was a pause that stretched like gum. Virginia had not one bit of training about how to converse in a situation like this. Early on Virginia had wanted to make peace. She'd wanted everyone to agree on how things were going to go. But talking to the woman married to your daughter's rapist was not a situation on her mother's hit parade of social how-tos and hot tips.

"Look," Betty said, moving closer. "I—I have been meaning…I've wanted…Well, we really haven't seen each other to talk since you returned the maternity clothes."

Harry spun past, a pied piper with several children following him, Tommy second. They all held musical instruments, everyone clacking and clanging so much that even Doris stood up and brought herself and her doll into the line. The place was bedlam. Virginia wished she were home in her kitchen with a cup of coffee. Or even better, in her mother's white tiled kitchen, the sun shining through the window, a plate of kuchen in front of her.

"There's no need," Virginia said, and she meant it. None of this was Betty's fault. If Virginia and Larry had been blind to what had happened, how could Betty have known? But a man didn't…do that. There had to be signs, didn't there? Larry could no more rape a child than land on the moon.

But when she looked into Betty's pale, honest face, Virginia understood that Roger Bradfield was a mystery not even his own wife could solve.

"It's—it just is," Virginia said. "There's nothing more we can do about it but move forward."

Betty tucked a gold strand of hair behind an ear. She was such a stunning woman, even pregnant. Virginia had never looked so put together when she was pregnant, except for when she "carried" Tommy. Such a tidy experience. Best pregnancy ever.

"They will be in school together for twelve years," Betty said.

"That they will." They would never get away from what happened, Virginia thought, not unless one family moved away. Given how deeply Larry and Roger were embedded in Saint Helen, a move wouldn't be possible until Larry retired. But by then, the children would be gone, and she'd be sitting in some boat in Florida wearing a sun hat and a floppy old-lady one-piece swimsuit.

"Maybe there is a way," Betty began. "To get things back to how they were."

Virginia looked up, but Betty had turned her face toward the children. Get back? How on God's green earth could they get back? Everything that had been in the "back" time had been some kind of lie. Virginia had loved Betty from the moment Larry met her and brought her home for dinner. Roger had been the perfect match. Perfect man. Personable, responsible, kind. And then.

"I don't know," Virginia said.

"Maybe you and me," Betty said. "We can meet with the children. Go to the park. The library. Maybe we…I could start up at the country club again."

Betty's face crumpled, and she brushed her cheeks with one hand. The poor woman had been painted with the brush meant only for her husband. But what else could she and Larry have done? Betty was lucky Larry hadn't called the authorities. Virginia's heart pounded hard in her throat. She had so many words to fling like knives, but instead she took another deep breath.

Tommy ran to her and flung himself into her lap. This strange, affectionate child. He wasn't one of hers, Virginia knew that. He was part hers, and the rest of him was Roger. Friendly, caring, gregarious. Worse things too, maybe. But Virginia knew she might erase that side of Tommy, keep him all Johnson. He'd never know the truth, and that lie would keep him whole, better, free. Things should be normal with Harry and at least Betty. Otherwise, cracks would form in the edifice they had constructed.

The children had all sat down around the stack of blocks. Even Doris was laughing, flinging her doll around.

"Let's start with the park," Virginia said.

Mary Jo Johnson
Summer 1954

JIMMY HAYES HAD been the first after Roger, and he'd been the only since, at least until he went to college in the fall of 1953. Soon after their first date, Mary Jo had slowly allowed Jimmy what he so clearly wanted, offering up her body in parts and in the expected order. This slow descent into sex lasted over a year, until finally, every weekend, sex was an expected part of the schedule.

"You have to find protection," Mary Jo said one night as Jimmy dropped her off. "Otherwise, we will never, ever do it."

She closed the car door without another word. The next night when Jimmy parked his parents' car at the edge of the park, she was not surprised when he produced a condom packet.

"Backseat bingo," Margie giggled when she commented on how many nights in a row Mary Jo and Jimmy saw each other.

Mary Jo told her to hush. This wasn't a game of chance, luck, or otherwise.

"He thinks you are one hot bombshell!" Diane joked during games, the three girls watching Jimmy jump high to catch an impossible football. "What do you two actually do?"

Diane stared at her, waiting, as if there were an answer she needed. Was Diane having sex too? They never talked about exact moves, strokes, pushes, parts. But on her cheeks, in the gleam of her gaze, a blush. Maybe Diane understood more than she let on.

Margie sat pale, stricken almost, turning her head away from the conversation as if it were a disease.

Mary Jo opened her mouth but then stopped, closed her mouth, bit lightly on the inside of one cheek. Talking about Jimmy might open other closed doors. She would never tell her friends anything. So she smiled and gave a quick wink, letting Diane imagine and Margie move onto other topics like skirts and hairstyles.

"You're beautiful," Jimmy said quietly after each time they had sex, stroking her face and hair, as if she weren't a girl who had had a baby.

Was she beautiful? Every weekend she put herself to the test. Football game, party, sex. Harvest bonfire, sex. Basketball game, party, sex. Picnic, sex. Swimming party, sex. The sex was carried out mostly in Jimmy's parents' car or his father's truck or at one of their houses during the miracle of either being empty. Mostly this was Mary Jo's house, as Jimmy had five siblings, all younger, all girls, with their friends swarming every room. But Mary Jo hated the times she and Jimmy found themselves alone at her house because the ghost of Roger Bradfield haunted the hallways, the closet, the rooms. He stomped down the corridors as Jimmy was over her, grunting. The ghost laughed, arms crossed, as he stared down at them bumping along on Mary Jo's twin bed.

He chuckled and shook his head. "You know you liked it better with me, honey."

Honey? Had Mr. Bradfield ever called her that? And had she liked it with Mr. Bradfield? How could that be possible? Mary Jo clenched her eyes and grabbed Jimmy's back, wanting the ghost to disappear forever.

But it was Jimmy, not the ghost, who left first. That last late summer day, he drove up in the used truck his father had bought for him and swung out of the driver's side, long legs in nice fitting dungarees. He had shaved and smelled like morning.

Mary Jo jittered, hands shaking. In the house, Tommy hid behind the living room curtain, peeking out to stare. He never took his eyes off her, waiting, she expected, for the day she would disappear. But now she forced herself to forget him. She met Jimmy on the steps and looked into his eyes, so dark, his face now a man's. She'd watched him grow up. He was grown up. He was leaving Saint Helen.

"Mary Jo," he said, taking her hands in his. Behind her, she heard tapping on the window. "I'm going to miss you so much. I'll think about you every day."

"I'll miss you too," she said, mostly meaning it. Not one day had gone by without him being only a phone call away. He walked or drove her to school. He took her to every game, at least the ones he wasn't playing in. Jimmy was there during holidays, celebrations, and shopping trips Mary Jo's mother asked them to make downtown, including the grocery store, his tall, strong body shielding her from Mr. Bradfield. He stood between Mary Jo and the world. Mary Jo and any other man.

Now she was alone again.

Jimmy ran back to the truck and pulled out his football sweater, a large SH stitched on the left front pocket. "I want you to have this. To sleep in," he said. "To remember me by."

Because her parents were suddenly on the front porch, he kissed her on the cheek, shook her parents' hands, and waved at Tommy who glowered behind the window. Bobby was nowhere in sight, as usual these days, locked in his room doing odd projects and blasting his trombone. He'd turned into a golem, the troll under their family's bridge, his face speckled with acne. But Mary Jo had the feeling he was watching Jimmy from his bedroom window.

A light breeze blew around and over them. A few leaves scattered on the driveway. Mary Jo waved one last time, and then Jimmy roared down the street. Mary Jo felt naked. She wanted to curl up and hide in her room, but instead she went inside for grilled cheese sandwiches and tomato soup.

For a few months, Jimmy wrote impassioned letters, telling her how much he missed her. Ohio State would be perfect if only Mary Jo were there. For a couple of school holidays, he'd made sure to drive up to her house before going home to his. There were parties and walks in the snow and movies. There was sex, the same as they'd always had, but somehow different, as if something was between them, sliding between their skin. Maybe it was distance. Maybe it was Jimmy's new life. A new girlfriend. Due to a freak storm, he didn't come home for spring break, and in his last letter,

Jimmy wrote about a job he'd taken in Ohio for the summer, coaching a football clinic for room, board, and stipend.

Great experience too, he'd written. Jimmy was eager to be a football coach. A teacher. Maybe a professor.

A smart step, he'd added.

She wrote back to congratulate him, and that was the last she heard, other than gossip that floated around town, probably started by Diane or Margie.

He has a new job and a new girlfriend.
He never officially broke it off with Mary Jo.
He's going to be a famous football player!
He's never coming home again.
Her heart is broken.

Jimmy was probably working at his new job now, she imagined, in the hometown of his real or imaginary new girlfriend. Her name was probably something like Missy or Candy. She was older, maybe a junior in college. Blond and lean with skin like butter. Or her name was Emily or Amelia. She was tiny with a doll's face and brilliant blue eyes.

Most important, nothing bad had ever happened to Missy Candy Emily Amelia. She'd never had a baby when she was twelve. Her whole life was in front of her, a spring field of corn, unharvested.

None of this was surprising. Jimmy was like that. He needed someone. He'd wanted Mary Jo before he'd really ever met her, and he'd kept her close the entire time they were going steady. She was his everything, until she wasn't.

Mary Jo felt his absence, but it was as if part of herself were absent, the part that Jimmy saw. The part of her that was beautiful and now was not.

One late night at the end of July, Tommy and Bobby asleep, Mary Jo read the latest book she'd brought home from the library, *Love Is Eternal*, an ironic title, she thought—but the story was about Mary Todd Lincoln. The house was silent, held cupped in a stretch of heat that had lasted two weeks. All the windows were open, and only an idea of a breeze pushed through the mesh screens. Her parents had gone to the country club that night for a summer soiree, cocktails and dancing. When they weren't home after midnight, Mary Jo walked the house to check the doors and lights, making sure the outside lights were still on.

Closing the book on Mary Todd Lincoln's struggles, Mary Jo got ready for bed. After checking on Tommy one more time, she turned off her light and looked out her bedroom window at the driveway, street, and creek. The moon was sinking, a nimbus of yellow clinging to the horizon. She felt as though she were in a ship, sailing away, heading into the unknown. Whatever was out there had to be better than this.

A car turned onto the street, casting shiny yellow light on the tree leaves. Above the noise of the engine, she heard laughter pouring out of the open windows.

The driver slowed and stopped at the bottom of their driveway, car idling. There was motion in the car, laughter, and first her mother—her drinking laugh high, arch, too loud—and then her father—steady and calm, even when he'd had a few too many—stepped out of the car.

"Thank you kindly," he said to the driver.

Mary Jo struggled to make out who it was, but then she got the answer.

"It was so wonderful to see you tonight," a woman's voice said. Betty Bradfield.

Mary Jo's heart stuttered and lurched. She pressed a fist to the center of her chest, barely able to breathe. Her throat hurt from something, maybe words she wanted to yell out the window.

Then she heard him, steady, smart, not drunk, the careful, calm one. "Take care, you two," he said, that voice in her ear as if he were in the room with her. "Larry, let me know if you want a lift to the club in the morning. Headed that way for a round of golf."

Her father patted the fender. Roger tooted the horn and slowly pulled away and headed down the street.

Her parents turned toward the house, laughing, happy, heads together.

"Oh, you are so tipsy," her mother giggled.

Her father said something Mary Jo couldn't hear. But she didn't know if it was because they were outside or because her heart was filling her whole body with a pounding rush of blood. Her ears whirred, her breath roared, each breath shallow, harsh.

They'd broken their promise.

They'd made friends with the Bradfields again. They'd said they wouldn't. That day they'd sat her down and told her the plan, her mother and father both swore Mr. Bradfield would never, ever come to the house again. They promised again and again, even as they sneaked her out of the house and drove her to Grandma Gert's in Charles City.

They lied. Maybe it was merely a car ride home, but it wouldn't take long. He would be here soon, maybe before she was able to escape. As the summer cracked hot into autumn, Roger Bradfield would be sitting on the back patio drinking bourbon and soda.

"Oh, mister, you are so silly," said her mother, stumbling up the front path below Mary Jo's window. Mary Jo could see her mother, four bourbons into the night, her eyes glassy, her smile too wide.

"Don't you know it," said her father.

Mary Jo had always known it, feeling a dull gray growing distance between her and her family and every single person on this earth but Tommy. But he wasn't hers anymore. From the moment she handed him to her mother and gotten on the school bus, her baby had started to drift away.

She was on her own.

Her parents laughed, clattering into the front door. Mary Jo heard it swing open and then closed, a little too hard. Quietly she stepped out of her room and leaned over the banister, listening to their too loud whispers and breathing in cigarette smoke and alcohol. Her parents clunked into the darkness of the house, not bothering to come upstairs and check on her, Bobby, or Tommy. Why would they? They had no need. Mary Jo was here, taking care of everything.

***

The next day, Mary Jo drove her mother's car to Diane's and convinced her to go downtown to the drugstore for lunch at the counter. Mary Jo had put on her white sleeveless blouse and her new blue cotton skirt. She'd spent time on her hair, something she'd been haphazard with since Jimmy moved away. Mary Jo was pleased that her time in the sun had made her arms and legs gleam, her skin a soft nutty color.

"My, you look nice," her mother had said as she walked through the kitchen. She was stirring a big pot of something, and Mary Jo had hoped it didn't mean they were having a party. "Pick up some egg noodles and two onions on your way home, would you?"

Used to be, her mother would do anything to keep her away from the grocery. When Tommy was a baby, they'd sometimes drive all the way to Franklin for flour and sugar to avoid running into Roger Bradfield.

Not anymore.

"Are we having a party?" Mary Jo had asked.

Virginia had eyed her over the top of the large pot. There was a pause, a one two, and then her mother said, "I'm taking this soup to someone who's feeling poorly. We're having chicken casserole, if you get me what I need at the store."

Mary Jo had nodded, but her body clenched. She could make an excuse when she returned home empty-handed. Or she could ask Diane to run into the grocery for her.

"What got into you?" Diane asked when she slid onto the seat next to Mary Jo. "And where's Margie?"

Mary Jo shrugged. "Don't know. Didn't you call her?"

"Nope," Diane said. "But it's okay. It's so crowded on the weekends. We'll be lucky to get seats ourselves."

Diane pulled down the sun visor on her side and puckered her lips as she stared into the small mirror, turning her head back and forth. She pulled out a gold tube of pink lipstick and smoothed it over her lips, touching up the corners with her fingers. Her father had forbidden her to wear lipstick, so she always put it on in the bus or the car or just before walking into a party.

"That'll do," she said. "Let's go!"

This past year Diane had grown an inch and filled out a little in the chest area, her blouses straining at the middle button. Suddenly the boys were more interested. No wonder her father was worried. She'd want that corner stool, the one visible from the front door, Mary Jo thought. Their unspoken plan suited Mary Jo; she could see everyone who walked in and pick from those who moved past Diane to her. It didn't matter, really, who it was, as long as he might last one year exactly.

Turned out it was Dave Miller, who pushed a freshman boy off his stool and sat by Mary Jo as Diane entertained Brian Peterson and Dick Wilson, who both vied for her attention by blowing straw wrappers at each other and ordering banana splits to tempt her.

"We should put them both in a sandbox and give them shovels," Dave said.

Mary Jo smiled at the image of the two football players throwing sand at each other.

Diane laughed, a tinkling, glittery glass sound. The boys blew more straw wrappers.

"Can I ask you to a movie sometime?" Dave said.

Mary Jo nodded, sipped her milkshake, chocolate, her favorite. Then she turned to Dave, gave him a look she had perfected with Jimmy, her eyes wide. In this light, she knew they were the color of honey. Her hair was smooth and dark and shiny, and she tucked one strand behind her ear. The light would be flickering against her pearl earrings. She leaned forward, titling her head down and then looking up into his face.

"Do you think you could do me a little favor at the grocery?"

Dave Miller all but wagged his tail. The counter girl delivered his burger and fries, and he turned his full attention to his huge platter of food.

Everything would turn out fine.

Jimmy Hayes
Summer 1954

JIMMY STOOD OUT on the field, whistle around his neck, hands on his hips. He wore a polo shirt that was wet enough to wring out and a pair of shorts. He felt like an idiot, of course, wanting nothing more than a T-shirt and dungarees, but the camp had a dress code, at least for coaches.

His group—a scrawny bunch of middle school Ichabods wearing pads and helmets—lumbered under the makeshift tent next to the 50-yard line, drinking water and cooling off, which was impossible in this weather. A dank humid dome hung over the field, and for about the hundredth time that day, Jimmy wished he'd never said yes to this job. To Ohio State. To Cammy, whose dad was the local high school football coach.

"Ten minutes!" he shouted, refusing to hide under the tarp with the kids or to talk one more time with the other two coaches about weight training or sprints, so he headed around back of the bleachers and sat down where he'd be hidden, if not cooler. There was no breeze, but the shade helped. Some.

He leaned back and rubbed his forehead. At first Cammy and then Cammy's summer plan was his perfect escape from Saint Helen. For about a week. But then he couldn't stop thinking about Mary Jo. And it was impossible to forget her where he was, right here, on a field. How many times had they rushed under the bleachers at Saint Helen High to make out for five minutes or an hour?

He didn't want to think about it or the way he could still feel her skin, see her smile. And then, when he least wanted to, he saw her eyes, the way she would look at him. Jimmy would have done anything for that look, the one that told him he was exactly perfect, for Mary Jo and the world. No one else had ever looked at him like that, not even Cammy.

How else could he explain their long relationship? He wouldn't be expecting Mary Jo's gaze, but then he'd turn a hallway corner at school. She seemed to heat and melt and pulse, like a fantastic unseen star beating out his name, a coded message for him and him alone.

Then there would be an after-game party, the whole weekend of parties and study times at the library downtown and dinners at her house, sometimes his. For years. At times, he'd get anxious, worry that he'd given himself over to someone he barely knew. Mary Jo was quiet, distant, faraway on some island only she had a boat and a paddle for. She didn't like to chat much—she would sit in a corner at a party—and although she was pretty, she was ordinary too, in most ways. Brown hair, brown eyes, nice smile, good figure.

But then she'd walk through a door and melt him, a girl with a superpower. When they were alone, she moved her body in ways, well, he'd never expected from anyone, ever, not even when he was married. Her skin was buttery, warm, soft, her legs and arms holding him tight and close, all of her saying, "Yes." Saying, "I know what to do."

It was like someone had given her the cheat sheet to the biggest exam of all.

He never told his friends, though when they were bragging about getting to third base with their girlfriends (not that Jimmy believed anything anyone on the football team said), he wanted to stand up tall, hands on hips, and say, "I'm having sex every week."

He wanted to wear a banner, be crowned sexual king. More than any other football player, farm boy, city slicker, show-off kid he knew, Jimmy was a real man.

"Don't ever tell," Mary Jo told him after the first time.

"I never—"

"If you tell," she said, "we will never do it again."

The air had closed around them. Mary Jo breathed into his neck, her breath sweet, like peaches.

"I won't—"

"You can't," she said.

He didn't, though he wanted to. But he wanted Mary Jo more.

A fly buzzed his head, and Jimmy swatted it away, sweat dripping down his neck. Seven minutes. And then four more hours. He might not make it.

Because then he had to go back to the room he was living in above Cammy's parents' garage. There was no sneaking down into the house at night and into Cammy's bed. Not that she would even allow that. He had access to her mouth and her breasts, but that was it. No hand rubbing over her panties. Not a swipe, touch, nuzzle, or push below her waistband.

Four more weeks of this. He might not make it.

Six minutes. He could run to the parking lot, jump in his truck, head to Cammy's house—no one would be home. He could empty out his room in two minutes. Out on the highway, roads clear, he'd be home in ten hours, tops. He could surprise his parents and then race over to Mary Jo's. Or he could stop at Mary Jo's first, pick her up, and press her to him, breathing in all the answers she had given him for years.

Five minutes.

Then, after an interminable dinner of fried chicken or succotash or pork ribs, he could take her away and disappear into her body.

They'd go right back to normal. He'd find a way to come home for every break. He'd sit in the Johnson's living room, dealing with Mary Jo's brother, Bobby, and all his annoying questions. Worse was the kid's staring. Holy smokes that kid had huge eyes.

But Mary Jo was worth it. Everything.

Jimmy wiped his forehead again, aroused despite the heat. Jesus. He missed her, but she was a trap, a silo, dark and forever. If he went home, he'd never leave.

Three minutes.

From the field, the sound of a whistle. Voices. The crunch of helmets hitting. At her job at her father's office, Cammy sat primly behind her desk organizing files. A fan blew on her face, not moving a strand of hair. She was that perfect.

Thank God, a cloud and then another slid across the sky, covering the blazing sun for seconds. What was he thinking?

Two minutes.

Jimmy stood up, smoothed his clothing, and wiped his face one more time. He wasn't going home to Saint Helen. He wouldn't until Mary Jo was gone, off to whatever life she would have, and knowing her, she would have one. And when he finally saw her years from now—she would be visiting from California because that's where she would be living—both of them would be so stuck in their own circumstances, they would only smile, nod, and give quick waves, the past a landmark they each drove by fast, not touching the brakes once.

Time.

Mary Jo Johnson
June 1955

THE NIGHT OF Mary Jo's high school graduation, there was a glitch. She hadn't understood until she arrived home, not knowing when Dave would arrive at her house after her parents dropped her off. Why would she think about it? She had it all planned out. There her parents went, off to the restaurant, Bobby and Tommy in the back seat waving to her. They would all meet at Edison's, sit at the huge family table in the middle of the dining room. Her Aunt Fiona would be there with her family, as well as Grandma Gert and Great-Aunt Edie, who'd both spent the night.

Dave should have been at her house already. His family was meeting them at Edison's too, and her mother had promised a large chocolate cake with vanilla ice cream. They'd all come back here afterward—Hazel due any minute to get things ready—and Mary Jo assumed it would be a late night.

Tomorrow she was headed off to Stanford to start a summer program for women.

"Got to get you gals ready for the men," her mother said. Mary Jo wasn't exactly sure what she meant, though Diane told her that all women wanted out of college was a husband.

"The MRS degree." Diane giggled.

All Mary Jo wanted was to get out of Saint Helen.

She waited in the living room, looking out onto the tree-lined streets, the leaves bright, dark green, and shiny. The weather had been mild, but heat was building, hanging on the horizon, waiting to smash everyone down. But she'd be in California, where there were ocean breezes and fog clinging to the summer-browned hills.

Behind her, she heard something shift, and she turned, clutching her purse and wrap, half-hoping it was Jimmy Hayes, returned, finally, from Ohio, just this once.

"I thought I'd find you here," Roger Bradfield said.

Mary Jo stared at him, her breath somewhere outside her body. She wanted to suck it back in and run, but she couldn't move or speak or cry out.

"You didn't think I would let you leave Saint Helen without saying goodbye?" He was smiling, but his words were twisted, poisonous.

"Dave—"

"I don't need long," Mr. Bradfield said. "And besides, I asked Dave to do a pickup from the store. You know he does some odd jobs for me now and again?"

Mary Jo found the ability to swallow. No, she did not know Dave did anything for Roger Bradfield. She didn't know Dave even knew him past the known facts of the grocery, the two banks, the farms. Who their age beside her was paying attention to Roger Bradfield?

She stepped back, but she was at the window and couldn't move any farther. The glass pressed against her hair, so nicely combed for her dinner out.

"Oh, you didn't know." Mr. Bradfield shook his head. "I guess you wouldn't."

His teeth gleamed. His hair was shiny, still dark, but now glinting with gray. She hadn't been this close to him for more than four years. But like always, his energy changed the room, the walls vibrating as he moved slowly toward her. She gagged at his smell: soap, aftershave, and a fierce need.

"You were always my favorite," Mr. Bradfield said. "I will never forget how sweet you were. Opened up like a flower."

He reached a hand toward her, and she flinched, closing her eyes. His fingertips grazed her cheek, and Mary Jo bit back a nauseous rage.

"Don't tell me you didn't miss me too," he breathed into her neck. "I could hear you thinking about me across town. You know I'm right."

Mary Jo almost gasped, swallowing back the sound. He was right. She had been thinking about him, at least sometimes. How could she help it? Each time Tommy turned to her, there was Roger Bradfield in their son's eyes, his cheekbones. Worse, each time Jimmy or Dave had touched her, she fought back a craving for Roger's first, horrible caress, the way he'd swept her skin with his fingers, enough so she could barely breathe.

Then she would be awash in shame for wanting the things that had broken her. And she was broken. She couldn't feel things she needed to, even though she kept trying. There'd been terror with Mr. Bradfield, but also something so intense and powerful she could almost float on it. Whenever he'd walked into a room she was in, she'd wanted to run away or toward him.

Right now she could imagine letting him surround her with his arms. He'd pull her gently to the floor and do things with his mouth and body that gave her such shame, such pleasure.

But no. No. No. This couldn't happen again. How could she live with another set of lies on top of the ones she was already living with? There was the baby who was hers and then not hers. The lie of every single day, Tommy never knowing the truth. She was rotten. To the core, her grandmother might have said. A bad apple.

She was leaving for her own new life, out of Saint Helen, and she would not bring along another baby she would have to abandon in one way or another.

As he moved closer, her breath stuck in her ribs, but she looked up into his face, seeing his lips, the pores on his nose, a too long eyebrow hair, dark and wiry. He needed a shower, his body stuck in a suit all day.

Mary Jo's body pulsed with ache and blood and hatred. As he brought his face to hers, her fingers moved across the window table, searching until she found it, heavy and solid and pointed at the edges. His eyes closed, and she grabbed what she'd been looking for. She smashed it hard against the back of his head. Once. Twice.

He roared, rearing back, and she used every part of her strength and smacked him against the cheek, hard, noting an instant bloom of red and blood. Then dropping the glass paperweight her father had brought home from California—the one etched with palm trees—she ran out of the house, no wrap, no purse, leaving the front door wide open. She ran as fast as she could, ignoring Roger Bradfield's yells from her parents' front porch, pretending she didn't hear him call out something about Tommy.

Her father would take care of Tommy. And if Mr. Bradfield ever did anything to him, she would come home and tell the entire town what he did. Then she would kill him with her own hands.

Mary Jo Johnson ran down the driveway and onto the street, as fast as she could in her celebratory graduation dress and nice shoes, hoping she would get to the intersection before Roger got into his car. Someone would be out watering geraniums or trimming overgrown rose bushes. Nobody would let her be dragged away, would they? Would they? She swallowed a sob and kept going. She strained to hear a car. She searched the road for a sign. Sucking in air, she hoped that in one second, two, Dave would turn onto her road and take her to the restaurant. She wouldn't even bring up him working at the grocery without telling her. She didn't care. Not anymore. All she needed was one more night. A few more hours.

Dirt gathered in her shoes. Gnats buzzed around her mouth and eyes. Sweat trickled down her spine, soaking the material around her waist. The heat of the day wrapped around her, urging her to slow, but she kept going. Mary Jo sped up, using her arms, flying down the street as fast as she could.

Tommy Johnson
September 1955

TOMMY DID AS his mother told him. He put on his stiff, brand-new school clothes, plus his new navy blue sweater. He tied his shoes as he was taught: *Over, under, around and through, meet Mr. Bunny, pull and through.*

He was good at tying his shoes, his laces tight, the loops exactly like bunny ears. His new book bag was at the foot of his bed, packed with his cap and the pencils his mother had bought at Marcie's five-and-dime. Before he left his room, Tommy picked up two toy soldiers: his Davy Crockett and a stagecoach driver, both from his latest town set up in the basement. He'd brought them up last night before his bath, knowing he would need them at school. If he put his hand in the bag while he was on the bus or maybe on his way out to recess, he'd feel better.

He didn't want to go to school, even if he and Harry Bradfield were going to be in the same class. He didn't care that Mary Jo and Bobby had done this before him. All he wanted was to stay at home and play. Or go to the park and swing, running around with Harry as their mothers sat on the bench and smoked. They never paid attention when they smoked.

"Don't be a little baby," Bobby had said earlier at breakfast, his face a mask of disgust. Or it was possible he couldn't smile because he'd been to the dermatologist the day before, the pimple ointment the doctor sent home making his face tight and stretched and fake. Shiny. A doll. A ventriloquist dummy, like that scary Charlie McCarthy. Or was it Bobby's anger that made him so ugly? "It's only school."

Tommy had looked into his corn flakes. School hadn't done anything good for Bobby. He hid in his room as much as possible and didn't ever go anywhere except band practice. He had one friend, John Pedersen, who lumbered over with his comic books that the two of them read in the basement. Tommy hated the way John smelled and wished Timmy Rawlins was still Bobby's friend. Timmy laughed a lot and smelled like dirt and peppermint, but they hadn't been friends for a long time.

"Tommy?" his mother called up the stairs. "The bus will be here any minute."

Tommy put his bag strap on one shoulder and then turned back, making sure he'd made his bed.

"You're a big schoolboy now," his mother told him after Mary Jo had left. "You can learn to make your own bed."

He'd watched his mother, and every morning he tried to do it the same, tucking the corners and smoothing the bedspread. It never looked right to his eyes, at least until he got home. He could tell his mother or Hazel had remade the whole thing.

Tommy stood in the doorway, looking toward Mary Jo's room, empty now, even though most of her things were still there. Her novels, the jewelry she didn't take with her to California, her stuffed cat and old doll, Flat Susan. Tommy sometimes went in and opened the jewelry box and stared before picking up one piece and then another. The sparkly pin Dave had given her for graduation. She never wore it, but Tommy sometimes held it up to the light coming through the window to watch the bright sparks of green and blue. A necklace their mother had given her, one pearl on a gold chain. Another pin from Jimmy, at least that's what Mary Jo told him. Tommy didn't really remember Jimmy.

"He was nice," Mary Jo had said while packing to leave for college. But her voice didn't sound like Jimmy was nice. Tommy wasn't even sure she thought Dave was nice. Maybe, he worried, Mary Jo didn't think he was nice, but then she had put down the sweater in her hands and grabbed him up, blowing air into his neck and making him screech.

He wished Mary Jo were here now, smoothing his hair and saying, "You're going to have a great day. And when you get home, you can tell me all about it."

Mary Jo barely telephoned, and she hadn't come home for Fourth of July or Labor Day. She sent him presents though. A stuffed bear wearing a Stanford shirt. A small football. A book about an Eskimo. But Tommy had almost forgotten what she looked like. Smelled like. That's why he sometimes opened her closet and smelled her clothes, grabbing her dresses and skirts in his arms and breathing in. If he closed his eyes, he could remember her. He could hear her, her laugh as she read him books at night.

Something huge and whole inside him wanted him to throw himself to the floor, fingers gripping the boards. He wished he could hold onto the door and never leave. Tommy didn't want to go anywhere without Mary Jo's smile. If he left his house right now, without her nod and wink, he would lose her forever. He could tell. It was true. Tears came to his eyes, and a wail he'd never been able to utter pulsed in his throat.

"Come right down here this instant!" his mother called up, impatient, that sharp nasal tone that always meant trouble, a sound four seconds away from a spanking. "Don't make me come up there."

Tommy sniffed, rubbed at his eyes. Mary Jo was lost from this house. From him. She was gone all away across the big world and not coming back. He might as well go to school and sit in Indian circles and learn to read. At least Harry would be there. Maybe he could go live with Harry in the big house they moved into only three blocks away. There would be snacks and lots of kids to play with. He wouldn't have to listen to Bobby play his trombone or sit at the table stiff as a board while his parents finished their meals. People would say things. Maybe at night someone would read to him. Or even better, someone would tell him a story he could believe. One whole true story.

That's all Tommy had ever wanted.

Betty Bradfield
Summer 1958

BETTY SIPPED HER cocktail, her third, though she was far behind Virginia Johnson and the other gals at her table, all of whom might be on their fifth. But really, who was counting?

"Cheers!" Betty raised her glass and gave a wink to Virginia, who leaned an elbow on the table.

"Cheers! And more of them to come."

Betty snorted and took another sip. Actually, Betty was counting all their drinks. She'd keep counting until she couldn't, which wouldn't be long. She was getting drunk, and the country club ballroom was hot and filled with noise. Dancers swung around the dance floor to the band music beating into Betty's brain. Why not drink? For the first time in years, she wasn't breastfeeding or pregnant. Finally she could smoke and drink without wanting to vomit in her hat. Better yet, her children—other than one-year-old Helen—were at her favorite aunt's house for a blessed two weeks. Betty had paid her babysitter Jean to take Helen to her house over-night, though she would have preferred the sitter to stay at theirs.

"It would be best for Helen to come to mine," Jean had said, her eyes strangely flat and implacable. "With the other kids at your mom's, I've got the perfect setup for her."

"We have the new television."

Jean shook her head.

Betty offered her more money, but Jean insisted in her placid way. After a lot of coffee and some aspirin in the morning, Betty would pick up Helen, who would be none the worse for wear. She loved Jean.

At the last minute, Roger had had to leave town on bank business. Or maybe it had been something about the new store in Franklin, which was causing all sorts of issues that kept Roger out day and night. As she hung up the phone, Betty had felt a swirl of disappointment tinged with despair. With the kids away, they'd finally planned a date for the two of them. A nice meal at The Farmstead and a movie. All gone in a second. Roger hadn't even come home to pack but simply called before he headed out of town.

"Enjoy your night of freedom!" he'd said. "I'll call when I get there."

Betty had waited for his call, but then, the kids gone, the house echoing, she'd taken up Virginia Johnson's invitation.

"Join us," Virginia had said. "Girls night out at the club."

There were no children to tend to and nothing to do. Betty had been beside herself. How should she occupy her time? She wasn't sure she even knew how to do that anymore, not with six kids running her ragged day in and day out. After Roger's phone call, she'd thought she'd simply go to bed early and sleep a normal eight hours. Get a good book and read as late as she wanted, wake up late, and smoke a cigarette for breakfast. Go to movie all by herself and eat a bag of popcorn and a box of gumdrops. Then she'd have come home to her empty house, walking from room to room to room searching for what? Her reason for being? Her life's purpose?

But instead, she was here with Virginia and her bridge group, the ladies laughing and dancing with other women's husbands.

"May I have this dance?"

Betty cut Virginia a look. It was Sam Boylan, recently widowed and constantly on the prowl, especially at the pool after his weekend golf games. And why not, really? He was in his late forties, two of his children off at school, and another—his girl—married with a child on the way. His time was his time.

Virginia didn't say a word, but one corner of her mouth rose.

Betty put down her cocktail glass. She and Roger hadn't been dancing in ages. Even when they came to the country club, he'd wave off her requests.

"I'd rather watch the dancers than be one. Go see if Don Randall will take a turn."

Betty winked at Virginia and stood, smoothing the front of her dress. "Don't mind if I do." She took his hand and followed him out to the floor.

Without a word, he put an arm around her waist, and they were off, spinning and twirling with the other couples. Betty leaned into Sam's shoulder, his suit crisp and clean and fresh. The room was packed, energy high, and Betty found she didn't have to think, allowing Sam to pull and push and turn. Wham, back in gear, feet moving.

Her heart strumming in her throat, a surprise smile on her face, Betty's skirts whooshed. The movement and air and pure fun of the dance made her laugh. Virginia waved from the table and raised her glass, winking as Betty glided by.

"You're a great dancer," Sam said in her ear.

Betty laughed again. She used to be a fantastic dancer, cavorting all night after a shift at the hospital. All those soldiers, barely recovered, wanting nothing more than a smile and some encouragement. Maybe a quick kiss in the corner.

"You should come to the club more often." Sam's eyes glowed with appreciation.

She almost said, *I'm here every weekend.* She wanted to say, *I'm here with my husband who won't dance with me, who sits us at the back table so he has a good view of the goings-on and the women. The girls.*

"I'll try," Betty said instead. Maybe she really would. She wouldn't be having any more children, that was for sure, a decision Catholic-to-the-core Roger would have raged about. But he never needed to know. It was her secret with her gynecologist, a former colleague at the hospital. During her last visit, he had prescribed a brand-new medication.

"In trials," he said. "My brother is a lead pharmacist on this one. Don't let the other ladies know. Not yet."

Miracle of miracles, she wouldn't be having another baby as a result of the pills she took every morning. Birth control, they were calling it. There would never be a way to control Roger. She was his wife. It was his right. It was their religion!

So be it. But inside her own body, she was in charge.

Sam gave her hand a squeeze. "I do hope you will. You are a joy to dance with."

The music played on, and he gave her a quick twirl. My word, did her skirt spin.

After Virginia dropped her off, Betty was too excited to sleep. Her whole body thrummed with the music, the beat in her fingers and toes and head. She hummed as she hung up her wrap and turned on the lights in the living room and kitchen before going upstairs, where she undressed, took off her makeup, put on her nightgown and robe.

Without thinking, she walked into Harry's room first to check to see if he were tented up with a picture book, sounding out new words from the light of his brand-new flashlight. Then she remembered. Harry wasn't here. Nor were Howie, Holden, Hayes, Hoyt. Or baby Helen. None of the H's, as Roger liked to call their brood, six children reduced to a capital letter. For a second, her entire body ached for her children, her insides that had carried them, as well as her arms, so used to having one or two in them.

Here, standing in the middle of the room Harry shared with Howie, she was emptied. Right now she wasn't a mother. She hadn't been a nurse for a decade. A wife? She wasn't what Roger looked at, not anymore. They even made love in the dark, on her side of the bed, the entire event lasting one or two minutes.

"Time for another baby," he'd say, kissing her forehead. "Who's next? Hiram? Hollis? Or another girl? Honor? Heather? Heidi? Hope?"

Roger would laugh and fall onto his back. He thought her fascination with H names was silly, but before she could even build up the necessary steam to be irritated, he was snoring.

Her husband would never know about the little pills, one a day, that would keep the H names at six. Roger would never have another child. But, of course, he did. Tommy, Harry's best friend. It almost didn't bother her now, except when she saw Roger staring at a girl, one about the age Mary Jo had been, barely twelve, hardly a moment past puberty.

Would he do it again? she wondered.

Then he'd turn to her and flick on his hundred-watt smile. No, a terrible mistake. Not Roger.

Betty closed Harry's door and headed downstairs. Getting comfortable, she sat in the comfy chair in the corner of the living room with a *Lady's Home Journal* opened to an orange cake recipe that would be lovely as a summer dessert.

Then she looked up, remembering that Roger said he would call. Maybe he had while she was out. If there was an emergency, he would have tried the club or even Jean's, knowing Betty might keep the babysitting date. But he usually called, even when he traveled by airplane through time zones. Even when he knew he'd wake her up.

"I know you need to hear my voice before you fall asleep," he'd say.

Suddenly she did want to hear his voice. Where was he again? Closing the magazine, Betty stood up and walked down the hall to Roger's office, flicking on the overhead light and moving toward his desk.

The Franklin store. Or bank. Roger had his fingers in so many pies these days, Betty couldn't keep track. Business was so good, they'd been casting around for an even bigger house so the kids could each have their own room.

"And we'll make sure we can add on," Roger had said. "Just in case."

He'd looked at Betty's belly. "We've been so blessed."

Betty eyed the desktop, searching for a letter or note about what hotel he might be staying at. Maybe he was staying with Dick Reed and his family. But usually he stayed overnight at the Franklin Arms, calling Betty from the lobby on his way out to meetings. All around him during the call, she could hear the clack of heels on tile, the hum of music leaking out of the bar, the ding of the elevator.

She sat down in his leather chair and flipped through his brand-new Rolodex, an amazing contraption that held all his contacts. So easy to find everything! Betty had half a mind to order one for herself for her recipes, typing them out so they would fit. How easy to cook with. She would ask Roger when he came home.

Rolling to F, she found the card for the Franklin Arms. She picked up the phone but then paused. Was it too late? It was almost midnight. But weren't front desks always staffed in bigger cities for late-night arrivals? People always getting out of cabs and whirring through revolving doors, leaves, rain, or snow flurries bursting into the lobby, like in the movies.

It was summer, though, and people would be out late, business happening after dessert and over drinks. Worse, maybe.

Betty dialed the number—long distance—and waited.

"Franklin Arms," the woman at reception said.

"I think my husband is a guest there," Betty began, feeling about as small town as she could be. A yokel. A hick. A sad woman left behind when her husband goes off to the big city. "Could you check and put me through to his room?"

"Name?"

Betty gave the woman Roger's name and waited. The house was empty, the light no longer cozy but sad, as if she were afloat on an emergency raft waiting for rescue.

"I'm sorry," the woman said. "No Roger Bradfield registered."

"Are you sure?" Betty asked, her voice throaty and insistent. "He always stays there."

"I'm sorry, ma'am." The woman was done with her. "He's not registered."

"Do you have any vacancies?"

"Yes, ma'am, we do," the woman said. "Regardless, your husband is not registered."

Betty thanked her and put down the phone. She picked up the cigarettes on Roger's desk and lit one. Regardless. Well. Maybe the Rolodex would have another Franklin hotel, but the F's yielded up nothing else hotel related.

Sitting back, Betty brought the Rolodex to her lap and flipped to A. Everything was so tidy, starting with Able Insurance. Probably Roger's secretary, Marva, had done all this work. No, Marva had left two weeks ago. What was the new girl's name? Katy? Kitty? They didn't last long with Roger, taskmaster that he was.

"They don't know about commitment," he told his family, all of them rapt. "You children take note. Do the work that is put in front of you. Don't shirk."

Kitty wouldn't last long. Not with that nasal whine she had, not to mention her habit of cracking gum, something Roger deplored. Betty had only met her once, but it had been enough. She'd almost winced when the girl started talking. Kitty was lucky she was pretty. Hopefully someone would take her out of the job market and put her in a house somewhere so she wouldn't answer anyone's phone and scare away the customers.

Beatrice Adams, Wheat Exchange.

Dr. Sorel Allston, Dentistry.

Carl Atkins, Apple Growers.

Betty stifled a grimace. The man had terrible breath, and there was no escape once you were pinned on your back, mouth wide open. Betty took a drag, letting the smoke drift around her. The night beat on. She flipped through A, B, and C, then suddenly dialed to R. Mr. Edgar Robinson. Rob's Tires. Rosemead Inn. Was that hotel in Franklin? Betty stared at the area code. Possibly.

Taking a quick puff of her cigarette, she exhaled and then picked up the phone and dialed. The phone rang five, six times before a woman answered, her voice tired, a bit wary.

"Rosemead Inn, Gladys speaking. How can I help you?"

"Hello, Gladys," Betty said. "I'm sorry to call this late, but I've forgotten what hotel my husband said he was staying in. I found this contact, so I hope I'm right."

"No trouble, ma'am," Doris said, back on point. "I can connect you to your husband's room. What's his last name?"

"Bradfield," Betty said, settling back in the chair, eager to tell Roger about her surprise night alone, the first in almost a decade. She wouldn't tell him about dancing with Sam and then sitting with him at a table for a final cocktail. She most definitely would not tell Roger how Sam had reached out a hand and put it over hers for a second.

But she would let her husband know about the music, the way it felt to whirl around the floor. Next time she would insist that he escort her onto the floor—

"I'm connecting you," Gladys broke in. "Thank you for calling Rosemead Inn."

Then there was a click, a hum, and a harsh *ring ring, ring ring.*

"Hello?" a woman's voice answered, her voice nasal and whiny. A girl, really. Katy. Kitty. Behind her, the low rumble of Roger's voice. "Who is it?"

In that instant of hearing her husband's voice, Betty was brought back by light speed and full body punch to the moment Roger first told her about Mary Jo.

Never again, he'd promised. Oh, he was so ashamed, crying at the kitchen table, head in hands.

I love you so much, he'd promised so long ago. *I'll love you forever.*

"Who is it?" Roger asked again.

Betty hung up, the phone receiver clattering in its cradle. She flung herself back in the chair and tried to find her breath. What now? What now? She couldn't lock herself in the nursery this time. All her children but baby Helen would ask questions. She couldn't plot her escape home to family, first her father and now her mother dead and buried.

How would she tell either of her brothers about Roger?

Her nursing skills were out of date. Maybe she could move everyone to Des Moines or Chicago, rent a house, and work in a doctor's office as a receptionist. At night she could take correspondence courses and get back up to speed. Betty saw herself sitting under a yellow desk lamp, her hair graying, frazzled, her eyes baggy with exhaustion. But there would be no other way if that were what she did.

At this point she was on her own.

Who was this man she was married to? How was it she was asking these same questions again? Child rapist, adulterer, liar, at the very least. She flipped through the Rolodex, fingers shaking, searching, searching, but for what? Evidence?

Betty started reading each card carefully. That was it. She wrote down the number for every single hotel, motel, inn, or country club. She didn't care about the long-distance charges anymore. Betty would call and find out when he'd been there and who he'd been with. She'd feign innocence and concern. She'd become Roger's secretary, needing to find him on urgent business, which it really was.

Then she'd search this office, and tomorrow before she picked up Helen from Jean's, she'd head down to the grocery. She'd find everything she needed, and then, only then, would she decide on her plan. Was she going to escape? Was she going to plan out the meals for next week? Was she going to poison Roger's Sunday roast? She had no idea what she wanted to do, though she wanted to do something. She didn't exactly know what, but as she wrote down number after number, she knew that by morning she would.

After a sleepless night and a quick shower and cup of coffee, Betty drove to Jean's to pick up Helen.

"What a sweet girl," Jean said, though she was looking curiously at Betty. Without thinking, Betty lifted a hand to her hair. Had she forgotten to brush it? Was she still wearing the kerchief she used when she put on makeup?

But her hair was smooth, brushed, and neatly twisted into a chignon.

Helen clung to Betty. More than any of Betty's children, Helen looked like her, from her hair color to the shape of her tiny toes. And thank goodness for that. Think if this beautiful, tiny girl had gotten Roger's prominent nose. That would have been a disaster on a girl. But like Betty, Helen had a pert Irish nose, her entire body compact, muscled, ready to work the earth. Ready to run.

"Did you enjoy your night off?" Jean said. Again, that stare.

"I did." Betty picked up Helen's bag. "But I'm ready to be a mother again."

"You can spoil Helen silly until the boys come home."

For a moment, they stared at Helen, the sun streaming on her, her hair a brilliant gold in the light. She was perfect. A literal sunny girl.

Jean looked away. "I won't be able to come to the house any-more." She moved a hand as if indicating some important reason. "But if you ever want to drop off the kids, they're welcome."

In that shaft of sunlight, Betty finally understood. After the trail of seduction she'd uncovered this morning, she could only imagine that plain Jean, with her long blond hair and surprisingly large bosom, had fended off Roger a few times.

Betty reached out and grabbed Jean's wrist. "I'm so sorry," she said. "I really am."

Then she tucked two twenties into Jean's hand.

"Say goodbye," Betty told Helen.

Betty hugged Helen, maybe even a bit too tightly.

Helen swiveled to look at Jean and raised a hand, waving in that floppy baby way. "Bye bye!" she said.

It wasn't until later, after Roger called to tell her he wouldn't be home until Monday evening, that it hit Betty. She hadn't let on a thing to Roger, keeping her voice light and airy. After the call, he had no idea that she had a clear understanding of his past months. Years, really, since that first horror of Mary Jo.

She'd put down the phone and listened to Helen babble in her playpen. Without warning, a sharp hand had reached into her chest and started to pull. Her hands, her feet went cold, and she started to shake.

Helen. Helen was a girl. A bright, beautiful baby who would grow into a brilliant, gorgeous girl and then woman. Right now, in her playpen, Helen was eleven years younger than Mary Jo Johnson had been when Roger did what he did.

What would she do when Helen got older? The last thing she wanted was for any of them to be harmed.

"Mama!" Helen called, waving a set of wooden keys that clunked together on their string keychain.

Betty had no idea what to do.

Mary Jo Johnson
September 1958

MARY JO AND her parents sat at a small table in the back of the main dining room at Ernie's in San Francisco. Her parents were dressed to the nines—her mother in a smart black hat with a white broach and a small mink stole, which had been the right choice for the chilly evening, fog hugging the coast. Virginia sipped at her second cocktail—a Manhattan.

"So delicious," she said, smiling over the rim.

Good thing they were staying in the city and not Palo Alto, Mary Jo thought. She'd hate to be the one trying to get her mother up to her room if she kept drinking like this.

Her father was in a dark blue evening jacket with a smart black tie and crisp white shirt, his glasses pushed down on his nose as he read the menu.

"I'm getting the Alfredo. It's their signature dish." Her mother put down her cocktail. "And the scallops."

Mary Jo was glad that her mother had opted out of the steak. If she had, they would have been subject to a long discussion about how Iowa beef was so much better than any other beef in the world.

"The sole sure looks tasty," her father said. "The lamb too."

"And what about a hearts of romaine salad?" her mother added. "Fine and fancy!"

Mary Jo nodded, uncomfortable in her new dress. When her mother announced they would be visiting before the start of the fall semester, she'd wired money into Mary Jo's bank account for a new dress or two. "So we can really have fun," her mother had said during one of her quick phone calls.

What Mary Jo didn't tell her mother was that she'd spent a lot of her monthly allowance on clothes. She never mentioned she was popular, a date Friday through Sunday every weekend. When she had a boyfriend, the weekend was invariably taken up with plays, games, and parties with their Stanford friends, but when she had broken up with one and then another and another, she'd had a constant stream of suitors and a need for new dresses.

This dress was a slim sheath that fell past her knees. The cinched waistline showed off her flat stomach, and the wide neckline emphasized her long neck. With all her running around, her weight had dropped.

The second her mother stepped off the plane and into the terminal, she'd taken one look at Mary Jo and smiled. "You're so slim!"

Her looks and size were better than her A's in English and Chem 1. She was such a good student that the mayor's son had borrowed her notes, returning them smudged but giving her his great broad smile. Sometimes she ate lunch with a known Communist, a visiting lecturer from Moscow, who asked her about "American values" over melted cheese sandwiches. Once she had even dated a murderer, though he wasn't a murderer when he took her out for dinner. That came later.

On her way across the country, Mary Jo had made herself a promise. Things were going to be different at college. She was not going to sleep with any men. Not one. She was not going there to get her MRS degree, as Diane had insisted.

"You'll get engaged and drop out," she'd told Mary Jo. "But at least you'll be in California."

That wasn't the plan, at least as far as Mary Jo was concerned. She was going to get her real degree and never get trapped, not by a man. Not in a room. Not in a closet.

"Did I tell you how we got this reservation?" her mother said after ordering and handing back the menu.

"Ginny," her father said.

Her mother looked up over her cocktail glass.

"How?" Mary Jo had been surprised. Once a Danish student, Jesper, had taken her to dinner here, but he'd planned it for months. Mary Jo and her dormmates at Branner Hall had agonized over her outfit. What to wear? What glove length? Opera or above the elbow? They settled on below the elbow. But black, very fancy, perfect with her emerald-colored dress.

When she and Jesper arrived, they were shown to a tiny table at the back next to the kitchen door that whapped every single time someone went in or out of the kitchen. *Whap,* during the appetizer and salad. *Whap, whap* during the entrée.

That had been their last date, Jesper sure, somehow, that Ernie's would do the trick. Not only would Mary Jo accept his proposal, she would sleep with him. Hadn't he arranged for his roommate's cousin's apartment to be empty and available? Hadn't he timed it all perfectly? The early reservation, the quick drive home. And then?

But Mary Jo had kept her promise to herself, the one she made when she left for California. And she'd kept it, playing the courtship game up to a point and then ending it when the man wanted more. A bad reservation at Ernie's wasn't enough to change her mind.

When her parents informed her they had a prime-time reservation at a good table, Mary Jo was impressed. Her father had always been able to do anything, even Ernie's.

"We lucked out is how," her father said. "Made a call at the right time."

Her mother shot her father a glance.

"But here's to you, Mary Jo." Her father raised his glass. "One year left of college. May it be a good one."

"This year you'll meet your husband-to-be." Her mother took another big swig and then turned to look back at the waiter, holding her glass high. "We can come back for a graduation and a wedding. We can bring the entire family with us."

"We won't be able to leave the state otherwise. Tommy almost packed himself in our suitcase," her father said. "He wanted to come in the worst way. 'Next time,' I promised him."

"When we meet your fiancé." Her mother watched carefully as the waiter took away her cocktail glass, her gaze sharp. Maybe she should follow behind the guy, Mary Jo thought. Bring the bottles back herself.

Mary Jo turned to her father, wanting to ask, "Is she like this at home?"

But she didn't. Her father was close behind, matching her mother drink for drink. Mary Jo would have to take them by cab to their hotel before heading back to Palo Alto.

"How is Tommy?" Mary Jo asked after the waiters brought not only her mother's drink but three romaine salads that were delivered as if choreographed by the San Francisco Ballet company.

"Heavens!" her mother said. "What a presentation."

"Did he have a good summer?"

Her father was already into his salad, but her mother sat back and picked up her drink. "He went to Camp Widiwagon for five weeks. Then to Scout camp. He's with your grandmother 'til school starts next week and we get home."

Mary Jo put down her fork. "He was barely home."

Her father kept at his salad, undone by the long romaine leaves. He picked up his knife, and Mary Jo was glad they weren't in France. Her friends at the dorm had told her, "Fold, don't cut your lettuce leaves."

"He's happier when he has an adventure. Such an active boy."

Mary Jo thought she might be choking on her salad, but it was emotion in her throat. She hadn't come home once during the summer, finding internships and jobs with local businesses. For two summers, she housesat for professors and could ride a bike to work. This summer she lived with one of her dormmates in a sublet, walking the five blocks to an office where she answered phones and filed invoices.

But her Saint Helen summers. The heat, her friends, the games. The water arcs in the back yard. Fourth of July. Her cherry tree and all the books she'd read, Jupey waiting for her at the trunk. Jupey had been gone for two years now, so Tommy didn't have her to rely on either.

Of course, it was the summer that ruined her life, but before that, she'd been happy. Hadn't she been? Summers were the best parts of her childhood, and Tommy wasn't getting that. Hadn't her mother promised to be a mother, Tommy's mother? Back then, in Mary Jo's bedroom, she's promised she would.

"He's a boy," her mother went on. "All he wants to do is dress up like an Indian or an astronaut or some such and yell and run around. If you thought Bobby was noisy, well, you don't know anything. Tommy is a one-boy band. He's—"

"Ginny," her father said. Her mother's name was almost all her father had said the entire night. Ginny. Ginny. As if she were lost.

Mary Jo looked down at her plate. The salad was sodden with olive oil, flecked with black pepper that looked like ants or dirt. Her stomach churned.

Her mother talked on about camps and school and new dungarees. They chatted about Bobby, who was at the University of Pennsylvania studying biology. He wanted to be a doctor, like Larry, but better, bigger. A surgeon. A brain surgeon. Unfortunately, he was still playing the trombone.

The salad plates were whisked away, and the entrées arrived, Mary Jo's mother astounded by the taste of the fettuccine dish, which to Mary Jo looked like a lump of stodgy whiteness. As she ate her filet mignon, she nodded when appropriate and chatted when necessary, but she was planning. She could see what would have to happen. She would graduate in the spring and find a job in the city. Then she would meet a man who would marry her after she told him about Roger Bradfield and Tommy. This would be the test. This would be what he would have to accept. Because after that, they would get married at the justice of the peace and bring Tommy to California. There would be no big wedding or party or family celebration. This man and she would find a place to live and start off their lives with Tommy. She would be able to unabandon him. She would save him from her mother.

"Some wine, dear?" her mother asked.

"No, thanks," Mary Jo said, wishing this meal were over.

"Another, please," her mother said, raising her glass high once again.

Mary Jo watched the waiters clear the table, sweeping crumbs off the white tablecloth. It would be a long year. But she had learned how to make plans and stick to them. She could wait it out.

After an excruciating dessert and coffee, Mary Jo stood on the sidewalk as her father maneuvered her mother into the back seat of a yellow cab. Her mother waggled her fingers in goodbye and then slumped against the seat. Her father closed the door and turned to Mary Jo.

He pressed a wad of folded bills into her palm, which Mary Jo slipped into her handbag.

"Thanks, Dad," she said.

"It was mighty good to see you. Christmas this year?" He held up a hand. "Don't answer yet. Let's talk next month before your birthday."

He gave her a tight, quick hug and then pulled back, squinting under the bright lights above them. His thick brown hair was thinning, enough that she could see his tanned scalp under his careful combing. He seemed smaller than ever.

"Dad," Mary Jo began without wanting to. But she couldn't stop from asking. "Did Roger Bradfield get the dinner reservation for you?"

Her father looked down, nodding. "Your mother mentioned our trip to Betty."

Mary Jo kept her face still, her eyes on his, not letting him see the roil inside her. "Okay," she said. "It was nice. Thank you."

He squeezed her shoulder, his hand warm. Even after all these years, she softened at her father's touch, believing in him, no matter what. Just as she had that long ago night when he delivered Tommy. "Hold on, MJ," he'd said. "Just a few more pushes."

She'd pushed, and Tommy had been born. Her father had been right.

Giving her a quick kiss on the cheek, her father walked around the cab, the door closing behind him. The car pushed into traffic and then headed up to the Fairmount Hotel.

For a moment, Mary Jo was weightless, invisible, ready to blow away over the waters of the bay. Everything that had created her was invisible, so much so that the man who raped her when she was twelve made sure she and her parents had a good table at a famous restaurant.

Mary Jo breathed in the smells of the city sidewalk and ocean breeze. Lights pulsed and glowed. Traffic lights shone red, green, yellow. In the distance she could hear the clank and rattle of a cable car.

All around her the hustle of living. People skirting past her, jostling her. And yet somehow, no matter where she went or how old she got, she was always still in the living room of her parents' home, both of them continually telling her that it wasn't his fault. That it was something that happened, like things do. A burned cake, a broken glass, a melted candle on the dining room table hardwood. An accident. A misstep. A freak occurrence.

They had promised they would take care of everything, easy as pie.

But they never had.

Mary Jo Johnson
Fall 1959

INSTEAD OF GETTING married after graduating from Stanford with a BS in chemistry, Mary Jo took a job with UCSF in the department of pharmaceutical chemistry, which broke her mother's heart and caused a month-long hiatus of phone calls and letters. Mary Jo ignored the silence and made plans. She was hired as a bench chemist, the second of only two women to work in the lab. She was given a more clerical role, tallying experiment results and getting coffee for the men—the chemists, as they liked to be called (sometimes the scientists), so special in their ties and lab coats. So important with their clipboards and data.

Half of her day, she performed chemical analyses of raw materials she assumed were being used in drugs. But she didn't inquire, doing only what was asked. She spent the afternoons getting the men coffee and filing paper.

Mary Jo was given a white lab coat with her name on the front, a salary, vacation days, and benefits. She made enough to rent a room at a boarding house in the Sunset district and go out with her college friends on the weekends. She made noodles and sauce on the hot plate during the week and watched television on the set she'd bought with some of her graduation money.

She wrote letters home to Tommy, sending him baseball cards she'd bought at Seals Stadium when she was on a date with her new steady, Ray, a Giants fan. Mary Jo had purchased three packs and allotted Tommy one a week. She hoped he was happy to open her letters, but she didn't dare think about that.

Instead she got dressed each morning, put on lipstick, a neat dress, and sensible but attractive black patent shoes.

"Great to have a gal in the office," Terry, one of the lead chemists, said her second day on the job. They were alone in the elevator, headed up to the sixth floor, which offered a view over the South Bay. He moved close enough that she could smell the coffee and cigarettes on his breath. He reached out, touched her arm. "A good-looking gal."

The elevator climbed slowly, one, two, three. Mary Jo began to sweat, a cold slick pooling at her waist, under her arms. Terry moved even closer, enough that she felt his heat from under his suit jacket. She shivered, turned her head, and stared at the metal wall and rows of buttons. Why were elevators always Otis elevators? Was there another company? Once her father had tried to explain the difference between hydraulic and traction elevators when the whole family was stuffed into a cramped, slow one in a Chicago department store, the box inching upward slower than Mary Jo could have walked up the stairs.

What had he said? She needed to remember.

"You're awfully sweet," Terry said. His teeth were yellowish, rabid, rabbitish. For a second, she imagined him with a carrot. But some rabbits were dangerous. Those back legs.

"Thank you," Mary Jo said, moving away a little, and then a little more as Terry kept reaching. His fingers were short, stubby, strong.

Finally the bell dinged, and the doors opened, pulling in laboratory air. Mary Jo scuttled out, wishing she weren't walking away from Terry, knowing his eyes were on her rear end. From now on, she decided, she'd leave the boarding house five minutes earlier so she could avoid Terry. If only I had a man, she thought, remembering Jimmy and how he'd always been there. Until he wasn't. And Dave, until he was fooled by Roger Bradfield.

But still. What she wouldn't do to put another man between herself and all the Terrys in the world. Terry would shut up if a tall, broad man stepped in beside her and stared at him. What kind of "gal" would she be then? Mary Jo thought. Not hardly. Not a gal anymore.

***

Two weeks later Mary Jo stepped onto the second-floor landing at her boarding house and almost ran into a man. He was dressed in work clothes, a black suit, white shirt, black tie, black wing tips.

At first, before she even glanced at his face, Mary Jo thought every part of him seemed dashing and shiny. He was the kind of man well tended to as a child, sent to the right schools, given a solid education. His mother would be like Mary Jo's own, but maybe not as big of a drinker. His father was a lawyer. Maybe a judge, given to long dinnertime lectures on justice. He had the same dark head of hair and flashing eyes.

"Whoa there," the man said, reaching out a hand. His tortoise shell glasses were literary, scholarly, and his hair was nicely trimmed, his fingernails short.

But as he steadied her, Mary Jo noted the threadbare suit, the tattered shirt cuff, the multiple polishes on shoes that could no longer be cured.

"Sorry about that," he said as they both righted themselves. "I have to head back to the office. Left a plan at home."

Mary Jo shrugged, found a smile, and then looked up at the man. He was tall, maybe six foot three. Maybe four. He was thin too, still clinging to a teenage metabolism, though from all the talk about weight at her family's table, she knew that wouldn't last.

Broad in the beam.

But his face. Handsome, deep smile lines, dark brown, almost black eyes. Nice smile, his lips full, but not like a woman's. Distinct eyebrows. So much hair, dark, curls fighting the careful combing he must have labored over in front of the mirror. She could almost imagine him taking a quick look into the small, cheap mirror the boarding house provided and doing a fast one, two with an Ace comb before rushing out the door.

He was tidy and clean, and he smelled like soap. Lifebuoy. He might have even done a quick afternoon shave, his skin fresh, without any evidence of a five o'clock shadow. He looked like he sprang from a large, rambunctious family, all boys, their mother chiding them as she served a hot meal. At the table, their father read a paper, peeking over the top to answer a question or tell the youngest to be quiet and eat his oatmeal.

The man gave her a smile, displaying a gap between his front teeth. Not bad but noticeable. Not fixed. The rest of his teeth were straight, white, and perfectly sized.

It was his nose, though, that caught her. Large, distinct, but not gross or vulgar. Nothing Jimmy Durante or Karl Malden about him. Nothing bulbous or knobby or unsightly. But profound and serious.

Mary Jo found her breath and smoothed her skirt. "Where do you work?"

"Standard Oil," he said. "On Bush Street. It's a long way back, so I better start."

"Okay," Mary Jo said. "Nice to meet you. Well, I'm Mary Jo."

"Michael," he said. "Michael Bradford."

After that meeting, Mary Jo contrived to miss Terry in the mornings and find Michael in the afternoons. If he didn't leave a plan in his room (she never saw him again during that time), he usually came home around five-thirty, which was when Mary Jo decided it was time to pick up a few supplies at the corner market. At first, she missed him, seeing him sprint up the staircase or leave the building, jumping into someone's waiting car or running down to the MUNI stop.

She would have followed him, but she didn't want to seem that desperate. But yes, she was. At the very sight of him and his barely-hanging-together shoes, her heart started beating fast, and her skin tingled.

Finally, one Saturday, she went downstairs to the mailboxes and found him standing in front of his open box, reading a letter. Mary Jo stilled, her breath caught, and watched him. The letter was pages long, the handwriting even but loose, as if the writer were happy. Maybe even carefree. Probably not Michael's mother. Virginia's handwriting was pointy and sharp, like her tongue.

When are you coming home?

You haven't been home in months!

We can't keep coming to you.

Mary Jo tucked those letters away in the box under her bed, writing back dutifully once a week to report on her work, the weather, and her college friends.

Sighing, Michael tucked the letter back into the envelope. Mary Jo headed toward him as nonchalantly as she could, forcing a "what a surprise to see you" smile on her face.

"Hey, there." She slipped the small key into the lock. There were three letters, at least one from her mother. She tucked them into her skirt pocket.

"Mary Jo, right?" he asked, and her hopes started to deflate. How could he know that she'd said his name to herself four, ten times a day: Michael Bradford, Michael Bradford, Michael Bradford.

Don't be owlie, she heard her mother say. She nodded. "Michael, right?"

Michael broke into a wide grin, his smile so big it took up his face. "At least we have good memories," he said, as if he had been berating himself on things he didn't have. Like what? Mary Jo wondered.

"True." She closed her mailbox. "Are you going out for the day?" Mary Jo looked at him, trying to keep a blush from cracking big and red on her cheeks. She smiled. "For once, it's not foggy."

Michael turned to the front window as if realizing there were an outside outside. "Holy smokes," he said. "I've been working all morning. I didn't even notice."

Something put an imaginary, forceful palm between her shoulder blades, urging words from her. "Do you want to take a walk in the park?"

Darn it! She could feel the blush creeping along her neck like a vine. She tilted her head and gave him a smile she knew from practice worked. It always had.

Michael slapped the envelope against his pant leg. He was wearing casual pants, nice and ironed, but again, worn. "Why not. We can take the bus. I better bring a jacket though. I don't trust the weather here. I can never read it. It doesn't make sense."

"Meet you back down here in fifteen?" she asked.

He flashed her another one of his high-magnitude smiles. Apparently they both had smiles that worked.

"Great. Be right back."

He loped toward the staircase and took the stairs two at a time. Mary Jo gripped her letters and headed to her room, head down, face pounding. She could do this. It didn't matter who wrote the long, detailed letter to him. Michael was the right one. No other boy or man in or since college had been. He was the one who would protect her, here and back at home. He would be better than Jimmy. Better than Dave. Michael Bradford would make everything turn out all right.

They walked in the park between the Steinhart Aquarium and the De Young Museum, circling the fountain and then sitting on a bench, watching cars slowly wend past the museum and the Japanese Tea Garden. The afternoon had turned golden, the air warm with cut grass and sea air. Both of them took off their sweaters and let the sunlight wash over them.

Michael had told her a little about his job as a civil engineer and his work on refineries in Richmond, across the bay, and in Pascagoula, Mississippi.

"That place is one hurricane away from disaster," he said, kicking at a rock. "But Standard Oil builds on. I really don't want to go back."

She gave him an encouraging look, but her body stilled. He couldn't go now. Not yet.

"How long will you be there?" The sun was hitting her face, and she knew her eyes would glow the color of honey. She blinked, keeping an interested look on her face, a half-smile of encouragement.

"Guys stay a year. Two sometimes. Then they get kicked back here, especially if they have children. It's part of the process." Michael shrugged.

Did he have a wife waiting? A fiancée? Was that who was writing him eight-page letters?

"I've never been to the South," she said. "I've heard New Orleans is something."

"They send us there too," Michael said. "Other than the weather, the hurricanes, and, well, the issues down there, apparently it's a good time."

"Don't forget the bugs. One of my dormmates at Stanford said there were cockroaches as big as dinner plates living in the trees."

Michael pushed his hair back from his face and nodded. "You are a smart one. Stanford."

She waited for him to say something about a failed MRS degree, a joke she'd heard at the office when the "scientists" thought she wasn't listening. But Mary Jo was always listening, just in case.

"I love California," she said. "We came out here during the war. I swore I would come back the moment I could. I hate the cold."

"You picked the wrong part of the state," Michael said, pointing to the sky. The fog was starting to flick in from the coast, wisping across the blue in white streamers.

"Palo Alto wasn't like this," Mary Jo admitted. "I should have gone to Pomona."

If she had, she'd be warmer. There'd be no Terry. Her parents wouldn't visit as often because there would be no jewel box city like San Francisco. Later, when she'd found the right man, Tommy would play on lawns as wide as parks, throwing balls with vast droves of neighborhood children.

But she was here. And with Michael, who could take her places.

"So you're from Colorado?" she asked. "You said University of Colorado, Boulder?"

"Born in Denver. Didn't go far."

He stood up abruptly, putting on his sweater and then holding out a hand. "Let's grab a bus and go to St. Francis Fountain. I could do with a burger and shake. Maybe two!"

He was as skinny as a bean pole. He'd never be broad in the beam. Mary Jo smiled and took his hand, the breeze catching her skirt and whisking her legs. "That's exactly what I want."

***

That became their weekly outing. Late Saturday morning, Mary Jo and Michael would meet in the boarding house lobby, sometimes wearing coats as the weather turned, and head to Golden Gate Park. They went to the aquarium, the museum, the Japanese Tea Garden, where they sat and drank green tea and looked out at the crowds walking up and over the curved drum bridge.

Later they would go back to St. Francis Fountain or head to Original Joe's for a plate of Joe's Special. Sometimes they went to Fisherman's Wharf, and early in December when crab season opened, they ate cracked crab and looked out at the bay spilling into the Pacific Ocean.

"You haven't told me if you're going home for the holidays," Michael said the second week of December. They were walking up Greenwich Street to Coit Tower after devouring a huge bowl of cioppino at a little dive on Pier 23. It had been the best bowl of soup Mary Jo had ever had in her life. She wasn't exactly sure what had been in it—something with tentacles maybe?—but the broth was tomato-y and rich and delicious, especially when she mopped up the remnants with a piece of fresh sourdough bread.

At one point, lungs heaving, she stopped, turned to look at the bay, sunlight glinting on the strangely still waters. Gulls called, spinning white over the waterfront. For a moment, Mary Jo pretended to not be catching her breath, the climb steep and not even half over. "Not this year," she said, pushing back the memory of Tommy's voice on the phone.

"Why?" Tommy had whined, tears behind his words. "I haven't seen you in a long time."

"Are you going home?" she asked. A couple of weeks ago he had talked about growing up in Denver. She had gotten the distinct impression he wasn't keen on visiting his mother, who lived in what might be government housing.

Michael nodded and gave a quick shrug. "Got to go," he said. "It's been a while."

I haven't seen you in a long time! Tommy howled in her mind.

They kept walking. "Will you be able to see some friends?" she asked.

"Hopefully. If the weather permits, I might make it to Boulder."

Swallows swooped overhead, but Mary Jo kept her eyes on her footsteps, knowing that each one meant she was that much closer to Coit Tower. She wondered how it was possible Iowa was so flat. Northern California seemed constructed of elevations, everything a triangle. Maybe she should walk more on her own, up and down the avenues or out by the Panhandle where things were flat or vertical.

"Sounds like fun." She forced her voice steady.

"Maybe." He didn't seem very happy about the trip. What was wrong with his mother? Or was it the person who wrote the long letter, the one she'd seen him reading that day by the mailboxes.

"My parents don't understand why I don't want to go home," Mary Jo said, relieved that things had suddenly flattened out. She stood still, letting the breeze twirl around her face. If she weren't so sweaty, she would be frozen by now. Exhausted and frozen. "They think all I want is to come home to where things are better. And, well, it's not better back there."

Michael nodded. "We all leave there to come here," he said. "The edge of the world. We could jump in a boat and paddle off."

Mary Jo turned to him and smiled. He was scrubbed awake by wind, his face pale, eyes dark. What was his secret? Was it anything like hers?

"Let's finish mountain climbing today," Mary Jo said. "Boats can be another weekend. Maybe we can start with a canoe. That I can do."

"You can?"

"And shoot a rifle. Better watch out."

Michael reached out and took her hand. He had big hands with strong, thin fingers. She'd looked at them when they were holding menus. His nails were clean, clipped close, his skin smooth and smelled of bayberry. So his sleeves were tattered. His person was in perfect shape.

"Come on," he said. "I can't wait to show you the view."

Tommy Johnson
Christmas 1959

UP IN HIS room, hiding from his mother's relentless holiday chore list, Tommy flipped through a stack of photos his parents had taken during his birthday party last summer. All of the boys sat around the dining room table as his mother carried in the big chocolate birthday cake with ten lit candles—nine for each year and one to grow on.

In the photo, his school and Scout friends sat at the table blowing into party horns, wearing pointed party hats, and cheering for the three-tier chocolate cake as it arrived at the table. On the dining room wall was the huge pin-the-tail-on-the-donkey game they'd played earlier, Harry winning of course.

"Horse's ass," Marvin Waddell had said, and not under his breath. No wonder no one picked him for kickball games at school. Tommy's mom had forced him to invite Marvin because he lived two doors down. Harry didn't hear Marvin but took his prize—a whole huge Hershey's chocolate bar—and waved it in Marvin's face.

In the photo, the table was mounded with presents, ribbons curled and shiny in the black-and-white shot. Before the cake and the frilled hot dogs and burgers and indoor games, they had all shot bows and arrows in the back yard, his parents having set up three targets and a gallon of fresh lemonade. After the party was over, his father took him and Harry on a canoe ride on the creek, the three of them carrying the canoe across the street and into the park.

It had been one of the best days of Tommy's life. Almost perfect.

Tommy held up the photo and blinked. For a second, he thought, why is Harry waiting for my cake?

But that wasn't Harry at the head of the table, wearing Tommy's brand-new horn-rimmed glasses and grinning like an idiot. Tommy was at the head of the table, and Harry was sitting next to Marvin, probably kicking him under the table

Tommy shrugged and laid the photo down on the pile, but then picked it up again. They looked so much alike. He'd never noticed it before, but they had the same eye color—though in black-and-white photos, everyone seemed to. They were about the same height, and both needed glasses, Harry's shiny and black. They even had the same strange habit of bending their elbows and holding them out like chicken wings as they ran.

"What's wrong with you two?" Mr. Kettwig hollered. "Run like boys, not birds."

At night sometimes, when Tommy couldn't sleep and didn't want to think about Mary Jo so far away, he pretended that Harry was his real brother, a swap for Bobby, who had left home for college and taken his horrible trombone with him, thank goodness. Harry was the brother he really wanted. In fact, Tommy could have swapped his parents for the Bradfields. Things were so much happier over there, all the kids running around, Mrs. Bradfield so pretty and nice, asking Tommy about his teacher and hobbies and plans. Mr. Bradfield came home with treats from the store, and on the weekends, he grabbed whatever kids he could, and they drove in the country or to Des Moines to see a film at the huge theater there. At the Bradfields' house, life was fun.

Tommy flipped through more photos. Presents, smiles, Tommy holding up the Stanford sweatshirt Mary Jo had sent him. There he and Harry were, pulling arrows out of the targets, both of them wearing the Indian headdresses they'd made at summer camp. Their hairlines were exact, their eyebrows two even and similar lines over their eyes. Look at their ears! No one in Tommy's family had lobes like that, dangling like flaps. But Harry did.

Without warning, tears pricked his eyes, and he wiped them away with the back of his hand. He shoved the photos back into their envelope. He didn't want to see any more. He knew what he would find. Something wrong had happened. He'd been left by everyone, even his parents who were still at home. But they weren't. They barely had time for him. They sent him away at every holiday and break. Camp, relatives, especially Grandma Gert's house. They seemed overjoyed when any invitation came in, not even listening when Tommy said he didn't want to go skating or to a park. He wanted to stay home and eat popcorn and watch *Lassie* and *Dennis the Menace* and maybe once, please once, *Alfred Hitchcock Presents*.

But his parents never let him stay up late.

From underneath his bed, he pulled out a shoebox, one he'd saved from his brand-new school shoes. Carefully he took off the lid, not letting the cardboard top rub the thin sides. Inside he'd placed every letter Mary Jo had written to him since she left for college. One a week, through summers and now her graduation. The last few months she'd been sending him baseball cards with players he didn't know when he got them but did now. Well, everyone knew Willie Mays. But now he studied the stats, memorized the rosters. Opening Day? Johnny Antonelli, Jackie Brandt, Orlando Cepeda, Willie Mays himself.

He picked up the stack of cards and flipped through them, imagining the men out on the field, the baseballs winging by like rockets. *Whack!* Caught in their leather gloves. He could almost smell the roasted peanuts.

After reading each of her letters, Tommy wrote back to Mary Jo, begging her to let him visit. He wouldn't be any trouble! He could sleep on the floor. He'd be as quiet as a mouse, even quieter. *Please, please, please, please!*

He wanted to go to a Giants game and walk across the Golden Gate Bridge. He wanted to cling on a cable car railing and lug up San Francisco hills. He wanted to sit at the front of a ferry boat and cross the bay.

But she never agreed. She wrote the word *later* about twenty times in her letters. Later. Now never seemed to come.

"Tommy!" his mother called up. "Dinnertime!"

A huge sigh filled his lungs. He exhaled. No one would hear him up here on the second floor by himself. As he put away the baseball cards, he picked up the envelope of photos again, the one that contained the shot with Harry and him at the table, both looking so happy. Both looking so much alike, as if they were more than best friends. As if they were brothers.

Michael Bradford
December 1959

"WHAT DO YOU mean?" Sylvia asked, staring at him in the living room of her parents' Denver home. The Christmas tree blinked on and off, red and green lights reflecting off the presents underneath. On the hi-fi, Bing Crosby's *Merry Christmas* songs bubbled out, annoying Michael so much he almost stood up to pick up the needle.

He resisted, staring instead at Sylvia's left ring finger. Against all his recent hopes, there it still was, on her finger, the ring he'd saved for and given her last summer before he headed out for California. She was going to finish her secretarial program and meet him…today, just before Christmas, her diploma packed away along with everything else she was going to bring to California. They were going to be married at Denver City Hall and then travel back to San Francisco and move into the apartment he was supposed to have rented but had not. All fall Sylvia had been writing to him about what they would need in the kitchen. She'd sent packages of linens and towels. She told him to buy a coffee percolator and a toaster.

All those Saturdays he was supposed to be apartment hunting and appliance buying, Michael spent with Mary Jo, exploring the city and eating out and going to movies. Saturdays turned into Sundays too, both of them reading the paper as they sat at the counter at Mel's. Then a drive to Marin over the Golden Gate. Or a ferry ride to Jack London Square in Oakland. They had played bridge with friends, Michael meeting her Stanford girlfriends and liking them.

For months Michael had ignored Sylvia's requests, her demands, and lived his life without anyone forcing him to do one damn thing.

Michael hadn't told Mary Jo about Sylvia. Not a word, yet she seemed to be sitting there between them, his secret human sized and waiting.

With a slightly shaking hand, Sylvia handed him a cup of eggnog.

"Thank you," he mumbled, noting Sylvia's mother's head bobbing at the doorway and then disappearing. Noises flared in the kitchen and then were silenced. First one door and then another closed.

Sylvia gripped her hands together, composed despite the tension, sitting like the actress she used to be in high school. Back straight, eyes on him.

Michael sipped, glad to have something to do other than sit in the awkward silence. He breathed in the brandy, but was unable to taste it, his mouth dry and empty. The liquid stuck in his throat, and he put down the cup, stomach burning.

He was going to have to start talking soon, ripping down the future bit by bit. Their plan was solid, iron clad. He could make a life with Sylvia, smart and fierce and full of energy. But then came Mary Jo, slow and languid, her smile taking an eternity to spread across her face. And when it did? Oh. And when she pulled away from his kisses and murmured, "You're my favorite," it was all Michael could do to not grab her and rush her upstairs, away from the porch of their boarding house. But he'd never been invited up to her room or her bed, though from the way she moved during their kisses, she seemed to know her way around a kiss. Maybe more.

"Not yet," Mary Jo had said.

"When?" Michael asked.

She'd given him a look, one that could have burned through water. "I've made a pledge to myself," she said. "Not until I'm married."

He'd felt his eyes go wide as he held the darkness of his engagement to Sylvia in his heart.

"But we can do this as much as you like," she said, kissing him again.

Michael wanted as much as he could get.

Now Michael took another sip of the terrible eggnog, his head beating from the alcohol he rarely drank. Marriage. Who was Mary Jo Johnson? She was from Iowa, of course, a place of cows and pigs and corn. She had two younger brothers, and her mother was a housewife. Her father was a doctor though, so he'd expected…what? She'd be a socialite with a diaphragm and a sex drive for days? She'd come up to his room like Grace Kelly did in *Rear Window*? A tiny but perfectly packed handbag-suitcase filled with a peignoir and slippers? Oh, and birth control.

"Sylvia," he began.

She looked down, right-hand fingertips on her left-hand ring. He'd had to save forever to buy the diamond, putting down twenty-dollar installment payments for almost two years. A slim, 18-carat white gold band with an emerald-cut diamond, a smidge under a carat.

She kept her eyes on her ring but said, "What happened?"

Michael leaned forward, wanting to reach out. They had slept together, often, and he knew the feel of her skin, the warmth of her body. There was no reason for him to wreck everything for someone he didn't know at all.

He was doing it anyway. Even from this sad Denver couch, his body was being yanked back to San Francisco by an invisible grip. Mary Jo's eyes. Her slow smile. Mary Jo laughing, the Golden Gate Bridge in the background. But who cared about that when she was in the frame.

Michael tried to swallow, froth trapped in his throat. It would be easier to die here on the floor, really, than keep going forward with this breakup. Behind him, he heard someone in another room trying to be silent.

"We've drifted apart," he began.

Sylvia shook her head. "You drifted away. To California. You left me here."

"We decided—"

"You decided. You found a job far away and decided to take it. You came up with our plan, and I've lived up to my side of it. I've finished my course. I haven't looked for a job because I was going to be married and relocating. I've told all my friends. We have wedding presents in the spare bedroom. I'm packed, Michael." Then she looked up at him, her dark eyes wide and full of tears. But she wasn't crying. "I'm sitting here waiting for my life to begin."

"I had to leave here," he said.

"You had to leave me."

No, he thought. Not you. He had never wanted to leave Sylvia. He forced himself to look right at Sylvia, unblinking.

She lifted her hands and then dropped them back into her lap. Two months ago he would have rushed to her side and picked up her hands, holding them tight. But that wasn't in him anymore.

"What am I supposed to tell everyone?" Sylvia asked finally.

Michael shook his head and put down his cup. Before he'd come to Sylvia's house, he'd told his mother about their breakup as if it had already happened.

"No surprise there," his mother had said, looking up over her crochet project, an afghan, one of dozens in the small, boxy apartment. "You don't seem to hold onto anything good."

Here it comes, Michael thought. The litany of how he'd failed during high school, ending up at a second-tier art school he'd left after his first year to start his engineering degree, something he thought his mother would appreciate. Maybe she had, but when he got his job with Standard Oil, she was back on the complaint bandwagon: *You're so far away, you never come home, you are ungrateful, worthless, barely a son at all.*

Maybe his mother had a point. Look at what he was doing now.

"Tell them it was my fault," Michael said. It was, of course. "You didn't do anything wrong."

Sylvia started to cry, tears falling on her hands. "Did you ever love me?"

"Of course," Michael blurted. "You know I did."

"But when did you stop?"

Had he? Didn't he feel the same way he always had about her? But if he'd loved her, how had there been room for Mary Jo to slip in? Love seemed so rigid, like something to dismantle in sections and put back together with no cracks or seams. Wasn't it more like sand, spilling everywhere? Getting loose and going where it shouldn't?

He couldn't tell Sylvia or anyone this.

Michael moved over to sit by her on the couch. He picked up her wet hands and looked her in the eyes, maybe the hardest thing he'd done. Seeing her upset made him want to run out of the house as if his hair were on fire, but he stayed. He sat. He waited.

"I'm sorry," he said. "I really am. But better now than to live together and then realize. This way we both can have a fresh start."

Sylvia pulled her hands away from his and took off the engagement ring. She looked at it for a second and then handed it to him, placing it in his suddenly upturned palm.

She shook her head. "I never really liked it," she said.

A rage skittered under his skin, enough that he had to breathe hard, once, sharp and deep. Swallowing, he stood and slipped the ring into his pants pocket, now ready to run. "Thank you," he said. "Say…" He looked into the dining room and kitchen, knowing that somewhere her parents waited. "I'm sorry."

Sylvia stood. With an awkward lunge, he hugged her quickly and then turned, finding the doorknob, pulling the door, and grabbing his coat from the coat rack. Then he was outside, the air thick with cold, but Michael Bradford was free. And he needed to call Mary Jo, fast. He needed to jump on the first available Denver/Salt Lake/Oakland train he could, even though the ride would take forever—or at least 40 hours with over thirty-three stops.

Standing on the sidewalk, he reached a hand into his right pants pocket. The ring, his broken promise; the ring, unloved. Michael turned it over with his fingers and started walking toward the bus station, where he would find a phone.

He was a terrible person. But a very lucky one. So lucky.

Mary Jo Johnson
Winter 1959–Spring 1960

THE MORNING OF his departure for Denver, Michael left so early to catch the train that he hadn't said goodbye. Mary Jo slept in, and it wasn't until midmorning that she found the letter. He must have slid it under her door on his way out.

On the front of the envelope, he'd written in his engineering school print: *Maryjo*, combining it into one name, the way he had from the start. With him, she'd become a new thing. One thing. Whole.

She picked up the letter and looked at it, tapping one edge in her palm. The paper *tick ticked* in the silence of her small gray apartment. There was likely nothing good in it. Michael hadn't rushed home to celebrate with his mother or visit with high school friends. Someone was writing to him with increasing urgency, the letters coming every other day, thick and dense with script. In fact, in recent weeks the envelopes were so stuffed with pages, Michael could barely tuck them in his back pocket.

She leaned his letter against a glass vase on the table and stared at it. She didn't have to open it. Why should she? Things were fine right now. Michael's mysteries and secrets could remain hidden.

Mary Jo turned from the table and went to the counter to make some coffee. She was about to sit down at her tiny kitchen table with coffee and toast when the phone rang.

"Don't open it," he said, breathless. "Promise!"

"Where are you?" Mary Jo leaned back, eyeing the envelope.

"Emeryville," he said. "Please, don't open it. I'll take care of it, I promise."

"Is it something bad?" Mary Jo sipped her coffee. "Should I know?"

"Listen, I've got to get back on the train. I'll call when I get to Denver. But promise me, okay?"

"I promise," Mary Jo said, and then Michael hung up.

She sat still for a moment, staring at the envelope, her eyes taking in every line of Michael's script. She'd just promised not to read what was inside, but how would that make things better? Shouldn't she know what she was up against?

Her kitchen flared with a brief, shallow stream of sun, then the room closed down as fog held the sky again. Mary Jo tapped her foot and then put down her coffee cup and picked up the envelope. Michael had made sure it was sealed, no easy place for a fingernail, letter opener, or knife to wiggle in. She'd have to try the tea kettle. Finally, Bobby's love of detective TV shows was paying off. If there was one thing she knew how to do, it was steam open an envelope.

Carefully she held the back of the envelope over the steam and moved it back and forth until, just like that, the flap peeled away a bit. Her cheeks flushed from the heat, her fingertips tingled.

Taking the envelope away from the steam, she placed it on the counter and carefully used one fingernail to open it, whole and intact. She turned off the kettle and thought of his words: *Don't open it! Promise!*

Opened. No promise made. She sat back down, unfolded the letter, and read.

Dear Maryjo—

I have had such a wonderful time with you these past months. Exploring San Francisco with you showed me everything. I would be the luckiest guy in the world if I could spend every day, every year with you.

But I never told you that before I left for San Francisco, I got engaged to my high school girlfriend. We've been together for years, and it seemed like the thing I was supposed to do. It was what was expected of me. It's what my mother wanted. What she wanted. What everyone wanted, so I did it, and then I came to SF and met you.

I'm sorry I didn't tell you. And I'm sorry that I'm never going to be able to tell you this in person. When I get back, I'm going to be married. Sylvia and

I are going to stay in a hotel until I can find us a place because I can't see you again, something I can't believe. I'm making the biggest mistake of my life. But it's too late.

I hope that you will find someone who deserves you because I don't. But I've made a commitment. I have to do this. I'm so sorry.

Love always, Michael

No wonder he didn't want her to open it.

Mary Jo read the letter through once more, memorizing the words, some sentences, not upset. She'd heard his voice on the phone. In her bones, Mary Jo understood how the story would play out. Michael would come home to *get* married.

She stood up from the table, leaving the envelope on the table, exactly where it would be when Michael returned, seemingly uno-pened, she none the wiser. Michael would walk in, tall and dark and handsome, his gleaming black hair swept off his forehead. His almost-black eyes would hold her, taking in every single part of her. She would breathe in his man smells of drafting pencils, velum paper, and shaving lotion. Mary Jo would float in his gaze and listen to his story, open-eyed. Michael would hold her hand, and he would watch her.

Sylvia Smith
December 1959

AFTER MICHAEL LEFT her, taking the engagement ring, and after her parents and younger sister, Marian, sat with her and held her hand, Sylvia went upstairs to the bedroom she had been sleeping in for twenty-five years, one she would be sleeping in for a bit longer.

In the corner by the window that looked out over the street were her packed suitcases, three of them, one for clothing and the other two for the wedding presents her parents, family, and friends had sent. After the planned wedding on New Year's Day—that appointment needed to be cancelled—she and Michael were going to head to the edge of the continent to start their life together, the one they had been planning since high school. They had their degrees and certificates. They were ready to start their lives.

The good news was, Sylvia didn't have to start anything.

She'd almost burst out crying when Michael had called it off, not from upset but relief. My god, she wouldn't have to go through with it. She wouldn't have to leave her family, her hometown, or her friends. With him.

Sinking onto her bed, not bothering to turn on the bedside light, she stared into the dusky gloom. But it wasn't only that. Last summer when he'd come home for a two-week visit, staying with his mother and coming over every day for dinner or for an outing on the weekends, she'd seen a change, something in his eyes, his mouth. A hardness, an angry word tucked away unuttered but still there. When Marian chattered on at the table, Sylvia saw how he gripped his napkin, his fork, how he'd stood up abruptly to excuse himself to go to the bathroom.

When they were on a walk in the neighborhood one night after dinner, they'd stepped into the street and a car hadn't seen them, brakes squealing to a jolting stop inches in front of them.

Michael gripped her hand and then flung it loose, running to the car's driver's side window and banging on the glass.

"Michael!" she called out, too shocked to do more.

"You imbecile!" Michael yelled at the driver, a woman with a small child in the back seat who began to cry. "You could have killed us!"

His face was red, a sudden sweat on his brow. His mouth was pulled back in a scary, hollow grimace, his eyes dark slits of anger.

"Michael!" Sylvia called again, but then he turned that same face on her, angry, unrecognizable.

"Get back on the curb!"

Stunned, Sylvia stepped back and waited as Michael berated the woman, who drove off weeping.

"Idiot women drivers," Michael said, taking her hand, though she could barely feel his touch, her body tingling, heart pounding so hard she heard each booming beat in her ears. "She has no business being behind the wheel of a car!"

After that, Sylvia couldn't help but notice his constant state of irritation at people: pedestrians, shoppers, movie-goers. Women drivers, colored bellman, Chinese grocers, Mexican gardeners. Her parents and sister. Even she drew giant sighs and eye rolls. He hated them all, everyone, at least when he was around Sylvia.

Downstairs, Sylvia heard her family's murmurs, a rumble of concern and speculation. The phone rang but was answered quickly. Soon the whole family would know, the neighborhood, their church. Sylvia imagined the gossip lines on fire, hot.

She imagined Michael's mother, that horrible, hulking woman. She was probably rubbing her hands in glee. Now she could have Michael for herself. Mrs. Bradford could clap her hands and berate him, as she would, even if she approved.

No wonder he was the way he was, irate, spiky, and full of hate. The good news was she wouldn't have to worry what would set this new Michael off, this Michael who had grown out of the quiet, shy boy she'd met in school at a play, the man who became some-one who made a big promise and then broke it. This man who had rage burning in him like a candle, a fire, a bomb. She wouldn't have to be there when it went off.

It would be embarrassing and awkward for a couple of weeks, and she would have to endure people's pity and shoulder pats and maybe even casseroles delivered to the front door, as if somebody had died. Fine. She'd do it. And then she'd go out and get a job. She'd find a roommate and move into an apartment downtown. Someday she'd find another boyfriend, and she'd have the marriage she'd wanted with a man she loved, but not with Michael, whom she no longer cared for.

Sylvia smoothed her hair and turned on the bedside light.

Mary Jo Johnson
March 1960

WEARING A HAND-ME-DOWN engagement ring and a cheap silver-plated wedding band, Mary Jo walked into the laboratory meet-and-greet cocktail party on the arm of her new husband. Michael had bought a new suit for their wedding mid-January, and he wore it now, the black material matching his hair, his eyes, the black pants making his legs look impossibly long and lean.

Introducing Michael to her colleagues—the men who asked her to get coffee—she walked the room until she found who she was looking for: Terry with his elevator hands.

Mary Jo tapped him on the shoulder and put on her best smile.

"Why if it isn't—" he began and then looked up at Michael, who was smiling, unconcerned and—Mary Jo could see—uninterested by the small man in front of him.

"Terry," she said, "I want you to meet my husband, Michael."

Michael reached out his hand, large, fingers long. Maybe, Mary Jo thought, he could wrap one around Terry's neck.

She smiled, as if this were a lovely, much anticipated greeting. "Terry and I tend to get to work at the same time, don't we? We have had some nice chats on the ride up to our floor on the elevator. I hate that elevator, don't you? Some days I wish they'd put in a new one, though I would surely miss our talks."

Terry was wide-eyed, not noticing that a woman had joined him. "Hello," Mary Jo said, talking fast. "Are you Terry's wife? I was telling my husband how Terry and I often ride together—"

"This is Darlene," Terry blurted. "Good to meet you, Michael. We—I told Bruce I'd make sure to introduce him to Darlene first thing. Talk later, okay?"

Terry almost ran off, Darlene giving Mary Jo a half-wave as she followed behind her husband.

"What's his story?" Michael asked.

"Not one idea," Mary Jo said. "Let's get some crab dip, shall we?"

Turned out, Mary Jo was able to quit her job in April, leaving Terry and her coffee services behind. By May she and Michael were making plans to move to New Orleans for Michael's new position. Standard Oil was paying for their moving expenses as well as their furnished apartment, so in the weeks leading up to their move, Mary Jo and Michael rode San Francisco like a horse. Dinners, movies, walks at Fisherman's Wharf and in Golden Gate Park.

In the evenings they met up with Mary Jo's friends and Michael's from work. They had dinners and played bridge and sat and talked around tables and smoked and drank martinis. Mary Jo wore the pearls her parents sent her for her wedding, which they'd had no time or opportunity to attend.

"When will you come home?" her mother asked. "We want to meet Michael. We barely know anything about him."

"Soon," Mary Jo said, thinking about the way Terry had scurried away from her, his wife in tow. But Terry was no Roger Bradfield. Roger would never run away like some mouse. He'd stand his terrible ground.

"We can come and visit you in New Orleans," her mother said. "That would be a nice visit."

"I promise I'll call when we are all settled," Mary Jo said. "We can make our plans."

But after that, she'd not communicated with her family. She was too busy. During the day Mary Jo packed up the few things they weren't going to sell, and at night they were eating fried shrimp at the Cliff House or drinking small dark cups of espresso at Café Trieste. Her hand in his, Mary Jo could almost believe in everything. Anything. She'd run all the way to the edge of the world and found exactly what she wanted. Why ruin it with a trip or a visit?

One afternoon, after packing up a box of letters, Mary Jo sat down and read the last one from Tommy.

Dear Mary Jo—

Hope you are doing very well. Say hello to your husband, Michael. I wish I could have come to your wedding. I could have seen the Golden Gate Bridge. Did you know it is barely older than you are? If it weren't there, how would people get places? By boat? I would like to go on a boat in the bay. Have you? What is it like?

Harry and I have been doing a lot of skiing, mostly in the fields between the houses, but over by the fairgrounds too. And it was so cold a month ago, the river froze solid. It was almost blue. And for days we were skating on it, though Mother had a hissy fit and made us get off the ice…

Mary Jo stopped reading and clutched at her throat, imagining the worst: Tommy standing still as ice cracked all around him. The sound of it, a freezing wrench of solids grinding against each other, and then the widening split and him falling in so deep no one could rescue him. Her mother screaming on the banks, Harry still and silent and still alive.

Standing, Mary Jo breathed back tears, an ache pounding in her face and chest and heart. She'd promised herself she'd bring Tommy to her once she had a husband. But now it was clear that wasn't enough. Not yet. How could she ask for him to live with her in New Orleans in a small two-bedroom apartment? Worse, while New Orleans had some class and style, it was the South, and such terrible things happened there. Was it a place to raise a boy? An Iowa boy, one who hunted, canoed, skied, and skated? A Boy Scout and an A student and a wiseacre. He'd be a true fish out of water.

She is always bossing me, Tommy continued. *That's why I want to come visit you. I don't care where you are. I'll be really quiet, and I won't bother you. Please let me come. Please.*

Say hello to your new husband for me and tell him what I said. I know he will understand.

Love, Tommy

Usually she wrote back the same day, but one day had turned into four. She struggled to take in a deep breath and then folded the letter and put it back in the box. She would write to him when they were unpacked. When they'd gotten settled, met some friends, started their lives in New Orleans. Maybe then he could come for a short visit. Mary Jo would test the waters and see how things went.

That night in bed, Mary Jo rested her head on Michael's chest, her arms around him, one of his around her shoulders. When she first pressed against him after their City Hall wedding and subsequent dinner out with friends, Mary Jo had held her breath, waiting for Michael to touch her body, pause, and then stop, his questions hovering under his palm.

Why are you so loose? Who have you slept with? Have you had a baby?

In her new husband's embrace, she felt as baggy as a blanket, frowzy, spread out, overused. She imagined her uterus like an old paper bag. Or a scarecrow face after a long summer, details erased, burlap ripped. Her breasts weren't pert and cute like other girls', her nipples darker, her flesh droopier.

Michael didn't seem to notice, his excitement clear, his breathing ragged, his embrace tight.

But when her husband touched her, Mary Jo felt Roger, always Roger. She heard him first too, expecting his words to come from Michael's lips, the way she'd expected them from Jimmy's and Dave's, yet then the men's strokes and words merged into one thing. They touched here and here. They wanted this and then that.

Her body, too, followed a pattern. Nerves. No, fear. Then excitement, a whoosh of feeling that what she was doing was wrong, forbidden. But then she liked it, wanted it, let go into it, following along with whatever the body over hers was doing.

Later came the guilt and worry. She was wrong and bad and had done a terrible thing. After their first time together, Mary Jo waited, but those feelings never came. Not with Michael. He was her husband, and even though she might not be able to ever tell him about Tommy—or bring Tommy to their home—the story on and in her body didn't need explaining.

"Everything okay?" Michael turned toward her, his eyes shiny in the darkness.

Mary Jo waited, thinking. She held her breath, imagining a scream might rip into the silence. But there was no upset. No noise. No fear. Michael was about to take her into a whole new life. He would protect her from all the Rogers in the world.

"More than fine," Mary Jo said, letting him pull her close again for another round, bringing her back to the beginning and the end, over and over again.

Tommy Johnson
October 1960

TOMMY GOT UP before his mother, slipping down the stairs and into the kitchen. The night before, he'd wrapped up two apples and a peanut butter sandwich and tucked them into the pantry in a brown grocery bag.

Now he grabbed the bag, another apple, and then drank some milk, making sure to wash the glass right away. Otherwise his mother would know something was wrong the moment she came into the room. She never left a dish undone, even on the nights she seemed really, really tired, which was almost every night these days.

Outside in the fall dawn, the sky was pushing through gray, a glimmer of orange in the east. Tommy pulled his bike out from behind the hedge by the side of the driveway, settled Bobby's old Boy Scout pack on his back, and started riding. He'd timed the journey last week. He could arrive at the bus station by 6:42 and catch the 6:50 bus to New Orleans, or, at least, in that general direction. The timing was so close, nothing could go wrong. He had food, money for a ticket and snacks if the bus ever let people out, which he hoped it would, and Mary Jo's new address. His plan was to call her from the station when he arrived. She couldn't ignore him then. Anyway, she'd be glad he was there, and her husband, Michael, would like him.

Tommy would make that happen. He would make it stick. He would stick like paste.

As he whizzed by, birds sang in the trees. Blackbirds. A late robin. Finches. The roads started to fill with cars, fathers off to work. Tommy had worried that his father would get a call to head to the hospital or the office, but the night had been silent. Tommy had slept with his alarm clock in his hand, turning it off at the first clang, his breath caught as he waited for his mother to come knocking.

No one woke up. Nothing rustled downstairs.

Now he was halfway to the bus stop and his new life. Finally he'd be with Mary Jo again. He could go to a new school and make new friends. Sure, he'd miss Harry, but Harry would visit every holiday and summer, and they could go fishing. There were tons of fish in New Orleans. Big, strange ones like marlins and barracuda. Fish with weird names like grunt and grouper. There were also hurricanes. Tommy wanted to see one of those.

Looking both ways, he carefully pedaled across Main Street and then turned left on Daniels, pumping as fast as he could. He had to make it. But as he was about to cross Franklin, he heard a slight tapping on a horn. He didn't look back, but the car came up beside him.

"Tommy," a man yelled. "What are you doing out here at this hour?"

Tommy refused to look over because he knew that voice. It was Mr. Bradfield. "Just biking," he yelled, pumping harder.

"Do your parents know you're here?"

Did his parents know anything he did? Maybe the big things like school, practices, sports, and friends. But second by second, minute by minute? They really didn't have a clue. Sometimes he wondered if he took his chemistry set to the attic and created a bomb if they'd notice if it went off.

"Tommy," Mr. Bradfield yelled, the car moving. "Stop."

Tommy didn't. He kept going, his legs exhausted. He needed to get to the station to make his bus.

"Where are you going?"

Where was he going? To Mary Jo, of course. To the one person in the whole world who really loved him. Or at least he thought she loved him, more than anything. She'd always told him that.

"I love you more than anyone in the whole world," she used to say when she tucked him in when she was visiting. When she called the house, she spoke to Tommy last, and for some reason, his parents didn't force him to hang up, never hissing, "Long distance" as they did with each other when relatives called.

"Tommy," Mr. Bradfield said. "Stop a minute."

There were no spare minutes. Tommy pedaled on.

"If you stop, I won't tell your mother. I promise you that right here," Mr. Bradfield said.

The car huffed alongside Tommy, wafts of heat and street grit hitting his face. He lightened up, coasted, and then braked, his tires gripping road and rocks as he stopped.

"I don't have much time." Tommy looked down the road, seeing all his minutes spill out like coins.

"That's where you have it wrong, son," Mr. Bradfield said. "You have all the time in the world. As I see it, you can make this particular trip any old time."

"I can't," Tommy said. This was stupid. "I need to go."

"Hold your horses, son. Let's put your bike in the car, and I'll take you wherever you're going. We can talk on the way."

Mr. Bradfield turned off his car and in seconds was loading Tommy's bike into the trunk.

"Get on in" he said.

Tommy was used to this deep voice, one from Sunday mornings at Harry's house, Mr. Bradfield urging them into the car so they'd make it to church on time. This was the voice from countless camping trips, Mr. Bradfield chopping wood and then building a fire for Tommy, Harry, and the Bradfield H's to cook over. Mr. Bradfield told the scariest stories as the fire burned to nothing and always managed to roast marshmallows perfectly, golden on the outside, melty on the inside.

Tommy could trust him to not tell. And maybe to get him to the station on time. Sliding off his Scout pack, he got into the car and closed the door. For a second, he wondered what Mr. Bradfield was doing out so early. He didn't look like Tommy's father did in the morning: wet hair slicked from a comb, button-down shirt, smoothly shaved face. Mr. Bradfield looked like he'd gotten out of bed, thrown on dirty clothes, and jumped in the car without bothering to comb his hair. But for what reason? And even stranger, there was a purse tucked into the well below the dash, a small red thing his mother might have taken with her when she went dancing at the country club. It took all Tommy had to not lean over and look in the back seat. Maybe there was other stuff there.

He didn't have to look around to smell things though. Was it lemon? Or spice? Something sweet like lollipops filled the car's interior.

"Good boy," Mr. Bradfield said. "Now, where to?"

"Bus station." Tommy looked up from the purse and kept his eyes on the road.

Mr. Bradfield started the car and took off, the window open, his left arm crooked out the window, as if he and Tommy were on a joyride, whatever that was. His father said that sometimes. "He's treating his farm like a joyride" or "This is no joyride."

This wasn't a joyride. Tommy knew that for certain.

"Got a travel destination?" Mr. Bradfield said.

Tommy wondered how he could avoid saying New Orleans. Maybe he could lie and say New York instead, but if he did, Mr. Bradfield would never let him get out of the car.

"I'm going to see my sister," Tommy said. There was no way Mr. Bradfield knew where she was right now. He wasn't paying any attention to Mary Jo. Probably the last time she came up in conversation, she was still living in San Francisco.

"New Orleans," Mr. Bradfield said. Tommy sunk into the seat. "That so. Quite a place. Been there on business. Had one of the best times of my life."

Mr. Bradfield flicked his turn signal and pulled up to the curb in front of the station. He turned off the car and turned to stare at Tommy. Tommy felt as though he were being pulled into an alien spacecraft by a tractor beam.

"Got enough cash? Expensive to get to. You have food for, what? Two or three days? And what about a cab from the bus station? Or is Mary Jo going to pick you up? She knows you're coming, right?"

Tommy shook his head. In the distance, he saw the silver shine of the bus headed toward them.

"And buses, well, they aren't what they used to be. All sorts ride them now. Who knows what you'll find under the Mason-Dixon."

"What?" Tommy's stomach started to clench as he listened to Mr. Bradfield list off the unknowns. Sure, he'd traveled. His parents had taken him to Des Moines four times. He'd gone to Davenport, Charles City, Cedar Rapids a hundred times. And once to Chicago. His parents had promised he could go with them to visit Mary Jo the next time they went to San Francisco, but there had been no next time. Tommy didn't know why.

"Very different in the South," Mr. Bradfield said, his voice lingering on South and not in a good way.

"Mason-Dixon?" Tommy said, assuming that was the focus of what was wrong. Was that a battle from the Civil War? Or something now?

Mr. Bradfield shrugged. "Go on. I'll take your bike back. Here." He pulled three twenty-dollar bills out of his pocket and handed them to Tommy. "You're going to need this. Get food at your stops. Little cafes by the station. And you can also tip the porters."

The bus inched closer, shiny and silver. People rushed up the steps and into the station. "Maybe you'll need to borrow my watch too," Mr. Bradfield said. "You need to keep time so you can figure out when to pull the cord to get off."

"The cord?"

"You don't want to do it too soon, or, well, folks will be irritated. Might cause a traffic accident too."

Tommy started to breathe fast, a bus-and-car pileup exploding in his mind, smoke, blood, and people screaming. Meanwhile, the bus came to a stop, and a bustle started on the platform. Tommy gripped the door handle, frozen.

"Come on." Mr. Bradfield opened his door. "Let's get you on your bus."

Tommy dropped his gaze to his lap, slumping against the seat. He wasn't going to New Orleans. He wasn't even going to step foot on the bus, shiny and silver in the morning light. He reached out his hand that clutched the twenty-dollar bills.

Mr. Bradfield shrugged and closed his door and put his hands on the wheel, ignoring the money. Neither of them spoke. The morning sun hit the windshield, and Tommy blinked against the light.

"Let's get you home." Mr. Bradfield started the car. "And this will be our little secret, okay. No one needs to know I picked you up this morning. No one needs to know you were heading to points unknown. All this is between you, me, and God. Got it, son?"

Tommy nodded, holding this strange morning inside, a tender secret beating like his heart.

The engine roared as Mr. Bradfield swung the car around and headed back into town. Tommy looked out the window, air on his face. Mary Jo began to slip even further way. In some ways, he could barely remember her. When he imagined his sister, he thought more about photos than her actual person. She barely wrote anymore and never called, so Tommy had to face facts. He wasn't going anywhere, at least not yet. But that was okay. He had almost ridden the bus right out of town, and now he had someone to carry part of his secret.

Mr. Bradfield knew. He didn't get mad. He understood. He was the only one who did.

Tom Johnson
May 2018

"TOM," HIS WIFE, Alice, called out one Saturday in late May. "Could you finally get to that box of your mother's?"

They were putting the house on the market in June, one month from the date Tom retired from his university teaching job, which ended half an hour ago when he turned in his last set of grades. Maybe it would actually end at his retirement bash the next weekend. But the point was, there was not going to be any transition time for the Johnsons. Alice was "sick to death" of the Wisconsin winters, so they were moving to a mud-colored adobe house in Santa Fe, cactus, agave, and cane cholla in the back yard.

But first the cleaning and thus, the damn box. Whatever Tom decided to keep would be put into the PODS storage unit on the driveway. Once full, the POD would miraculously disappear and then arrive on their New Mexico driveway, as if delivered by aliens.

If only it were going to be that easy. No move was.

After their mother died, Tom and his siblings had converged at their mother's place in Naples, Florida, and packed up what little remained. It was up to them to ready the unit for the next old person. Much of their mother's furniture—the heavy wooden pieces from the big house in Saint Helen—had been sold four years ago when she moved to a stepped-up care unit when she began failing. Until then, she'd dressed sharp, as always, dresses or skirts for lunch and dinner in the dining room and occasional car rides to the Naples Yacht Club, her membership active since 1969. She wore her pearl earrings and necklace and her wedding and engagement rings. Virginia Johnson had a standing hair appointment every

Wednesday at ten in the morning for two decades. She'd kept a growing number of potted plants that were neatly tended and invited her neighbors over for tea and cookies once a week, all of them sitting under an indoor arbor of palms and ferns.

But by the time she died from heart failure, there was no one left to remember her but her children and their children. Her friends, sisters, and extended family were either dead or scattered across the country. Her neighbors had passed over long before Ginny had. She would have been irate she hadn't made it to one hundred years old.

"Missed by a month!" she'd have whined. "What a shame."

Once they all arrived, they realized there wasn't much to do. Their mother hadn't wanted a funeral or service of any kind, so after divvying up what little there was and after meeting with the lawyer and signing papers, Tom returned from Florida, driving Virginia's seven-year-old Lincoln filled with boxes of keepsakes Mary Jo and Bobby had convinced him he needed, photo albums from his childhood, those years from about 1955 onward when he was essentially an only child.

What a trip down memory lane. There he was, a Boy Scout, an Indian chief, an astronaut. Tom, winner of the annual Saint Helen spelling bee, three years in a row. Look at all those big white teeth. There he was with the Bradfield clan, all of them shrieking under the arcing fan of a backyard sprinkler. There he and his father were in the canoe, their hats and mittens on for a fall paddle.

Every year was exactly ordered, January through December, not a season out of turn. It would have been a sin to toss them out, so into the Lincoln they went. He'd guessed what Alice might want, taking with him those bird plates she had always admired, a few of the teacups his Grandma Gert had collected, a gilt-edged box from Ginny's one and only trip to Italy.

Tom headed home in the Lincoln, boxes and a potted plant in the back seat. He'd assumed his son, Nick—a college student— would want the car. Free, its biggest selling point. But Nick stood in the driveway dumbstruck.

"There's no way I'm driving that car," Nick told him. "People will think I'm working for the feds." He looked in the back seat. "But I'll take the plant."

For the next few months, Tom opened the boxes, pulling out an album, a paperweight etched with two bucking broncos, a serving spoon, and then closed the lids on the past. Finally he crammed everything he couldn't deal with into one box and stored it in back of the storage rack. Case, or in this instance, box closed.

Mom, he'd scrawled on the top with a half-dead black Sharpie. Jesus. This is how we end up, he thought. Dead and gone with one box of crap no one else wanted. Now as he pulled the softened, moldering cardboard out onto the garage floor, he decided that this move would be his true winnowing. He'd get rid of anything Nick would refuse to have. Tom would move to Santa Fe with two flannel shirts, his Tesla, and their dog, Sadie. And Alice, of course.

Out on the driveway, Alice and her best friend, Kris, lugged a covered bookshelf to the PODS container. Then an office chair. Then boxes of books, mostly from his office. At least he'd been diligent about packing those. Both women gleamed in the sunshine, Alice tall and shapely and still blond, as if she could run out to the tennis court and play the several sets of tennis she used to. Shame about her hip. And knee. Getting old wasn't for the young. Pretty soon both of them would be bionic.

Tom laughed to himself as he pulled up the stepstool and positioned himself in attack mode in front of the box. King of the mountain, he thought. King Mountain.

Out of the box first was the album he'd looked at carefully before, the many shots of little boy Tommy, he of the big teeth. He put it to the side. He flipped through a few others, deciding that Nick might end up wanting the shots of his grandparents, the big old house in Saint Helen, Tom as a boy. Then a teenager. Then a young man off to college, a college graduate, a newly married man.

But after setting aside a plastic Charlie Brown figure, circa 1956, he picked up the box and took it to the side of the garage Alice had identified as the "get rid of" pile. He arranged a set of coasters, a needlepoint with "Home Sweet Home" in red thread, and one album filled with shots of their parents' friends at parties. As he was about to fold up the box, he saw an envelope tucked into the side. More photos. For a truly unsentimental person, his mother had been insane about the photos.

Leaning against the wall, he pulled out the photos and began to flip through the stack. There he was again, older now, sometime in the mid-seventies, sitting on the lanai of his parents' condo. He had sure made some desperate fashion choices. So much polyester. Look at those bangs! And all that hair! Sitting at the table with a drink and a smile. On the lawn holding a just-picked avocado. On the boat showing off his catch, a flounder, a big one. Sitting at the dining room table with…wait, that wasn't Alice. Tom looked closer and then pulled his reading glasses out of his shirt pocket. That wasn't Alice at all. And it wasn't him either.

He flipped back through the other photos. Not one of these photos was of him. Remembering his mother's habit, he flipped to the back of a photo of the "not him" smiling, an arm around Virginia. There, in his mother's careful cursive, was a name. The man in the photo was Harry Bradfield.

For a second, Tom was caught in time, an old memory at the back of his mind. Had he seen this photo before? Or had he seen another photo that had confused him? Harry, Tom or Tom, Harry? When had that happened?

Tom closed his eyes, forcing himself back, back, back. A party. An envelope. He'd been in his bedroom, looking at birthday photos, feeling an emptiness he could still imagine all these years later. His siblings had left the house, his parents so much older than all his friends'. His longing for Mary Jo. So many years ago, he'd flicked through shots of him, Harry, and all their friends. But he'd stopped at Harry. He'd seen this resemblance before.

This time he could do something about it.

"You're coming to Madison?" Tom said, his phone clamped between his shoulder and cheek. He was taking a break from sorting, now in the back yard watering the rose bushes. He was going to miss these, years of his life invested in each varietal.

"Was going to call you this week. Weird you called."

Not as weird as what I'm going to ask you, Tom thought. "Birds of a feather."

"What my mom always said," Harry said. "Or was it 'peas in a pod'?"

They both laughed. All their childhood, they'd been together, in the same classroom or troop or team. They'd spent so much time at each other's houses, it was hard to know where they actually lived. Only college had separated them: Tom heading to Madison for his degrees in history, and Harry to Harvard to study business. An H university, of course. Harry had worked in Manhattan for a time, but eventually he was pulled back to Iowa to take over his father's ever-expanding grocery store chain and banking businesses.

Sometimes Tom wondered if his own academic achievements—MA, PhD, tenured professorship, published books—seemed slightly sweet, perhaps pathetic, to the tribe of H's that ran and owned most of Saint Helen and other parts of Iowa. Roger and Betty had moved to Naples too, but Roger had died shortly after Tom's father, and Harry had swooped down to Florida and taken Betty back home.

"She can see all the kids and grandkids," Harry had told him. "Kate loves having her here."

And who wouldn't? Betty had always been kind, and even as age crept up on her, she kept a sense of humor and her wits, at least until recently. Harry had built a huge house on the edge of town, set back from the street, property obscured by plane trees and beeches and large swaths of emerald grass. If a passing traveler looked closely, he could see the tennis courts, swimming pool with guesthouse and cabana, barn for animals who didn't have the faintest idea they lived on a farm, the construction sleek, rock solid, the stalls more like movie sets for carefree critters.

"I'd have you stay with us," Tom said, "but Alice dismantled the guest rooms, Nick's former room, and the family room. We're sleeping on a mattress and pulling clothing out of suitcases."

"She really wants out of there," Harry said. "And who can blame her?"

Harry and Kate had a house in the suburbs of Phoenix and a condo on Oahu. The moment a polar vortex grabbed hold, off they jetted to warmer climes. All the Bradfield H's—at least, all but Helen, Harry's only sister—their kids, and even sometimes Tom and Alice enjoyed the Bradfields' warm and warmer hospitality.

"Come to the Edgewater. We'll drink whiskey and look out at the lake. Then we can eat a two-pound steak at the restaurant."

Tom was trim, still, but his cholesterol? Well, he wouldn't tell Alice. This would be his last Madison hurrah.

"Call me when you get in," Tom said, a flare of nerves in his chest. Maybe by the time Harry arrived, he thought, I'll know what to say.

Harry had reserved a table at the Edgewater Hotel's Boathouse, a bar with casual dining. When Tom arrived, Harry was already sitting at the wood table, looking out over Lake Mendota. The sky was blue with a haze on the horizon, the water triangled with sail boats. The sun stretched down the sky, pushing into the haze, everything slightly orange, the leaves of the trees glinting gold. God, he was going to miss this state.

"There he is." Harry stood up and pulled Tom into an embrace. His friend smelled successful. All of him buffed and shined with the most expensive ingredients. His hair recently cut, his clothes dry-cleaned and professionally laundered. He was a man out of the *How to Live Successfully* catalogue, hard copy. Tom, clearly, had only read the online edition.

"Looking good," Tom said, watching as Harry motioned to the server who had been prepared to bring over the Macallan triple cask 18 and two glasses.

They settled in, let the server pour. The air spun around them. Tom heard snatches of laughter, music from the beach, cutlery clinking behind the bar. His heart pounded in his chest like something wound, one of those silly toys he'd had as a child. A monkey clanging metal cymbals. Taking in a deep breath and picking up his glass, Tom allowed himself to really look at Harry, half-expecting to see something new. Maybe a clue or a sign. But instead, all he saw was Harry Bradfield, his oldest friend. Tall like Roger, long arms and legs, and finally, a little paunch, a ring of fat not even hiking and tennis could get rid of. Time had caught up to Harry too.

"Old times," Harry said, reaching over to clink Tom's glass. Tom almost sniffed in his first sip, a smell like earth and hills and peat.

"Old times," Tom said. "How is life in Saint Helen?"

"Same. But different. Strip malls and opioid addiction. But still the harvest and the festivals and the football games. We're staying the winter this year."

"Why's that?" Tom took another small sip, savoring the liquid as it burned and glided over his tongue.

"My mom can't travel anymore. It's too confusing for her and hard for us. We don't want to leave her with caregivers."

"I'm sorry," Tom said, shaking his head. All his childhood, Betty Bradfield had loomed, half-angel, half-movie star. Her smile had wattage. She'd never been anything but kind and warm to him, especially during high school when Tom had felt distant from his own parents. They never "got" anything.

The server came back with a cheeseboard full of cheddars, brine-washed double-creams, a local muenster. A basket of crackers and sliced sourdough and bowls of pickles and olives made the idea of a two-pound steak impossible. Also impossible was bringing up the photo almost burning a hole through Tom's breast pocket.

"You got to love Wisconsin," Harry said. "Though I'm still not sure why you picked this state over Iowa. Why you turned down the University of Iowa's offer is beyond me."

They were silent for a moment as they gathered their cheeses. Wisconsin had been perfect. Initially he was 250 miles away from his parents, at least while they were still living in Saint Helen. And by the time they'd moved to Naples, the 1,500 miles between Tom and his parents was freedom. Plus, his mother had never taken to Alice, raising her eyebrows or rolling her eyes at Alice's very liberal proclamations about, well, everything: parenting, politics, government, reading material.

Worse, it seemed, Alice's shape had never pleased Tom's mother either, who liked *her* people to be long and lean, with no bottoms or tops, all evidence of flesh hidden. While athletic, Alice was round and busty.

"Broad in the beam," Tom had once heard her mother whisper to Betty.

"There's some poem about fences making good neighbors," Tom said with a shrug. "Wisconsin was like that fence in terms of my parents."

Harry looked up and nodded. "Say no more. But my god, this cheese is fantastic."

Tom forced down a bite and wiped his mouth. He paused as the server refilled their water glasses, taking in a breath of the fresh air, lake-whipped and crisp.

"I've got a pretty weird question for you," Tom said.

Harry looked up from his plate. "What else is new?"

Tom pulled the photo from his pocket. He slid it to Harry, who wiped his hands and picked it up. He cocked his head. "When were you and Kate together like this…at my parents'? No, that's your parents' place in Naples."

Harry brought it closer to his face, adjusted his glasses, and stared. "No, wait. That's me, isn't it? But…" He looked up at Tom and then back at the photo. He stared at it some more and then put it down, shaking his head. "I'm not sure what your question is."

"It got me thinking about things," Tom said.

Harry sat back and took a deep breath. "Such as?"

"For as long as I could remember, there was something broken in my family. I ran away once. Or almost. Your dad caught me trying to take the bus to New Orleans."

"What?" Harry picked up an olive and then put it down. "I'm surprised he didn't take you there himself. He always had a soft spot for you. Talked about you up until the end."

Tom stung from a stab of sadness and regret, imagining himself on his bike, headed toward his sister, the person who loved him most in the world. He still had all the letters she'd written to him, though there hadn't been one for a very long time. Later, he'd loved being with his father out in the woods camping or hunting, but his father had worked hard up until the minute he'd retired. But Mr. Bradfield? Tom could still see him staring out his car window, face rapt, serious, as if whatever Tom was up to was worthy and important.

"He might have. Instead he dropped me back home and never said a word to my parents."

Harry tapped the photo. "So this. What do you think it means?"

What did it mean? Tom wasn't sure, though he'd invented scenarios. No way Roger Bradfield and his mother had an affair. Most of the time, she'd been polite but distant, turning her attention to Betty. Later in Florida, they'd all grown close, retired and happy, golfing and fishing, drinking out on the lanais, the pool water lapping before them.

Maybe Roger Bradfield had gotten a rural woman pregnant, one of those farmwives Larry Johnson got on his high horse about—all their large bottoms and heart problems. Roger had come to Tom's father to ask for some kind of help. Deliver the baby in secret and so forth. Somehow the Johnsons ended up with the baby. Or it was more complicated than that. A friend was involved. So who?

"I'd ask Mary Jo, but she hasn't been well lately. Jenny called to let me know she was having some tests. Bobby and his semi-secret partner are hiding out in his retirement community. He hasn't seen Mary Jo in years. I don't have anyone else to ask."

Harry picked up the photo again. "The resemblance is uncanny. I never saw it. At least, not like this. But worse, we somehow both had that stupid rock star haircut."

"We were pretty groovy."

They laughed. Tom took a bigger sip of whiskey than he should have.

"God, my dad," Harry said.

"What do you mean?" Tom asked.

"This pisses me off," Harry began. "When Dad died, I thought, *finally*. From what I can tell, he'd been the touchy-touchy type all his life. Grabby hands. He'd have lasted about two seconds in today's business world. He was that way his whole life, even when he could barely get out of bed. After he died, it was done. No more facility staff or nurses complaining. All of that was over. The guy might have been old, but he never stopped trying."

Tom could still hear the other men at picnics and barbecues saying, "That Roger. A true ladies' man."

"It was always a barrier between my parents. But it wasn't like I could ask. There was this look my mother periodically lobbed at my father. Really, now it's clear it was revulsion. There were times I thought maybe she'd left him, though it was always explained as an emergency trip to help some relative or another. One *emergency* lasted half of ninth grade. Another long mess happened when Helen was in high school. Later, somehow, miraculously, my dad was back at the center of her world every time. It was an assembly line of emotions like clockwork."

Tom shrugged. "He had a lot of charm. When he talked to you, it was like, bam. He was there. One hundred percent."

"Charm," Harry said. "Is that what they call it?"

"Now it's a crime," Tom said. When he first started teaching, it was common practice for male professors to find their girlfriends and then wives from the student pool. Now it was a Title IX infraction. The last few years, Tom had held office hours in the department's common area.

"Make it to retirement without a lawsuit," Alice had said. "We don't want to spend our money on lawyers."

She had only been half-kidding.

Harry was silent, sipping his drink. Then he said, "People always did think we were related."

"Brothers," Tom said.

"I shrugged it off every time. You were my best friend. Of course we look the same. Why wouldn't we?"

"Something happened," Tom said.

"I'm not sure what." Harry finished his whiskey in a big gulp that would have had Tom coughing into next year. Then he poured another.

"Could you ask your mother?" Tom asked.

"That would be some conversation," Harry said, voice sharp. "Hey, Mom, did Dad…" Harry took a swig. He was flushed, his eyes watery. "Then there was that…thing with Helen."

"That thing," Tom said, trying not to ask what really had happened to Harry's sister. Helen had acted out—as they would say now—in high school and had been packed off to a girl's school in Lausanne, Switzerland, her junior year. Maybe it was drugs or boys or overall bad behavior. Tom didn't know. She'd never come home, not for graduations or weddings. Not even for Roger's funeral. Everyone else had been there, the church packed cheek to jowl.

"Talking about Dad brings up Helen."

Tom shot Harry a look, but his friend waved him off.

"Long, horrible story. But the point is, talking about Dad makes my mom think about the people who left her. She starts talking about all the dead people in her life, working herself into a state."

Tom lifted a hand. "Bad idea."

Sighing, Harry ran a hand through his thinning hair. "It would be my last resort."

"Have you ever done one of those DNA testing kits?" Tommy asked. "My niece Jenny discovered she's still one hundred percent European."

"No surprise," Harry said.

"Not with her parents, though she hoped her father had hidden Native American blood in his lineage. Apparently there were some remote skeletons in those closets she wanted to fossick around in."

Harry looked at Tom and held his gaze. "Will a scientific answer change anything?"

Maybe it would. Maybe he and Harry would fall out over the outcome. Maybe he'd suddenly want all the H's to know about him. Or maybe he'd wish he could confront Betty, wringing out details. Maybe he'd disrupt his sister's quiet life as he demanded answers about his past.

But more than anything, Tom wanted an end to the pinging sadness from his childhood, a pain beating inside him, an emptiness neither Alice nor Nick had stripped away. He'd had a great career, a fantastic family. A good life when all was said and done.

He and Alice were off to their next, maybe last adventure, the desert calling. But he needed to know the big why of all of it, now, before it was too late.

"Maybe it will help me make sense of things."

"Jesus," Harry said. "And I thought this was going to be the fun part of this visit."

"It's not over yet," Tom cracked.

Tommy lifted his glass, and Harry did too. Here was to whatever was coming.

Mary Jo Johnson
June 1961

SHE SAT IN her mother's kitchen, a fan whapping hot air around the room. It was a desperate hope, but she prayed she wouldn't throw up, at least until she was upstairs in the bathroom.

"Drink some water, dear," her mother said as she cut open a watermelon. The cracking ache of the sound made Mary Jo turn her head, the noise reminding her of fruit and juice, which made her want to throw up even more.

"Do you have any soda crackers?" Mary Jo asked.

Her mother let the watermelon halves sit on the counter as she opened the pantry to find the crackers.

"Anything else?" Her mother looked at her as she placed a plate in front of her. The four dry crackers seemed dangerous, but Mary Jo had to eat something.

It wasn't like this the first time, she wanted to say to her mother, almost reaching out a hand to keep her nearby.

Why is it like this now? she wanted to ask. *Am I being punished for Tommy?*

But in this household, there was no first-time pregnancy. There was only this time—Mary Jo's first pregnancy, Mary Jo a first-time mother—and this time she had such bad morning sickness, morning stretched from the moment she woke up until about ten at night. When the nausea finally abated, Mary Jo ate all she could, knowing that a queasy, unbearable ache would return first thing in the morning.

"The picnic will take your mind off things." Her mother started cubing the watermelon, yanking out the red flesh as if in some kind of medical dissection. Already in the cooler, fried chicken that Virginia began cooking at 6 a.m., a thick, oily smell that wound up into Mary Jo's bedroom. There were deviled eggs and freshly squeezed lemonade, and right now, her father was loading up the hand-cranked ice-cream maker.

"Too bad Bobby couldn't come home this summer," her mother was saying.

Bobby had taken a summer job at a laboratory between his junior and senior years, living with a roommate in downtown Philadelphia, a fellow he'd met his freshman year. Ronald. Richard. Something with an R. All Mary Jo remembered was the guy's bangs, cut straight and lying on his forehead like a Turkish carpet.

"That roommate. Strange boy," Virginia said. "Takes all kinds."

But Bobby was cut loose. No way he'd come home for picnics or command performances at dinner parties. The last time he'd returned, he'd brought back his guitar, the instrument now abandoned and silent in his old bedroom closet. Thank God he hadn't brought his trombone. Someone might convince him to play.

"But it's good experience," her mother went on.

Mary Jo looked out the window. Summer blew crisp and clean in the back yard. Dressed in dungarees and a striped T-shirt, Tommy walked back and forth across the lawn, batting at grass with the pointy end of an arrow. *Whack, whack.* Grass tips flew. He'd barely said two words to her since she and Michael had come to visit, not that she really blamed him.

Her mother bustled at her usual speed. Mary Jo closed her eyes against Virginia's velocity.

"Most of the neighbors will be there." Her mother shot her a look. Mary Jo sighed, not ready for an encounter with the Bradfields, any of them. How many children had Betty had at the end? Six? Seven? All with names that started with H. What a ridiculous letter. Hubert, Humphrey, Hortense, not that these were the kids' names. Mary Jo really didn't know them, aside from Harry, Tommy's best friend. Plus, there was that great big space between child five and six or six and seven. Mary Jo couldn't remember and really didn't care.

But she didn't want to see any of them. She could easily get out of going, citing her condition, her nausea, her fatigue.

"Everyone is so looking forward to seeing you," her mother said, giving her a harder, sharper look as she packed the picnic basket with napkins and cutlery. "After being gone for so long without a visit."

"Mother, I told you Michael was getting settled at his job. We didn't have time to go rushing all over the country."

But they had rushed around New Orleans. Standard Oil had brought in so many young couples, most with no children or only one. Babysitters were a breeze to get and so cheap! There were nights out on Bourbon Street, bridge games with way too many drinks, and trips to visit plantation houses or the beach.

Some days Mary Jo would almost pinch herself, amazed that her life had turned out like this. She was not trapped in Saint Helen. She was with her young, handsome husband (though Michael had put on at least fifteen pounds since they were married). His pay was steady and the cost of living so reasonable, they had extra for weekend trips and new furniture.

And then she got pregnant, despite all her efforts to avoid it.

"Don't you want a baby?" Michael had asked when Mary Jo brought up condoms, the rhythm method, both.

"Of course I do," she had told her new husband who hadn't noticed a thing about her wrecked and used body. With Jimmy and Dave, Mary Jo hadn't thought about being ruined. They had been boys with not one clear idea about sex between them. But Michael was a man who'd had a fiancé and other girlfriends before being engaged. But Michael hadn't said one word.

Having a baby was different. How would that go? She'd walk into a doctor's office and have to admit this was not her first baby but her second. The doctor would notice the stretch marks on her belly and thighs. She would have to tell him about her first pregnancy symptoms (none, really). And maybe worse, she'd have to skirt around the fact that her father had delivered the baby at her grandmother's house.

"Just not now," Mary Jo had told Michael. "Let's wait until we move back to the Bay Area. We're having such a wonderful time."

Michael had agreed, allowing the week off sex during her ovulation and using condoms, if necessary, which it always seemed to be. And he seemed fine with her hands, her mouth, though more than eager when the week was up, especially on weekend mornings.

Something had gone wrong though. She'd had the days wrong. Or a condom broke. It didn't matter how it had happened, just that it had. No matter what, Michael couldn't know that this wasn't her first pregnancy, so one week after she missed her period, Mary Jo went into action and found a gynecologist none of the Standard Oil wives used, a Negro doctor, if truth be told, with an office outside the city limits. What did it matter? Dr. Thompson would keep track of things, and when she went into labor, Mary Jo would have Michael take her to the closest hospital. Whatever doctor was on call would deliver the baby. No one would ever have to know about Dr. Thompson, who'd simply nodded when she said, "My first baby was put up for adoption."

Mary Jo wasn't scared. She'd done this before.

So here she was, sitting at her mother's kitchen table, bilious, fat, and hot, sweat sliding down her sides, a baby roiling inside her. Her second baby.

"Maybe I should stay home," Mary Jo said. "Michael can go. You can introduce him to everyone."

In a swift instant, her mother gave her *the* look. How well Mary Jo knew it, the reprimand from her entire childhood. The look that told her to stand up straight and put a smile on her face. Oh, but first, comb that hair and then put on a proper pair of pants, not those filthy dungarees.

"Pretty girls are happy girls," her mother always said.

What will the neighbors think? the look said in all caps, strident, insistent, intense.

"Fine," Mary Jo said. She stood and handed her mother the soda crackers. "Please pack these."

Then she left the kitchen to get ready for the picnic.

The weathered wooden tables under the great beech trees were laid out with so much food, the sight of it made Mary Jo want to walk back to the car. Heat in a baking car was better than oozing, sugary hams, leaky egg salad, and syrupy brown baked beans. On the grass that fanned out from the shade, grills were fired up, and the men were stationed in front of them, turning great slabs of ribs, whole chickens, pork chops the size of dinner plates. Everything billowed with grease and smoke.

"We don't have to stay." Michael was so kind, so gentle. "I don't care what your mother says. She doesn't scare me."

Mary Jo swallowed down whatever was trying to come back up, half of it Saltines, half fear. "It's okay. We can sit in the shade. We can mingle. Then we can escape."

But it wasn't that easy. Mary Jo's father swept Michael into the band of men barbecuing meats. Then Tommy pulled him into a race with a spoon and an egg. After making sure her mother saw her chatting with all the country club ladies, Mary Jo pulled a folding chair to the edge of the conversation and sat in the densest part of the shade with two soda crackers and a glass of Coca-Cola.

"Works for everything," her grandmother said earlier, patting her hand and then giving her a bubbling paper cup. Her grandmother seemed smaller, frail, thin as paper. Mary Jo would have never survived Tommy's birth if it hadn't been for Gert whispering in her ear, "You can do this, MJ. You can bring this baby into the world, whole and perfect. Push, MJ. Push."

They'd never been able to really talk about it. In fact, she'd never been able to talk about Tommy with anyone, not since those first few weeks with her mother. Sometimes Mary Jo wondered if she'd made up the whole thing, except, of course, there was Tommy right now running around with all the other children, half of them seemingly Bradfields. Only four people in the entire world knew about her baby, and one of them—the baby—didn't remember. Not even Dr. Thompson mentioned her first pregnancy, only writing *multigravida* on her chart, a word Mary Jo noted when she flipped to the page when he left the room. Multiple pregnancies. She knew it because of her father's work. Even if Michael saw it, he wouldn't have a clue what it meant.

Mary Jo sipped her Coca-Cola, wishing she could look out to the picnic without seeing the reminder of all that had gone wrong in her life, starting with Roger Bradfield. Sometime during this trip, she'd put an end to his interference in her life. If he came near her or talked to her, she'd hiss in his ear, "Leave me alone."

If she saw him go near Michael or Tommy, she'd say, "I live across the country. I'll tell everyone your secret."

Maybe she'd finally call the police, though it was probably too late for that. But she could call them anyway.

Two crows flutter-jumped in the tree, a leaf swooping to the grass in their wake. Mary Jo swallowed back a surge of nausea, from this pregnancy or her first, she couldn't tell. She took another sip of soda, letting her grandmother's remedy do its magic.

A quick, strange breeze blew, scattering napkins and one straw hat. She smiled, feeling sleep wash over her until she noticed that Roger Bradfield was headed toward the center of the playing field, the spoon-and-egg race now shifted to a game with a ball. Tommy turned toward him and smiled, a big smile she hadn't seen her entire visit but one she remembered from when he was a little boy. She'd come in the house to see him, and there he'd be, all teeth and bright eyes. Now he was aiming it at Mr. Bradfield, who ruffled his hair. Then Tommy made a gesture, and Mr. Bradfield turned toward Michael, who slicked back his thick, dark hair and then stuck out a long arm. They both laughed, sunlight sparkling against their glasses, both dark-framed.

Two tall men with thick, dark hair, long arms, big noses, glasses.

Mary Jo's mouth went dry, and she put her cup on the lawn, leaning forward. Bradfield. Bradford.

Her breath came fast and shallow, and she felt tears take over her entire face, stilling her into a stunned surprise. Had she done that on purpose? When she came upon Michael at the mailboxes, had she recognized him? Had she thought, here is another Roger Bradfield, especially for me? Here is a Roger I can have for my very own.

On the field, Michael was animated, smiling, hands on his hips. Roger was nodding, moving his hands. A true conversation between men, between equals, between twins separated by birth.

Her marriage was this lie she'd told herself over and over again. She'd left Roger Bradfield behind in Saint Helen, hadn't she?

Hadn't she? She'd found a man who was offering her an entirely new life, nothing close to her childhood…abuse. None of them had taken care of her the way she should have been sheltered. She'd been a child, barely older than Tommy was now.

How could they have done that to her? How could they have put her back into her life and expected her to be normal or whole or happy? And how could Roger Bradfield walk up to her husband and talk to him? How could he even be near Tommy, a child he'd never recognize or care about.

Seeing her watching them, Michael waved. And then Mr. Bradfield waved, a smug, strange, satisfied look on his face. He put his other hand on Tommy's shoulder. Even from here, she could see his fingers pressing hard.

It was too late. Mary Jo would never be done with any of this.

They kept waving, expecting her to what? Stand up and come have a nice chat? Tommy finally looked at her and started to wave too. Heat whipped her body. Her head pounded. Her swollen ankles throbbed. Roger Bradfield winked and clapped Michael on the shoulder.

Mary Jo leaned over and threw up between her feet.

Mary Jo Johnson
October 1962

CUBA WAS SECONDS away from bombing the United States, but Mary Jo was less afraid of the nuclear missiles rushing to prime US targets than she was of Michael, who had taken to throwing furniture, plates, and books around their small house.

Last night, as heat hugged the neighborhood despite the grainy darkness, he'd come home from work in a rankle, exhausted and hungry, and swiped the lamp off the buffet when she asked him to hang up his coat instead of throwing it over the back of a chair.

With one arm whisking fast across the teak, whoosh. The lamp flew, hit the wall, the glass base shattering on the wood floor.

Jenny had started to scream in her playpen. Mary Jo stood in the middle of the living room, hands to her mouth, eyes wide.

He's coming for me next, she had thought, her heart beating out a warning in her ears. The room stilled, Jenny whimpering. At barely one year old, Jenny had only a couple of words, Mama, doggie, Nanna, none of which were needed now. But Mary Jo couldn't look at her child, not wanting to see her fear.

Mary Jo had swallowed, clutching her freezing hands. Sweat poured down her back and pooled in the waistband of her panties. She closed her eyes, braced her body, readied herself. Enough had happened to her in her life, but no one had ever hit her. Not her parents. Not her boyfriends. Not even Roger, who had done everything else.

When she opened her eyes, Michael was no longer in front of her but rather sitting at the kitchen table waiting to be served. He'd crunched over the broken lamp bits to get there. He picked up the carefully folded napkin, flicked it wide, and laid it in his lap.

So now, even though Pascagoula, Mississippi, was less than one thousand miles from the various nuclear silos in Cuba, Mary Jo was fixed on her china, crystal, and ashtrays. What would go next? Anything might fly.

Tonight she was prepared. She'd put Jenny to bed early, stashed away anything breakable, and now Michael was penitent, sorry, sitting at the kitchen table eating her macaroni and cheese with bacon, a secret recipe from her next-door neighbor Susan.

"Fills up Hank, and there's enough for leftovers. Put some crushed potato chips on top," Susan had said. "And a big iceberg salad. Perfect."

Mary Jo had taken Susan's advice, and she'd also made a chocolate sheet cake with buttercream frosting, Michael's favorite.

She had served herself, but she could barely eat, something wrong, every sticky, chewy bite a potential choking incident. Breadcrumbs lined the top of her mouth. Her hands shook.

"How was work—" she began, but Michael put down his fork.

"I am so sorry," he said, reaching out to take her hand. "I don't know what has been going on with me. It's—it's so damn hot here. I want to get us back to the Bay Area."

Mary Jo stared at him, finding breath in her lungs. "Yes?"

"They said two years tops."

He dug back into his meal. Unlike New Orleans, their second posting, Pascagoula, was hot, flat, and boring. There was no nightlife or fun outings with martinis. While there were bridge games and shopping trips with the new flock of Standard Oil wives, Mary Jo found the conversation the same—who bought what, who was cooking what dish, who said the next wicked thing. And now they had Jenny. Mary Jo couldn't bear to leave her at night, wanting to be there when she woke up, first for feedings and later when she was scared by a noise or the dark. Sometimes Mary Jo curled up on the spare bed in the nursery and slept with Jenny instead of going back to bed with Michael.

Every single minute with Jenny was a miracle, not that there were minutes to squander on anything exciting. Not in this town.

Michael shoveled his food in fast, as if he'd grown up in a large family and had to race to get his fair share. Or maybe he was worried the house would fold around him like a circus tent. A week ago she'd told him to slow down, and he had slapped his hand on the table, the cutlery rattling. His angry reaction that night and yesterday had to be about nerves and anger. Not to mention the world was about to end. Mary Jo had turned off the news because she couldn't stand it. If bombs were coming, she didn't want to know. Let the world blow up while she was doing the dishes.

"This is great," Michael said, dishing out a second helping.

Mary Jo gave him a small smile and speared macaroni with her fork, twirling it on her plate.

He wasn't truly violent. He'd never hit or shoved her. And he loved Jenny so much, picking her up and talking to her with funny voices. Michael loved Mary Jo too. Maybe they didn't have sex as much as they had when they were first married, but he had barely been able to wait until she'd healed after Jenny.

"Tonight?" he'd asked for weeks.

"The doctor said six weeks," Mary Jo said, turning away from her husband. Actually the doctor had said, "I tell women to set their own timeline. Four weeks usually does it."

She took care of Michael with her hands, hoping that he would let her be for a couple more weeks. After six weeks came and went, she told Michael the doctor had given her the all-clear.

Mary Jo had expected their marriage to go back to the way it had been. After all, she had Jenny on a tight feeding schedule, had lost her pregnancy weight, and was happy to have sex. But after a few nights of lovemaking, Michael seemed distracted, upset, irritated. When she woke up in the night, he was wrapped in the sheet on his side of the bed like a caterpillar in a cocoon.

And here they were. Hard words and a broken lamp between them.

Outside crickets or cicadas or some whiny bugs were screaming by the windows, a whirring ratchet of sound. She didn't know what any of the bugs here were, other than cockroaches and sand flies.

"Maybe you can put in for a transfer home?" she asked, laying down words as if she were setting tiles. One wrong move and disaster.

Michael looked up from his plate and beamed. "That's my girl," he said. "I'll make sure to see about that tomorrow. Back in the Bay Area, everything will be better. We can get away from—" He waved one hand to take in the room, the neighborhood, the town. Maybe the entire state.

He reached out and touched her hand, putting it in his and holding on tight. Here he was, the man who had taken her all over San Francisco. Here was the man who had sat by her on the cable car, his head back as he laughed at her stories.

If only they could go back in time to the months before he went back to Denver and returned with a used ring. At the time, she'd been so relieved, she let Michael slip it right on her finger, a perfect fit. It wasn't until later that she thought of the other woman. And now Mary Jo thought about her all the time. Did she know she'd dodged a bullet? Did she wake up every morning thanking Mary Jo for taking him away? And look at the other woman now, out shopping, a new ring on her finger. Look at that hat she has on. A pillbox like Jacqueline Onassis, powder blue to match her eyes. Her handsome new husband worked in finance or science. Maybe he was a doctor. Michael had told her she was pretty but not as pretty as Mary Jo, which was likely a lie.

"Definitely not as smart as you, my Stanford grad," Michael said. "You're the smart one. Doctor's daughter."

A woman didn't have to be smart to find a good husband, Mary Jo thought. That was luck. Or a gift from one god or another. It was chance or happenstance. For a long time, Mary Jo had thought she was one of those so blessed. Look at her husband, an artist and an engineer. But that was before Michael had moved her from New Orleans to a refinery town in Mississippi. Before he broke the lamp. Before he stared at her hard when she said the wrong thing, enough times that she kept quiet as much as she could.

That was before she questioned herself, wondering if she'd tried to find the worst thing that had ever happened to her and make it happen over and over again. But hadn't they fallen in love?

Hadn't he loved her, enough to travel all the way to Colorado to break up with a pretty woman almost as smart as Mary Jo?

Could they find that place again? Or was it lost, like everything else?

"Maybe we work on getting Jenny a baby brother," Michael said, serving himself another lump of macaroni.

"That would be nice." Mary Jo wished she meant it. Something in her voice gave her away, and Michael's eyes were on her, alert, ready, flashing with the spark of lamp throwing. Her heart pounded, and she struggled to swallow and then find her most useful smile. "I mean, with all that's going on. Cuba. Wouldn't it be nice for this all to be over? What if it never is?"

Again Michael reached out, stroking her hand as he ate the rest of his dinner. She tried not to flinch. He reassured her. Kennedy might be a scumbag plastic Ken doll, but he was the president of the United States, and that stood for something. Cuba would back down. A wretched little island. Everything would go back to normal. All Mary Jo had to do was have faith. She had to believe. She had to hang on.

"Any dessert?" Michael asked, letting go of her hand and sitting back in his chair, his eyes on her. "I could go for something sweet."

Val Bradford
April 1970

VAL BRADFORD'S MORNING was filled with ache, her fingers pulsing at the joints from too much crocheting the day before. Two doses of aspirin did nothing. Exhausted, with dirty dishes in the sink and crumbs on the counter, Val slumped lumpy in front of the television. No matter which way she turned the dial, there was bad news, a mirror to the badness that was in her fingers and now in her body, a heaviness in her lungs that burned with every cough.

She'd made so much noise coughing, she'd missed part of the broadcast.

"Houston, we have a problem."

At least that's what she thought the newscaster had reported.

"Val, did you see what's going on?" Ethel called as Val realized their astronauts were in trouble. "Oh, Lord, bring those astronauts home safely. We need to do something. Well, I don't know what. My word."

"They're closer to the Lord out there," Val yelled into the receiver, Ethel's deafness making each conversation a hardship. "Better reception."

Ethel was stunned into silence, minor miracle. She had a mouth on her, Ethel. Couldn't shut up most days, telling Val this and that, acting like she invented the universe. Worse was that she didn't pay attention to most of what anyone else told her, probably because she didn't hear it in the first place. Maybe Ethel imagined she could tend to the astronauts herself. But Val strained to not contradict her neighbor, seeing as Ethel took her to the grocery store every week and out to lunch after. Ice cream too.

Sometimes Ethel even slipped her a dollar here and there when Val's food vouchers ran out at the end of the month. Val's own fault for eating too much, though she'd never admit it to anyone, much less Ethel.

"The power supply is dwindling," Ethel hollered. "Those poor men are going to run out of air, food, and water."

Hadn't God made the world out of air and water six thousand years before? Anything was possible. In his corner, Perky peeped and squawked. Blue and gold, the bird was the only thing cheery in this ugly square room.

"Exactly," Val mouthed to her bird. "Ethel is so dramatic."

Perky stared at her with his dark eyes and then pecked at his cuttlebone. *Tap, tap, tap.*

"They were hit by a meteorite," Ethel went on. She had more information than Chet Huntley.

"That so?" Val wanted to hang up and watch the television, exhausted as she was from yesterday's session with Barbara as well as washing the front room windows and hanging her new curtains. Good grief, she was tired. How many hours had she put into her projects? She'd made the curtains herself out of a lovely lemon-colored fabric that she'd bought when her cousin Virginia took her to the five-and-dime's fabric counter. At least she wouldn't have to look out her window onto the stark, dull street below. The cars, the hoodlums. All those crazy people who lived in her building and the one across the street. Always drunk, wearing T-shirts and dungarees and holding liquor bottles.

The damn nerve of them with all their constant noise.

"You heard about Lucille?" Ethel was saying.

"Sure did. Funeral's on Saturday. Hard to believe she's gone." Years ago, back when they were all younger and had husbands who were alive, they played bridge on Wednesday afternoon. Ethel, Belva, Lucille, and Val. Smoked cigarettes, drank gin, and played for pennies.

"I'll call Belva. We can all go together. Strength in numbers."

"Chicken's coming out of the oven" Val said, coughing into her fist. "Talk tomorrow, Ethel."

"Better hurry before it dries out. It's about one minute between juicy and embers."

God love her soul, but Ethel was a know-it-all.

Val hung up the phone and sat back, her breathing swift and shallow. There was no chicken in the oven. There had been no time for cooking, what with the curtains and her damn lungs and aching fingers. Also, she'd recently gotten her teeth back from the dentist, and they throbbed against her gums. She'd have to go back for yet another interminable appointment.

Sloppy work. And for that amount of money? She should have a smile like that shiny young actress, Ali MacGraw.

Val laughed at her thought, coughed, and then settled, her large body fitting snug into her stuffed wingback chair, the one she'd brought with her through each move. She'd made a slip cover a few years back, but that was wearing as much as the original upholstery. Didn't matter though. The chair fit her just right, something worth carting all over Denver. From the house she'd lived in with her husband before he died, and then each successively smaller place, to here, her public assistance apartment for the aged. Small apartments at a reasonable price, sixty and older. Not that anyone was following the rules. Her neighbors let all their family members move in. Babies even. How was anyone supposed to tolerate babies at this point? Worse, there were nightly helicopters and sirens, the police searching for the criminals who lived right under Val. Or next door. The humping and bumping, banging, shouting, night after night, enough so that she had to wear rubber earplugs to get a couple hours of sleep.

Truth was, though, she barely fit into the chair, snug at her hips, the flab pressed on either side. Five more pounds on her old, aching bones and she'd be forced to buy another, not that there was any money for that expense. She needed to reduce. Last time Val went to the doctor, she'd only lost a quarter of a pound, and her blood pressure was through the roof.

"Mrs. Bradford," young Dr. Smernoff said as he whisked in and out. His diploma on the wall. University of Nebraska, 1958. He'd only been practicing for a little more than a decade. "You're setting yourself up for a cardiac incident."

Cardiac incident, Val thought now as the local newsman pointed a stick to a spaceship diagram.

The phrase sounded like a television show. *Next up! Cardiac Incident!*

Val reached down to her sewing basket, finding her tatting project, a lovely little doll dress. For her Tricia's birthday. Such a sweet child. Not like Jenny, who had taken one look at her the one and only time Val had been invited to visit and said, "You're fat."

"They will then fling around the moon." The announcer turned to a diagram that looked like something a child would concoct before building a toy rocket.

"They don't have one damn clue what they're talking about. Right, Perky?"

Perky stared at her with his black eyes.

Maybe she should work on her crazy print dress, though all that wildly colored fabric would make her look like a lumbering circus as she walked, not that she did much of that. Thank God for Ethel and Belva. And the monthly check from that brat kid of hers, Michael. Not always a brat. He wrote. He sent money and presents. He called on her birthday and holidays. But he'd left Denver for Boulder, and Boulder for the world and had never come back.

Yesterday she'd dialed his house three times. No answer. It had been three weeks since any contact. But maybe it was best she didn't talk to her son. When he did answer the phone, she could hear how he was tolerating her.

"Oh, really?" he'd say when she told him about her projects and plans. "Sounds like you're keeping busy."

In the background, family noise. A television. Mary Jo's voice, a high-pitched whine, if you asked Val. The titter of the three girls.

How had her boy ended up so far away and with a woman who didn't even like Val? Once, a long time ago, he'd loved her, held onto her neck as she carried him to bed, whimpered as she left the room, leaving the closet light on. His curly black hair, his dark black eyes. Maybe he had grown into a storky string bean, at least until after college. Those ears! Like his father's, large with fleshy earlobes. And his nose? A bit like hers, at least until he had his deviated septum fixed, like that's all the doctors did. Ha! He looked like Charlton Heston afterward, movie star handsome.

But Michael had been so smart. And talented. Could draw anything. After high school, he'd gone right to art school, and Val was sure that his paintings would end up on museum walls.

But he'd come to her after his first year and told her he was off to Boulder. Engineering.

"I have to make a living," he said, eyes on the dinner she'd made him. Stuffed cabbage leaves with tomato sauce, his favorite. "I'm ordinary. Nothing special. No real talent. I need to get a real job."

"That's not true!" Val felt something inside her pang. "Remember those play sets you painted in high school? All those hoity-toity parents talked about them during intermission."

In fact, it was all Val could do to keep from walking around the lobby telling everyone it was her son who had such talent: "The ocean? That sea monster? My son created them all."

Once she started to say something about the towering statue in Act Three, but the woman next to her rushed into an exclamation about her own child. "My boy is playing Perseus. He memorized all those lines."

"My goodness," Val had said, not finding the right words to compete with the woman's tall blond son in his tunic and sandals. And there had been a lot of lines.

Yet even after all these years, at the back of one of her dresser drawers were the photos she'd taken of Michael's handiwork. But now that stage, that high school, that boy were all gone, residing nowhere but in her memory.

So now what did she do? Now that she was no more than an obligation and bad memory? From the moment he called until the second before he hung up, she couldn't shut up. Every phone call. It all came out in a rush, Val unable to stop complaining. Her back, her fatigue, her teeth, her overall health. She had no money for improvements. For fabric. For food.

Worse, she'd start in on him, the one she wanted more than anything.

"You don't visit."

"You don't call enough."

"You don't send money. Don't you know how I live? Do you know what it's like for me at the end of the month? Have you seen the vegetables in the discount bin? Rotten, wilted, brown."

After those calls, she'd maybe get a twenty-five-dollar check in the mail. After some of the calls, the ones when she got angry and said things she shouldn't have about his father, his wife, his job, his bratty older child, she got nothing. And he didn't call again for months.

When he finally did, Val would try to make nice, but the next thing she knew, she was complaining all over again.

If she kept it up, he'd put her in a home, like the one her former neighbor Jane lived in, stuffed into a wheelchair all day with the windows closed. God, the smell of that place! Val visited once and wished she had a mask to clamp over her nose and mouth. The bathroom smells; the odors of aging bodies and imminent death.

Even this place was better than a home, which was the wrong name. Prison, more like.

Perky cheeped, cracked a sunflower seed, shell flying.

"Messy bird." Val sipped her beverage, part apple juice, part rum. She wasn't supposed to drink anything, but the alcohol made her body stop shouting.

On the TV, a diagram of the space module's possible return to Earth's atmosphere, the newscaster's optimistic words not matching his expression.

If the astronauts made it around the moon and then Earth, they would surely die anyway. Fire. Calamity. Disaster. Enough already. She pushed herself to standing and turned off the television set, the picture crackling with static and closing down into a small white eye and then nothing.

Val sat down again and reached to the table near her chair and turned on the transistor that Michael had sent her the year before for Christmas. A's versus the White Sox. But there was only static, no matter how she turned the dial. Even the airwaves were against her.

It was impossible to leave one world for another. She had escaped her dried-up dreams in Buffalo—love, family, home—

only to meet her husband her first week in Denver, a man who'd never loved her and then died when Michael was nine.

As soon as he could, Michael had left as well, creating a family he loved better than Val. How was that possible? Why hadn't he married that Sylvia, the girl who'd lived here in Denver? Val had heard she'd married a dentist and lived a fine life. Michael had gone off and picked Mary Jo, a spoiled brat who'd had everything handed to her on a silver platter. Those snooty parents with their country club and fishing boat. God, the look on Virginia Johnson's face when she first saw Val. Couldn't even be bothered to hide her disgust. Well, Val had hoped Virginia's daughter would have been better than that.

She wasn't. Mary Jo never wrote or called, only addressing the girls' letters that came less and less often. Never included one damn word of her own. So who did Val have now but a bunch of friends who could really not care less?

No move ever worked. Her mother had left Poland for an American world of slaughterhouses or ironworks for the men and ordinary drudgery or worse for the women. A place where they were all called Polacks.

Val closed her eyes, felt her breathing, each inhale as if she were pushing up a slab of concrete. One breath, two. Another. Later there would be a pork chop—probably wormy and dry—and maybe a little ice cream. Before that, she would finish the dress for Tricia's doll and maybe her print dress. The day was warming, and she could open the windows and let the breeze whisk her into a better mood. With Perky's bright eyes on her, she'd make into the evening and, God willing, tomorrow.

Maybe the astronauts would too.

But for now, Val drifted, finding her big body sitting next to the Apollo crewmen, her hands on the controls as she pressed the right buttons, the ones that would work.

"You come home," she said after the engines engaged and hummed. She patted their astronaut-suited hands, boys inside these suits, all of them so young. "You come back to me now."

Mary Jo Johnson
July 1970

WHEN MARY JO'S Grandma Gert called, it was rare, fast, and succinct, her grandmother caught in the time when long-distance calls were a terrifying luxury. When Mary Jo was little, her grandmother still had an old-fashioned phone, one with a conical-shaped earpiece and a stand with the dial at the base. Now, as she listened to her grandmother's voice, she saw the old house in Charles City, Gert standing in the hall next to the tiny telephone table, the earpiece pressed tight to her right ear.

"You'll have to speak up!" she'd yell. "I can't hear a word you're saying."

Now, of course, Gert had a modern rotary phone, three of them, this one in her parlor, where Gert was no doubt sitting.

"The girls," she asked Mary Jo. "How are they doing?"

"Very well," Mary Jo said automatically, though, in fact, they were. Jenny was almost ten, a loud, wild girl with a great sense of humor. Her little sisters, Tricia and Joy, looked up to her admiringly, or at least, Joy still did. Tricia seemed to lurk in the background a bit now, one eyebrow raised as Jenny ate up the scenery. How did an eight-year-old raise an eyebrow?

"How are you, Grandma?" Mary Jo asked. "Are you feeling better?"

"At this age, any day I get up is better," her grandmother quipped. Last fall Gert had broken her hip and spent two months in rehab. Virginia had been in an uproar about getting her mother moved permanently into a facility, but Gert would have none of it.

When her two months were over, she moved home, had new handrails installed, and dug in.

"Are you getting out—"

"Let's stop the chitchat," Gert said. "I have something on my mind."

Her grandmother began talking about the past and secrets and time to pay the piper. Mary Jo pulled out a dining room chair and looped the extra-long phone cord in her hand, pulling it so she could sit down at the table. She picked up her pack of cigarettes, tapped one out, and lit it.

"What is it?" she asked on her exhale, though Mary Jo had owed the piper a lot for a long while.

"I'm not going to beat around the bush. Have you ever talked to Tommy about his history?"

Mary Jo tapped her cigarette, ashes falling into the old cereal bowl she used as an ashtray.

"We decided—"

"Your parents decided twenty years ago," Gert said. "You are a grown woman with three—four—children, and you can do what is right."

"It wouldn't be right, Grandma," Mary Jo said. "It's been too long."

All these years, Mary Jo had imagined telling Tommy the truth, but she'd never been brave enough to say a word.

"He's only twenty," Gert said. "There's still time for him to forgive you."

"What did I do?" Her throat tightened, tears in her eyes. She hadn't done anything. Things had been done to her. All the adults—even her grandmother—had made the decisions. Why did she need to be forgiven?

"I don't mean that," Gert said. "What I mean is that he will have that wound inside him. In the deepest part of himself, he has always known he's not Virginia's son. He knows there's something you aren't giving him. What you can give him is the truth before it's too late."

Mary Jo took a drag off her cigarette, the inhale biting, raw. She brought a fist to her mouth, pressing back a cough. Since day one,

Tommy knew in his bones that something was wrong. Mary Jo hadn't helped anything by making him her favorite person in the entire world.

"But it might be too early, Grandma," Mary Jo said. "He's not yet started his life. When he graduates—"

"Have you been saying that since you left home?"

"Saying what?" Mary Jo heard her lie.

"'When' sentences. When I graduate. When I get married. When I move away. Then I'll tell Tommy the truth. I know you, Mary Jo. I've known you since before you were born. I saw you push into the world, starting from your mother's pregnancy. You are stubborn, MJ. You know what you want. You want to help Tommy."

"But he's fine." Mary Jo stubbed out her cigarette, breaking it into the bowl. "He's doing well."

"He won't always be."

Mary Jo slumped in her chair. She listened to her grandmother talk on about lies bending people's hearts and souls. As if Mary Jo didn't know that. Sighing, she looked around her perfect ranch house in the tony East Bay suburbs. Michael had moved up the ranks at Standard Oil, getting them first home to the Bay Area—a tiny house in Richmond—and then with his promotion to project management division chief, they'd bought this sprawling fixer-upper he'd spent every weekend on for eight years.

Now she could look out the window to a perfect swath of emerald lawn and their own swimming pool, the pool cleaner scouring the watery perimeters like a robot cuttlefish. The girls could all swim, even Joy, though her strokes were more doggie paddle than anything else. This summer they'd all turned the color of hazelnuts, their hair glinting with sunlight.

Each of her children had their own bedrooms, twin beds festooned with pink and yellow and, for Joy, a luscious blue. Joy and Tricia shared a bathroom, but Jenny had her own. Michael and she shared a master bedroom with an attached bathroom with two sinks. And her kitchen? Double ovens, a dishwasher, a hot water dispenser, and a separate freezer.

"You've done very well," her mother had said when they visited.

What did that mean? Mary Jo wondered then and now. She'd done well to find a man who could buy her a double oven? Maybe her mother was right. But what her mother didn't know was that there was a price for everything.

"Promise," her grandmother said, her voice loud and crotchety. "Promise me you'll tell Tommy the truth."

Outside, scrub jays soared blue past the window. The pool cleaner shot a strange plume of water that arced over the pool and splattered on the hot cement. Cicadas rang incessantly, a soundtrack for the hot yellow sun. From the back of the house, little girl giggles. Mary Jo's heart hardened into a dark lump. Right now, post-lunch and waiting for their afternoon swim, they were three little girls, innocent and open. But that wouldn't last. It never did. In two years, Jenny would be as old as Mary Jo had been when she had Tommy.

"I'll tell him, Grandma. I promise," Mary Jo said, though even as she spoke, she knew she was lying.

Turned out, Mary Jo never had to tell her grandmother she hadn't told Tommy the truth. That winter, her grandmother died of pneumonia. Stubborn to the end, Gert had ignored her respiratory symptoms until it was too late. Mary Jo got away with her lie, though that didn't make her feel better about not wanting to go the service. Traveling to Iowa during the dead of winter was a perfectly good excuse. But the real reason was she couldn't see Tommy. And she didn't want to see Roger Bradfield, who years ago had crept back into her parents' lives, he and Betty both. He'd be at the house, pouring stiff drinks, spouting platitudes, and shaking hands. He'd be that annoying friend who said, "Thank you for coming," to guests, even though the only attachment he had to Gert was an illegal one.

Whether she attended the service or not, Mary Jo held onto her grandmother, even now. All these years later, her hand still gripped Gert's as it had with each contraction. For always, her grandmother's face would be in front of her own as her body contracted and tore and opened. When it was finally all over, her grandmother had laid Tommy in her arms for the first time. But it hurt too much to remember his tiny face, eyes shut, mouth already sucking. Her first baby, one she'd never been able to claim. Not like she had her girls.

When her mother called a second time about the funeral, Mary Jo could barely keep from crying, guilt gilding her voice as she consoled her mother on the phone.

"I really want to come to her service, Mother, but the girls…No, he really can't take off work…I'm so sorry. You know how much I loved her."

At least that wasn't a lie.

Her grandmother had left each girl one thousand dollars that Michael decided to invest in the stock market.

"A friend gave me a tip," he said one night after dinner. The girls were in the family room watching television, the brand-new color set Michael had insisted on, a Japanese brand Mary Jo had never heard of, Sony.

"Don't you think we should put the money away for their college educations?"

Michael took in a long, slow breath, his jaw clenched. Her heart fluttered, and she sat back in her chair. There was still time to keep him from erupting. Mary Jo swallowed and brightened, finding a slight smile to fasten to her face. She was a Mrs. Potato Head of passive looks. If one didn't work, she could quickly try another.

"But if you have a good idea," she said, "of course, it would be wonderful to make more."

Satisfied, Michael wrote out the check, the full three thousand dollars she'd deposited only the week before. Mary Jo saw it disappearing. Poof! Like smoke. She was relieved she hadn't mentioned the money Gert had left to her alone. Ten thousand dollars in a check made out only to her. It was as if Gert had known something was wrong. So instead of putting it into the joint account, Mary Jo had walked out of Bank of America, driven over to Crocker Bank, and opened a new account in her name. If she hadn't, Michael would have pulled it all into this harebrained scheme. This way she could pay for a college education or two. Or maybe something else. Plane ticket. Four of them.

The dining room thumped with one beat, two, the rising heat of her husband's irritation, but then Michael's mood took a better turn.

"It's a sure thing," Michael said. "You wait and see. We'll be able to pay for all their college expenses. Maybe even cover their weddings. Three girls."

He smiled at Mary Jo, the look that told her he still wanted a boy. His lips were happy, but there was accusation in his face, the intensity of his eyes. *You haven't given me what I want most!*

"It's very exciting," Mary Jo said, feeling dread all through her body, her bones filled with it. "I'd better get the bath ready for Joy."

She stood up and walked toward the family room. She'd made it through another night, so far. There were still a few hours left.

The money evaporated into nothing but zeroes. Michael explained it as a market fluctuation. Mary Jo listened while rinsing dinner dishes and putting them in the dishwasher, turning to him to nod encouragement as he continued.

"It doesn't matter, really. Things are going so well at work. But it would have been nice to have a little nest egg for each girl. A surprise."

"It would have," Mary Jo agreed, wishing she could suck back her words.

"What do you mean?" Michael said.

"What you said." Mary Jo wiped her hands on the dish towel and searched her face for a smile, but her mouth wobbled. "Things are going so well for you at work. It doesn't really matter."

"Really? *Really?*"

She braced herself against the counter and tried to hide her shaking knees. "I know you did your best."

"My best? This wasn't anything to do with me." Michael stood up from the counter, hands clenched at his sides. "I'm not responsible for the stock market, am I? I'm not in charge of society, am I?"

"Of course not." Mary Jo strained to keep her voice steady. "I never said—"

"Don't contradict me!" Michael's voice rose. From the corner of her eye, she saw her children file out of the family room and head to Jenny's bedroom, closing the door behind them with a tiny click.

Now was the time to be silent and still. Mary Jo put a hand on the counter and tried not to breathe. Sometimes this worked, the sliding into her shell, eyes closed, her entire body rigid.

"How dare you tell me how to invest my money, money that comes into this family. You don't have any idea how hard it is to be in charge of everything."

Michael lurched out of the kitchen, past the dining room, into the hallway. All Mary Jo could think was, *the children*. Michael swung into the master bedroom and turned around the room, arms spread wide.

"Look at this mess! You can't even take care of the one thing you need to. This house!"

Earlier in the day, Mary Jo had been working on new dresses for the girls and had left her sewing table open, exposing thread and scissors and bobbins. On the floor, a pattern piece. On the dresser, her tomato pin cushion.

"I'll put it all away. I'm sorry. I got caught up with dinner preparations."

"You can only do one thing at a time? How could you possibly even think to tell me what to do? How to do it?"

He came closer to her, his face white with rage, skin flushed, eyes wide. But then he flung open the sliding glass door and grabbed a frame that held photos of all three of the girls, the faces Mary Jo fell asleep to every night. Michael tossed the frame like a Frisbee and then lunged for the alarm clock. It cracked metal on the concrete patio, the bell clanging.

Grunting, he hulked methodically through the room, picking up and flinging things Mary Jo cared about. She rushed toward her sewing machine, but he moved in front of her and grabbed it right out of its table.

"Michael, please," she begged, but he lugged it over to the door, and with a wicked turn, wind-up, and release, he pitched the machine over the step and onto the patio where it thudded hard near the pool.

Mary Jo heard its important parts break—needle, presser foot, hand wheel, spool pins—metal bobbins rolling and bouncing like coins. But her husband wasn't done, picking up her cut pattern pieces, paper still attached to the fabric with pins. Out went her thimble, pinking shears, packs of bias tape, sewing box.

Her daughters cried in the next room.

He yanked open her top dresser drawers and began to toss out her lingerie, nightgowns, and bras. At first she tried to pull what she could around her, a sob stuck deep in her chest, a cry she was familiar with. But then she stopped her gathering, swallowed back her tears. Mary Jo wasn't hurt. Neither were the girls. They'd survived his rage once again.

Mary Jo sat down on the bed, lace panties and an old maternity bra in her lap, watching her husband at his insane efforts. It was too late to save the things she needed and loved best, but she would make it worth her while. This was how she'd gotten her clothes dryer and the dishwasher. He'd tossed and broken all the dirty dinner plates the night she'd had a fever and been unable to cook or clean; the next day, she'd gone to the builder's supply store and ordered the KitchenAid dishwasher. The day his weekend shirts smelled musty, and he'd ripped down the clothesline in the back yard and burned the clothes in the laundry basket in the outdoor incinerator, she'd called Sears Roebuck and had them deliver a dryer, their best.

This is how it went. After he'd thrown out every last thing and calmed down, his rage dissipated, he'd rush out of the house, sometimes to his car, sometimes just walking down the street. When he returned, he would be so very sorry. Oh, yes. The apologizing would begin. She'd never forgive him for anything he'd done, but she would get that Italian Necchi machine she'd seen on display at the fabric store. So sleek. The instructions came in English and Italian. And there were free introductory classes Wednesday afternoons.

Mary Jo wiped her eyes with her old bra and smoothed her hair. This would be over soon, so she waited. She'd make him buy that sewing table too.

They girls called it "the night the sewing machine flew." It was filed near, behind, before "the afternoon Jenny's room was destroyed," "the night the phone book hit its target," and "the Saturday Tricia ran around the swim club grounds and didn't avoid getting slapped."

As the years went on, the stories about Michael's upsets could literally fill a book. When the bridge group ladies complained about their husbands, Mary Jo heard the humor in their voices. "Oh, that Michael. You can take the truck driver out of the cab, but you can't make him stop shouting, 'Shit, goddamn.'"

Everyone laughed.

She never regaled them with true stories about what went on behind closed doors, but they'd seen Michael chase Tricia into the parking lot and slap her into next Sunday. They'd been on the Girl Scout trip with Jenny and watched Michael hoist one of the girls out of the river when she'd been told five times to stop hanging onto the river raft. He'd yelled at the swim coach and thrown a sign into the water, narrowly missing kids doing their warm-ups. Mary Jo was sure her friends, neighbors, and acquaintances assumed that what Michael did out of the house was only worse inside it.

They weren't wrong. There was a dark ugliness in Michael that he tried to shovel out of himself, but there was an unending supply, a River Styx of rage. So far, though, she'd managed to keep things quiet, undercover.

She had to do something.

When Mary Jo read the job announcement at the library downtown and then took and passed the assistant test, Michael began to churn, a roil that was about to overflow. She gripped the dining room table so hard her fingernails turned white, but she kept the easy patter going.

"It pays well enough. And I only have to work one day a week to be able to enroll in the pension."

He wiped his face with one hand, his breathing slowing. "That kind of stupid job has a pension?"

She nodded, looking at him with her best blank face. "And the kids can check out as many books as they'd like. No limit for family. They can come with me, too, and sit in the library while I work. Jenny can take Tricia and Joy to the grocery store for a snack. You can have some time with your weekend projects."

Michael looked at her with his dark eyes, waiting for a fumble he could pounce on. Mary Jo forced her face still, save for her perfect little smile.

"That doesn't sound too bad," Michael admitted. "But not more than once a week. You're needed here. As it is, you can barely keep up."

At first when she began working, Mary Jo was sure he'd take her keys or hide her purse. Or even throw a fit and tear down the house before she left with the girls. But instead he stayed in bed, sleeping in on the Saturday shift she'd signed up for. The girls were wide-eyed, partially frozen, looking down the hallway as they ate their cereal, waiting for their father to roar down, arms wide.

Like church mice, they filed into the big station wagon, Jenny in the front seat next to her. Mary Jo was tempted to coast down the driveway to make their getaway silent. But gritting her teeth, she turned on the engine and backed out like normal. Michael did not come running out of the maw of the garage, fists clenched.

Once she'd settled Tricia and Joy at the large round table in the children's section and Jenny at the table closest to the checkout desk, but in the adult section, Mary Jo sat with June Simms, the head librarian, in her office. The hush of the library surrounded them, June studying Mary Jo's file.

"Stanford," she said, raising an eyebrow. "Impressive."

Was it? If she'd ever gone on to do anything, maybe it would have been. Maybe she could have stuck it out with the chemists, doing more than making coffee and fending off Terry. Maybe she could have forgotten about Michael and why she needed him. She hadn't been brave enough to do that. Or anything. But she was here now.

"It was an experience," Mary Jo said. "Really prepared me to be a mother."

June looked up and barked out a laugh. "Right. So the library. Let's get the ladies at the desk to show you the checkout procedure."

From nine until twelve, Mary Jo followed behind Lucia Davis as she checked out books. There was a very specific order to putting the cards into the machine, dated for library records and the patron. Later there was the reshelving. As she walked by, her girls stared at her, mouths open in what seemed like surprise.

A couple of hours in, Jenny led her sisters into the bathroom and then out the door and down to the grocery store where she was to buy them each a treat to eat after they finished their lunches, which they carried in brown bags to eat outside on the bench in the back.

Mary Jo stood behind the desk, taking the books, pulling out their cards, running them through the machine. Then she stamped each with a date and handed the books back to the patron.

"See you next time," she said.

She greeted neighbors and women from the bridge club. She felt something on her face she could barely remember, her muscles moving in a strange way, enough to make her cry. But she wasn't sad. Not at all. She was happy, here in this nest of books, her children with her, safe. So that's what it was. She was smiling.

On the way home, Mary Jo gripped the wheel, the cage she wore around herself reforming.

"When we get home," she said, "don't make a lot of noise. Go to your rooms and put away your books. I'll start dinner."

"Will he be mad?" Jenny asked.

Mary Jo glanced at her oldest daughter, pale-faced, pale-haired, wide-eyed. "I don't think so. But let's make this an easy thing. Then we can spend every Saturday this way, all right?"

She glanced in the rearview mirror. Tricia and Joy nodded, both with a small stack of books on their laps. Joy was almost asleep, her eyes barely open.

Gliding into the open garage, Mary Jo counseled her girls one more time, and they all slipped into the house as quietly as they'd left it. One, two, three, the girls went into their rooms and closed their doors. Mary Jo put down her things and pulled out the casserole she'd made the night before and put it on the counter. It had a lot of hamburger in it, a concoction of tomatoes, noodles, and cheese, hearty enough that Michael had never complained. With a big salad and a loaf of garlic butter sourdough, he might not even explode until after dinner.

Quickly she washed the dishes in the sink, washed the vegetables and set them in the rack to dry, and then did a sweep of the house, stacking magazines and newspapers and fluffing pillows. She set the dining room table and then told the girls to clean their rooms. Mary Jo opened a couple of windows, letting the air carry away the stale house air, feeling the breeze on her face. Outside Michael was in a T-shirt and work pants, digging drainage around the back of the house. He was focused, intent, and for a minute, she could see the man she fell in love with. There he was, standing on the Golden Gate Bridge, staring into a future that must have been better than this.

"So how was it?" he asked at the table, washed up, a smudge of dirt still on one cheekbone.

"The girls certainly enjoyed the reading," Mary Jo said. "More casserole?"

Michael nodded, holding out his plate.

"When do you get paid?"

"On the fifteenth and thirtieth." Mary Jo said. She'd be unable to deposit her paychecks into her secret account, though she had stashed away some holiday money her parents had sent her. She had almost fifteen thousand dollars. But she couldn't think about that now.

Michael tucked into his casserole. The air in the dining room lightened. Even the glow from the light fixture above seemed to burnish her family, the table, the entire evening with gold. But she was braced, keeping an eye on the girls, begging them silently not to chatter or complain or ruin everything, but they'd been trained by their father's rage. Quiet, compliant, fear in their bones, they acted like normal girls. Pretty, smart, average girls living in a normal family. No one would ever guess, except the people who had heard Michael, seen him tossing their world around whenever he saw fit.

This Michael tonight, though, was not that Michael. He was a normal father eating his meal after a long day of home improvement projects. And somehow, the night ended with Michael asleep on the couch in front of the flickering television, the girls tucked safely into bed, and Mary Jo reading a newly checked-out library book in bed.

Maybe things were getting better. Maybe things would work out.

Michael Bradford
December 1950

"YOU LOOK LIKE a gangster," Bud said when Michael slid too far on the front seat of Bud's Chevy. Michael pushed back toward the door and then closed it, the truck rattling. His dress pants were slick and old, worn shiny in the seat, bought years before.

They were also about an inch too short—hem let down until there was no hem left—but the black socks helped hide the floods. But Michael wore a new black sweater, black shirt, and tie. His thick black hair was as slick as his pants, and he hadn't shaved his upper lip for three weeks, despite his mother's constant morning chiding.

"You look like a damn dago," she said.

Michael had brought thumb and forefinger to his upper lip in a move he hoped would own one day, once he had a full, thick mustache.

"Or maybe an ugly black caterpillar." She laughed, a grating sound he hated.

But no matter what she said, he almost had a mustache. Sparse and patchy but on his face and visible. He wished he were Italian, blessed with facial and chest hair, but unlike Bud and Ray, Michael hadn't packed on muscle or sprouted enough hair in the right places, except on his head, where he was nothing but wild black curls. In a swimsuit, he looked like a twelve-year-old, hairless, smooth, thin-chested. His body reminded him of an aspen: white exterior, tall, spindly, but with a crown of leaves.

"Shut up and drive." Michael put his coat on the bench between them and lit a cigarette, the process still new and exciting. His lighter clicked and sparked in the cab.

He looked over at Bud, who was knotted up in one of his father's ties as well as his father's old suit.

"My mom's going to hand me my head on a plate if she smells smoke. She comes out for a sniff test every time I use it."

"It's a work truck," Michael said.

"You know my mom."

Michael rolled down the window, letting in the brisk air. For about an hour this afternoon, it felt like snow, the sky heavy with frozen possibility, not that anything would have stuck in town. But then the weather passed, the temperature hovering somewhere in the mid-thirties.

They were dressed up for the special dinner after the last rehearsal. The stage, set, and crew were ready for action tomorrow, so the drama teacher, Miss Foote, was hosting a dinner at Cherre-lyn Café, the whole place set aside for them.

Michael wouldn't be this dressed up again until Sunday night for the after-party at Carol Pokraka's house. She was the official Madwoman of Chaillot, but really, not mad at all.

"How many mad women are there in Chaillot?" Bud crooned.

Michael turned on the radio, adjusting the dial.

"Every woman is a mad woman," Michael said, wondering if he meant it. His mother was mad, that was for sure. When her piecework and mending work dried up—not surprisingly, she managed to insult most of her clients—Val grew restless with rage, the past two years like living inside the eye of a tornado.

At night, a couple of glasses of wine in her, she let loose, first at the world and then at Michael.

"Worthless!" she would cry out. "You don't care. You don't notice all that I do."

She would stomp and crash around the apartment and call out names. Michael hid in his bedroom and read *Captain America* and *Human Torch* comics. But every day, Michael endured the repeated litany of her dissatisfactions and dislikes: men, bastards, spics, Jews, dagos, niggers; uppity, showoff women in single-family houses; families, hers specifically; husbands one and two; and then Michael.

Skinny, stupid like his father, that bastard Injun, good-for-nothing. Dead. Leaving her behind with nothing. Nothing.

No one loved her enough, the right way, with care and tenderness. No one saw who she was, nurtured all her talents, helped her get a dress shop going, a crafts or woolens store. Wasn't she talented? She could have been a true quilter, an artist.

"You are throwing your youth away!" she cried out from her chair. "You don't even know how to live!"

Michael tried to live. He palled around with Bud and Ray and all the kids he'd grown up with. First thing last year, Bud pulled him into stage crew. Michael was in charge of the set design, and for *The Madwoman of Chaillot*, he'd painted the castle walls and applied all the glitter and gold.

Besides that, he had a thing for a member of the cast, Sylvia Smith, the Madwoman of Passy. Somehow she managed to look good in her ridiculous hat and white ball gown.

"You really did a good job on the set," Sylvia had said this afternoon after the run-through. "So pretty."

"You going to the dinner?" Michael asked, his face flushing. He focused on his tool bag, feeling about as smart as his father's old hammer.

"Of course." She smiled at him, her lips bright red. "I'll see you there."

She walked away and then turned back. "Silly character."

I'll see you there, Michael thought now. *Silly character.*

"Don't go getting any crazy ideas," Bud said. "I saw you looking all moony over Sylvia. She's going steady with Bill Bailey now and probably forever."

"I know," Michael said, but despite what Bud told him, he understood what Sylvia's eyes were saying. It wasn't about going steady with anyone.

"I mean it, Michael."

Michael sucked on his cigarette and nodded, cool air on his forehead, smoke in his eyes.

***

"There you are," Sylvia said, first thing, as if Bud had been lying about Bill. Her right hand was on Michael's arm, her slim, pale fingers squeezing tight. He wished he had on a decent pair of pants, and at the back of his mind, he heard his mother's hiss: *You look like a dago.*

He could also imagine Bill's laughter about his floods, his wild hair, his scraggly mustache. But Bill was nowhere in sight, only a table with two open chairs, Sylvia leading him there.

Michael turned back to Bud, who shrugged and then seemed to look around the room for the disappeared boyfriend, Bill hiding behind a potted plant.

But nothing. Bud winked.

Sylvia sat down, put her napkin in her lap, and looked up at Michael expectantly. She was tall and thin with big, dark eyes and dark hair that curled around her heart-shaped face. Her neck was long and slender, her lips full. Of all the Englewood High School drama department actresses, she was the one who could make it out in California, in Hollywood, her face on a billboard.

She'd picked a table with most of the Madwomen (three girls were sharing the role of the Madwoman of Saint Sulpice: Connie, Frances, and Shirley) and their dates from the cast: the Broker, the Juggler, Dr. Jadin, the Sergeant. Michael knew Ralph Early—the Juggler— pretty well from calculus and everything else: pep band, orchestra, forensic club, student council, junior play, and now senior play.

"Michael!" Ralph gave him a salute, his blue eyes wide behind his glasses.

"Where's Bill?" Michael asked Sylvia as he sat down, quiet enough so only she heard.

Sylvia fidgeted with her napkin, her cheeks flushing.

"The play can't go on without one of the prospectors," Michael said.

But before Sylvia could answer, one of the cast members, Dick Wolf, raised his glass. "For the discriminating theater-goer!"

They all raised their water glasses. Michael smiled, feeling hopeful. Maybe Sylvia and Bill had broken up? Maybe he actually had a chance? Sylvia smiled at him, and there was her hand on his arm, a light, constant pressure.

As all his friends laughed and cheered, Michael wanted to feel happy. He could imagine what that felt like, and he wanted to grab it. But no matter what good thing came into his view, he always felt the hug of something wrong, a feeling he understood from experience, each time he walked into his apartment and saw his mother smiling.

Nothing good ever came of that. Nothing good came of anything.

Mary Jo Bradford
August 1977

WHEN MARY JO realized Michael was really sick, she began to forgive him. She unpacked her resentment, mistrust, and fear, emptying herself of almost twenty years of feelings because he would never return from the hospital. He was to have exploratory surgery to find the cause of his stomach pain, something hidden, an illness that kept him from eating or working on projects or working in general. A pain that kept him internal, self-absorbed, uncaring about the messes and arguments and disturbances in the house. A pain that kept him awake at night roaming the house, a skeleton specter. None of the tests—those that invaded him from his throat and his behind—had revealed a single clue. And yet the man was folding into a paper napkin, fragile, fluttery, insubstantial.

The morning before Mary Jo drove him to the hospital, he laid on the floor of the living room, a man floating on the raft of his clothes, the fabric spread out around him. She hadn't had the heart to suggest new pants. His belt needed three more holes. Even his shoes looked two sizes too big.

As Mary Jo finished packing Michael's suitcase and then walked into the living room, she noted Jenny sitting on the couch pretending not to stare, but Mary Jo watched her eyes flicker over her father's body. Tricia and Joy were at swim practice, a neighbor arranging a carpool for the Bradford kids and all their activities. Jenny had asked to skip practice today, wanting to what? Watch? Come with? Mary Jo didn't want to ask.

"All ready," Mary Jo said, finding the strings of her smile and pulling them.

As Michael rolled onto his side, pushed himself up, and then struggled to stand, Jenny jumped off the couch to help him. Her face shone like a sunflower, full of hope and summer. Mary Jo clutched the doorjamb, willing herself to stay upright.

"Thanks," Michael said, putting his hands on his daughter's shoulders to right himself. His hair was standing up, his curls askew. He was forty-one years old and still had a full head of hair and not one gray strand, but now, curled into a C, he looked closer to seventy.

"Can I come?" Jenny asked. "I can help."

Michael stared at her, and maybe, for once, he didn't see all her flaws, the ones that worried him, her weight, for one. At puberty, she'd blossomed in all the worst places and not in an attractive way. One night Michael sat her down and showed her a photo of his mother, Val, at twenty: heavy, smashed into a dress, arms like pork tenderloins. Jenny had been ashamed, slinking away from the lecture, but when she lost seven pounds, Michael bought her a new dress for a spring party.

But there were things she'd never be able to lose, such as Val's nose.

"If it gets bigger," he'd told Mary Jo, "we'll have to come up with money for plastic surgery. She can't end up looking like my mother."

Mary Jo hadn't harbored any love for Val Bradford—dead now these past three years—but Michael was overreacting. There was no possibility Jenny would end up like Val. Yet Mary Jo bit her tongue. At least he was watching Jenny. He noticed her, even if his gaze was negative and biting. He was paying attention. Under Michael's watch, no one would hurt her.

"Jenny," Mary Jo said now. "I need you to be home for the girls. I'll call as soon as I can."

Her oldest daughter nodded, biting her upper lip, an unattractive habit, worse because her lips were cracked and chapped. Sometimes the child worried her lips bloody, but now was not the time to bring up that.

For the first time in decades, Mary Jo wished her mother were here, standing next to her, tapping her toe impatiently. *Let's clean up this mess*, Virginia would say. She'd wrangle everything into a smooth-flowing stream. In fact, if Virginia were here, Mary Jo and Michael would already be on their way. Jenny would be busy at some chore, and soup would be bubbling on the range. Virginia would stay home with Jenny and deal with her lips and maybe even her stomach and hips. Her hair, her bangs, her need for deodorant, daily, maybe more. Probably they'd go out shopping for a proper dress, new nylons, nice party shoes. Barrettes, headbands, hairspray. New underwear with elastic that held. A new bra that fit. A lipstick, barely pink.

By the time Mary Jo returned, Virginia would have fixed all the problems she could, her own hair still in place. Michael's illness, though, wouldn't be one of them.

"It will be fine," Michael said, his face pale, drawn, haggard.

Mary Jo could see that not even Jenny believed him.

By the time the doctors closed up Michael's surgical incision, they knew the worst. The cancer hadn't been in any of the places they'd searched or tested. Instead it was on the outside of the stomach. At least, that's where it had started. Now it was everywhere, spread to all his organs, maybe even his brain.

After Michael woke up from surgery, Mary Jo sat by his bed, wiping his mouth after he sipped water from the straw and arranging the blankets, even though they were tucked around his feet. At first he didn't say much, nodding or shaking his head when she asked him questions. But as the anesthesia wore off, he asked for his pipe, which Mary Jo filled and tamped. When she handed it to him, he didn't want it lit, content to hold the bowl in the palm of his right hand.

Finally he said, "I know about Tommy."

She froze, her eyes on the cup she was placing on the hospital tray. She swallowed and then breathed in. "What do you mean?"

Michael closed his eyes and sucked down a gulp of air. Then he exhaled and looked straight at her. "He's your son."

That was a sentence she never expected anyone in her adult life to say. *Tommy* and *son* were never put in the same location, not even in her head. He'd been her baby, and then he wasn't. He'd never been her son. All of that was behind her, but from the ache in her chest, even now, even here, Mary Jo saw how stupid that idea was.

"Who told you?"

She sat and looked at her husband, her angry, dying husband.

"Roger Bradfield. That day…at the picnic."

Mary Jo sat back in her chair, the tray clattering. That horrible man. That horrible, horrible man.

"What did he tell you?"

"He said you had a baby out of wedlock. He wanted me to know. To be sure that I understood you'd been through pregnancy before. That you'd be okay. Nice guy, huh?"

Michael closed his eyes and brought his free hand to his chest, as if to check if he were still alive. Mary Jo couldn't move. Roger Bradfield wanted it to be clear she was damaged goods. He wanted to claim her as his. He'd been there first. He didn't want her to have any life at all, even after all she had given up.

"Did he tell you who Tommy's father was?"

His eyes still closed, Michael shook his head.

Almost every single rotten part of her wanted to tell Michael, even though he lay on his deathbed. Here, she thought, take this. It's what you deserve after all these years of us hiding from your rage. This next sentence would be for the girls, all of them crying in the closet as they hid from the yelling and flung crockery. This was for Mary Jo's lost hopes and dreams of a normal family. This was for the space that never opened up for Tommy. She used to think that was her fault, but Michael had known. He'd known! All those years, he'd known her worst secret. How many times had she mentioned her worry for Tommy? Michael had never suggested a visit or invitation to join them on a trip.

But she'd never brought it up either.

Mary Jo leaned over, breathing close to Michael's face. He smelled stale and sour, his breath full of the poison inside him.

The words were on her tongue, ready, aimed. But he was asleep, his fingers peeling away from the pipe. Mary Jo took it from him, set it on the bedside table, and walked out of the room. She had to call her friends and family. She had to get her daughters here before it was too late.

The next day, Mary Jo was able to get all the children in to visit him. But as she was leading Tricia and Joy to the waiting room—Jenny had come in the morning—she started as nurses and doctors ran to his room. Her heart pounding, she settled the girls in chairs and then walked back down the gloomy hallway. But it was too late. Michael had snuffed out like a candle the moment she'd left the room.

Her hand over her mouth, Mary Jo stood over her husband, his face still holding onto the pain of the past few months, dark circles under his eyes, a pinched look around his mouth. Maybe some of that was the secret he'd let loose. Mary Jane had imagined she'd been carrying it all these years alone. Why hadn't he said anything? Or would he have thrown the world around instead?

She put a hand to his forehead. Someone had closed his eyes, and he looked as he had when asleep. How normal he'd seemed to her then. A man asleep. Not someone who could spin his emotions into fire like a magician. But now he'd never be angry again. He'd never fight against the thing he'd been fighting against his whole life.

"You can sit for a while," a nurse said, and Mary Jo did, reaching for Michael's hand, which was already starting to cool. His hands had never been cool, always warm to hot. When they were first married and living in San Francisco, she'd be wearing flannel pajamas, socks, and mittens, and Michael would be flat on the mattress, stark naked, covers off.

Mary Jo squeezed his hand, desperate for him to squeeze back. Come on, she thought. You can't be dead. You're too angry to be dead.

It was impossible that Michael should simply stop, he of the upheavals and upset, though in recent years, he'd calmed. Maybe two years had passed since anything had flown in their house. No sewing machines, phonebooks, shoes, or books. The girls had stopped tiptoeing past the family room when he was resting on the couch. Michael and Mary Jo had enjoyed their evenings, sipping cocktails and eating pretzel sticks in the time before dinner. He told her stories about work, and she filled him in about the library and the girls' activities. He managed to go to events without causing a scene. People forgot how he'd chased Jenny or yelled at the coach. Life seemed perfect for a couple of floaty California years, years like those she remembered from San Clemente back in the forties. Sunlight and oranges and blond summer hills.

Until this summer. Until August.

"Should we call anyone for you?" another nurse asked.

Mary Jo shook her head but then said, "My girls are in the waiting room."

"I'll sit with them and call the social worker," the nurse said. "Take your time here."

Mary Jo nodded. The nurse patted her arm and left her with her husband's body.

Time. One minute Mary Jo was escaping Iowa for California. The next, she was in a wrestling match with the unknown woman in Denver for Michael. She'd won, taken the literal ring! And then for years, she was fighting against him. Her children were born and grew up. The past became hazy. She barely thought about anything before college, even Tommy—Tom as he was called now. Tom Johnson, PhD. He didn't need to be saved anymore from anything. It was too late to bring him home. They'd all finally found their places, the past the past.

Behind her, the clacking of trays and the squeak of rubber-soled shoes. Nurses whispered in the hallway. Michael seemed to have relaxed, his face softening, his hand cooler, nothing beating inside him. Whatever she'd been wanting when she met him, she didn't need it anymore. No one was after her. No one was trying to catch her in an elevator or linen closet. She could take her husband's belongings and her children and go home. Mary Jo would call her supervisor at the library and ask for a full-time job.

Still holding her husband's hand, she took in all that she could. His nose, the one he worried Jenny would inherit. His dark eyelashes. His almost black hair. His lips, parted slightly, as if he might suddenly take a huge breath. For a second, Mary Jo waited, hoping all of this was a big mistake. But Michael did not breathe in, turning to her to say, "What the hell is going on?"

No, this was it. The last time she would look upon her husband's face. He wanted to be cremated, so she needed to say goodbye to him, their marriage, their entire history, back to the day she first saw him at the mailbox. How wrong she'd been about him. But her plan had worked, hadn't it? In his horrible way, he had saved her. Had he kept living, maybe things would have smoothed out for good. But leave it to Michael to do things the hard way. Leave it to him to not let the good things happen.

Leave it to Michael to wait until the truly bitter end before letting her know he had accepted her worst thing, just in time for it to be too late.

The only good news about any of this was that he'd taken her secret into death. As far as Mary Jo knew, there was no one he could tell now who would matter.

Behind her, the rustle of the curtain that surrounded his bed. Already people were ready to take him away. Mary Jo leaned down and closed her eyes, breathing in his skin that still smelled like the soap at home, Dove. She kissed his cheek, tucked his hand back on the bed, and left the room, needing to find her daughters.

Tom Johnson
July 2018

"IF YOU WANT to come visit," his niece Jenny said, "do it now. Soon. Our trip to Copenhagen in June was an eye-opener."

"What do you mean?" Tom asked. He sat in his new living room in the Santa Fe house. Alice had decorated in earth-tone shades ranging from sand to rust with periodic "pops" (as she liked to say) of turquoise, teal, and gold. Once done with the interior, Alice had turned to the scrubby back yard. Outside right now, she and their new gardener were wrangling a yucca. Wind blew Alice's graying hair free from her ponytail, her hair a sparkly nimbus around her head. The daylight was bright, the sky a deep blue. Tom yearned for snow.

Jenny sighed. "While I was talking to a gate agent, she went to the bathroom and got lost in the terminal. I was actually called to the courtesy phone. Before that, she refused to leave her hotel room unless I was with her. No matter where we went, I'd turn around, and she'd be wandering down some museum hall or another, not knowing where she was. Once I went into her room, and she was standing there staring at the bed like a zombie."

"How long has she been like this?" Tom asked.

"A while." Jenny paused. "Maybe years."

"Why didn't you let us know?"

His niece laughed, soft, remorseful. "I didn't notice. Or pretended not to. Classic case of denial. It took a couple of the people on the tour to point it out to me. Daughter of the year, right?"

"Don't beat yourself up."

"Hard not to," Jenny said. "Who else can I blame? But we have an appointment with a neurologist in two weeks. I'm pretty sure this isn't old age. At least that's what my husband keeps telling me."

Tom half wanted to hang up. He'd waited too long. Now that Mary Jo was losing her mind, she might not remember what had happened sixty-eight years ago. Or would she? Didn't folks with dementia lose the present first? Last in, first out?

In the yard, Alice and the gardener plopped the yucca into its hole. Wind pummeled the palms near the big window. Alice brushed the hair off her face and then saw Tom watching her. She waved. Tom waved back as he listened to Jenny tell him about the blood test and MRI and CAT scan Mary Jo would have to have.

The test Tom and Harry had taken was clear. No question, they were half-siblings. They shared, what? Twenty-something percent DNA. Harry had been stunned, and Tom asked again if he could talk to Betty. But the week before the results came in, Betty had had a series of mini-strokes and was still in the hospital.

"Let's wait on that," Harry said, Tom hearing not a small amount of relief in his friend's voice. Maybe the past wasn't something Harry really wanted to dredge up.

Tom wouldn't push in that direction, thinking he had other options. He needed to remind Jenny to share her information with him. Time to build the DNA family tree. When he'd clicked on all the links, he'd hoped he'd find a list of matches: half-brothers and -sisters, aunts and uncles, cousins and second cousins ready to spill the beans. But nothing.

"She's already complaining about all the tests," Jenny was saying. "It's not going to be easy."

"Can Tricia help?" Tom asked.

"Help? From Brisbane? You mean, fly all the way home for her mother?" Jenny's voice tried to swing on some sarcasm but landed solidly in self-pity. Tom didn't blame her for that either.

Tom shook his head. "Look, I'll come out. Two weeks, you said?"

"Really?" In her question, he could hear all the times she'd been the one to organize and plan. Had no one helped her? What about her husband? Her kids? Well, Tom certainly hadn't, but that wasn't his job, was it? Mary Jo had left him all those years ago, never coming home for any length of time. Her loyalties had been elsewhere, not to him. Maybe he could have been a better brother, but for so long, she'd had Michael. And then her girls. And now, it would seem, just Jenny.

"Let me talk to Alice, but I should be able to stay with your mom and help out with the appointments. Send me the schedule?"

Alice and the gardener were lugging another plant, this one taller, fronds flinging back and forth. His wife had planted at least twenty new trees and now had thoughts about volcanic rocks and various native shrubs. His absence during a quick trip to the Bay Area wouldn't ruffle Alice in the slightest. She might not even know he was gone.

Jenny agreed to the plan, and they hung up. Slipping his phone in his pocket, Tom walked to the window to watch the planting of this next tree. He hadn't told Alice about the DNA test, waiting until he had all the information, figuring he had time. Now he might never find out the truth. Poor Mary Jo.

Tom put on a hat and headed to the back door. He should help with the tree. And he also should call Bobby before heading out to California. Bobby was a weird old bird who sent Tom and Alice stilted Christmas cards and wrote odd emails with even odder attachments: *Iowa water sources tainted. No frogs for Saint Helen's ponds* or *Golfing Causes Cancer—It's the Lawns and What We Treat Them With.*

Once Bobby sent Tom a video of himself playing in a geezer band, wailing on the trombone, if that was, in fact, what someone could do on the instrument. Tom had no idea his brother still played.

But Bobby had all his wits about him. And he might know more about Tom's origins than the DNA test. Bobby might be the only one left who did.

Mary Jo Johnson
September–December 1977

THREE WEEKS AFTER Michael died, Mary Jo woke up out of dead sleep, her heart pounding so loud, it seemed to come from outside of her body, a gong banging in another room. Blinking, she took in a ragged breath, waiting for her body to calm. Then she reached out. For a sad second, she felt Michael's weight in the bed next to her, a heaviness on the other side of the bed that she understood from seventeen years of marriage.

He was back. He was back.

Mary Jo turned over to face the nothingness next to her and sighed, grief and relief mingling in her throat He was finally gone. But where was he? He couldn't really be the ashes in the box up at the Queen of Heaven mortuary. Or could he? Was he a ghost, haunting the rooms, his old life? Or was he in heaven? Or hell?

If he did come back, she wouldn't waste time and would ask, "Why didn't you tell me you knew about Tommy?" Who cared about the afterlife or heaven or even God? She needed to know why he'd kept her secret a secret all these long years.

He'd gotten her at the end.

Mary Jo turned onto her back and stared at the ceiling. From down the hallway, she heard footsteps and the sound of kitchen cupboards opening. Pushing back the covers, she got out of bed and grabbed her robe. Joy stood at the sink filling a mason jar with water. Mary Jo watched her, wondering if her youngest was sleep walking. But then Joy took the glass with two hands and drank the entire thing.

Mary Jo watched her, mouth open. When Joy was done, she turned to fill the jar again.

"Are you feeling sick?" She put a hand to Joy's flushed face. She wasn't warm but rosy.

Joy didn't seem to have time to answer. She gulped down more water until Mary Jo took the jar from her and put it on the counter.

"I'm so thirsty," Joy said, avoiding her mother's gaze and reaching for the water. "This happens at night. Then I pee like crazy."

Mary Jo hadn't heard this nighttime ritual before, but tonight was the first night she hadn't taken one of the Valium pills her father had prescribed before he left. "Not too many," he said. "Enough to get you back into the swing."

What else had been going on at night? She glanced at the clock on the stove. Two a.m.

"Fine," Mary Jo said. "But give yourself a break. Come on. Let's sit at the table."

"Can I have some toast?" Joy asked. "I'm starving."

Mary Jo got out the bread and the toaster, while Joy sat at the table watching her. Her long blond hair was messy, the whites of her brown eyes slightly red. But she was Mary Jo's most beautiful child. She had Virginia's long, lean body. Joy would grow up into a woman who would look elegant in a sheath dress and sandal flats, a stylish leather purse in the crook of one arm. Michael had never worried about Joy's nose or body. Not for one second.

Joy ate four pieces of toast and then another jar of water. Her face was an odd color, flushed, as if she were on some kind of drug, a child in an opium den.

"We're going to have to go to the doctor tomorrow," Mary Jo said. "I don't think it's normal to be so hungry and thirsty in the middle of the night."

Joy nodded as she crunched through the last crust on her plate.

But what was normal? Mary Jo wondered. Was there a manual she could read about living in the time after a spouse died? What about the children? What were they supposed to do?

"Get them ready for school," her mother had said before she went back home to Naples. "Get them new clothes and shoes and enroll them in activities. Maybe a good club. In a couple of months, they'll be back on track."

A moment fluttered by so fast, Mary Jo couldn't catch it. She thought, should I tell my mother what Michael said about Roger? Should I get Roger on the line now with Mother here and let him have it? Tell him the secret her husband had kept to his deathbed?

But then Virginia was opening the phonebook to search for an able housecleaner. "Just a good spritz around here will make you all feel better."

Would a clean house and drama club really make things better? Mary Jo wondered. But she called the school offices, put her daughters into after-school programs. She enrolled Jenny in a driver's ed class. When she wasn't working at the library—now three days a week—she poured over Michael's papers and waited for the death certificate, life insurance payouts, and final paychecks to come in. A coworker at the library recommended her husband as a financial advisor, and Mary Jo met with him, hoping that he could do more with the money than she could. She even turned over the money in her secret account, never used, twenty-two thousand dollars, all hers. No need to hide anything from Michael anymore.

Mary Jo watched Joy chug the last of her water, her eyes glittering. After she'd swallowed every drop, Joy went to the bathroom and urinated for what seemed like minutes.

There was nothing normal about this.

But the next morning and night, and the next day after that, Joy seemed to recover from her vast thirst. To be sure, Mary Jo avoided taking sleeping aids and slept on her back, ready to spring out of bed should Joy head into the kitchen to drink up the world. At night alone in her room, an old story her father had told her about a patient tugged at her memory. The girl had been twelve. Something had happened. Her kidneys? Or was it her pancreas? She'd wasted down to nothing and died before taking the medicine that could have saved her.

But Mary Jo didn't get on the phone to ask her father about that old story. Things were better. A week passed. Another. And another after that. Joy's normal color returned, her eyes clear, focused. No more nighttime water-and-toast binges. Crisis averted.

Still holding her breath, Mary Jo kept going through the motions of a life until she was living again. School started, and it turned out Virginia had been right. They were back on track, all of them partially relieved that Michael was no longer there, a terrible tripwire in their house, a war that only ended when he died.

How sad was that?

Or maybe they understood they had no choice. Mary Jo didn't really understand, but day after day after day, things started to get a little bit better. Life was on track. They were invited next door for Thanksgiving and for Christmas Day.

Mary Jo exhaled.

Then the day after Christmas and the long food festival at the Smiths' next door, Mary Jo woke to Jenny crying out.

"Mom! I can't wake Joy up! Mom!"

In the bright morning light, Mary Jo blinked as she rolled out of bed, stumbled, ran, finding Jenny standing over Joy, one hand on her sister's shoulder. Tricia sat on the edge of Joy's bed, clutching her hands.

"It's like she's permanently asleep," Jenny cried. "Like she's stuck in a bad dream."

"Call 911," Mary Jo said. "Now!"

"This is the worst case of juvenile diabetes I've ever seen," the doctor said from behind his desk. Three hours before, Joy had been admitted from the ER to the hospital. Limp, unconscious during the ambulance ride, she'd come to after receiving intravenous fluids. Doctors and nurses bustled in and out, pushing the curtain that surrounded the bed open and closed, open and closed, the metal sound grating on every nerve Mary Jo had left.

Finally a nurse had guided Mary Jo to the station where she filled out papers, and then to this doctor's office, where she sat, clutching the forms the nurse had handed her and her car keys, something she'd grabbed on the way out, forgetting she was coming by ambulance.

"When did these symptoms first appear?" the doctor—Crawford—asked. He glared at her over his reading glasses.

"This morning—" Mary Jo began.

"This is the first time you noticed anything?"

"Well," she began. "A few weeks ago…"

"You didn't think to take her to her regular doctor?" Dr. Crawford began to write down what could only be a litany of horrible things. *Negligent mother. Dangerous home environment. Call social services?*

"She had some symptoms, but they disappeared. I thought they were gone. Some kind of fluke. It's been a really hard time," Mary Jo said, sniffing, the act of doing so bringing on real tears, which she batted at with the back of one hand. "My husband died at the end of the summer. I've—I've been trying…"

She stopped and looked toward the window, storm brewing. Outside, 1977 churned toward its end, the sky full of dark gray clouds. Live oak limbs waved, shucking leaves that tapped against the glass and flew off. In a matter of days, they'd all be living into a year Michael Bradford would never see or experience.

"I'm sorry for your loss." Dr. Crawford's tone changed, a tinge of kindness under his words. He put down his condemning pen and looked at Mary Jo, his eyes dark and hard on her. "We've likely caught this in time before any real damage was done. Your daughter will make her recovery here, and before she goes home, we can get her stabilized on insulin treatments. She'll have to come back for education classes and follow-up appointments. Regularly."

Mary Jo stared at him. Diabetes. Of course. That was it. The story her father had told her. One of his medical school teachers had been treating a farm girl. The doctor had ridden to the farm to drive her to the hospital to see a visiting doctor who carried with him an experimental drug, insulin.

"Listen," he'd said to her parents. "The Mayo Clinic has a new treatment. It might be risky, but it's worth a try."

The parents had looked at each other and sighed. Their thin, exhausted girl was their only child. Her face was the color of a ripe tomato, and she slept almost all day.

"I'm sorry," the farmer said. "But she's been through too much."

Of course the poor thing had. But hadn't they all? Mary Jo's year had been too much. Nothing but the worst had happened. Wanting Joy's symptoms to truly disappear had been too much to hope for. Wanting Michael to not only calm down but live a long and happier life was too much as well. Wanting to have all that she wanted without the bitter rind of the world far exceeded anything Mary Jo deserved.

"Will Joy be all right?" Mary Jo asked, gripping her hands together. Her father's story hadn't ended well. The parents never agreed to the treatment. The farm girl died days later.

Dr. Crawford was back to his intense gaze. He tapped his pen, nodding. "You are going to have to have a complete lifestyle change. The entire family. When someone gets diabetes so young—" He looked at the file. "Nine years old. Well, it's an adjustment that diabetics have to make. No sugar. Regular meals. Exercise. Safety precautions in the home so something like this never happens again."

Mary Jo breathed in, relief filling her body. So maybe there was hope. This she could fix. This she could change. Unlike everything that had happened to her, here was something Mary Jo would overcome.

"I'll do whatever you tell me," Mary Jo said. "I surely will."

Dr. Crawford watched her, something like belief in his face. But he didn't nod. He didn't smile either.

Roger Bradfield
May 1985

"ROGER," FATHER CALVINO said, "I'm here for your confession."

Confession? Roger's eyes were closed, but the word banged in his head. He tried to open his eyes, but it was too much work. Let me be, he wanted to say. I have nothing to confess. I've done nothing wrong. Besides, the blasted priest was here before. Not long ago. Today even? Yesterday? Roger had stopped counting hours, not noticing light and dark in the care facility where it was always light somewhere.

But the priest. First the confession, which Roger had already done or at least thought about it: ignored his wife, worked too hard, forgot the poor, the sick, the needy. Wasn't kind enough, maybe. But that was bullshit. He'd given so many people their lives. His wife, his kids, his employees at the store, stores, bank, banks. He'd made all their lives better.

He wanted to sit up and grab old Father Calvino, shaking the man into performing another ritual. What about some kind of minor sainthood, patron saint of the giving of income, property, health, wealth? Saint of prosperity and plenty. Saint of progeny.

Roger wanted to smile, but he wasn't sure his mouth would cooperate. He had so many children. He'd done as God commanded and spread his seed. He was a farmer of children.

What would they all do without him? Things weren't going well out there. Case in point: the blasted priest.

The priest kept moving forward. Roger was anointed, an oily smudge on his forehead. Before the Last Rites, Communion, which Roger tried to avoid, pressing his lips tight. Damn wafers. Lamb of God wafers, he thought, wishing he could laugh, but that was harder than a smile.

"He really can't swallow," Betty said from somewhere in the room, close by. Was she still here?

Then God Almighty, finally the Last Rites. *Through this holy anointing, may the Lord in his love and mercy help you with the grace of the Holy Spirit. May the Lord who frees you from sin save you and raise you up.*

Damn straight, Roger thought. Raise me up and get me the hell out of here. And by here, he meant this body, his body, which was so heavy and unnecessary at this point. Hadn't he done all that he needed to do on this earth? Hadn't he made progress with a capital P? Wouldn't God welcome Roger Bradfield into heaven with open arms—no St. Peter needed—and have him pull up a chair? Wouldn't God want to talk business?

The rites were over. Roger felt the priest move away, heard Betty jabbering about something. Oh, he felt so strangely whole right now. This was a righteous death, Roger understood. After a good, long life, he was being rewarded. Sure, he was dying, but his fine mind was intact, his life an example of how to live on this earth. He was leaving without owing anyone anything. His only regret was not being able to see all his children before he left. He wanted to stroke their heads, the soft hair they'd had as children, shiny and new. Yes, he regretted that. But nothing else. Not one damn thing.

Bobby Johnson
July 2018

BOBBY JOHNSON SAT in his family room in his favorite chair, a Svago Zero Gravity recliner, a soft and expensive chair in soft brown leather. In his right hand, his second drink of the night, bourbon and soda with ice. In front of him, the television emitted soft, comforting music, this a show about rescued slow lorises in the first segment, the second on sloths. Ironic, Bobby thought, taking a sip of his drink. Sloth or slow loris. He could be either, take your pick.

On the couch next to his fancy chair, his former college roommate, longtime companion, and now husband, Richard, sat with his drink, a vodka tonic, the bottom of the glass wrapped in a paper napkin. His face was rapt as he watched the amazing once-a-week occurrence of a sloth shitting at the bottom of a tree. Progress! Soon it could be returned to the wild. In his lap, a magazine with a crossword puzzle. The night would go on like this for another couple of hours until Bobby turned off the television and they went to bed.

"Good night," they would say, kissing each other and sleeping the sleep of old men with arthritis. But bedtime was a long way off. There were sloths and then that Irish cat veterinarian show to watch.

"Oh, goodness, they are adorable," Richard said, hunched over a little, his once-thick brown hair thinning They were two old men now.

Bobby didn't answer, not that Richard really expected him to. Though they had lived together since the mid-seventies, the situation had often been precarious, one or the other of them heading to a hotel when visiting parents or family arrived. It wasn't until 2014 when Pennsylvania changed the marriage laws—and coincidentally after Virginia died—that they'd gone to Philadelphia City Hall to be married along with hundreds of other gay couples. It was their party now.

No one other than Tommy knew about Richard. No one had ever really asked, assuming Bobby was too strange to have a relationship. This, Bobby knew, was probably close to the truth. He won the damn jackpot, lottery, pot of gold when some dormitory system paired him with Richard. The only miracle Bobby had ever experienced.

Like his parents before him, he'd have someone to be with until the end. They would legally and officially sign papers and make decisions for each other. Richard would be there to take Bobby's box of ashes home and then toss him into the trash. Or put him in an urn. Maybe his niece Jenny would find a purpose for him. Fertilizer?

"What's so funny?" Richard asked.

"Go back to your sloths," Bobby said.

Over the years they'd traveled to Europe, Iceland, Australia, and Botswana. Before they'd moved to this senior complex, they'd had a summer garden and a greenhouse during the winter. They'd made a life Bobby never thought he'd have.

Bobby avoided having to watch another sloth shitting at the base of whatever damn tree it was because his phone rang. Tommy's name popped up on the screen. That was a surprise. He gathered his drink and phone and pointed to the porch. Richard barely nodded, enraptured by the large, limpid eyes of Geraldo, the rescue sloth. Bobby shivered—moths were crawling up and down the sloth's back. Nature was disgusting.

"Tommy?" Bobby closed the sliding glass door behind him.

"Hey," Tommy said. "You have a few minutes?"

Bobby sat at the glass table, facing the green space and wending concrete paths of the community. Outdoor lighting threw glowing yellow tents around the communal pool. In the trees, the rustle of birds. At least he hoped they were birds and not sloths.

"How are you?" Bobby asked.

Tommy was silent for a second. Bobby could almost see his shrug. His younger-brother-not-his-brother was slouched somewhere, his now not-thin body draped the way it always had been, arm over chair back, legs crossed. Maybe he had a drink too, even though it was still early in Santa Fe. No matter what, he was still a Johnson, drinking in his bones. His eyes that were Mary Jo's dark eyes must be intent, staring into a room.

"Not bad," Tommy said. "But I have a fairly strange question for you."

Bobby sat up a little and took a sip of his drink, swallowing hard. Of course Tommy did. The real question was why it had taken him so long to ask.

"Strange," Bobby said.

"Odd," Tommy said.

"Okay." Bobby took another sip and looked out to the darkening trees. Now he would rather be looking at a sloth.

"Long story short," Tommy began, "and no preamble here, Bob. No other way to do it. Turns out that Harry Bradfield and I are half-brothers."

Bobby dropped his glass. He dropped his phone, the screen shattering. In that instant, he saw his sister sitting in the nursery talking to her baby. Nursing her baby, holding Tommy in the way Bobby had seen other women do but with their children. How could she have known to hold Tommy like that? She'd been a child. A child. All the blood seemed to pool in his heart. He was back in the hallway, spying on his sister, the darkness holding him. But now the sorrow did too.

All these decades, Bobby had believed Jimmy Hayes had been the baby's father, young though he might have been. Jimmy had been an athletic boy, one all the kids looked up to, handsome, smart, and funny. Bobby had never been able to take his eyes off Jimmy Hayes, every single part of him moving as one piece, as if his whole body knew what each part wanted and moved in concert.

Jimmy Hayes was the first boy Bobby had adored. And also the first boy (certainly not the last) who ignored Bobby completely.

Finding his breath, Bobby sat back into the past, seeing his sister holding the baby in that quiet room. Jimmy was the father. That's what he'd thought. Mary Jo and Jimmy, a tragic story about misguided youth and parents making hard choices. Their parents had found out, probably that one night when he'd been packed up and sent to Timmy Rawlins's house in the middle of dinner. Things had changed by the time he returned the next day. He'd felt it. He'd almost smelled it in the dense, silent air of the house. But what could he have done about it? He'd been a kid. A sad, lonely kid, whose sister had gotten pregnant by her boyfriend.

The story Tommy suggested was another story altogether.

"What is it, Bob?" Richard asked as he yanked open the door. "You are as white as the Ghost of Christmas Yet to Come."

Bobby couldn't answer.

"Is it your heart? Where's my phone?" Richard turned to head back inside. "Is it your heart again? I'm going to call 911."

"No, no." Bobby's voice cracked. "I got spooked. A bird."

He pointed at the tree, his hand shaking.

After Richard helped him clean up the broken glass and poured him another drink, Bobby settled in the patio chair and called Tommy back, making sure to keep his face from the phone's broken screen. But no matter what, this call would bloody them both.

"I have a story," Bobby said. "Long story short."

"Long story short," Tommy said, his voice ready for the misery.

"What are you going to do?" Bobby said after he'd told him his side of the tale, which wasn't really a side but a sliver, a refracted slant of light, yellowed with time. In a few years, no one would be able to see it at all.

Tommy was slow to answer, likely stunned. Or horrified. Both would make sense. "I told Jenny I'd go out to help her get Mary Jo to her neurological tests. Seems as though she's fighting against a diagnosis."

"Hard to blame her for that." Bobby didn't want to know anything about his brain. He hoped to flicker out all at once, a sudden, completely dead star.

"Agreed," Tommy said, his voice full of words he didn't say.

"Are you going to tell Harry?" Bobby asked.

Again, a pause. Bobby had always envied Tommy's casual happiness with Harry, his best friend. But now it would seem that friendship hadn't been an accident but insurance, protection against this very moment. If either Tommy or Harry found out, they'd hold the secret close to protect the other.

It was late in this story, almost the end. Roger, Betty, Virginia, and Larry were dead. Mary Jo's mind was full of static. Bobby's ticker was one big fright away from broken. Poor Joy. Maybe Tommy and Jenny—and Tricia, wherever the hell she was now— would have more story to make.

"I'm going to see what I can find out during my visit. Then, well, I'll have to tell him."

Bobby was the silent one now. Inside the house, Richard was turning off most of the lights. Tomorrow they would go to the botanical garden for an hour and then split a soup and sandwich at Bleu Door downtown. They'd go to the library and then the grocery store and stop in for the weekly happy hour in the community room. Bobby hoped to repeat this day with Richard as many times as possible, and he wanted to remember it. Inside, he shook with sadness for his once-beautiful sister. His stunning, gorgeous, glowing sister.

"She's the smartest of you all," his father had said one night soon after Mary Jo was accepted at Stanford University. "Boys, both of you keep your eyes on her."

Mary Jo Johnson
January 1993

MARY JO SAT next to the hospital bed, cupping Joy's right hand
in hers. There was a large window in the private room. The muted
orange glow of an unusual January day poured in through a window and picked up the gold in Joy's hair, the warmest thing about
her because Joy was dead.

Mary Jo stroked her daughter's hair, ignoring the bloody saliva
on her chin, a trail left from when the nurse removed the ventilator
tube. Without all the machines attached, Joy seemed more conscious than she had for the five days she'd been in a coma, resus-
citated at home by the paramedics and then rushed to the ER, all
for nothing. Now, Joy still and soft on the bed, Mary Jo gazed at
her most beautiful child, her youngest, her favorite.

She had been alone with Joy for minutes, maybe a half-hour;
the nurses finally stopped trying to get her to leave the room.

"Let her have a minute," Mary Jo heard Cristina, the head
nurse, say. "It's her daughter. Her baby."

Out in the waiting room, Jenny, Tricia, and Joy's husband,
David, waited along with friends and relatives. Someone was
making important calls to the undertaker, but Mary Jo wanted
nothing to do with that. All she wanted was to sit by this bed,
maybe forever, always clutching Joy's hand.

"Mom," Tricia had said when she'd arrived from Australia the
day before. "I read her chart."

"Is she going to come out of this?" Jenny asked.

"They've done all they could," Tricia said. But what did she
know? Mary Jo thought then. Tricia was a pathologist and studied

dead people and their post-mortem problems, though her recent focus was skin, the leathery brown samples from reckless sunbathers. But while she trained, Tricia had cut and sliced people after the worst had happened. The worst had not happened here, not yet.

Tricia pulled Jenny out of the room, but her words carried all the way to Joy's bedside. "Joy is brain dead. They didn't get to her in time."

"What do you mean?" Jenny asked.

"Her brain. It's like—it's like pink yogurt. It's lost all its…structure." Tricia cupped her hands around a soggy but imaginary brain.

Mary Jo held her breath, thinking of the folds and twists of a brain where memories were tucked and hidden.

Jenny was silent for a long beat. "So why the five days in a coma?"

Tricia had no answer for that, but within an hour, the doctor in charge gathered the family and suggested removing the machines keeping Joy alive.

"Now they tell us," Jenny hissed. "What is wrong with these people?"

"Catholic hospital," Tricia said. "Death is forbidden."

When the nurses let the family into the hospital room after pulling out the tubes, disconnecting the bags, and detaching the wires, Mary Jo reached out to touch Joy, running her palms down her hair, touching her face, murmuring to her as she had when Joy was a baby and couldn't or wouldn't sleep. Her dark eyes were glassy, staring up at the ceiling, enough that Mary Jo almost glanced up to see what her daughter was looking at. Was she hovering somewhere in the room, a ghost freed of her body? A spirit watching?

How, Mary Jo wondered, could Joy's essence be gone? She waited, hoping Joy would sigh or smile or curl toward her as she had when Mary Jo took her back to bed after a 2 a.m. feeding. What riches.

As Mary Jo waited, Jenny, Tricia, and David cried and held and touched Joy's body. David grasped her thin waist, placing his head on her chest. "When I did this at night, she would say, 'Umph,' and put her hands on my head."

Mary Jo wanted to reach out and stroke his hair too, but she held back. How could he not have seen this coming? How could he have let her go to bed and not noticed that that evening would be her last conscious time on earth?

How could he! Mary Jo wanted to shout as she stood, pointing her finger. But she would have to point a finger at herself too. After one particularly bad insulin reaction, Mary Jo had swallowed whole the ER doc's comment.

"In a few years, diabetes is going to be perfectly manageable. No more highs and lows. No more needle sticks. You won't have to wait long."

With the doctor's cutting-edge information in hand, how could one ice-cream cone or candy bar matter? A little insulin would even out Joy's blood sugar. Mary Jo ignored the flyers for diabetic summer camps or weekly meetings, especially during the years of puberty when diabetics go off the rails. She and Joy went out to dinner, ate desserts, celebrated with cake. Joy had never evened out, balanced. Up and down, up and down, Mary Jo ignoring things until they had to rush to the hospital. And then all of that repeated until Joy wasn't her concern but David's.

Point, point, point.

David clung to Joy's dying body.

Jenny and Tricia finally let go of their sister, last hands on shoulder, shin, foot. Mary Jo looked at their sad faces, slumped bodies, searched for the pieces of Joy in both of them. The arched eyebrows, brown and full, the small chins in oval faces. They hugged each other, turned toward the bed one more time before backing away slowly, letting go, walking out the door.

David placed one last hand on Joy's face and then left as well.

Mary Jo couldn't move or let go of Joy's hand. Her ears rang and rang and rang; lights flickered in the corners of her vision, surrounding Joy like a halo. She had never seen death like this before, watching its every single move. She didn't see her father die, not there for his last breath, though she did watch him fade away for his last ten years: first his eyes, then his ears, and then his mind, Parkinson's taking over his body one sense, one ability at a time.

When Bobby called her the night he died, Mary Jo had barely registered the event. Larry Johnson been gone for years.

In her mind, her father was walking the corridors of Saint Helen Hospital, chart in hand. He was laughing at a catch, a trout as big as the world. Or he was in Grandma Gert's house, urging her to push Tommy out into the world. He was smiling at her from across countless dinner tables.

"You're the smartest of all my kids," he said once, twice, many times.

When Bobby told her how their father had died—quietly, no fuss—a small question mark opened up in Mary Jo's chest, and then before she even knew what question she wanted to ask, it faded away. The past, like everything else, was disappearing. Right now she could barely remember her own husband. Maybe she'd been forgetting about Michael before he was even dead, missing his final passage. But now she was breathing in the last air her child had breathed before she stopped breathing at all.

Mary Jo leaned over and ripped a white tissue from the box near the bed and wiped away the saliva trail. Joy's skin was getting cold, but Mary Jo didn't take her hands away, feeling the soft hair, the scars. Joy was still pink-skinned and open-eyed. She was still her daughter.

Mary Jo brought Joy's hand to her lips and kissed it, closing her eyes. This hand. Once so small. When she was six months pregnant with Joy, she and Michael took the girls to Saint Helen. Jenny and Tricia ran wild in the back yard, playing on the grass and in the woods. Fat, hot, and sweaty, Mary Jo sat on the back porch, tense, anxious, certain Roger Bradfield would pop up any second. Her parents seemed nervous too, sitting down to tell her unusual stories. It had been harvest time in her father's backyard garden, and he brought baskets of vegetables to the kitchen for Virginia to can. He saved the oddities for Mary Jo though.

"Look at this, MJ. This squash looks like a foot."

She held the zucchini in her palm, two bulbous toes curving away from the body of the squash. Dried blossoms curled over the ends of the "toes" like diseased toenails.

"Dad!"

He shrugged but didn't stop. Every day he had something else: Siamese twin pumpkins, bulging mutant tomatoes, corkscrew pole beans, two-headed sunflowers.

That summer every grown and birthed thing was somehow wrong. Mary Jo sat silent, looking at her father's offerings, holding her stomach. She didn't believe in omens, but she was starting to, each day a hanging shank of heat and bad garden harvests. Though once she returned home, she forgot about the garden oddities. Everything was going to be all right.

The morning Mary Jo went into labor, Michael called his boss at Standard Oil, and they dropped Jenny and Tricia off at the Sandells' before heading through the Caldecott Tunnel into Oakland. Now Mary Jo almost smiled, remembering Jenny standing in the driveway, her mouth a surprised O. But then, she hadn't had time to react, so busy was her body trying to have the baby. It was rush hour, and her contractions were coming faster and faster, harder and harder. By the time they reached Merritt Hospital, Mary Jo's water had broken. She'd panted, gripping the side of the door. As attendants helped her out of the car, Mary Jo had glanced at Michael. His face was white, and he still held the steering wheel as if he had miles to go.

There wasn't time for one more mile. Twenty minutes after they arrived, Joy was born. She was so red and so blond, hair a glittering white sheen on her head.

Michael stared down at the baby in Mary Jo's arm, relief and irritation in his expression. "Another girl. Well, we had a deal. A boy, you name him. A girl, I name her…And her name is Esther. Esther Elaine."

Esther? Why would he do that to a sweet baby girl? There was so much baggage in that name. Biblical or, at least, Old World. When the baby and Mary Jo came home from the hospital, Mary Jo would change her tiny baby's diapers, kiss her fingers and toes, and try out the name. "Esther…Essie…Tessa."

Jenny and Tricia came up with a rhyme that helped for about a month: "Esther the pest, the tee-legged, toe-legged, bow-legged best pest in the West."

Mary Jo and the girls sang to little Esther in the morning as she sat in her highchair. She would bang her cup on the edge of her tray and smash a banana slice into her bow-shaped mouth.

One day when the baby was eight months old and Michael was at work, Mary Jo snapped. She called the county and officially changed her daughter's name, naming her for what this baby felt like: joy. When holding this baby, Mary Jo couldn't feel the part of herself that was broken.

When she'd returned home from the bank where she'd dealt with some paperwork, Mary Jo battened down the hatches. Michael would come home, she'd tell him, and something would break. Maybe a lot of things. But all he did was look at her, his eyes dark, his gaze long. Mary Jo clenched, wondering if she should run or cower. Then he sighed and said, "When's dinner?"

Soon it was as if Esther had never existed. The family had Joy now.

One night, a good night, she and Michael were sitting at the dining room table while the girls watched television, and he reached for Mary Jo's hand.

"I'm glad we had the third," he said, shooting a rare smile down the hallway. "I wouldn't know what to do if something happened to one of them."

More than the strange vegetables in her father's plot, Michael's words were bad luck. This was tempting the gods, the ones that could strike. Some peasant part of Mary Jo wanted to spit in the corners of the room or incant protective spells. She felt like the gypsy woman in a B movie, sitting in her wagon warning of danger. The Jewish people had rules for this, kissing their fingers or touching doorjambs.

But for a while, until Michael died, things were all right, getting better, good. Mary Jo thought her fears of mutated babies and childhood accidents and family tragedies were exaggerated. They weren't. The years, though, healed things. After Jenny and then Tricia went off to college, Mary Jo and Joy moved into a comfortable, quiet rhythm. Mary Jo looked forward to coming home from the library to sit with her daughter on the couch, watching television and laughing at the silliness of the shows. In a strange way, she felt more intimate with Joy than anyone else ever, except for all those years ago with Tommy in the nursery, their secret a bubble around them.

With Joy, each day of those years seemed long, each meal important, each conversation crucial, each look Joy gave Mary Jo a clue to a secret she would never fully grasp. But every day also meant Joy could get another cold or the flu. Mary Jo studied her daughter's blood sugar levels as if they were weather reports, wondering, what will go wrong now? By the time Joy was eighteen, she'd endured two eye lens replacements. The doctors had removed one kidney and one ovary, both with tumors. One summer Joy's weight plummeted to eighty-five pounds for no reason. For three hot months, Mary Jo watched everything her daughter ate, each cracker, every tuna salad sandwich, every slice of cheese, hoping it would help. Slowly Joy gained the weight back, meal by meal, Mary Jo hovering.

After each health crisis, Mary Jo would think, was that what I was worried about? I'm sure it was. That's all I'd been fearing. That's all that will happen. That was the last thing.

Joy met David her first year at college. During the summer after their sophomore year, they moved in together, and it was nice, for a while, to let someone else worry about illness and blood sugar levels. When the couple decided to get married, Mary Jo dipped into the insurance money Michael had left and gave them the best wedding she could. She and Joy shopped for everything together: dress, shoes, goblets to toast with, the knife to cut the towering wedding cake. There was so much hope, Mary Jo might be able to cut a big slice and nibble on it for years.

I'm so stupid, Mary Jo thought now, stroking Joy's cheek, cold under her fingertips. How could she have forgotten what she knew best: Love never pays off.

So of course she and Joy would end up here, together. What else could Mary Jo have expected? When Joy and David departed for their Hawaiian honeymoon, Mary Jo had watched their plane arc into the sky and thought, she's on loan. I'll get her back.

Here in this hospital, Joy had arrived home, back in the place she began. She was as close to Mary Jo as she had been during that hot Saint Helen's summer at her parents' house. With no disasters left in the offing, Mary Jo sat back in her chair and rubbed Joy's ankle. This was the last time they had together, and she wanted to remember it all, every smell, every touch. The room was quiet, no metallic hum, no wheezing pumps. Mary Jo was with her last baby, her Esther, her Joy. She breathed in her daughter's scent, still there under the hospital patina: the baby oil rubbed into her tender skin, the henna she applied to her hair days earlier.

Mary Jo cupped the side of Joy's head and then pressed her hand. Joy was as still as fallen snow. The January light drifted onto her body in a final goodbye.

"Mom," Jenny called from the door.

Mary Jo closed her eyes, squeezed Joy's hand one last time, and stood, turning away from her daughter, the light, and into what remained.

Virginia Johnson
April 2014

LARRY HAD NEVER lived with her here, this second stage of the assisted living community. They'd first had a lovely three-bedroom apartment with all the latest appliances and a large, enclosed porch. After his stroke, Larry had moved directly into the nursing facility, a loud, clattering place she hoped to heck to avoid. Her task was to die from years rather than illness.

After Larry was gone, she decided to transition to this apartment with its two bedrooms and a view. But the kitchen was a fake kitchen: a microwave, a sink, a fridge. With neither stove nor oven, Virginia was dependent on the staff to bring her meals. She could have gone nightly to the classy dining room. Men had to wear a suit jacket. Women dressed up, pearls and diamonds and heels. Windward Park for Seniors was a cut above, expensive to buy into. Exclusive. But why bother calling a staff member to help her clatter into the dining room in her condition?

She'd just sit here in her housedress and scarf. There was still the view, the ocean lapping against the shore, the evening sky and the water the exact same color, a dark aqua that shimmered.

"Mother?" someone was saying, and Virginia realized she was holding the phone to her ear.

"Bobby?" Oh, that poor, strange boy.

"It's Tom, Mom," her younger son said. "How are you?"

How was she? Probably the same as she was the last time he called, just older.

"Not bad," she said, lying. The only thing keeping her alive was, what? Desire to see how it all turned out? Maybe it was already done. "You and yours?"

"Good to hear," Tom said. "We're all fine."

Virginia almost hung up. What else was there to say? Worse, what else would she say if she had to keep listening to Tom breath into the phone. All these years, and she'd never told him the truth about his life. The lie between them was as big as the world.

"Thinking about coming down for a visit," Tom said. "Like to see you this year."

Don't, she wanted to say. Don't come visit me now or ever. Let me live out this terrible lie alone. Let me watch nothing good continue.

When Larry was alive, Virginia could handle Tom's visits to Naples with his dumpy little dough wife, Alice, who talked only about plants and children. As he had always done, Larry solved problems by forgetting about them. Wasn't it beautiful outside? Look at that sky. The fish are jumping!

Larry kept them all busy on the boat and at the country club. But she couldn't look at Tom anymore and see anything but what she did wrong. That would solve some problems, create others. She laughed a little.

"Are you all right?"

"Never better," Virginia said. "Oh, my dinner has arrived. I'll talk with you next time, Tom."

"When—"

Then she did hang up. Her front door opened, and a young woman—they were all young—rolled in with a tray. Virginia breathed in steamed meat and bad vegetables. Maybe there would be a nice brownie.

Later in her bed, cleaned up and tucked in by a lovely young woman wearing all pink, Virginia wished she could go back. Back and back and back. She'd float into that house in Saint Helen and pick up the carving knife she had just used on the ham. Ignoring the Christmas partygoers, she would walk up to Roger Bradfield and tap him on the shoulder as he started up the stairs heading toward her little girl. A child. Mary Jo. Virginia would hold up the long, sharp knife, let it glint in the dim hallway. She would watch the blood drain from Roger's handsome, florid, rubbery face. Flashing her knife in front of him, she would say the magic words that would make him disappear from Saint Helen forever.

Tom Johnson
August 2018

LATE WEDNESDAY AFTERNOON after hours of testing at the hospital, Jenny had dropped Mary Jo and Tom back at the condo. Parking near the front curb, Jenny had bustled in and put together a cheese plate and a bowl of cut fruit but then headed off, needing to, well, get the hell away from her mother. Tom could hardly blame her. Mary Jo was argumentative, sullen, and exhausted on top of everything else. Now she sat in her recliner in the family room, gripping a bourbon and water, their mother's drink. Or, rather, Virginia's drink.

After today, Tom understood alcohol was on the forbidden list for dementia patients. Good luck prying spirits out of his sister's tight clutch.

"I don't think you'll make it until dinner unless she has her drink," Jenny had said. "I'll meet you two at the restaurant. I made reservations for 7:15."

Tom felt a thrum of nerves at the thought of driving anywhere with Mary Jo, her behind the wheel or otherwise. Maybe worse, he suddenly didn't want to be trapped in this condo with his sister at all, a response that surprised him. All his life, he'd wanted to see Mary Jo, but now, with what he knew, he wished he could ask Jenny to take him to Oakland International.

"Sounds good," Tom had said.

Jenny had patted his arm distractedly. "Thanks so much for coming. I'm not sure I could have gotten through it all by myself."

Then she was out the front door, the latch clicking behind her. Tom sighed. No one could have gotten through that appointment alone. While a SWAT team of four practitioners took Mary Jo into a separate examination room, a social worker and a gerontological nurse practitioner asked Jenny and him questions about Mary Jo's behavior.

Tom mostly stayed quiet, as he didn't have anything of substance to add. But he listened to his niece recite Mary Jo's decline, starting with the things that went south first. Holiday cooking—some pumpkin pie disaster—first. Then there was the time she boiled broccoli for so long, all that was left was a scorched pan. Hardest to believe was that Mary Jo wasn't reading like she used to. Tom hadn't noticed, but Jenny said that even though Mary Jo had gripped a book as they walked into the appointment, she'd been "reading" that book for months, the corner of page fifteen folded down indefinitely.

After both meetings, Mary Jo had a PET scan and some blood drawn.

"We'll be in touch," the social worker had said to Jenny, no hint of a diagnosis or lick of humor in her voice. This was not going to be good news.

Tom took his time locking the front door, reluctant to go back to the family room where Mary Jo held court with her drink, which was likely already consumed. If Bobby was right and Mary Jo was his biological mother, in twelve years, this might be his own future.

From the family room, a sudden blast of television. Fox News, Mary Jo's favorite channel. Tom pushed his hair back from his forehead. It was going to be a long night.

His phone vibrated, and he pulled it out of his pocket. Harry.

Looking back at the family room, Tom unlocked and opened the front door and went out to the porch, blinking against the slanted evening sunlight.

"Harry," Tom said. "You saved me."

Instead of a laugh, he heard Harry sigh. "Not my forte these days, but I aim to please. Thought maybe you'd be in the drinking time. It's after five there, right?"

Tom laughed and moved onto the strip of lawn in front of Mary Jo's place and under the shade of a crepe myrtle tree. "What's up?"

"Have you looked at the DNA site recently?"

"No," Tom said, suddenly thinking about dementia and heredity again. The company offered up all sorts of medical tests that Tom had opted out of. Maybe Harry hadn't. "Bad news?"

"Hard to say," Harry said. "But we have company."

"What do you mean?"

"Looks like a couple of half-siblings out there. I have an email in my inbox I really don't want to open. Someone 'wanting to connect.'"

"Jesus," Tom said, not saying what he was thinking: Who else did Roger Bradfield rape? But he hadn't told Harry what Bobby had seen all those years ago. Not yet. Not until he talked with Mary Jo.

Tom could almost hear Harry shaking his head. "This was one full can of worms we opened."

There was no blame in his oldest friend's voice, but Tom felt horrible that he'd dragged Harry into this mess. Maybe he could have figured it out on his own, but how? He sighed. "I don't know what to say."

"Who does, man? This shit, well, it's going all the way back. It predates us. Let's see what we can find out. I'll read and answer the email. I'm going to have to bring in the other H's sooner or later. And what about Mary Jo? Have you talked to her yet about those days?"

The night before, Mary Jo had rambled on about their childhood, stories about Jupey and how the dog ate the currant berries off the bushes before Virginia had a chance to harvest them for jelly making. The big furnace that rumbled through the house like a monster. Her childhood friends Diane and Margie and their many children and grandchildren, several of whom were in medical school or scuba diving in Bermuda or teaching English in Florence, Beijing, Berlin. The picnics at the city park on holidays. The pork—the best in the world. The beef—the best in the world, too, really and truly.

She was packed with information, but when she tried to set the table, she couldn't seem to remember the word for fork. Last night he'd watched her shuffle back and forth, pulling down a plate, a cup, another plate, a fork, once she remembered what it was. She referred repeatedly to the instructions Jenny had left her for heating up the lasagna, reciting the steps—Press one for time. Enter five minutes. Press start—before Tom took over and got the meal going.

As he had waited for the lasagna, he'd looked around the condo. He hadn't been here for years, and it was heavy with late 1990s décor and design, Mary Jo cramming as much furniture from the slick, enormous rancher she'd sold as she could. Big white tiled counters with dark grout, too-bright fluorescent lighting on the ceiling, wrought iron railings that wobbled when gripped. If this condo was any kind of metaphor for his sister's life, things were no longer holding together. Even the plants outside were wilted, blooms faded, leaves brown.

There was no need to wait for the test results from today's visit. Mary Jo had some form of dementia, pure and simple. But maybe because the past was really the present now, he still might be able to get the story out of her. His story.

"I'm going to talk with her now," Tom said.

"Won't be easy," Harry said. "I'm just glad I don't have to have this conversation with my mother."

Betty Bradfield would have had things to say, Tom knew now. There was no way she couldn't have seen this side of her husband. Not unless she'd tried really hard not to. He took in a deep breath. "I'll call you tomorrow."

"Good luck," Harry said.

"You too," Tom said, finding it hard to believe he was referring to Harry's emails with their potential half-siblings. He was going to have to tell Alice everything. Tonight, or tomorrow. Tomorrow. When he got home, for sure.

They hung up, and Tom slid his phone into his back pocket and headed to the family room to talk with Mary Jo.

Mary Jo Johnson
September 1993

AFTER JOY DIED, Mary Jo's coworkers at the library and her bridge friends all said the same thing: "Don't make any big decisions for at least a year."

Mary Jo lasted nine months. Then she called the mother of one of Jenny's friends, a successful real estate agent, who sold the sprawling rancher off-market, well over asking price. Mary Jo had to move out in a month.

Jenny was furious, white-knuckle house hunting with Mary Jo, taking her to every available condo in the county.

"It doesn't have a patio," Mary Jo would say. "It's so dark."

"Who cares?" Jenny said, throwing her purse into the car. "You should rent something for a while."

"Capital gains tax," Mary Jo said, hearing her accountant's voice come out of her mouth. "If I buy right away, I can roll over the Proposition 13 assessment. I barely pay any property tax. The rate will move with me."

"Jesus, Mom," Jenny said, sighing. "What were you thinking? This is like Olympic-style home buying. Or some kind of contact sport. I'm actually sore."

What had Mary Jo been thinking? It wasn't about the real estate market. Mostly, it was she couldn't spend one more night in that house with all the ghosts. Michael and Joy roaming the halls, banging their sad gongs. Every window, door, room, faucet had a memory. But there were practicals too. What did she need with a swimming pool? It made her nervous when Jenny's boys came over to swim anyway. All she had to do was turn away and disaster would strike. And all that yard and its seeming miles of lawn? She wanted nothing to do with it. Mary Jo needed a clean slate and start.

Finally, at the end of a hellish property-viewing weekend, Mary Jo walked into a condo on a wide street. Near the front door, hydrangeas, rose bushes, and an enormous crepe myrtle. Hanging on the front door, a precipitous fall wreath of red and orange leaves, even as all around them, summer crackled in the nineties. Heat waves rose from the asphalt.

"This looks nice," Jenny said. Either she had regained her usual happy demeanor, or she was going to hard sell this place. But the front did look inviting.

Inside, the house hummed with air conditioning, something Michael never installed in their home.

"Fog comes in every summer night," he'd said. "Nature's own."

She'd wanted to yell at him during those five days of the summer no one could sleep, the heat hanging in their house like an unwelcome guest. Mary Jo had been too hot to complain. Or she didn't want to deal with what happened when she did.

But this condo? The inside air was crisp and cool and clean, filling the three bedrooms, two and a half baths with comfort. And there was a patio with an orange tree at the back and jasmine climbing the back fence.

"I want this one," Mary Jo said. "Call Cecilia. We need to write up an offer."

For a second, Jenny seemed to want to argue, but then she pulled out the cellphone she'd purchased for emergencies—which this was—and called the agent.

After the movers, Jenny, and all her friends who helped out had left, Mary Jo sat alone in the very first place she'd ever purchased alone. After eating some cheese and crackers, she'd worked all evening putting away her clothes and toiletries and finished off the kitchen. Now she sat in her office surrounded by cardboard boxes, the most important one in front of her.

Mary Jo opened it and pulled out the slim manila envelope with Michael's engineering school writing still on it: Birth Certificates. Car Title. Social Security.

Michael would have no idea that she'd put his Statement of Death by a Funeral Director form inside, alongside their youngest daughter's, David sending her a copy. David, off to his own life, selling the house he had shared with Joy and moving to Las Vegas. Soon Mary Jo would never hear from him again.

One by one, she opened and read through each document, noting dates and times and places. Over the years, Mary Jo should have discarded the old car titles and the extra copies of Michael's birth certificates and her parents' wedding license, but she'd added in the new documents, making sure everything important was safe.

Finally she got to the one she'd slipped in after Michael had died. This piece of paper had been a mistake, an error, something her parents had to fix, and fast. Exhausted after driving back and forth to Grandma Gert's, delivering Tommy, and working out the entire plan, her father, the usually unflappable Dr. Larry Johnson, had made a terrible mistake. Somehow, when they took the baby in for an exam after his "surprise birth," her father had told a young hospital volunteer with the pad and pen that the baby's mother was Mary Jo Johnson. Later, when the certificate arrived by post, Larry had rushed downtown the next day to fix the mess, the new certificate arriving the following month.

Mary Jo had found the original birth certificate later on her father's desk, shoved under his glass paperweight. Without asking, she'd slipped it free and kept it all these years. She'd brought it with her to California, and with each move, she'd made sure that the evidence Tommy was hers came with her.

She traced her and Tommy's names with a finger, together here on this paper, the only place that held the truth. Her grandmother, father, and even Roger Bradfield were gone; soon everyone who knew the real story, including herself, would be nothing but dust.

Outside the streetlights flicked on, sudden moths flinging themselves around the bright bulbs, dots of them hitting the screen. She was alone in the quiet, nothing but the past around her. She should burn this certificate, right now. What if she fell down the stairs tomorrow, breaking her neck? Jenny would find this. She would call Tommy and Tricia and Virginia. All the careful secret keeping would go up in terrible smoke.

Downstairs the phone rang. Probably Jenny, checking in.

Mary Jo folded up the certificate and slipped it back into the envelope, just for now. She could throw it away later.

Tom Johnson
August 2018

TOM SAT NEXT to Mary Jo, the television on before them, the screen as big as any he'd seen. He had a drink too, but a weak one.

"How about a refresh?" Mary Jo asked during a commercial break, pushing herself to the edge of her chair and clutching the arm.

"How about we go outside and sit on your patio," Tom said. "It's cooled off a bit. Besides, there's something I want to talk to you about."

Mary Jo looked at her glass.

"I'll get you a halfie," Tom said, using their mother's term, though Virginia had pretended halfies didn't count. She could have as many as she wanted after 5 p.m. "I'll meet you out there."

He took his time fixing Mary Jo her drink, barely splashing any bourbon into the glass before adding ice and water. In his shirt pocket, the photo of Harry and Alice seemed to burn into his skin. He'd also printed out the DNA report, but now, given the way Mary Jo was acting, the numbers and charts seemed a bit too technical.

Outside, the air was loosening its grip on the day's heat. Shade slanted over the patio, the oleander and orange tree leaves gleaming. Mary Jo sat at her outdoor table, staring vacantly, but then turning toward him when he closed the screen door. There she was, dark eyes flashing. She was right here, the sister he had always known.

Tom put her halfie on the table and sat, scooting toward her, both of them looking out toward the trees and the driveway beyond. Putting down his own drink, Tom fished out the photo and put it on the table. Mary Jo looked over her glass at it, still sipping, and then pulled the glass away and paused.

"You look so young," she said. "When was that taken?"

"The seventies," Tom said. "The hair is a giveaway. An outgrown Beatles hairdo."

Mary Jo picked up the photo, holding it close. Her hands had been affected by the same arthritis that had twisted Grandma Gert's hands. Virginia's and Aunt Fiona's too. Gnarled. That was the word. Mary Jo gripped the corners, blinking as she examined the shot.

"Such a good-looking young man," Mary Jo said, putting the photo down.

"But it's not me," Tom said.

Mary Jo cracked a smile. "Of course, it's you."

She pointed one finger at Harry, tapping the table next to his face.

"But it's not. It's Harry Bradfield," Tom said. "I found the photo in some of Mother's things before Alice and I moved. I thought it was me too, but where was I? Looks like the Bradfields' place. And why was I sitting next to Kate, my arm around her?"

"That's not Alice? Surely it must be."

"It's Kate, Harry's wife."

She put down the photo and took a sip, grimacing, Tom thought, at its watery taste. "Nice afternoon, isn't it?" she said.

"Harry came to visit, and we had a chat. We went over some things from our childhood."

Mary Jo gripped her glass, looked toward the birdhouse that Bobby had given her years ago when he was on his carpentry kick. Someone, maybe Jenny or her husband, had hung it on the orange tree. Tom, Alice, and Nick had received one as well.

"No birds have ever moved in," Mary Jo said. "I saw a wren fly in and out once."

"We decided to do a DNA test," Tom said, ignoring birdhouse talk. "The results came back."

She looked at him, taking in an audible breath.

Tom pulled out the folded sheet of DNA, a table he'd created from his and Harry's tests. Carefully he unfolded it in front of Mary Jo, knowing she might not understand. But he'd been a teacher long enough to know he needed to get to the point.

"Harry and I share about 23 percent DNA," Tom said, barely able to keep his voice steady. "We're half-brothers." He stopped, not wanting to get into segments shared.

Mary Jo looked at the paper, her hand curled around her drink.

"The shared DNA comes from Roger." Tom sat back. "But that left a mystery."

His sister dropped her eyes from the paper and looked to her left, bringing her glass to her lips but not sipping.

"We should get ready for dinner." Mary Jo put down the glass and tried to scoot back from the table. Her plastic chair scraped the concrete, the table wobbled. Tom put a hand on her shoulder, pressing a little. She sagged, sat back. A robin began to belt out a whinny and then beat itself out of the trees and flew off. The air stilled.

"I called Bobby," Tom went on. "I told him what we'd discovered. He had a story from those days. Something he saw. You and me, when I was a baby. In the nursery."

At that, Mary Jo shuddered a little, breathing quietly, slumping like a used-up scarecrow, faded and limp, straw coming out everywhere. House finches began to flutter in the bushes, calling to each other. The trouble was a crow on top of the garage next door. Somewhere an irrigation system shuddered out its cycle. The crow beat into the sky, leaving silence in its wake.

"Will you tell me the story?" Tom asked.

"There's nothing to tell." She avoided his gaze, gripped her hands together, shaking her head a little.

"Please, Mary Jo," Tom said. "It's time."

She remained silent but not still, her eyes sharp and keen and moving, as if she were listening to her past like a radio show. What was happening in her brain? Was her refusal to give him what he wanted her personality or her disease? It didn't matter, he realized. He had to know the truth. If he didn't find out now, he never would.

"I need to know, Mary Jo. All my life I've known there's a story beyond my grasp. Nothing ever felt…right."

Finally Mary Jo looked up at him with terrible dark eyes. With effort, she pushed herself to standing and left the patio, the sliding screen door clicking behind her. So that was that, thought Tom. He'd come all this way, lived his whole long life, and he would never have the truth. But then Mary Jo came back with an envelope in her hand. She sat down and slid out a stack of papers, going through a couple before finding what she wanted, a folded piece of paper.

She handed it to Tom, who opened it to find his birth certificate. But not the one he'd seen before. And then, slowly, his sister, Mary Jo, told him what happened.

They were late to set out for the restaurant, the story of what Roger did barely laid out. Flustered, Mary Jo wiped her eyes while moving through the condo, finding and then losing her purse, her car keys, her sweater.

"Let's cancel," Tom said as he followed her to the car. "We need to talk more about this."

"I don't want to cancel," she said. "Jenny's expecting us."

"She'll understand," Tom insisted, fastening his seatbelt and cringing as Mary Jo backed out of the garage. Brake, accelerator. Brake, accelerator. "At least once she hears the story."

The car lurched, Mary Jo gripping the wheel. "She will *not* be hearing this story."

"Maybe not tonight—"

"Not ever!" Mary Jo swung wide into the street without looking for oncoming cars.

"Why don't you let me drive," Tom said, though all he could think about was *Not ever!*

But Mary Jo ignored him, on some kind of autopilot Tom hoped he could trust. She'd lived here since just after Joy died, separated from most of her family, only one child nearby. The others? One child taken from her, one who died, one living in another country. Though part of him wished twelve-year-old Mary Jo had fought for him, he had known Virginia Johnson through and through. She made decisions that lasted.

"I don't think I can go back to normal after this," Tom said. "Eventually Nick is going to have to know."

With an awkward jerk, Mary Jo took an exit, fast, speeding on the long exit and into a circle, the road leading under the freeway.

"There's no need for anyone to know now." Mary Jo faced forward. "Wait until I'm dead, which won't be long based on all those tests today. Jenny wants me dead anyhow. She and her husband want my money."

Tom shot her a glance. "That isn't true. Jenny—"

"What do you know about anything here?" Her voice was as hard as a slap. "You've visited twice in twenty years."

"You left me. You left me and barely ever came back." Tom's face flushed, and he was surprised to feel himself blink back tears. How old was he? Five?

"Too painful." Mary Jo's chin jutted out, and she leaned over the steering wheel.

Tom nodded, stung, angry too. She and Michael hadn't visited often, and somehow Mary Jo's visits to their parents never coincided with his and Alice's. Not such a mystery now.

"I'm sorry," he said.

"Everyone should be. This is a sorry business."

Tom turned toward the window. They had left the crowded freeway and were headed the wrong way, that was for sure. The tree-lined streets widened, and as Mary Jo headed west, they narrowed, wending up oak-covered hills awash in gray dusk light. Soon they would be in Oakland Hills.

"What can I do?" he asked.

Mary Jo didn't answer, her face still and wet.

"Pull over," Tom said. "Stop."

With a shudder in the car and her body, her hands shaking on the wheel, Mary Jo bumped up onto the right-hand curb, both of them lurching as she braked. Tom bit his tongue and clung to the Jesus handle (as their father used to call it) while catching his breath. Mary Jo sniffed.

"I wanted to know who I was," Tom said finally. "I always knew something was…up. Now I understand, but there's more. It's bigger than you and me."

"Let me die first," Mary Jo said. "Let me be gone to tell the rest of this story. Let me jump out of a window first."

"Everything isn't about you, Mary Jo," Tom said. "It's about me too. It's not really something I'm thrilled about, but my family deserves to know. My son especially. Harry's family too."

She turned on him then, her eyes glittering in the dark. "You have no idea what it was like with Roger Bradfield. He was a monster. I've spent my entire life trying to forget him. The whole thing. It was hard. I loved you. You were my baby, and they took you. Told me to live my life. So here it is. My life, what's left of it. You've waited this long. Wait a few more years. Maybe months if you're lucky."

Mary Jo waved her hand and then brushed tears off her face. Just then, her cellphone began to ring, Jenny's name on the screen.

"Tom," Jenny, his niece, his half-sister, said. "Is that you?"

Was it? Tom thought.

"Where are you?" Jenny asked.

Hell, if I know, he wanted to say, but instead he clipped the phone into the holder on the dash. He'd imagined that when he told Mary Jo, the world would somehow right itself. He'd see things in different colors. The crack, the fissure in his life would mend, he and Mary Jo finally able to talk truly.

But the truth had come too late. He would never have the closure that self-help books and therapists touted. He'd go back to Santa Fe, tell Alice the story, prepare to tell Nick at some point, and most likely never see Mary Jo again.

"I don't know where I am!" Mary Jo yelled into the phone.

Neither did Tom.

Jenny Bradford Pine
August 2018

JENNY STOOD OUTSIDE the restaurant, screaming—slightly—into her phone. Somehow her mother had gotten lost on her way to Luna, a restaurant she and Jenny had come to weekly for years. They were so well known to the host that they were seated at a specific two-top, given the same server. How could her mother have gotten so turned around?

"Mom! Mom!" Jenny yelled. She'd pulled up an app she'd also downloaded to her mother's phone, LifeSave, so they could track each other. Finally it had come in handy, Jenny talking on the phone while navigating via the app.

"You're approaching Main. Tom, do you see it?"

"I do."

"Turn right," Jenny said.

"Right?"

"Correct," Jenny said, using better communication skills, a practice that also came in handy when teaching high school kids. But this was ridiculous.

On the screen, her mother's car millimetered its way up Main Street. She was still nine blocks away from the restaurant, having managed to somehow end up two towns over. Jenny had finally called, hearing the relief in her uncle's voice when he answered.

"Thank god" was all he'd said.

"Okay, head up Main. Mom?"

"I hear you."

"Head up Main and get in the middle lane."

Jenny leaned against the wall, exhausted. What a day. First the appointment and now this. She'd already alerted the host that they were going to be late, and her mother was so slow at meals, Jenny wouldn't be able to leave for well over two hours.

She wished she'd left the country like Tricia had, even though most days, she wanted to slap her sister into tomorrow. Or, at least, she thought about it.

"Okay, stay straight." Her mother's car icon seemed to stall right in the middle of the street. "Don't stop in the intersection. Keep going—yes, into the parking lot. Keep going. That's right. I'm standing out front. Find a parking spot, and I'll wait for you."

Her mother and uncle made yes noises, and Jenny hung up, seeing her mother's car crawl through the parked cars, searching for an open spot. Finally her mother lurched into place, and then the two of them were walking toward the restaurant. For a second, Jenny was caught, confused, seeing something she hadn't seen before.

Her mother and uncle were walking in unison, their gaits, their swing of leg, crook of arm exactly the same. At that moment, they both looked up and saw her. Neither of them smiled.

Dinner was silent, except when Tom started talking about Nick and his post-college plans. "I'm not sure I would call them plans. More like hopes. Dreams. Expectations."

"We all figure it out somehow," Jenny said, realizing she had very little to say about her much younger cousin. She'd met him when he was an infant, a five-year-old, and then an almost teenager. They hadn't converged for Grandma Ginny's funeral because there hadn't been one. Or for Grandpa Larry.

"Well, if he ever comes to town, let me know."

Jenny's children had never met Nick, barely knew their uncle. Where were her two kids right now? She wished she had an app for that, though her older son would sooner be physically injured than tracked via GPS. Was Dom in Berlin? Or London? She almost looked at her watch, as if time could predict his movements. But out in the world he was, living the activist/journalist life. Her younger son, Sam, was steadier, working as a park ranger on Mt. Diablo, living with his psychologist girlfriend and their cat. Around him, Jenny could breathe a little more easily.

Her uncle nodded. Meanwhile, her mother was making hash out of her entrée, picking the cheese and prosciutto off a pizza.

"Don't you like your meal?" Jenny asked.

"I don't like pizza."

Jenny and her uncle looked at each other and then away.

"Sorry about being so late," Tom said. "We got to talking."

Jenny's mother kept scraping off cheese and then licking her fingers loudly.

"Mom, you love this place. I thought the directions were in your blood."

"It was night," she said. "And we were talking."

Neither her mother nor uncle spoke further, both intent on their meals. Maybe now wasn't the best time to bring up her mother's test results, some of which had come by email right before Jenny left for Luna. She had power of attorney and medical power of attorney for her mother, so everything came through her. She'd already set up the first appointment in the Memory Care Center.

"This is horrible," she'd said to her husband.

Steve had squeezed her shoulder. "Do you want me to come to dinner with you?" he asked. "I will. I'll help you tell your mother."

Jenny had let him off the hook, but now she wished she'd agreed. Steve always knew how to fill the silence in a social situation. And as for the results? She'd arrange to go back to the condo tomorrow or the next day and sit down with her mother and uncle and explain everything.

"How are you liking Santa Fe?" she asked her uncle. "Is it too hot?"

Tom looked at her, and she was stuck by how closely he resembled her mother. Well, not really, but their eyes pierced Jenny the same way, gaze intent, sharp.

"Not as hot as you might think. It's high altitude."

Jenny had been to Santa Fe once; for the week she and Steve were there, her hair had felt heavy, lank, and then, also, electric.

Her hair almost lifted off her head from the static. For that reason alone, she'd stay in the Bay Area, no matter how much she liked pottery and art and Mexican food.

Like that, there was nothing to say. The meal churned on. There was no way to casually bring up that her mother had vascular and Alzheimer's dementias. Her uncle would go home tomorrow afternoon. He'd flown out to help, as he said he would. He and her mother had a visit, but it didn't seem to have gone very well, the silence between them full of something Jenny couldn't name. There was a fourth person—a shape or shadow—sitting at the table, crowding out conversation and talk, smothering them with a dull heaviness.

"Do you need a ride to the airport?" Jenny asked.

Tom shook his head. The server came to their table with a fresh basket of bread and then refilled their water glasses. Her mother glanced at Tom and then went back to her pizza madness. Then she dropped her fork.

"I want some vanilla ice cream. I don't want to eat this anymore. I'm done with it."

Jenny wanted to argue. She wanted to talk about nutrition and blood pressure and heart health. But did it really matter anymore? When things got to the end, shouldn't we be allowed to have exactly what we wanted? What, really, did cholesterol mean for her mother now?

She turned and looked back into the restaurant. "Waiter?"

Tom Johnson
August 2018

"BAD NEWS FIRST, please," Alice said. That was the type of person she was. Rip off the bandage. Jump the fence before looking. Get the hard things over with fast. If there was something good afterward, lucky her.

"My parents were not my parents," Tom said.

For a moment, they sat in silence on their back patio, looking out toward the night brilliant with stars. In the fire pit, the wood embered. Alice pulled the Navajo-style blanket around her shoulders as a chill drift of air settled around them.

"That's not bad news, is it?" Alice said.

"Maybe not," Tom said.

"I'm sorry." Alice leaned over to touch his knee. "I don't know what I'm saying. I'm sorry. And, really, what are you talking about?"

"It's a long story. A sad one."

"Sad? You're serious? You are serious."

Alice sat back, her eyes unwavering and on his.

"That's why I went to visit Mary Jo and Jenny. I needed to find out more. And I did."

Tom took out the folded piece of paper from his front pocket and opened it. Alice took it and leaned close to the lantern, reading.

"Oh, my," she said. For a while, she held the paper in front of her and then sighed. "Mary Jo. My god. But who is the father? Not—"

"Not my dad," he said, "not Larry. It was a family friend. It was Harry's dad."

"Roger," Alice said, no question.

Tom shot her a glance. Alice shrugged. "He was creepy. Always watching. I saw how he looked at women. Mary Jo, in fact. Me too. At our wedding reception. I made a note to keep out of his way."

Tom shook his head, and Alice reached out to him again, keeping her hand on his knee this time. "I keep saying the wrong thing. He was your father."

"Biological father," Tom said.

For a moment, neither of them spoke. Alice wiped her face with the back of her hand. Tom nodded.

"It's ugly. But there's good news, remember?"

"What is it?"

"Harry's my brother," Tom said.

Alice laughed, though she almost sounded as though she might cry. "Of course he is. Makes sense. It was always there, wasn't it? You two somehow understood."

"And Jenny and Tricia are my sisters." Tom paused, hearing that sentence for the first time. He had sisters.

"This is hard to take in. I can't imagine how you feel."

Tom sat back, listened to his wife talk, and answered her questions. The night closed around them. Alice patted his arm, sat back to exclaim, and then listened to the story another time. The more he told it, the more it came true. He was the product of rape. His mother was his twelve-year-old sister. His family spun a lie that had held for sixty-eight years. His best friend was his brother. All but the last should have thrown him for a terrible loop, but Tom felt better, as if he'd been breathing with one lung and was now breathing with two. He kept thinking he should have a breakdown of some kind or needed to call a therapist, but when he arrived back in New Mexico, he'd felt strangely at peace. Calm, as if he'd been waiting for exactly this news—no matter how bad—to save him. Maybe it had.

Eventually Alice stood up and kissed him on the forehead and went into the house to close things up and get ready for bed. For a few more minutes, it was he and the bats, the creatures that flickered and swung in the sky and the dark mystery of night. The fire died; the stars popped brilliant. Tomorrow would be another summer day.

From now on though, Tom had the answers that had always eluded him, the key to a puzzle he would never finish. This story would be carried on in Jenny and her boys and Tricia. In his own son, Nick. In Harry and his siblings and their many, many children. In those other half-siblings who roamed the planet, all springing up along the path Roger Bradfield took during his long, very wrong but prolific life.

At least Tom had the pieces and parts, the information that explained his life. They wouldn't make things better, but they helped make things whole.

He stood and folded the blanket and went inside, turning off the lights as he went deep into the house, headed toward his wife.

JESSICA BARKSDALE INCLÁN

Mary Jo Johnson
May 2019

THE MOON HAD carried away the cat food.

Mary Jo wandered the rooms, looking for the kitchen, the cupboards. The cat. Where was the cat? She had a cat. Would it last the long night without food? Where had the moon put it?

In the kitchen she opened a drawer, the handle hard in her hand. She pulled away, blinking into the fake kitchen with the shallow metal sink and white microwave. This wasn't a real house, her house. That girl had sold her place to strangers. They'd all stolen it. A truck had come to take her best furniture. Worse, it was probably put out on the sidewalk for people to riffle through. She couldn't find any of her favorite things. Where were her clothes? Her jewelry?

She shuffled back out to the main room, searching for her cat. She had a cat. Would it last the long night without food? It was probably hiding deep in the memories she tried to catch in her hand. There was one. Mary Jo reached out to grab it. Her husband. She'd had one, hadn't she? He'd left her though, disappearing like smoke, taking her memories with him.

Mary Jo fished out another, a big one, the story of her baby brother. How had anyone believed? They promised she could take care of him. He'd been hers, right?

"Mrs. Bradford?"

They were finally here to take her to him, her baby.

"What are you doing out of bed? Come on now. I have some medication for you."

Mary Jo walked next to that person who would protect her from the monster who waited for her, hunched, dark, and pressed against her.

Where's my baby? she asked, but no one answered.

When had she last seen the baby? Did he disappear when she went away? Was he still in her arms? Or back at the stolen house? She remembered him there, sitting in a chair, looking at her, his eyes so dark, like his father's. He never called. He had the cat. He would know where the cat food was.

"Let's visit the bathroom first," the person said.

Mary Jo shivered, scared to be in the dark, in a small space, alone with a stranger. She wanted to scream, but then it was over, and she was pulled into another room.

"That's right. Get back in bed. Here's your pill…Well done. Okay, I'll be back later."

Mary Jo's mother was tucking her in, patting her arm. Virginia looked down at her, smiling for once, offering her comfort. Mary Jo clutched at her, but her mother left anyway, a door closing somewhere.

She wanted to tell her the baby and the cat would starve without her.

"It will be all right," her mother said. "Go back to sleep. It's still nighttime."

The moon was out, looking at her. That's what the moon did. It came, and it went, like everything. It showed itself, and then it hid, dead to the planet below it. They would all die. Everything died anyway. All the chatter died away. That baby, that boy, that man stopped asking his terrible questions. Wanting something from her. Needing what she didn't have. Not anymore.

Where was the cat? She must find the food. Where was it? Where was the monster now? Where was he hiding? Why wouldn't the moon show her? What waited for her in every dark corner?

What next? Mary Jo wondered. What next?

Jenny Bradford Pine
August 2021

"SHE ALWAYS SAID, 'Tom was my baby.' I thought she meant she treated you like her baby. She made it sound as though Grandma was too busy with her life and gave the raising to Mom. It was like this big gift they gave her, as if you were this amazing toy. Something was off, but I didn't notice. It was one of those family stories I accepted."

Jenny sat with Tom on her deck looking out toward towering cypress and redwoods and, beyond them, the San Francisco Bay. Towering trees, Jenny thought, the exact words the real estate agent had used last week when drafting the listing. Jenny and Steve were selling a house in the blazing post-pandemic real estate frenzy.

"I *was* her baby," Tom said. "I wish she'd been able to tell me earlier. When it didn't need to be a secret anymore."

"That's not how she worked. It's not how Grandma worked either. But frankly, it's amazing they pulled it off. All these years.

"Did you ever—" Jenny hesitated. "Think to ask?"

Tom tapped a palm on one knee. "We weren't a talking bunch. Plus, I didn't know the question. Not 'til the photo."

Jenny looked at her uncle—her half-brother, she had to remind herself. Finding Tom named in her mother's will should have been the first clue. Sometime after Joy's death, her mother had changed the terms, at least according to the son of Mary Jo's attorney, who had taken over his father's practice.

"Call your uncle," the lawyer said. "I can do it if you want. But why don't you tell him. Then we can all talk."

Jenny and Tom were talking now, hadn't stopped for days, enough that Tom flew out to talk some more and meet with the lawyer himself. In the house, Steve was whipping up his famous polenta dish. Tom would stay with them a couple of nights and then head home. Maybe Jenny and Steve would fly down to Santa Fe after the holidays, now that the idea of flying was something to consider again. Right now the coast was almost clear. They'd all been vaccinated, had stockpiles of KN95 masks, and there were talks about booster shots. Even her mother had been vaccinated in the months before her death. Mary Jo had lived through the pandemic, but Jenny wasn't sure her mother had even known it was raging.

"The whole story is pretty hard to believe," Tom said.

Yes, both the pandemic and their family story. Jenny nodded, turning her mother's engagement ring on her right-hand ring finger, noting the slight dig of the diamond with each revolution. Strangely, it fit perfectly, this small, simple ring that her mother had rarely worn. In Mary Jo's will, she'd specifically left it to Jenny, not Tricia. At first Jenny had put it in her jewelry box but found herself slipping it on one day and not taking it off, a reminder of her mother's now unbelievable life.

Sometimes Jenny held out her hand, watching light flicker and glint off the stone. Despite his rages, how her mother must have needed her father, he the solution to Mary Jo's tragedy. Anger was easier to deal with than Roger Bradfield's abuse. Easier than her own parents' betrayal.

In the cypress tree, nuthatches scrabbled up the thick bark and called out *meep, meep.* The late-afternoon wind whisked slight fingers of fog through the canopy, the sun round and orange as it slipped behind the hills.

Tom was right. The whole story was almost impossible to accept, and yet Jenny had known all along. In so many ways, her mother had tried to tell her. Tom had been her baby. MeToo was part of her history. A man had done things to her. When Tom told her the truth, Jenny cried out, "Of course" and "I don't believe it" almost at the same time.

"How did Tricia take the news?" Tom asked.

"She asked when her part of the estate was coming," Jenny said. "Same thing she did when Uncle Bobby died and she found out there was a bequest. 'What's the holdup?' she asked."

Tom laughed. "She has her priorities."

What Tricia had were boundaries and an unforgiving nature. Maybe one day she would be interested to know the facts about her mother's death and more about Tom, her uncle turned half-brother, but to Jenny, it seemed perfect that her sister stayed across the world and far away. Things were a lot easier with her gone.

"Seems like I had two different childhoods at the same time," Tom said. "One real and one not."

"That's probably true for me too," Jenny said. "I had the story where I was the oldest child. And then the hidden story where I was the second child. The story where I had only sisters, and one where I had a brother. One where my mother had been…"

"Raped," Tom said.

They both paused. In the kitchen, the shake and rattle of pans and then a waft of tomato sauce.

"You know I met him," Jenny said. "They took us to the yacht club. Then he and Betty came to visit a couple of times. We have family photos with him sitting at a restaurant table or in our home, looking right at the camera. In life too. He stared. He was a watcher. It was unnerving but also, well, exciting."

"He smiled a lot," Tom said. "Not a care in the world."

"Roger Bradfield had two different lives."

"More than two," Tom said. "But I'll tell you about that later."

Jenny shot him a look but was relieved to not learn anything else, at least for a while. She shook her head. "He seemed to know the thing inside I wasn't saying. He was compelling. I guess I liked him."

"Me too," Tom said.

They laughed. "MeToo," Jenny snorted.

"I *also* liked him," Tom clarified. "I think I loved him, at least for a while. He was nothing but kind to me at times when I needed it."

Jenny didn't say that Roger lived only one life, the one where he was right. Roger was front and center, king of the castle, doer of good deeds, giver of wanted affection. Kind and compassionate. Righteous. From what Jenny knew, he held onto his accolades and died holding them tight. What Roger Bradfield remembered wasn't what Jenny's mother remembered, at least when Mary Jo could remember anything. What Jenny and Tom remembered was different than Roger's and Mary Jo's constructions of the past, and different from each other's too.

What was the use of memory when no one remembered the same thing? Everyone connected to this story had been on an island of their own thoughts, and then that island was eaten away by storm and water and sun until nothing remained. By the time Mary Jo died, she couldn't talk. Her eyes didn't dart back and forth. She was taking in nothing, as far as Jenny could tell. Whatever memories Mary Jo had were buried deep inside, maybe gone.

All they had were these moments now, sitting outside in the summer air, talking about their lives, the past, their families. All of it would disappear, but they had a chance to live into the future built from what was happening now. Maybe she and Tom could bend the story toward a happier ending, if they were lucky. They could start with small things, like this afternoon, this talk, this meal.

"Dinner," Steve called from inside the house. "Come on in."

Mary Jo Johnson
August 1948

THE GRASS HELD onto the summer heat of the day, though the evening air flickered through the thin green tips, brushing Mary Jo's face. The moon hadn't even tried to rise, hiding behind the horizon. She and Bobby lay on their backs on the lawn behind the house, looking up into the darkening sky, their fingertips touching. Her braids loosened, Mary Jo's hair spread around her in a halo. Out on the patio, the adults were laughing and drinking, telling stories, their words rushing together like a lullaby.

"There!" Bobby whispered. "Another one."

They were counting shooting stars and lightning bugs, Bobby winning. He'd seen two of each so far, though Mary Jo had hope she would start seeing her own.

"That child needs spectacles," her mother had said the other day. "Can't see the hand in front of her face."

But Mary Jo liked the fuzzy world around her, the way that everything seemed magic. She was about to open a door in the haze and step into another world. That was what growing up was. One day she would peek through a secret portal in a magical place at the edge of Saint Helen and disappear and never come back. She'd leave her entire childhood, her parents, and even Bobby behind, though he would do fine all by himself. Look at him now? Seeing everything Mary Jo couldn't.

"Another one!" Bobby pointed. "Oh, Mary Jo, look. And a lightning bug, right there, above you."

Mary Jo reached up, felt the spark, the glow, the short season of heat and light burn into the palm of her hand.

Acknowledgments

MANY THANKS TO the folks who read this novel in parts and as a whole as it grew. Shout-outs to Andrea Clausen, Sarah Blaser Murray, Julie Roemer, and Laura Petersen. Warren Read, Mishele Maron, and Kris Whorton read much if not all of a couple of drafts, and I so appreciate the time they gave me.

This novel would never have happened without a novel that hasn't made it to print, at least not yet. It is a sweeping, historical, generational tale that needs more time (or maybe a quick burial). I extracted this story from that one and developed it, so I want to thank all the folks who have already met Grandma Gert and her story, including Darien Gee and Kent Meyers.

Bill Burleson pulled this story from the literal pile, and I've so appreciated his upfront, honest approach to publishing. What a joy to work with him.

My love and appreciation to my husband, Michael (no similarities to the Michael in this story), for his constant support of my writing. My sons, Mitchell and Julien, were there to listen to me whine a little and provided walks, talks, and love. Kris Whorton keeps listening and listening and listening. I'm pretty lucky.

Finally, thanks to you who are reading this now. You got to the end, and that's usually a good sign.

About the Author

JESSICA BARKSDALE INCLÁN is the author of the poetry collection, *Grim Honey*, and the novel *The Play's the Thing*, both published in 2021. Her short story collection *Trick of the Porch Light* is forthcoming in Fall 2023. Her other work includes the novels *Her Daughter's Eyes*, *The Burning Hour*, and *When You Believe*.

She taught composition, literature, and creative writing at Diablo Valley College in Pleasant Hill, California, and continues to teach novel writing online for UCLA Extension and in the online MFA program for Southern New Hampshire University. She lives in the Pacific Northwest with her husband.

You can read more about her work at www.jessicabarksdaleinclan.com.

More books by Jessica Barksdale Inclán

The Burning Hour
Faced with the driest fire season on record, the Mapps must place their trust in a government less than honorable, while Nick Delgado struggles with regulations and familial expectations to become the man he needs to be.

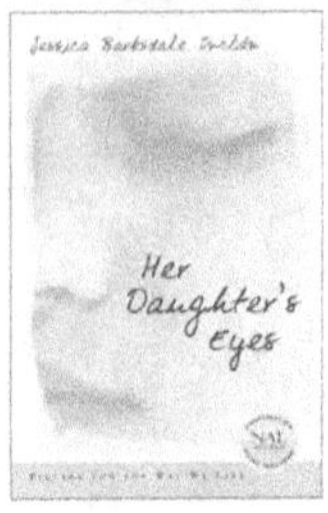

Her Daughter's Eyes
A moving novel of chances made and chances lost, Her Daughter's Eyes is a story for everyone who has known what it is like to feel alone in the safest place of all—home.

The Instant When Everything is Perfect
Mia thought she had everything—a thriving career, a wonderful husband, and two beautiful sons. But illness shakes her out of her comfort zone when her mother is diagnosed with breast cancer.

Grim Honey
These poems follow thin paths of grief, up through steep switchbacks and down rocky declines, where for a moment, we can pause and remember before moving on.